JOEL AND FAMILY

JOEL AND FAMILY

Book 2 of the Joel Series

Ted Louis

iUniverse, Inc.
New York Lincoln Shanghai

Joel and Family
Book 2 of the Joel Series

Copyright © 2007 by Ted Louis

All rights reserved. No part of this book may be used or reproduced by any means, graphic, electronic, or mechanical, including photocopying, recording, taping or by any information storage retrieval system without the written permission of the publisher except in the case of brief quotations embodied in critical articles and reviews.

iUniverse books may be ordered through booksellers or by contacting:

iUniverse
2021 Pine Lake Road, Suite 100
Lincoln, NE 68512
www.iuniverse.com
1-800-Authors (1-800-288-4677)

This is a work of fiction. All of the characters, names, incidents, organizations, and dialogue in this novel are either the products of the author's imagination or are used fictitiously.

ISBN: 978-0-595-44639-1 (pbk)
ISBN: 978-0-595-88963-1 (ebk)

Printed in the United States of America

CHAPTER 1

I poured myself a cup of coffee and sat down at the kitchen table. Hildy was busy fixing the breakfast the boys would be enjoying shortly. It had now been three months since I had adopted the boys. I had never been happier. I now had a sense of purpose. Hildy also seemed to be happy with her new life as the boys surrogate grandmother.

"Hildy, we need to talk about how we're going to take care of the boys this summer," I said. "They finish their school year the middle of May. That's only 16 days away. I think we're going to need some help. I can't expect you to be the sole caregiver for five active boys while I'm at work."

"They are a handful," she chuckled. "But you're right. I'm not as young as I used to be, and I don't think I can watch them and do all the housework and cooking at the same time."

"Well, perhaps we could find a nanny to help out during the summer. Maybe not a real nanny but someone who could help you out and still take on part of the responsibility of the boys," I said. "There might be a college student home for the summer who would be able to help out. Do you know any of your friends who have college kids that might be interested? I think Eric is going to have the same problem with JR."

"I'll ask my girl friend Janice. She has two daughters going to University of Texas. Both of them were studying to be teachers the last I knew. They might be interested in earning some money and getting some first-hand experience working with kids," Hildy said thoughtfully. "That might solve both yours and Eric's problems. I'll call Janice right after we get the boys off to school."

I had just settled down with the morning newspaper when TJ crawled up on my lap and hugged my neck. "My, you're up early, little one," I said, kissing the top of his head.

"Uh-huh, I couldn't sleep," he mumbled into my chest. "My tummy said it was time for breakfast."

Giving him a squeeze, I said, "Why don't you go wash your hands and face while I wake up your brothers. By that time Hildy will have your breakfast ready. How does that sound?"

"Okay," he said, slipping down off my lap and then padded off to the bathroom.

As I entered Joel's bedroom, Samson lifted his head over the side of his basket and looked at me, making sure I was a friend before he hopped out and stood beside the bed looking at Joel. I gently shook Joel and Samson helped by licking him on the ear. That woke him up in a hurry. The first thing Joel did was to hug Samson.

"Good morning, boy," he said. "Oh, hi, dad."

"Get washed up, Hildy has breakfast almost ready," I said, shaking my head, knowing I had taken second billing to a dog.

Samson followed me into the twins' and Chris' bedroom to make sure I got them awake also. They jumped out of bed at the mention of breakfast.

It is amazing how much Samson has changed since Joel first found him. His leg has healed nicely, although he does still favor it. The treatment to rid him of heart worms was a very bad time for the boys. The treatment almost proved fatal for him. It involved a medicine which contained arsenic and it made him very sick for about two weeks before he began to recover. His coat now shows no sign of the mange he had when we found him. It has a normal healthy shine. He is just a normal healthy mutt. With the money I spent on his veterinary bills I could have bought an AKC registered prize winning champion show dog. However, I don't think the boys would have had as close an attachment as they do to Samson. I must admit that the mutt has grown on me too.

He is still very much Joel's dog. He loves all the boys, but you can tell there is a special bond between him and Joel.

After breakfast, I walked the boys down the lane for them to catch their school van. As I gave all of them hugs and reminders to behave themselves at school, they hopped on the van and were off. The weather was so nice I almost decided to play hooky and stay home from work. April and May are two of the best weather months in south central Texas. It is not too hot and it never gets cold. It is ideal for outdoor activities. Reluctantly, I gathered my stuff together and went to work.

"Happy May Day, boss," Carol said as I entered the office. "Here are a couple of contracts you need to look over and there was a call from William Weller again. He would like for you to call him back. He said it was important."

"I'll bet I know what he wants. He's been bugging me for a couple of months," I told her. "When Foster comes in, have him see me. I'd like to talk to both of you."

I had just finished reviewing the contracts Carol had given me when she told me Foster had arrived and would be in as soon as he got a cup of coffee. The contracts would stretch our already-stretched resources to the limit or beyond, but would bring in a considerable amount of revenue. I always hated to turn down consulting work, but if Foster couldn't come up with some more consultants, I didn't see how we could take on the additional work.

"'Morning, Crane," Foster said, cheerily, as he walked into the office with his big mug of coffee he was famous for carrying with him at all times. "I see you have the Halverson and Becket proposals. They could keep 12 to15 staff busy for the next year and a half."

"Yeah, I see. But do we have the staff to make it work? I thought from your last staff report that everyone was already pretty much committed to existing projects."

"That's true; they are. I think that I have a way of getting the staffing we need to do both of the projects. There's a small consulting firm in Austin that's having trouble staying afloat. I know Jim Carson, the owner, and have talked to him about either subcontracting some work to him or absorbing his staff into our company. I think he would prefer to subcontract, but my preference would be to hire his staff. That way we have much more control over how the projects are done. Jim is a damn good project manager, and I'm confident the people he has recruited are first rate."

"Why don't you contact him and set up an appointment when we could meet to discuss things with him?"

Just then Carol walked in. "Sorry I'm late. That phone has not stopped ringing since I walked in this morning."

"The way the business is growing we should probably think about getting you some help. I know the tech assistants can help out once in a while so you can at least get away for a bit, but still doesn't give you much time for us. Foster and I can keep you busy just doing our stuff, let alone doing all the things the consultants need you to do. Anyway, think about it.

"The reason I wanted to talk to both of you is related to that William Weller who wants me to call him back. He is a senior partner from one of the Big Five consulting companies. They want to buy ACC. They have made a very attractive preliminary offer for the company. In fact, it's much more than what we have valued the company at. Most of that is, of course, for the 'goodwill'. They are very much aware of our reputation for quality work and want to cash in on it by buying us out rather than starting up their own office here. What's your reaction?"

There was a brief silence before Foster said, "What would happen to all the people? What about Carol and me?"

"I haven't discussed any specifics with him. If I should decide to sell, I would make sure all of the staff be given the option of remaining for a period of not less than one year. The only reason I'm considering the offer is that I'm finding it more and more difficult running the business and taking care of five active growing boys. With summer coming up, the boys will need even more of my attention. They need me to be with them. They need a full time parent."

"When would all of this happen?" Carol asked.

"The timing of any buyout has not been discussed. We need to carry on as if it were not going to happen. We have to take care of business and give our clients the best we have to offer. I've not made a final determination to sell and you will be the first to know as soon as any decision has been made. Also, I would appreciate it if the rest of the staff does not hear of this until the decision is made. I thought the two of you should know since I depend so heavily on you."

"Thanks, Crane," Foster said. "I know it's your decision alone, but for what it's worth I would prefer to keep working for you. This business has flourished in the last year or so and I think it has a lot to do with the professionalism and dedication to the clients that has been characteristic of your attitude. It's infectious with the staff."

I called Weller after Foster and Carol went back to their work and agreed to meet with him next Monday. He was going to fly in from London just for our meeting. "I guess these guys are really serious about the buyout if they are willing to spend a couple thousand or so to fly in just for a few hour meeting," I thought out loud.

The rest of the day was spent with the minutia that occupies most of a manager's time that those aspiring to the job never think about. I was ready when it came time to leave. I wanted to be home when the boys got off the school van.

The van was a little late in arriving so I had time to park the BMW and walk down to the gate to welcome the boys. The van arrived a couple of minutes after I got there. TJ was the first off the van followed by the twins and JR with Chris bringing up the rear. When the driver started closing the door, I panicked. Joel had not gotten off the van.

"Where's Joel?" I asked, looking at the other boys.

"He went home with John," TJ said.

"Why did he do that?"

"I don't know," TJ replied, as he started up the lane to the house.

"He said he had some homework that John and him had to do," Lenny volunteered.

I was a little upset as I walked back up to the house. The first thing I did when I got there was to ask Hildy if Joel had told her he was going to John's house after school. When she said he had not told her, I really became upset. This is the first time any of the boys had done anything that I thought I might need to punish them for. What would be the appropriate punishment, I wondered? I guess it is time to sharpen the parenting skills.

I tried to be calm as I called the Gordinier house. "Pauline, this is Crane Johnson. I understand that Joel is there. May I speak to him, please?"

"Oh, hello, Crane," Pauline answered. "Yes, Joel is here. He and John are doing some homework they brought home from school. Just a minute and I'll get him."

"Hi, dad," Joel said, cheerfully.

"Joel, I'm a little disappointed you didn't let us know you were going to go home with John tonight. I was worried about you when you didn't get off the van."

"I'm sorry, dad. I guess I forgot to call you. Can you come get me about six o'clock? We'll be done with our homework by then. Thanks, dad, I love you. Bye."

He hung up before I could even say goodbye to him. This was not like Joel. Something strange was going on.

I got to the Gordinier's house a couple of minutes before six. As I rang the doorbell, I had not decided what I was going to do with Joel, let alone what I was going to say to him. Bruce answered the door.

"Come in, Crane. It's been a while since you've been here. It's good to see you again. Have a seat. I'll tell Pauline you're here."

"I really don't have a lot of time, Bruce. I just came to pick up Joel. Hildy'll have supper ready by the time we get back."

"Okay, then, I'll go tell Joel to get his things together."

Pauline came into the living room where I was and we chatted for a few minutes before Joel came in carrying his school books, stuffing them into his backpack.

"Hi, dad," he said, giving me a hug.

"Are you ready to go? Do you have everything?"

Joel hugged Bruce and then Pauline before he and John dashed out the front door giggling like a couple of school girls. He had dumped his backpack in the back of the BMW by the time I had said goodbye to everyone. John gave him a quick hug before he saw me and turned a bright red.

I wrapped my arms around John, giving him a hug also. "It's all right, son."

"Thanks, Mr. Johnson," he said into my chest, returning my hug.

As we drove home, I gently scolded Joel for not calling either Hildy or me to let us know what he was going to do. I tried to get across to him we were worried about him and if anything happened to him we would be devastated.

"I'm really sorry, dad," he said quietly. "I won't do it again."

When I looked over at him I could see a tear running down his cheek, but, strangely enough, he had a funny little smile on his lips.

I still hadn't decided on what form of punishment made sense for his transgression when I punched the remote to open the gate to the property. Something was going on, but I couldn't put my finger on it. As we rounded the curve in the lane leading up to the house I saw eight or ten cars parked on the drive.

Parking the car in the garage, I again looked over at Joel who was unbuckling his seat belt.

"Happy birthday, dad," he said, and kissed me on the cheek.

"You little stinker, you did this on purpose, didn't you?"

"Yeah, we fooled you," he giggled, as he hopped out of the car, grabbing his books.

I had no more than stepped inside the back door when I had my arms full of TJ and surrounded by the other three in a group hug.

"Happy birthday, daddy," TJ said in my ear. "Hildy said I did a good job 'cause I didn't tell you."

"You sure did," I said, setting him down. "You all fooled me."

The family room was crowded with people including Dr. Sam and his wife Carol, Eric and JR, Darcie and her friend, who I would later find out was Mel, and Foster and Carol from the office. Jack and his wife and three kids were also here. Harold Nicholas and his son Joey were here. Bruce and Pauline had evidently followed us because they and their kids came in the front door shortly after I had greeted everyone.

I don't know where Hildy had hidden all of the food that was now spread out on the kitchen table and counter tops. I had seen no evidence of it when I left to pick up Joel.

"Hildy, I know this was all of your doing. I didn't think anyone knew when my birthday was," I said, as I gave her a hug and a peck on the cheek. "Thanks."

"Actually, it was Joel's idea to invite everyone and he wanted to make it a surprise. I hope you weren't too hard on him for not calling you about going to John's tonight after school. That was the only way I thought we could get you away from the house while everyone arrived. Bruce and Pauline were in on it too."

It turned out there were fifteen kids and fourteen adults including Hildy and me. I think there was enough food to feed twice that number. Everyone had brought some kind of dish for the party, but I think Hildy had prepared the majority of it. There were salads and casseroles, relishes and chips, meats and gravies, potatoes and all kinds of vegetables, breads and rolls, but I didn't see any desserts.

We encouraged the kids to take their plates outside to save wear and tear on the carpets. Sam had brought some folding chairs and tables so there was plenty of room for all of them to sit. Hildy saw to it they all had enough to eat and drink before she filled her own plate. The dining room table was meant to seat twelve but we were able to get all fourteen adults around it by squeezing everyone together. There was hardly a need for a place for Hildy and Carol Greene. They were up seeing to the kids more than they were seeing to their own meals. Carol was loving it, she didn't get to see her grandchildren very often and to her a house full of kids was heaven.

Darcie sat next to me and told me about Mel. They had been dating for several months. He was working for Southwestern Bell as a manager in their IT department. It sounded like it was getting to be serious between them. You could tell by the way they looked at each other.

"Crane, I want you to know I submitted my resignation to my boss at CPS today," Darcie announced.

"Oh, really? Why?" I asked.

"I can't be part of an organization that cares so little for the kids that they are supposed to protect. The final straw that broke the camel's back came this past weekend. There was a four year old boy who was starved to death. The family had been reported to CPS three times in the last twelve months. The first two times the case worker investigated, but never even saw the child in question. The first report to CPS was that the boy had been beaten and had two black eyes. It was also reported that the boy was forced to drink out of the toilet to quench his thirst. The case worker reported the accusations were unfounded. The third report of abuse was not even investigated and the people reporting the incident were informed by letter from the regional director's office to the effect they should keep their noses out of it, that CPS knew what they were doing.

"The boy died Sunday in the hospital after being taken there when he lapsed into a coma. He weighed less than sixteen pounds when he died. We have since received a report he had his mouth taped shut with duct tape, also his hands were taped to his crib to keep him from getting out of bed. He had been forced to lie in his bed for so long he had developed bed sores. The only good thing, if you can call it that, which came out of this, was the two other children were taken from the house and placed in foster care."

There were tears in my eyes to match the ones in Darcie's eyes when she finished telling the story. "I cannot understand how anyone, let alone a parent, could cause a child to be harmed. It is just unthinkable," I said.

Her story put a damper on the party for a while but the sound of the kids laughing and having fun outside soon brought things back to normal. It seemed like there was a steady stream of them trooping in to get more food. Much as they tried, the supply of food did not entirely disappear. The adults did not do all that badly when it came to eating either. I know I was stuffed by the time I finished.

Just when I thought I could not eat another bite, Hildy literally wheeled out on a cart a very large, two layer, rectangular chocolate frosted cake with thirty lighted candles. As she did, the assembled crowd began singing *Happy Birthday*.

"Make a wish, daddy," TJ said.

"Yeah, make a wish," echoed Joel.

"I don't know what I could wish for. I have almost everything a man could want, five wonderful boys that I can call my sons and friends that fill my life with joy," I said, and then tried to blow out the candles. TJ helped. I did have one wish that I did not share with the assembled crowd.

Hildy cut the cake and gave me the first piece. She then cut the children their pieces and Carol Greene helped by adding ice cream to theirs. Even after cutting twenty-nine generous pieces of cake there was still a third of it remaining.

Joel sat his cake plate down and stood up as if to make a speech. "Dad, we told everyone not to bring you presents. Is that all right?" Without waiting for my answer, he went on, "But we wanted to give you something."

With that he stepped into my study and brought out a wrapped package and handed it to me. My hands were trembling as I carefully removed the wrappings to find a box about a foot long, ten inches wide and an inch or so thick. As I started to remove the lid of the box I was surrounded by all five of my angels. When the lid came off I found a professionally taken, beautifully framed photograph of the five boys posed on the new staircase.

I couldn't find my voice for a minute.

"Don't you like it?" TJ asked, looking into my eyes which were now filled with tears.

"It is the best present I have ever received," I whispered. "When did you get this taken?"

"When you went to Dallas a couple of weeks ago, Hildy had the man come and take the picture," Joel answered.

"And you guys kept this a secret that long? I can hardly believe that," I said, giving TJ a squeeze. "Thank you so much, I will treasure this forever."

I got up and gave each of the boys a hug and a kiss on top of each head before they went back to eating their cake and ice cream. I passed the photograph around the room for all to see.

I think TJ was glad when everyone started going home. Jack's little girl Sara followed him around like a puppy dog again. The same cannot be said for Larry and Lenny. They spent most of the evening with Linda and Cassie Gordinier. It looks like I might have to have 'that talk' with them or at least begin their education into the facts of life. Samson was the only member of the family who was absent. The crowd of people was too much for him. He hid in the bedroom until almost everyone was gone before he poked his head around the corner.

Because it was a school night, our guests with children started leaving around eight o'clock. Carol Greene insisted on helping Hildy clean up and get everything put away. Sam, Eric and I stood out on the patio talking while my boys and JR played. Carol came out and joined us for a few minutes after finishing with Hildy. It wasn't long before she gave me a hug and wished me a happy birthday and then she and Sam left, leaving Eric and me standing there. About fifteen minutes, later Eric called JR and told him it was time to go home. JR started to complain, but his dad gave him the look that said 'don't even think about it'. JR turned to the other boys and gave them all a hug before rushing to me for a hug.

The boys went to their rooms to get their baths started while I went to talk to Hildy.

"Thanks for all the work you did to get the party organized. I don't know how you got the boys to keep the secret as long as they did," I said, as I gave this large woman a squeeze.

"It was my pleasure. The boys helped out a lot and so did everyone else. Crane, you have some very loyal friends who hold you in high regard," she said. "What do you think the odds are the boys will want another piece of cake before they go to bed?"

"I think the odds are very high," I said laughing.

"I think I know what your secret wish was," Hildy said, looking me straight in the eyes, as I sat down in a kitchen chair.

"What?" I asked.

"It was probably that you wished you had someone nearer your own age you could share your life with. Am I right?"

"That's close."

"Crane, I've known you and worked for you for, what, nearly seven years. In all that time I have seen you throw yourself into your work and for the last six or seven months into saving these boys from the clutches of CPS. You have never considered your own needs. It has always been some thing or some one. I may be stepping over the line as an employee …"

"Oh, Hildy, you're much more than an employee. You're a part of this family. You should know that."

"I know I act that way sometimes, and I'm glad you don't mind. Getting back to what I was saying, there is someone who is very interested in becoming closer to you. And from what I can tell, you are also interested in reciprocating. I can't say it would be my preference, but more than anything, I want to see you and the boys happy."

"Am I really that obvious?"

"No, but I know you pretty well, and I guess I have always been able to read people."

"Daddy, did you like your party?" TJ asked, as he jumped into my lap.

"It was the best party I ever had and do you know why?"

"'Cause the cake was so good?"

"No, the cake was great, but it was because you and your brothers are my sons."

The boys did have another piece of cake as Hildy and I thought they would.

"Now, I know one little boy who is going to be a tired little boy if he doesn't get to bed soon," I said, picking TJ up and starting toward his room.

He put his arms around my neck and giggled softly into my shoulder. I carried him back to his room and sat him down on his bed. Joel was just leading Samson back into the bedroom after taking him out to do his business before settling down for the night.

I sat down on the bed and reached over to give Joel a hug and his kiss. "Thank you, guys, for the surprise party. I'll never forget it. And the photograph, I will treasure as long as I live." I tucked them in after receiving a hug and a kiss on the cheek from each of them.

The scene was repeated in the other boys' bedroom. This time I received three very wet kisses and a group hug from the three of them. "Goodnight, my angels, sleep tight. I love you."

The bed beckoned me as I buttoned up the house for the night even though it was still early. It was not even 9:30 when I slipped under the covers.

CHAPTER 2

Tuesday morning came after a restless night. Too much food at the party and that extra piece of chocolate cake with the boys when they had their snack had my stomach giving me fits all night. Even if it weren't New Year's, I resolved to cut down on the amount of food I consumed. I must have put on weight since the boys came into my life. At least that's what my pants were telling me.

After I got the boys off to school, I decided to take a look at their trust accounts to see whether I needed to make any adjustments to their portfolios. The trusts had been established on January 12, 1995 and I had not paid any attention to them except in a cursory manner since then. I retrieved the morning paper from the kitchen, opened to the stock quotes and circled the stocks the accounts were invested in. To not play favorites, I had invested each account in the same five stocks.

I booted my computer and brought up the spreadsheet that had the details of the accounts. Within a few minutes I had the new value of the trusts.

I had invested their trusts rather aggressively, and it seemed to be paying off. The only conservative stock in the portfolio, WAL-MART, did the poorest of the lot. Being the computer nerd that I am, most of the stocks were in the high tech area. The $2.5 million trust I started in January for each of them was now worth a little over $3.6 million after nearly four months. After reviewing the results and researching the stocks on the internet, I decided not to make any changes in the trusts at this time. I did resolve to pay more attention to the trusts at least once a month or whenever I received information of a negative nature concerning the individual stocks.

I called my broker to check on my portfolio since it was a bit more complex being a mixture of stocks, bonds and cash that changed more frequently than the boys' accounts. I wanted to find out what it was worth now that I had distributed over ten million to the boys. Roger Burton had been my broker for about 16 years. He started handling my stock purchases after my parents died. He did the same for grandfather. He had instructions to reinvest any dividends back into the company that paid it and to deduct any brokerage commission from the interest paid on my bonds.

Roger was able to give me the balances within seconds of when I called him. "This is the way it breaks down Crane. Stocks: $83,322,085.73. Face value of Bonds: $5,000,000 earning interest of varying rates from 6.25% to 9.00% giving an income per year of $390,000.00. Cash in your brokerage account of $71,232.45."

"Thanks, Roger, if you hear any good stock tips let me know."

"Yeah, sure. With the way your stocks have performed you should be giving me the tips," Roger quipped before hanging up.

Satisfied that the boys' and my future finances were sound, I decided it was time to head off to work. As I settled down to the business of ACC I got a call from Ezra Bernstein about the status of my civil suit against Judge Clinton and Joyce Gerhig.

"Crane, these guys want to settle out of court in the worst way. You said you didn't want money. Is that still your thinking?" Ezra said.

"I don't need the money. All I want is for them to publicly admit that they lied about me in order to get even because of their past indiscretions for which they were censured," I said.

"I think I have a workable solution, if you approve. I have already approached their attorneys with it and they both believe their clients will agree."

"What is it?"

"In a nutshell, it calls for Judge Clinton to resign. With Judge Riley referring perjury charges against him he doesn't have too much choice. The next thing they will do is to purchase a full page ad in the *Express-News* explaining their behavior and apologizing to you. You will, of course, have the final okay on the wording of the ad. They will also pay all of your attorney fees, which are not inconsiderable. After all, I have been working on this for the last three months. The last thing they each will agree to do is pay to you a sum of $1. How does that sound to you?"

"If they agree, I don't see any reason to continue with the suit. The one condition I would put on the ad, other than my approving the language, is it should be positioned in the first section of a weekend edition. Sunday would be best, but Saturday would also be acceptable. This would allow for the widest possible readership."

"That's a good idea. We don't want them to hide the ad back in the classified section where very few people would see it. With those suggestions, I will see if I can work out the final agreement with their attorneys," Ezra said, before ringing off.

The rest of the day was fairly routine, and I was able to get away in time to meet the boys when they got off their school van.

Joel got off the van giggling, "I came home tonight."

"Yeah, you stinker, you really had me fooled last night," I said, as I gave him a tight squeeze. JR and the others soon followed him off the van and all received their hugs before we walked up toward the house.

We had barely gotten started when Samson came bounding down the lane and jumped into Joel's arms causing him to drop his book bag. The boys quickly surrounded Samson, petting and hugging him, and in return they were getting licks from a very happy dog. At my urging, Joel put Samson down and we again started to the house. Samson must have covered ten times the distance we did with his constant circling the boys, running up the lane, then back to us. He was in constant motion, showing his happiness that his boys were home.

Everyone disappeared into the bedrooms to change clothes and wash up so Hildy would give them their afternoon snack. They could tell what it was going to be because the house was awash with the aroma of freshly baked chocolate chip cookies. It didn't take long before all of them were sitting at the kitchen table, drinking milk and pillaging the large plate of cookies. I did get one without my hand being mistaken for a cookie.

"Thanks, Hildy," Joel said giving her a hug after he and Chris had rinsed all of the glasses and stacked them in the dishwasher. "Those were super!"

"Dad, the school sent home a note I was supposed to give you," Joel said as he rushed into his bedroom to retrieve the note.

"Oh, I hope he hasn't gotten into trouble at school," I said to Hildy.

"No, I'm sure he hasn't," Hildy replied.

"Here," Joel said handing me the paper.

I quickly skimmed it and was at once relieved. It was a notice that Corinthian Academy was going to go co-ed next year starting in the new high school class that is being added and would consider adding co-ed classes to other grades in the future depending on the demand. The freshman class would be limited to 25 girls the first year to see how that worked out before the decision to add more was made.

After Hildy read the note she looked at me and said, "I think that's a good idea. I worry the boys don't get enough exposure to girls their own ages. They need to learn how to socialize with girls even if they don't have any attraction to them now. That is, all but the twins and the Gordinier girls, Linda and Cassie."

"Yeah," I said, laughing. "They seem to have found quite an attraction there. I think they may be a little too young, but I don't see any harm in their current apparent infatuation with them. They really are a couple of cute little girls."

Later in the evening, after I had checked all of my troop's homework, Joel came and squeezed in beside me in my lounge chair.

"What's the matter, son? Do you have something you want to talk about?" I asked, as I put my arm around him.

"Well ..."

"You can tell me anything or ask me anything. You know that."

"I guess so ... It's just ... I don't want to be a tattletale."

"Whatever it is, it's bothering you. That probably means it's something you're not comfortable with. Is that right?"

"Yeah, but you might get mad if I told you."

"The only way I would get mad is if whatever it is would hurt you. I never want you to be hurt, ever again. I love you guys too much to ever see you get hurt."

"I love you too, dad."

He sat there quietly for several minutes. I decided to let him initiate the conversation I knew he wanted to have. After a while he turned his head to face me and looked into my eyes with his beautiful azure eyes as if to assure himself I meant what I had said. Satisfied, he laid his head on my chest before he began to tell me what was bothering him.

In a voice I could barely hear, he began, "One of the eighth grade boys said he's gonna bring some marijuana to school tomorrow. Some of the other boys and him are gonna smoke it after lunch. They want me to smoke it too. I don't want to, but I don't want them to make fun of me and think I'm a baby. I don't even like the smell of smoke. My old dad used to smoke cigarettes all the time and sometimes he smoked marijuana. He always hurt me worse when he did that."

Joel began sobbing at this point. I wrapped my arms around him and held him until he quieted down.

"Son, you have a very difficult problem to solve. On one hand, if you smoke with the other boys they won't make fun of you or call you names, but you would be doing something you don't want to do. That would probably make you feel bad. On the other hand, if you tell them you don't want any part of smoking the pot, you will be doing what you really want to do, but they will probably call you a baby or other names. Neither choice is without a price.

"Let's see if there is a way to find a third solution. What if there were no marijuana? Would this solve the problem?"

"Yeah, but ... but ... Glenn said he was gonna bring it."

"What if a teacher found it before lunch?" I asked, filing the name Glenn away for future reference.

"How'd they find it?"

"If someone told, say, Mr. Coulter, maybe he could find it and then you wouldn't have a problem, would you?"

"No ... but ... I can't tell him. I'm not a tattletale," he said, firmly looking at me.

"I know you're not. Do you think that if I just happened to call Mr. Coulter and just happened to mention that I had heard someone was going to bring marijuana to school tomorrow that you would be tattling?"

"Well ..."

"I would never tell Mr. Coulter that you told me. You just did what I hope you always do when you have a problem, and that is to come to me and talk it out. Now, why don't you run along? I think I hear Hildy getting your snack ready," I told him, as I kissed the top of his head.

"Thanks, dad. I love you."

"Me too, son."

I waited until the boys had finished their snacks, brushed their teeth and I had tucked them in for the night before I called Paul.

After we had exchanged pleasantries, I got around to the point of the call.

"Look, Paul, I have some information that an eighth grade student by the name of Glenn is going to bring some marijuana to school tomorrow and I was wondering if you could make sure it finds its way into the right hands."

"Oh, I'll bet I know the young man in question. There are two boys named Glenn in eighth grade but I would be willing to wager it's Glenn Parsons. He is a bit of a bully and is on the verge of being a disciplinary problem," Paul said. "The forms you signed, like every parent, give the school the right to search the locker, backpack and person of any student in the presence of an administrator and a faculty member. I think we can handle the problem."

"Paul, I would appreciate if my name never got mentioned in any of this. I don't want it to affect the boys."

"No, Crane, you will not be mentioned when I talk to Mr. Pierce in the morning. But thanks for the heads up. Keeping drugs out of the school is becoming more and more difficult."

After I hung up, I got to thinking it would be a good idea to have a talk with all of the boys about my feelings on drugs. It's just one of those parenting things I'm learning as I go. "I wonder what other things I need to do to be the good parent I want to be," I muttered out loud, as I headed off to bed.

The rest of the week went by quickly. The marijuana problem had been solved by the student in question being assigned to ISS (In School Suspension—a fancy name for isolating him so he had no contact with other students during school hours) for the remainder of the school year and was barred from returning to the Academy for the following year.

The weekend turned out to be great. The weather could not have been more perfect. The boys and I swam and played their favorite game, which mainly consisted of dunking me. We went fishing on Sunday afternoon. They were getting better at fishing, except for TJ, and he didn't have the patience to tend his line for more than a few minutes at a time. He was more interested in watching the other boats, the jet skiers and the water skiers. Even the sail boats caught his attention. By the end of the day, we had caught enough fish for a decent fish fry.

When we got home, the boys went swimming, while I was left with the task of cleaning the fish. Since Hildy left us to fend for ourselves on Sunday evening, I started a fire in the barbeque pit in preparation for grilling the fish. Checking the refrigerator for something to serve with the fish, I found some ears of sweet corn still in the husk which would be great when grilled. I threw together a salad and some garlic bread I could heat up on the grill, and supper was almost ready. I'm sure Hildy could have made a much better meal than I had put together. I laid no claim to being a gourmet cook. The boys didn't seem to object. There were no leftovers.

Monday morning arrived sooner than the boys wanted, but they were soon off to school and I was off to work. I had the meeting with William Weller at ten to discuss their interest in purchasing Alamo Consulting Consortium. I had mixed feelings about the meeting but was willing to listen to their proposal.

Foster came in to see me shortly after I arrived at work. He got right to the point.

"Crane, I talked to Jim Carson this weekend when I was in Austin. He would still prefer that we didn't buy his company, but was open to the idea. I don't know if it would make good business sense to buy it. I can't see us buying it and then shutting it down just to get his consultants. The only way it would make sense is if we kept the office open as the Austin branch of ACC."

"That does have some appeal," I said. "Did you discuss any amount he might want for his company?"

"He did throw out a figure, but it was way out of line. We are four times as large as he is and he wants almost as much as what ACC is valued at. I'm sure he would be willing to negotiate since at the present time he has but one contract open and it only occupies three of his staff."

"Let me think about it. I have that meeting with William Weller shortly so the point may be moot. That reminds me, I need to get started. I told him I would meet him at his hotel at ten. He's staying at the Hyatt down on the Riverwalk so I'd better get a move on. I'll let you know what results from the meeting with him," I said.

The desk clerk directed me to Weller's suite on the top floor of the hotel. It seems these guys go first class all the way. Weller was a tall, handsome, athletic-looking man in what appeared to be his late 30's or early 40's. He ushered me through the sitting room of his suite to French doors that opened onto a balcony overlooking the Riverwalk giving a marvelous view of the waterway. It was a great place to hold a meeting.

We had just exchanged greetings and were sitting down when room service arrived with coffee and a selection of pastries. I accepted the coffee but turned down the pastries with great difficulty. However, the tightness of the waistband on my trousers reminded me I needed to control my eating habits. I had to learn that just because the boys were able to take in large quantities of calories without putting on excess weight, that did not apply to me.

"Let's get right down to business," he started. "We want to buy your consulting firm and are willing to pay top dollar for it. We have done our homework and believe by purchasing your business instead of starting one of our own from scratch would save us at least two years of start-up costs.

"You have an established reputation and a broad client base that would take us time to build up. We believe San Antonio and the central-Texas area have good potential for the consulting business for the foreseeable future.

"It is my understanding you have 32 consultants working on projects at the present time. Is that correct?"

"Not exactly, we have 43 now on projects plus 6 technical assistants who prepare the mundane project reports and update project plans. We also have requests from two companies that will require we add even more consultants. It may be as many as 12 or 15," I told him.

"Hmm, my information seems to be a little out of date. That may change things a little," he said, as he consulted his Franklin Planner flipping through several pages before he continued. "This is what we propose. We will pay you $14.5 million for your business and assume any and all debts of the company. In addition, we propose to retain you as a senior consultant with a guaranteed annual compensation of $100K for a period of five years. For this we would expect you to assist in the promotion of the business and be available in the office on average five days each month."

"That seems to be a very generous offer," I said. "I do have one question. What would happen to all of the people working for ACC? I feel responsible for them. I would want to be assured they have the option of at least one year employment with your firm."

"I don't think that would be a problem. One of the reasons we are interested in ACC is that you have been able to attract some of the best and brightest talent in the South to come to work for you. We would be most anxious to retain them."

"Listen, Mr. Weller, I'm not prepared to make any decision today. I will need to consult my accountant and my attorney to see what impact this would have on my tax liability and on my future financial situation. There is also my family to consider."

"I thought you were a bachelor."

"I am," I said, laughing softly. "I am not married, but I have five adopted sons."

"You, sir, have my deepest sympathy. I have one teenage son and he is driving me to drink."

"I'll be back in touch with you by the end of the week, after I have talked with my advisors, to let you know whether or not I am interested in pursuing the matter any further," I said.

On the way back to the office I stopped off for an early lunch. I took the opportunity to call Gerald Cousins and Carlos Martinez on my cell phone to set up some time to talk to them about the possible sale of the business.

Foster was in my office almost before I was seated. "Well, what did he say?"

"Their offer is very generous, but I haven't made any decision yet. I have to talk to Gerald and Carlos before I could think of making a final decision. I did tell him that I expected them to retain the current staff for at least a year if I did sell. I got Weller's assurance they would do that. They believe our people are highly qualified, and that's one of the reasons they are interested in buying us out."

Shortly after Foster left my office, Carol told me Hildy was on the line. That was unusual. She rarely called unless it was something important. Thankfully, it was only to ask if I were going to be home all evening because her girl friend Janice's daughters were home from college and would be available to be interviewed tonight. I had nearly forgotten about asking Hildy to set something up with them. Other things had been occupying my mind.

I called Eric to see if he were still interested in talking to one of the girls about watching JR during the summer break. He said he was so I invited him to stay for supper and then we could both talk to them. I also wanted to talk to him about the possible sale of the business. Up to this point I had not spoken to anyone other than Carol and Foster about the possibility. I notified Hildy we would be having guests for supper and then decided to head for home even though it was a little early.

Hildy was surprised when I showed up early. On the way home I had decided to tell her I was considering the sale of the business.

"I thought something was on your mind," she said, when I told her. "I thought maybe it was Eric. What would that mean for Janice's girls this summer?"

"I don't think anything would change that arrangement. It will take a while to work out all of the details if the sale goes through. Besides I think it is a good idea to have some extra help around here and give you a break. You need to have a vacation sometime also."

The boys were overjoyed that JR was going to stay for supper when they arrived home. They were less enthusiastic about the possibility they might have a "babysitter" over the summer. The grumbling did not last long. Their afternoon snack took precedence.

Eric arrived just before six o'clock and was greeted by JR on the front driveway in his usual way by jumping up into Eric's arms to be carried back into the house. It always did my heart good to see the loving relationship between the two. I had asked Eric at one time how JR was coping without his mother. Eric had responded that his ex-wife had never really wanted a child and she virtually ignored JR. He said that although JR asked about his mother once in a while he never obsessed on the fact she was gone. I guess seeing my boys didn't have a mother made it seem more natural to him.

Becky Sue and Mary Jane Lively arrived for their interviews right at 7:30. "My God, why do Texas parents tag their daughters with double names?" I thought. Regardless of their names, the girls were quite good looking and well mannered. Their southern accents were so thick they could be cut with a knife. I silently hoped the boys didn't pick that up.

Eric and I talked to the girls and told them what we were interested in having them do. We tried to lay out everything we could think of so there would be no surprises if they took the jobs. This process took about three-quarters of an hour before we were satisfied.

Becky Sue was 20, and Mary Jane had just turned 19. They had completed their junior and sophomore years in college respectively. Both seemed to be mature and interested in working with the boys. Of course they had not met them to this point. Becky Sue was majoring in Secondary Education while Mary Jane was majoring in Elementary Education.

After Eric and I had finished talking to them, I asked Hildy to talk to them also. I thought she could provide us with the female perspective. Then it was time to introduce the boys.

They had been doing their homework while we had been talking to the girls. They seemed to be a little shy at first when we introduced the girls but soon warmed up to them. It wasn't long before they were talking to them like old friends. The boys insisted on giving the Livelys the grand tour of the place.

When the tour was over, Hildy had the boys' snack set out. She had made a large bowl of fruit salad and whipped cream to top it.

Joel came up to me and whispered, "Can they have a snack with us?"

"Why don't you ask them if they would like to have some?"

He did and they accepted. In fact, we all joined in. It is a good thing Hildy prepares enough to feed an army.

"Becky Sue," I said, as they were getting ready to leave, "do you think you would be interested in helping out with my five boys?"

"Yes, I think I am," she said. "They seem to be such young gentlemen."

"They are very well behaved and for that I'm glad. I will need to talk to the boys and to Hildy and get their opinions. I will let you know tomorrow what our decision is. It has been very nice meeting both of you," I said, shaking her hand and escorting her to the front door.

Eric had been having the same conversation with Mary Jane.

The family meeting went pretty much as I had expected it. The boys had all taken an immediate liking to both of the girls so their vote was for hiring both of them. Hildy also was enthusiastic about the way the girls came across. My vote made it unanimous for Becky Sue. Eric and JR had come to the same conclusion for Mary Jane.

"Okay, guys, it's bath time. It's past your bedtime already. Now scoot!"

"Yes, it's time for us to get home also. JR, go get your books and let's get moving. I'll never get you out of bed in the morning," Eric said.

When I went in to tuck the boys in, TJ was already sleeping. I brushed the hair off his forehead and kissed him goodnight. I even patted Samson on the head and told him goodnight. I looked forward to this ritual with the boys every night. It meant they were safe for one more day.

I repaired to my study to take care of some paper work I had brought home from the office. I got to thinking about the way Eric reacted to my telling him about the possible sale of the business. I should say the way he didn't react. It struck me as rather odd at the time, but now that I had time to think about it, it was really strange. Although it had not been part of my thought process on the sale, it would make a relationship with him less strained not being employer/employee. I'll just have to see what Gerald and Carlos have to say tomorrow.

•

CHAPTER 3

The meeting with Gerald and Carlos went very well. We spent the majority of the morning discussing the various legal, financial and tax consequences of the sale. It all came down to what I really wanted to do. The responsibility of the boys was weighing heavily on me. They needed a fulltime parent. Of course, they loved Hildy but she was not their mother and she had her hands full keeping house and cooking for all of us.

I made up my mind that the best thing for me to do was to sell the business at the offered price. It was a fair price for me and the conditions to be placed on retaining the consultants was fair for the employees. The condition that they would assume all debts of the company and continue to pay my ex-partners wife for the deal we had to pay for his share of the business made it even more enticing. With that settled, I called Weller to let him know of my decision to sell, provided all the details could be worked out. I gave him Carlos' name and phone number to call to work out the legal framework. I also gave him Gerald's information in case there was a need for financial data on the company. It was agreed we would try to complete the sale by the end of June. That gave us a month and a half to work out all of the details.

After Gerald and Carlos left I remembered to call Becky Sue to let her know we wanted her to come to work for us. We agreed she should begin work next Wednesday. The boys only had to go to school to pick up their report cards and then would be off the rest of the day. I think the salary I offered her was more than she expected, but I knew she would earn every penny looking after five very active boys.

As usual I left in time to get home when the boys got off the van. Samson knew that when my car arrived home it would soon be time for the boys to return, and he would head down to the gate to meet them. If we had to wait more than a few minutes, he was a dog in constant motion, running to the gate then back to me again and again until the boys arrived. He couldn't wait for the gate to fully open. Instead, he would squeeze through as soon as there was a space big enough for him to get through. Whichever one of the boys was first off the van got the tongue licking of his life. Although Samson loved all of the boys equally, Joel was first among equals.

Darcie came to pick up JR because Eric had to go to Dallas for the project up there. She fairly bounced into the kitchen where I was talking to Hildy. You could tell she was bursting to tell us something.

"Guess what! Mel proposed to me and I said yes," she bubbled.

Hildy and I stood there for a moment with our mouths open in surprise. Hildy was the first to recover. "That's wonderful! Have you set a date?"

"Congratulations," I finally said, recovering my senses.

"Thanks! Yes, we are going to get married June 24. It is going to be a small wedding with only a few friends and family. Of course, you all are invited."

"Where's it going to be?" I asked.

"There's this quaint little Presbyterian Church in Fredericksburg where his mother lives. We have been going there almost every weekend. The pastor is a young man with an amazing presence. His sermons speak to your heart directly from his heart. Mel grew up with him."

While Hildy and Darcie discussed marriage plans, I decided to get JR ready to go home. I just hoped that Darcie had enough of her senses intact to get them home safely.

Sitting down to one of Hildy's delicious meals, I announced to the table that I was going to have to start my routine of swimming laps every morning if I were going to continue to eat like the boys. I also vowed to give up snacks with them. I made my vow public so that I would feel bad if I didn't stick to it.

After supper, Joel asked me if I would help him study for his year-end tests. Of course, he knew I would. Anyway, about all I had to do was to look over his amazingly organized notes and papers he had on every subject and read a question off, and he would answer it. I don't think he missed more than a couple of questions over the course of the hour and a half we spent reviewing, and those he was able to answer with a little hint. I knew he would do well on his tests when we were finished.

The next morning at work, I received a call from Weller saying they wanted to send a team in to do their due diligence on Tuesday. After I agreed, he said there would be a team of five senior people. Two would work with Gerald on the financials while the other three would be working with Foster and the other consultants going over the current projects and statuses.

Upon completion of the call I asked Carol to set up a meeting with all the consultants for Monday morning at nine and to arrange for the out of town people to attend by conference call. I knew everything would be set up perfectly. I was going to miss having Carol's efficiency in organizing my workday when I was no longer the boss.

The rest of the day was filled with the usual routine which consisted mainly of mountains of paperwork that passes over a manager's desk. Now that the decision had been made to sell the company, I was almost glad. Maybe I would be able to get back to doing some "real" work. Actually getting to solve client problems again was very appealing to me at this point. Oh, I got to review all of the project proposals for the company and to add my insight and experience to them, but it was not the same as doing the original work on the proposal. Nor was it as satisfying as working at the client site getting your hands dirty writing code, analyzing and solving unexpected problems or changes to what the client had asked for. It got my blood racing just to think about it.

Eric picked up JR that evening. I asked him if he and JR would like to go fishing with us on Saturday. Before he could answer, JR made the decision for him. I didn't know JR was listening but once he heard that was it, they would be going or there would be one very unhappy boy. I told them we would try to leave the marina around ten and return about two and, if we caught enough fish, we would grill them.

I was glad they accepted because I had ulterior motives. I wanted to have a talk with Eric where we would be fairly free from distractions.

Saturday morning, as I was swimming my laps, which I had faithfully done each morning since I had announced I would, I saw something out of the corner of my eye as I made a turn. Stopping to shake the water out of my eyes, I saw it was Chris.

"What are you doing up so early, son?" I asked a little surprised.

"You said you was gonna swim so I thought I would too. Is that all right?"

"Of course it is. I'm glad to have the company. Come on, I have about fifteen minutes to go."

I knew Chris was a good swimmer, but I didn't know if he could keep up with my longer strokes so I slowed them down so he could keep up. After about ten minutes, I could tell he was beginning to tire so at the end of a lap I decided we should quit. I didn't want him to get too sore from all the exercise. I also wanted to give him the satisfaction of keeping up with me. We got out of the pool and I dried him off with the only towel I had brought out before drying myself.

"Okay, you go jump in the shower and wash the chlorine off and I'll go see what Hildy is fixing us for breakfast."

"Super."

I made the detour to the kitchen, but before I got there I could tell by the smell that she was fixing waffles and sausage. She said she needed about 15 more minutes before she thought she would have enough fixed to keep ahead of the boys' appetites. That gave me just enough time to grab a quick shower before I woke the other boys.

They were reluctant to get out of bed until they smelled the aroma of waffles and sausage. That brought them wide awake, and it didn't take them long to wash up and make their way to the breakfast table.

Saturday had come none too quickly for the boys. They were beginning to love the water, and anytime they knew they were going to get out on the boat they could hardly wait.

Before we left the house, I made sure the boys all had applied a liberal supply of sun block. I didn't want to have any sunburned boys when we got home. It was a good thing we had the van. By the time we had all of the lifejackets, fishing poles, tackle boxes and coolers, along with the boys, it was bulging at the seams. All the boys had seated themselves and had fastened their seatbelts except Joel. He was saying goodbye to Samson. They both looked at me with a pleading look in their eyes that said, "Can I come too?" How could I refuse?

"Okay, get the other lifejacket out of the garage. It may be a little big for him, but if he falls overboard, it will keep him afloat until we can rescue him. And make sure he does his business before he gets on the boat. There are no trees on the boat."

We got to the boat just before ten. The marina had prepared the boat for our arrival. They had removed the tarp that covered it but had not put up the canopy. I decided to wait until the sun was higher to put it up. They had also filled the gas tanks so we wouldn't run out while in the middle of the lake.

About half way through loading our gear onto the boat, Eric and JR arrived. That interrupted the process while everyone greeted each other. It didn't take long to load the rest of our gear and Eric's. Joel took Samson into the trees before they joined us.

Before we left the dock, I made sure everyone had his lifejacket on and secured. I steered the boat to a spot not too far from our house where we had some luck landing fish last week. Although the boat was rated for twelve people, the eight of us, all the gear and a dog looking into every nook and cranny made the boat seem crowded. At first Samson was not sure he liked the gentle rocking of the boat. He was a little unsteady on his feet for the first fifteen minutes or so before he got acclimated. It wasn't long before he was curled up at Joel's feet.

Eric and I got the boys' fishing gear out and baited the hooks before we helped them cast their lines.

"Now be careful when you cast. I don't want to have to dig a fishhook out of any of you. That would not be fun for either of us" I told them.

When the boys were all settled down to the business of fishing, I turned to Eric and said, "I think we need to talk."

"Yes, we do."

We left the boys and went to the stern of the boat and sat at the small table on the port side. Neither one of us said anything for a minute or so. Finally I screwed up the courage to start the conversation both of us wanted to have.

"Eric, you said at one time that you were attracted to me and I told you I felt the same way. I also told you I would do nothing that would jeopardize my ability to adopt my sons. Well that obstacle is out of the way and my sons are secure in my home. The other obstacle, to me, at least, is the employer/employee relationship and that will soon be taken care of."

"I still feel the attraction for you, Crane. How do we go about establishing a more personal relationship?"

Just then TJ said, "I'm hungry. Can we have something to eat?"

"Sure, I think Hildy packed some fruit and juice for a snack. Let me see if I can find which ice chest it's in."

Fishing was quickly put on hold while everyone consumed the apples, pears and grapes that Hildy had packed. The apple juice also disappeared in record time.

When the boys went back to fishing, Eric and I resumed our conversation.

"Crane, are you ready to become involved? You have standing in the San Antonio business community. Any hint of scandal would ruin that. You know how provincial they are. Even in the short time I've been here, I have seen how prudish they can be. I'm not even sure they approve of your adopting five young boys. You know how they love to gossip."

"I wish I could say yes and know I really mean it. What I do know is that I'm lonely. That may sound strange with five active boys filling my life. But I need the company or friendship or maybe even love of another adult."

"I know what you mean. When I moved here I didn't really want any entanglement. I was getting over the bitterness of the divorce and I thought all I needed was JR. And that was true for a while. Now that we have settled in, I find myself yearning for someone to relate to on an adult level."

"I caught a fish. I caught a fish. Daddy, I caught a fish," JR hollered.

"Take it easy, son. Keep your line taut. Reel him in slowly. That's it, you're doing fine. As soon as you get him close to the boat, I'll net him and bring him aboard," Eric said to his son.

When the fish was finally on the boat, all the other boys had to stop and congratulate JR. The first fish of the day was always a special moment. It didn't take long before the boys were back to fishing and Eric and I were back to our conversation.

"How do we get started?" he asked.

"I guess we just need to get some time alone. Set aside some time for ourselves."

"Yeah, I guess we need to take our time. Much as I would like to get to the 'good stuff', I think it's best that we take it slowly."

As the boys caught more fish we were interrupted more and more often. Both TJ and JR caught a couple but soon tired of fishing and were more interested in watching the other boats and playing with Samson. There were an unusually large number of sailboats out on the water today. I later found out they were practicing for the race scheduled for next weekend.

Around noon I asked the dumb parent question, "Anyone hungry?"

I was nearly trampled as they reeled in their lines and made a beeline to the ice chests. Hildy had packed a variety of sandwiches including ham and cheese, roast beef, and tuna salad. Carrot and celery sticks, hardboiled eggs, chips and bananas rounded out our picnic.

"Didn't Hildy give us dessert?" Chris asked.

"The bananas will have to do, son, at least for now. Hildy said she was going to prepare a special snack for us when we get back so you'll just have to wait a little while," I said.

By two o'clock the boys had caught their limit of fish and were ready to go home. I started the motor and headed back to the marina. The boys had a fun time as we headed back, every boat we passed they waved and hollered at. In return most of the boaters smiled and waved back. One guy on a jet ski came along side our boat and talked to them for a minute or so.

"Can I ride one of those?" TJ begged.

"Maybe some day you can. In a few years, when you are bigger," I responded, barely able to control my snicker.

"Okay," he said, and went back to the other boys.

It didn't take long to unload the boat. I think the boys were thinking of the special snack Hildy was preparing for them at home. Samson was equally happy to be off the boat. He headed for the nearest tree.

Eric and JR accepted our invitation to come and have the grilled fish with us. Even with my boys' appetites, I didn't think we could eat all of the fish we had caught.

As I drove the van into the garage, I said to the boys, "You guys go jump in the showers and wash the fish smell off."

"Do you want me to help, dad?" Joel asked.

"Thanks for asking son, but I can handle it. You go help TJ get cleaned up."

I was unloading the last of the tackle when Eric and JR arrived. When they got out of the car, I asked, "Do you want to go take a shower and get rid of the fishy smell?"

"That sounds like a winner. I put us in a change of clothes just in case we went swimming or something, but a hot shower sounds like a better idea," Eric said.

"Well, I hope there's some hot water left. The boys are in the showers now. You know where the spare bedroom is. You can use it or the shower in my bedroom. Take your pick."

I finished putting away the tackle and empty coolers and put the one containing the fish by the back door. I hoped I could get Eric to help me clean them later. As I walked into the kitchen I saw what the special snack was that Hildy prepared. It was a "turtle" cheese cake. She was going to top it with caramel and whipped cream. I gained weight just thinking of all the calories.

That didn't stop the six boys and Eric from enjoying the high calorie treat. With Eric's almost obsessive exercise routine he could afford to indulge, but my less rigorous routine didn't burn as many calories. Instead I went and took a shower.

Eric agreed to help me clean the fish while the boys played three on three soccer (more like kickball). It gave us another chance to talk privately. During the cleaning process, I learned he liked to go to the symphony but had not done so since he moved here because he didn't like going alone.

"The first two years I was in town after college, I had season tickets to the San Antonio Symphony," I told him. "I quit going also because it wasn't very much fun going by myself."

"They have a special program next Saturday that I would like to go to, but I hear it's sold out," he said.

"Hey, if you want to go, I think I can get tickets."

"How? They're sold out."

"Well, I contribute to the symphony every year even though I don't go anymore. They always hold back a few tickets for patrons in case they want to go at the last minute. It's a little late to call today, but I'll call first thing on Monday to see if I can get a couple of tickets."

"Great, it's a date!" Eric said.

I felt almost giddy at the prospects of a 'date' with Eric. It had been a long time since my last romantic adventure. As I thought back on it, the flood of unpleasant memories I had suppressed for so long overwhelmed me. I guess I showed the pain on my face.

"What's the matter, Crane? You look almost ill. Are you all right?"

"Yeah, I'm fine. Just some bad memories surfaced. I'm all right, really."

It wasn't long before Joel approached with the other boys. "Can we have some soda to drink? We're thirsty," he said, panting.

"I don't know about soda, but I think Hildy might have some juice if you ask her."

They raced off to quench their thirst and I turned back to the fish-cleaning and Eric. "Did you notice that Joel seemed more out of breath than the other boys?"

"Yeah, he did seem to be panting more than the others. It could be an allergy. It's past Mountain Cedar pollen season, but maybe it's mold or ragweed," Eric said.

"Well, I need to schedule physicals for the boys before they start their summer sports activities anyway. I'll have Dr. Sam check him for allergies when we go. I suppose I'd better set up an appointment for them next week."

Our meal was excellent. The taste of freshly caught fish grilled over a mesquite fire is heaven on earth. Hildy's side dishes only added to our total enjoyment. Eric was a witty and charming dinner guest. I was really beginning to look forward to next Saturday's concert.

It wasn't long after we ate that Eric said to his son, "JR, it's time we headed for home. Your Aunt Darcie expects us for church in Fredericksburg at ten in the morning. Say goodbye to the boys and let's get going."

As JR hugged each of the boys and went to find Hildy in the kitchen, Eric thanked the boys and me for the great day. We followed Eric back into the house to round up JR. He was having a very serious conversation with Hildy as we walked in. She gave him a big hug and a kiss on the forehead.

Eric received a hug from each of the boys before he and JR got into their car. I shook his hand and he held it longer than normal as we each said our goodbyes.

Next Saturday seemed a long time off.

CHAPTER 4

Monday morning I had three important items on my agenda. The first was to get appointments for all the boys to get physicals. I rushed to work and got there about a quarter of nine. That gave me barely enough time to call Dr. Sam's receptionist to set up the appointments. Thankfully, I was able to get them set up for first thing Thursday morning at nine.

The second item was to hold the meeting with the consultants to inform them of the sale of the business. I expected there would be some consternation from the staff and I was right. After I made the announcement there was complete silence for a few seconds and then it was pandemonium. It seemed that the 26 consultants present in the room were all speaking at once. I couldn't hear the other 17 on the conference call for the commotion in the room.

When I finally got order restored, I started taking questions one at a time alternating between the room and the conference call. Most of the questions centered around job security. I reassured them they would be given the opportunity to stay on for at least a year. That satisfied the majority of the questions, but the meeting continued for almost an hour and a half before most of them were satisfied. I left them with the invitation to come see me or to call me if they had any more questions that came up later. I would try to make myself available to them as much as possible.

When I returned to my office I called the symphony business office. I told the receptionist what I wanted and she transferred me to Fritz Schlather. Fritz was the business manager for the symphony. I had known him since I had a season pass the first couple of years I was in San Antonio.

"Crane, it's good to hear from you again. I am remiss for not calling and thanking you personally for your generous contribution this year. How have you been? We haven't seen you at any concert recently."

"I'm well, thanks. Look Fritz, what I'm calling for is to see if you have any tickets available for Saturday's performance. If you do, I would like to have two."

"We always hold back a few tickets for last minute patrons and I just happen to have a pair. You will have to share a box with the Dills if that's all right."

"That would be fine. I have served on a couple of committees with Jason and Rebecca. They're good people."

"We are also hosting a gourmet dinner at the Rodeo Club if you're interested. It starts at six and costs $125 per couple. If you want I can reserve a couple of spots for you."

"That sounds great. I haven't been to the Rodeo Club in probably four or five years. I do remember they have an excellent chef. Reserve a couple of seats for us. I'll be by to pick up the tickets later today. And thanks, Fritz."

After I hung up, I called Eric to tell him of the plans.

"What is the dress for the occasion?" he asked.

"You would probably feel most comfortable in a tux," I replied.

"I guess I'll have to go rent one. I haven't worn a tux since I got married. Do you know of a good place to rent one?"

I gave him a couple of suggestions and then hung up.

Throughout the day a few of the consultants stopped by my office to clarify issues that pertained to them individually. Most of the questions were about non-salary items such as health insurance and our tax-deferred savings plan. I was able to answer the majority of the questions, but some I had to tell them I would have to find out the answer and get back to them. I was able to get away long enough to pick up the tickets from the symphony office.

As was my habit, I left the office in time to meet the boys' school van when it dropped them off. Only one more day of this before they would be out of school for the summer. It was such a warm afternoon we decided to take a swim before our supper.

We played a game the boys has made up they called 'dodgem'. The rules were simple. We divided into two teams of three players. A volleyball was the weapon. If you were hit by the ball you had to sit on the side of the pool until only one person was left. Since I was the biggest, I was handicapped by being forced to throw the ball with my left hand (I'm right-handed).

One by one the boys were eliminated. First TJ, then Larry, Chris and Lenny followed to the sidelines. Joel and I were the only ones left. He was good at ducking under the water just in the nick of time to avoid being hit by the ball. Our battle went on for several minutes before he faked me out and as I came up from under the water I was hit on the shoulder by the ball.

Joel was immediately surrounded by all the others being hugged and congratulated on his great victory. I joined in the celebration.

We played several more games with Chris and Lenny each being victorious. I did suggest to the boys that they not pick on TJ because he was an easy target and let him stay in the game a little longer. I did this without TJ hearing me tell them. It made him glow with pride when he wasn't the first to retire to the sidelines.

As we exited the pool, I noticed Joel was again breathing hard, much harder than the other boys. When I asked him about it, he brushed it off saying he was just tired. It still concerned me, and I was determined to bring it up to Sam when we saw him on Thursday.

Tuesday was a complete loss at work. The due diligence team arrived and occupied most of my morning. Two of them descended on Gerald while three others interviewed me, Foster and the other consultants in the office. They looked through all ongoing projects as well as recently completed ones. They planned to be here the rest of the week at least.

I was glad when it came time to go home to meet the boys' van. When I got home I discovered they were already home. I had forgotten that school was to be dismissed early. They had already changed clothes, washed up and were enjoying their afternoon snack when I entered the house. I expected to get a hug from them, but they were too occupied with the strawberry shortcake Hildy had fixed.

After supper I asked the boys if they wanted me to read to them. The weather outside was turning rather foul so outdoor activities were out. They agreed with enthusiasm. Since we had finished our last book, I chose a new one from my library, Daniel Defoe's *The Life and Strange and Surprising Adventures of Robinson Crusoe*. When everyone was settled with TJ leaning at my side and the others sitting or sprawled on the floor, I began.

I was born in the Year 1632, in the City of York ...

We got through most of Chapter 1 before I could tell they were getting restless, so I decided we had enough for the night. Besides I think they heard Hildy in the kitchen and expected their snack was being prepared.

Chris again joined me for my swim Wednesday morning. It was my intent to let the boys sleep in since they didn't have to be at school until nine and then only to pick up their report cards. I had only done a few laps when he swam up beside me. He kept up with my reduced strokes for a good ten minutes before he tired. When I noticed he was beginning to struggle I suggested to him that he go jump in the shower and then wake his brothers. He jumped out of the pool and dried off with my towel and ran to the patio door. When he arrived at the door, he turned, flashed me a big smile and waved before entering the house.

Becky Sue arrived at the gate as the boys were about finished eating breakfast. I buzzed her in and made a note to put in a temporary code for her to use so we wouldn't have to let her in every morning.

"Good morning, Joel and Chris and TJ. I can tell who you are, but you two, I'm going to have problems with," she said, looking at the twins.

"The easiest way to tell is, if you can catch them eating, Larry is right-handed while Lenny is left-handed," I said. "Come to think about it, that's not too hard after all. They seem to be eating most of the time."

"Dad!" they both said, frowning at me.

"Becky Sue, why don't you stay here with Hildy while I take the boys to school to pick up their report cards? She can familiarize you with the place and show you where everything is. We should be back by around 10:30."

It seemed like every parent had brought their child to the school today. It was difficult finding a place to park. As I drove into an empty spot, Darcie drove into the space beside me. She brought JR because Eric was off early to fly to Dallas and Mary Jane wasn't going to start to work until tomorrow.

The boys grabbed JR and ran off to their classrooms to get their report cards. That gave Darcie and me a chance to talk.

"What are you going to do now that you've left CPS?" I asked.

"I haven't decided what I'm going to do. The wedding plans are taking up most of my time right now, but after we get back from the honeymoon, I'll have to get serious about looking for a job. Mel would like for me to stay at home. He is a little old fashioned. That's one of the things I love about him. I'd like to stay involved with kids. There are so many out there that need help. I can't turn my back on them as if they no longer exist just because I don't work for CPS anymore. I don't know how, but I want to help. There must be a job out there that will allow me to do just that."

"I'm sure there is," I said.

We chatted on for about forty-five minutes before the kids started drifting out of the school. The boys didn't immediately come to the van. They were busy saying goodbye to all their friends. Eventually they made their way to where Darcie and I were. They all handed their report cards to me at once. Joel had made the "All A Honor Roll" for the second semester. I was very proud of him and I let him know it with a big hug. The others didn't receive letter grades like the middle school gave. They had received "Excellent" or "Very Good" in all their subjects. Each one in turn got a hug and congratulations as I read their card.

We drove home with the boys all excited that they didn't have to go to school for about three months. It was going to be a hot day, and all they could talk about was going swimming when they got home.

"Hey, I don't know, guys. Maybe Becky Sue doesn't swim. I never thought to ask her if she did. I'll check with her when we get home. Okay?"

Their response was a half-hearted, "Yes, dad."

I didn't need to worry. When we got home I found out Becky Sue was a Red Cross trained life guard. She had brought her swim wear just in case the boys wanted to go for a dip. Needless to say the boys were thrilled.

As I drove into work, a thought began nagging at the periphery of my mind. I really didn't know just what it was until I reached the office and sat down at my desk and gave it a chance to come to the surface. When it did it hit me like the proverbial ton of bricks.

"Of course!" I thought, as I picked up the phone and called first Gerald and then Carlos to set up a meeting for nine Friday morning. I was feeling really good knowing the decision I had made, if only I could make it happen. Gerald and Carlos would have to tell me if I could.

I didn't leave at my usual time since I didn't have to be home to meet the boys when they got off the van. I regretted my delay. The evening rush hour traffic was horrible. It took me half an hour to get from my office to highway 281 to go home. I vowed I would not make this mistake again. I had gotten spoiled leaving early with the excuse that I had to meet the boys. Oh well, it wouldn't be that long before I would only be coming into the office five days a month. I suppose I could put up with the traffic for those few days.

Nobody met me as I drove the BMW into the garage except Samson. I scratched his ears and walked in the back door. I greeted Hildy and proceeded toward the family room. As I approached I could hear Becky Sue reading to the boys. TJ was tucked under one of her arms as she read to them from *Alice's Adventures in Wonderland* by Lewis Carroll.

Everyone's attention was fixed on Becky Sue. They didn't notice me until Joel looked up and said, "Hi, dad."

I got my usual hugs from them as the reading session broke up. Becky Sue started gathering up her things in preparation for going home.

"Well, how was your first day?" I asked her.

"I think it went very well. We had our swim and the boys showed me around the property. I didn't know boys could eat like they do. They said you read to them sometimes so I decided it would be a good idea to do that also. You have such a great library. I hope you don't mind that I got one of your books."

"No, feel free to use any of the books I have in there. The boys really like having someone read to them. And by the way, I have to take the boys in to get their physicals tomorrow morning and I would like for you to watch them in the reception area while I'm in the exam room with them."

The boys walked Becky Sue to her car and each one gave her a hug before she left. As she drove away, TJ wrapped his arms around my waist and started sniffling.

"What's wrong, son?" I asked, very concerned.

"She makes me think of my mommy," he sobbed. "Can we go see mommy again? Please?"

My heart nearly broke as I answered him in a choked up voice, "Sure we can. How about if we go tomorrow after we get done at Dr. Sam's?"

"Okay," he said, wiping his eyes with the back of his hand.

I talked to Hildy about TJ's reaction to Becky Sue. She didn't think it was too unusual seeing that his mother was only a few years older than she was and did resemble her somewhat. She thought TJ would get over it in a few days, but thought it was a good idea to visit the grave site again.

TJ seemed to need a little more loving than usual. He needed to be in constant touch with either Hildy or me. He sat on my lap as we watched a *Peanuts* special on TV before I sent them off to shower and get ready for bed.

The next day we left for Dr. Sam's office as soon as Becky Sue arrived. I had remembered to give her a code so she could get in without us activating the gate. TJ was the first to give her a big hug. Fortunately, the traffic was not too bad and we arrived at Sam's office just a few minutes before nine. Finding a parking place was the worst part about having to go all the way downtown for anything during the day.

I filled out all the paperwork for everyone except Joel. His file was already thick with all the tests he had been through over the past months. The other boys had not been seen by Sam as patients.

Joel was the first to be examined. Dr. Sam did all the usual tests. When he got to the point where he was listening to Joel's chest and breathing I told him of my concerns about Joel's shortness of breath.

"Well, I wouldn't worry too much about it. Joel has grown almost two inches in height and gained thirteen pounds since the first day he was here. It is not unusual for a growth spurt to have that effect on a young boy. He has also entered into puberty which could cause some of that. I'll have a few extra tests run on his blood sample to see if anything has changed since the last one. If that doesn't show up anything we could put him through an allergy series."

TJ wanted to be next. I don't think he had ever had a physical like Dr. Sam was giving him. He was having a great time until it came to take the blood sample. He was having no part of the needle. No amount of coaxing could convince him it wouldn't hurt. Finally, I went to the waiting room and got Joel, hoping he could convince TJ it would be all right and not hurt.

It took Joel a few minutes but he succeeded in convincing TJ to let Sam draw the blood. Joel held one of his hands and I held the other. When it was over and Sam put a Band-Aid on his arm, he wore it like a merit badge, showing it off to his brothers in the waiting room. He did snuggle up to Becky Sue after his bravado wore off.

Larry and Lenny wanted to have their physicals together, which was not surprising to me. They giggled like a couple of little girls through most of it. When it came time for the blood sample, Larry could not watch while his or Lenny's was drawn. Lenny, on the other hand, was fascinated with the process, asking Sam all kinds of questions and watching intently as Larry's and then his own sample was drawn.

Chris' physical went off without a hitch. The whole process for all five of the boys took nearly two hours. I could tell they were getting restless so I suggested we go get an early lunch. That met with thunderous approval.

Becky Sue and I herded the boys a couple of blocks down the street to a Tex-Mex cafe which I knew was a good place to eat and was friendly to kids.

As we sat down, the waiters began bringing an endless supply of tortilla chips and salsa. They would no sooner set one basket of chips down when it was "inhaled". It wasn't long before the waiters learned and brought four baskets of chips at a time and an equal amount of salsa.

We consumed an enormous amount of food between the seven of us. I must admit I did my share of the eating. I always liked Tex-Mex food. I think Becky Sue was amazed at the amount of food the boys were able to put away. By now I was used to it. Of course we had to have the obligatory praline as we left the restaurant.

"Are we still gonna go see mommy?" TJ asked.

"Yes, TJ."

"Can we take her some flowers?" he asked.

"I think that would be a good idea. There's is a flower shop a couple of blocks over and I think we could do with the walk after all that food," I said.

The large array of flowers on display at first overwhelmed the boys. TJ was the first to arrive at a decision as to what he wanted to get. "Can we get these white ones?" he asked, pointing to the carnations.

That brought immediate acceptance from the other sons.

Joel thought for a minute and then asked, "Maybe we could add four red ones? One for each of us?"

"Why don't we add a pink one for Chris? Your mom was not his, but you are his brother now. Is that okay?"

TJ ran to Chris, gave him a hug and shook his head to indicate yes. I looked at Becky Sue and saw she was just barely holding back the tears. She is going to fit in just fine, I thought, because she wears her heart on her sleeve like the rest of us do.

We waited while the lady behind the counter assembled the dozen white, four red and one pink carnation into a beautiful arrangement with ferns and baby's breath. TJ insisted on carrying the bouquet to start with but soon relinquished it to Joel after a couple of blocks.

It was rather quiet as we drove to the cemetery. It was either their full stomachs or the anticipation of seeing their mother's grave again, reinforcing the fact she was dead.

I parked the van as close to the grave site as I could, but we still had to walk a ways to it. As we approached her plot, Chris began to hold back. It was then I realized that he may never have been to a cemetery before, let alone visited a place where a person was actually buried.

The other four walked up to their mother's headstone and placed the flowers at the base. I put my arm around Chris as he watched his brothers talk to their mother's monument as if she were there listening to them.

"Son, your brothers loved their mother very much. She loved them also. It makes them feel good to come and talk to her. Do you understand?"

"Uh-huh," he said quietly, as he slipped out from under my arm and went up to the headstone.

As he touched the headstone, I heard him say in a voice barely above a whisper, "I wish you was my mom. Maybe you would have loved me too."

I nearly lost it right then and there. Becky Sue did. She rushed back to the van wiping the tears from her eyes as she went.

When the boys were finished, we headed back to the van, Joel with his arm around TJ's shoulder and Larry and Lenny on either side of Chris with their arms around him.

Since it was getting late, I decided to call Carol and tell her I would not be in today at all. I had planned to go to the office this afternoon. She said everything was fine at the office, but there were a couple of emails I should look at. Everything else could wait until tomorrow.

Friday morning was going to be hectic. I had the meeting with Gerald and Carlos, as well as a final meeting with the due diligence team before they went back and reported their findings.

I was nearly late for the nine o'clock meeting with Gerald and Carlos. They were waiting for me when I arrived. "Sorry, guys, there was an accident on 281 that had traffic backed up for miles. It seemed like the police were doing everything in their power to prevent traffic from moving long after Air Life had taken the accident victims away. Let me get a cup of coffee and I'll be right with you."

Carlos followed me to the coffee pot and poured himself a cup also.

"How's everything going with the sale? Any problems working out the contract?"

Carlos responded, "No, everything seems to be going smoothly so far. We are beginning to refine the language of the contract. I would guess that all the details should be worked out by the end of next week or early the following week."

"On the financial side," Gerald began, "the one area which still needs to be worked out is how to allocate the profits of the company that have accrued to you prior to the end of June but have not been realized. I have been working with one of their accountants and I think we are close to agreement. I don't see that it could hold up the sale though."

"Good," I said. "Just how much will I realize from the sale after taxes?"

"That's hard to say exactly but my best estimate is Uncle Sam will take about 22% of the proceeds above your basis for the company. I estimate your basis to be about $4.5 million so that means the taxes will be about $2.2 million. Your net should be about $12.3 million. Now that does not count your drawing account that you haven't touched this year. The taxes have already been paid on it so it's yours unencumbered. It amounts to nearly $275,000. By the time we allocate those unrealized profits you should receive something around $12.6 million give or take."

"Thanks, Gerald, that's what I needed to know," I said, taking a deep breath before continuing. "Here is what I want the two of you to help me with. I want to set up a tax-exempt foundation for the purpose of helping children, like my sons, to get adopted. I want to call the foundation 'Adoption Services for Exceptional Children' or ASEC. It will provide yearly grants to couples or individuals who would not normally consider adoption because of their financial situation but would provide loving homes if money were not a consideration. I intend to seed the foundation with $10 million to start with. What do you think?"

They both sat there with open mouths and disbelieving looks on their faces before Gerald recovered enough to say, "You mean you're going to give away $10 million just like that?"

"Gerald, you know my finances even better than I do. You know I can afford it. It will probably help with my tax situation also."

"Crane," Carlos said, "who's going to run this foundation? When do you need it set up? Are you crazy?"

"I will be in charge overall. I have someone in mind to run the day-to-day operations, but I haven't approached that person about the job yet. I also have a second person in mind to act as a consultant to the foundation. Second, I would like it set up and ready to go by the first of August. And to answer your last question, yes I probably am.

"I will be the president and chairman of the board and I would like for each of you to serve with me if you have no objections. I will receive a salary of $1 per year. As directors you will receive compensation for your time at your standard rates or whatever you deem to be fair."

"Crane, I would be honored to serve on the board," Gerald said. "If serving does not require extensive absences from my business, I, too, would be willing to receive the $1 salary."

"I echo Gerald," Carlos said.

"Thanks, I was hoping I could count on you," I said. "I hope I can invest the seed money in some fairly safe corporate bonds that will give a return of about 10%. That would give us about $1 million to deal with each year less any salaries and other expenses."

We tossed around a few more ideas before the meeting finally broke up. After they left, I called the two people I wanted to be part of the foundation and asked if they would stop by the house Saturday afternoon around one o'clock to discuss a proposition I had for them. Despite their questions, I wouldn't reveal what I had in store for them.

Later in the afternoon I met with the due diligence team before they returned with their recommendations. From what I could determine from them, the results were most favorable. In fact, some of the team seemed down right excited about the proposed purchase.

On the way home, I started to get excited about what was going to happen tomorrow, not only with the foundation but the 'date' with Eric.

CHAPTER 5

I didn't know how the boys would react to my not being home to tuck them into bed on Saturday night. When I explained to them that Eric and I were going to the symphony, they hesitated for a minute before Chris piped up, "Can JR stay all night with us?"

"I don't know, son. We'll have to ask his dad. I think Darcie was going to stay with him," I said. "I'll call Eric and see what he says. Okay?"

At supper, I discussed with Hildy what she thought about taking on another boy to take care of while we were out. She didn't seem to have a problem with it. All she wondered about was where he would sleep. When I suggested they use the three beds upstairs in the new large bedroom, it was met with enthusiasm from the boys. It would be like camping out.

When I called Eric after supper to suggest JR's stay on Saturday, he, at first, was hesitant saying that Darcie already said she would stay with him. He told me he would have to talk to Darcie and get back to me.

About fifteen minutes later, he called and said it was fine with Darcie. She said Mel and she would come and help out with the boys until they went to bed, then they would go back to Eric's place for the night. That would take some of the responsibility off of Hildy.

I also made a call to Jack to see if he was available for lunch on Monday. "It's been a long time since I bribed you with a lunch," I said.

"I know this isn't just out of the goodness of your heart," Jack replied. "You know I have never turned down one of your bribes, but I would like to know what it is I'm being bribed for this time."

"You'll just have to wait and see. I have a proposition for you that I think you will be interested in. I'll come by and pick you up around noon. See you then," I said, as we hung up.

I put the boys to bed and gave them a special hug and kiss since tomorrow night I would miss doing it for the first time since they came to stay with me. I think I was more affected by the thoughts of that than the boys were.

As I was putting them to bed, I noticed Joel had a couple of bruises on his arm. "How did you get those bruises?" I asked.

"I don't know. I got a couple on my legs too, see. I guess I just bumped into something," Joel said.

"You're going to have to be more careful. I don't want anyone to think that I have been beating up on you," I laughed.

"No, you wouldn't do that," he said, wrapping his arms around my neck and giving me a kiss on the cheek. "You love me, I know that."

I didn't sleep well. There were too many things running through my mind that I needed to take care of tomorrow. The foundation was foremost in my mind but not far behind was the time I would be spending with Eric. It was after two the last time I looked at the clock.

I still got up to swim my laps. I had been very diligent about my efforts to get back into better shape and to try to remove an inch or so from my waistline. I wasn't too surprised when Chris joined me a few minutes after I got in the pool. I was getting used to him swimming with me in the mornings. He didn't always get up in time but at least a couple of times a week he seemed to make it. About ten minutes was his endurance limit. When I noticed him tiring, I would suggest he go jump into the shower and then get the others up for breakfast.

The morning seemed to drag on as I waited for my guests to arrive after lunch. A few minutes before one the gate buzzer sounded. I activated the gate opener after verifying it was one of the people I expected. The second car was close behind. I went outside to greet my guests.

Paul Coulter was the first to step out of his car. "Crane, it's good to see you again. Your call the other day was so cryptic I have been in a state of anticipation every since."

Darcie and Mel pulled up right behind Paul's car.

After the introductions, I led them into my study. I had Hildy prepare iced tea and some cookies for our meeting. I wanted to put everyone in a good mood for my sales pitch.

"I know you have been wondering what I had in mind when I asked you to come here today. I have a proposition for you to consider. But first I need to give you some background.

"Paul, you may not know this but I am in the process of selling my consulting company.

"What you and Darcie both don't know is what I intend to do with most of the proceeds from the sale. I've talked with my lawyer and have instructed him to process the paperwork necessary to set up a tax-exempt foundation with $10 million from the sale. That foundation is why I asked both of you here today.

"Darcie, I know you will be looking for a job after you return from your honeymoon. The foundation I am creating will have as its sole purpose to find suitable parents who are willing to adopt older kids who might not have the opportunity in the normal course of events and to facilitate those adoptions. The foundation will provide ongoing financial support for those couples or individuals who don't have the financial resources. I want you to run the day-to-day operations. I know you cared deeply about the kids you came across working for CPS; that's why I want you to help me make this successful.

"Paul, you probably wonder what you could do for the foundation. You once told me about your experiences with the foster home system. I want you to act as a part time advisor to keep us from becoming a 'private' CPS.

"Now, I know you probably have a lot of questions. Some I can probably answer, some I can't because the plan is just coming together."

"When is all this supposed to happen?" Darcie asked.

"I would like things to get started as soon as possible. I know it will take a while to get everything going, but the foundation will be official August first," I said. "If you agree to serve, we'll work out your compensation."

"Sounds interesting," Paul mused.

For the next hour I tried to answer all the questions they had. At the end, I think I had convinced them that what I was proposing was feasible. I told them to think it over and to let me know in the next week or so if they were interested. I got their assurances they would seriously consider my proposal and let me know.

It was a little after two when my guests left. That gave me enough time to take a swim with the boys before I had to start getting dressed for the dinner and symphony. We had a great time in the pool, playing all the games that the boys had made up. Their favorite was still the very first one we had played when they came to live with me—king of the hill. Their laughter rang out across the lake. I was sure people on the south shore could hear their glee as well as mine.

"Okay, guys, dad has to go start getting ready to go to the symphony. Why don't you go see if Hildy has a snack for you? But first, go rinse off the chlorine and get out of your swimsuits. I think Hildy was going to bake some peanut butter cookies," I said, as I lifted TJ up onto the side of the pool.

They ran off for their quick showers and I went for a longer one. I shaved again even though I had shaved before breakfast this morning. It was just after 4:30 when I finished in the bathroom. Eric was not due until around five. I took my freshly dry-cleaned tux out of the closet and removed it from the plastic bag. Going to my dresser, I retrieved my stockings, tie, handkerchief, shirt studs and cuff links. Hildy had laundered my formal shirt and hung it on a hanger. It was starched to perfection. My patent leather shoes were the last item to join my ensemble.

Seeing everything was ready, I returned to the dresser and found a pair of bikini briefs I had not worn in several years and put them on followed by an undershirt. I don't know what possessed me to wear those briefs. I guess I just wanted to be a little daring.

It took me nearly fifteen minutes to dress after everything was laid out. The most time was spent putting in the shirt studs and trying to tie the bowtie. It had been several years since I had tied one and it took some time to remember all the correct twists and turns to make it come out right. Grandpa had taught me how and he always said you had to hold your mouth just right to tie one. I don't know if I did, but I know I made some awful contorted expressions before it was tied right.

"WOW!" Joel said, as he looked up and saw me enter the kitchen.

"Crane, you look fantastic," Hildy said, as she stepped up to me and straightened my carefully tied tie and brushed my shoulders. I could remember as a kid my mother doing the same for my father when they had to go to a fancy dress affair.

"Yeah, dad, you look pretty," TJ chimed in.

"Thank you, I think," I told TJ, as I tousled his hair.

"I never seen you dressed up like that before. That symphony must be a real fancy place," Chris said.

Larry and Lenny just stared at me as if I were a stranger before they said in unison, "Cool, dad!"

Just then the doorbell rang. It had to be Eric and Darcie, but I didn't know how they got through the gate. The boys followed me as I went to let our guests in.

JR was the first to enter when I opened the door. "Hey, Mr. Johnson, you and my dad are dressed like twins," he said before being surrounded by my boys and hustled off to the kitchen so they could finish their pillaging of the peanut butter cookies.

"You guys are going to knock them dead in those outfits," Darcie said giving me a hug.

I shook Mel's hand who was next in line. Eric was the last to enter. It was a good thing or I would have stood there with my mouth open unable to say anything to the others. Eric was stunning in his rented tux. I had always thought he was a handsome man before, but tonight dressed in a tux, he could easily have been a model or a movie star. I just shook his hand and ushered everyone into the living room. By that time I had recovered my powers of speech.

I told Darcie and Mel to make themselves at home. Hildy was planning to grill hamburgers for the boys for supper, and they were going to 'camp out' in the new upstairs bedroom. Eric and I wouldn't be back until after midnight.

We took the BMW. As we approached the gate, it reminded me to ask Eric how they got through it without a code.

"Oh, one of your boys gave JR a code."

We made small talk as we drove to San Antonio. It was never hard to talk to Eric. He had such an easygoing attitude and he easily kept up his end of the conversation. Traffic was not too heavy so we were able to get to the Rodeo Club in plenty of time to park the car and find our table. Dinner was to be served at six so there would be plenty of time to get to the performance which was to start at 8:30.

We were to be seated with the Dills, with whom we would be sharing a box at the concert, and the Belkins. I remember being introduced to the Belkins some years ago.

As we took our seats at the table a waiter approached and asked if we would like a cocktail or a glass of wine. I looked at the menu card on the table and saw we were having beef as the main entrée so I ordered a bottle of Beaulieu Vineyards Cabernet Sauvignon Private Reserve 1987. This is an excellent wine just coming into its maturity this year.

Before our wine arrived the Dills showed up. "Rebecca, Jason, it's good to see you again. It's been a couple of years, hasn't it?"

"Crane, it's been too long," Rebecca said as she gave me a hug.

I shook hands with Jason and then introduced Eric. "I'd like to introduce Eric Levin. Eric, this is Rebecca and Jason Dill. Eric works with me and is a single father like I am."

I saw the strange look that Rebecca gave me, but she hesitated to say anything until after they had finished greeting Eric.

"Now, Crane, what's this single father thing you mentioned? I never heard about you getting married."

"Rebecca, it's a long story, and some day I'll have to tell you the whole thing. The short version is that I adopted five boys between the ages of six and twelve. Four of them are biological brothers. The other one is not. They all came from abusive homes. They have been in my care for going on nine months."

"How in the world do you manage to take care of them and work at the same time," she asked.

"I have a wonderful woman the boys have adopted as their grandmother. She lives with us and provides the feminine touch the boys need. She is an amazing woman. I could not do this without her."

"That's great, Crane. Eric, how long have you been in San Antonio?" Rebecca asked.

"I've been here about six months. I used to live in Houston before my divorce. My son and I moved here to take a job with Crane's consulting company. Our sons became good friends immediately," he answered. "They go to the same school."

The waiter arrived with our wine at that point. He offered a taste to me before he poured Eric a glass. It was superb. It would definitely complement our meal. The Dills decided to order the same wine.

The Belkins arrived just as the waiter was about to leave. He took their wine order and left. After the introductions were made all around we settled down to pleasant dinner conversation. Jerry and Patricia Belkin were an older couple in their mid-sixties, but they were delightful to talk to. The six of us had a very enjoyable dinner. The company was great and the meal was outstanding. From the Caesar salad prepared at our table side to the crème brûlée, everything was absolutely delicious. I vowed I would not wait as long as I had to visit the Rodeo Club again.

Eric was a hit with both couples. His witty conversation throughout the meal kept everyone in great spirits. I was in awe and admiration of him and his easy manner. Often during his banter he would place his hand on my forearm as if making a point. I don't know if it was intentional but it certainly made a point with me.

I was sorry when the meal was over and we had to leave for the symphony hall. Eric and I thanked the Belkins for the delightful company telling the Dills we would see them at the symphony and departed for our car.

"Crane," Eric said squeezing my arm as we approached the car in the parking garage, "I don't know how the rest of the evening will go, but I have so thoroughly enjoyed myself. It's been a long time since I have spent a meal in such gracious and hospitable company. I feel like I've known these people all my life. Thank you."

As we got into the car I said, "The Dills and Belkins are good people. They're not your typical rednecks you sometimes find in the upper social strata. That doesn't mean they would understand or approve of a relationship between the two of us. Caution is the best course of action."

"Of course, Crane, I would never do anything to jeopardize your standing in the community."

We got to the symphony in plenty of time to find our box and get settled before the Dills arrived. Again the conversation among the four of us was light and non-controversial. Soon the curtain came up and the program began.

I had not paid that much attention to what was going to be performed until I looked at the program as the orchestra began to play. I was pleasantly surprised that the first part of the program consisted of music from Bizet's opera *Carmen*. The second part after intermission was selections by Tchaikovsky. *Carmen* was my favorite opera and my favorite music from it was from *Suite #1* called *Les Toreadors*. If it didn't get your blood stirring I don't know what would.

At intermission we had a glass of champagne with the Dills. It wasn't good champagne but the good thing about it was it didn't make you want to have more than one glass. It gave you a reason to stay sober so you could drive home safely.

The music was great. The orchestra played with feeling and technical accuracy. *Les Toreadors* was played with the passion I think Bizet would have applauded. I remember how much I used to enjoy coming to hear the music, but how much I hated being there alone. With Eric there beside me, I enjoyed the experience so much more. I almost hated to see it come to an end.

We said our goodbyes to the Dills, thanked them for making the evening so enjoyable and headed for the car. As we settled into the car Eric surprised me by leaning over and kissing me on the cheek.

"Crane, I can't remember when I've enjoyed myself more. Thank you for making all of this possible."

"I must say it's been one of the most enjoyable, if not *the* most enjoyable, times I've spent. The Dills and Belkins added to my enjoyment, but being with you made it special," I said, as I took his hand and squeezed it. I decided I had better get started home before I got too maudlin.

It was almost midnight before we got out of the city and headed for home. Our conversation on the way home was kept to safe topics. Neither one of us knew exactly how to proceed. I drove Eric to his house since Mel and Darcie had driven him to my place earlier.

When we arrived there was an uncomfortable silence. Neither one of us knew what to say. "I'll come and get JR in the morning. I hope he wasn't any trouble," Eric said trying to make conversation.

"Oh, I'm sure he was fine. The boys should be up and have breakfast by nine," I said.

Eric leaned toward me. I leaned toward him. It just seemed natural that our lips met. His kiss was soft and at the same time intense. I responded instinctively to the kiss.

"Thanks for a great time tonight," Eric said huskily, after we broke apart. "I think I'd better go."

"You are very welcome and yes, I think I'd better go, too. I'll see you in the morning."

As I drove the few miles back to my house, I kept wondering why I hadn't invited Eric to spend the night with me. I knew part of the answer. I wasn't ready to admit to myself that I was gay and I wasn't ready to try to explain it to the boys.

I set the house alarm and went into my bedroom to change out of my clothes. When I turned on the light I noticed a lump in my bed I knew was TJ. I turned off the light and went into my bathroom and turned on the light. I quickly slipped out of my clothes and into my pajama bottoms before walking over to the bed and sliding quietly under the covers trying not to wake him up.

"Hi, dad," TJ said sleepily, as he slid over to me. "I missed you."

"I missed tucking you in also," I said and kissed his forehead. "Now go to sleep, it's late."

He turned over and curled up into a ball like he always did when he slept and was asleep before I had a chance to pull up the covers. Unfortunately, sleep did not come to me as quickly. I mulled the events of the evening over in my mind and was very pleased with all that happened. It wasn't a night of wild sexual ecstasy, but a very comfortable night for starting a lasting relationship based on friendship, mutual respect and physical attraction.

I was awakened the next morning by a pair of soft lips kissing my cheek. "Good morning, little one. Did you sleep well?" I asked.

"Yeah, when you came home. I was 'fraid you wouldn't come home," TJ said, as he wrapped his arms around my neck.

"There's no way I would ever leave my TJ," I said, rubbing my nose against his. "Did you have fun playing with JR last night?"

"He's lotsa fun. Hildy let us stay up late and play and ever'thing."

"That's great. Why don't you go see if your brothers are awake? I'll bet Hildy will have breakfast ready soon. Eric is going to come get JR after breakfast."

TJ hopped out of bed and went to seek out his brothers while I jumped into the shower for a quick one. I decided I would give myself a break from swimming laps this morning. I justified it by reminding myself how good I had been for the last few weeks, and besides my tux had not been too tight around the waist last night.

The boys were just coming out of their bedrooms after washing up and putting on some clothes when I opened my bedroom door. This was cause for all of them to get their morning hugs and that included JR.

"Good morning JR. Did you have a good time last night?"

"Yes, sir, we did lots of neat stuff. I wish I had a brother so I could sleep with him. Chris said I could be his pretend brother."

Hildy must have been up early cooking. She had fixed a mountain of scrambled eggs, sausages, hash brown potatoes, biscuits with jelly, orange juice and milk. I grabbed a cup of coffee while the boys served themselves. I just hoped there would be some left by the time everything had been passed. It is amazing the amount of food one additional boy can make disappear.

After breakfast I helped Hildy tidy up the kitchen. "How were the boys last night? Did they behave themselves?" I asked her.

"They were very well behaved. They seemed to really enjoy JR's company. They had so much fun, laughing and playing and being rowdy without being destructive. Darcie and Mel were great to have here too. They're going to be fantastic parents someday. You could see how much Mel enjoyed being around all of them. He acted like he was one of them sometimes," she chuckled.

"TJ said they got to stay up late. What time did you finally get them to bed?"

"It was about a quarter to ten before they got into bed, but it was probably after ten before they really got settled down and to sleep."

"I found TJ in my bed when I got home around 1:30. He's still a little insecure about me leaving him no matter how many times I've told him I wouldn't."

"Yes, he puts up a brave little front most of the time, but underneath he is still afraid he'll lose you like he lost his mom."

When the front door bell chimed I knew it had to be Eric. I shook his hand and ushered him into the kitchen where I offered him a cup of coffee. He declined but went to Hildy and gave her a big hug.

"Thanks for taking care of my little rascal. I hope he wasn't any problem."

"He was no problem at all. He had a ball playing with the others. You may have a hard time getting him to go home. He said something about wanting a brother …" she said, with an evil grin on her face.

"I don't see that in the cards," Eric responded.

They stayed about another hour before Eric was able to convince JR it was time to go. Reluctantly, JR agreed but only after he got a promise from his dad that he could come back again sometime.

Everyone was tired and didn't put up a fuss when I suggested they get their showers taken and get ready for bed about eight o'clock. It was just barely dusk when I tucked the last one in bed. I think they were all asleep before I left their bedrooms.

I didn't skip swimming my laps Monday morning. Chris didn't join me. All the boys were still sleeping when I finished my exercise. After I finished showering and getting dressed I went in and woke them up. They resisted getting up until I told them Hildy had fixed pancakes and bacon for breakfast. Food is a powerful motivating factor for growing boys.

Becky Sue arrived just as I was leaving for work. She told me she was going to give the boys another swimming lesson this morning since it was supposed to be so nice out.

Carlos called me sometime after I got to work and wanted some clarification on a couple of points about the foundation, but indicated everything was going well in his efforts to get it set up and running. I spent the rest of the morning taking care of the seemingly endless paperwork required to run a business. Foster was visiting one of our client sites in Houston so Carol and I were handling his duties.

I did get away in time to pick up Jack for lunch. I drove to a little hole in the wall place that I knew served some of the best chicken fried steaks in San Antonio.

"Oh, I see you're really going all out to bribe me," Jack said sarcastically.

"Just you wait. If you don't like the food here, I'll bribe you with another lunch at a place of your choice tomorrow," I told him.

The place was definitely unimpressive when you walked in. It was impeccably clean but the furniture was old and not much of it matched. I led Jack to an empty table near the wall trying to get a little privacy so I could talk to him. We had barely taken our seats when a very large older woman approached and threw her arms around me.

"Crane, you naughty boy, you haven't been here in months. Don't you like momma's food?" she chided me.

"Momma Sara, I've been so busy and haven't been able to get here. Excuse me, I'd like to introduce my friend Jack. Jack, this is Momma Sara. Careful, Momma, he's a cop," I laughed.

I went on to explain to Jack that I had eaten almost every day in Momma Sara's place for nearly a year while I did a project for a company down the street. I was a young kid just out of college and she sort of took me under her wing.

Momma Sara left without taking our order. I knew what she was doing but Jack wondered what was going on. He hadn't yet seen a menu so he didn't know what he wanted to order.

While we waited, I started to tell Jack about the foundation I was going to set up. He thought it was a wonderful idea but wasn't sure why I was telling him so much about it so I got to the point.

"I want to use you to vet the people the foundation proposes to assist. I haven't worked out how to do it yet, but I need someone with police connections I'm sure. If you have any ideas I would like to hear them."

"Are you willing to pay for this service or is this a volunteer effort on my part?" Jack asked.

"We will definitely pay. I just don't know how we would go about it. Would I pay the police department or can I pay you?"

"Look Crane, I have been talking with my wife about setting up my own private investigation operation. If your foundation is willing to pay, you could be my first client. I have become more and more frustrated with the political in-fighting in the department."

"Jack, I hate to see you give up your pension, but that's your decision. The foundation will pay you a retainer of $50,000 plus any out of pocket expenses. I want you to think it over before you give me your answer. Talk it over with your wife. The foundation will not be in operation until the first of August and it will take us some time to get up and running."

Momma Sara arrived with two large platters holding her mouth watering chicken fried steaks, mashed potatoes with cream gravy, and corn. One of her waiters was right behind her carrying a tray with freshly baked hot rolls, tall glasses of iced tea and a bowl full of lemon wedges.

"Wow!" Jack exclaimed. "If I eat all of this, I'll have to find a place to take a nap this afternoon."

It was a struggle, but we ate it all. That made Momma Sara very happy. She gave both Jack and me a big hug when we got up to leave. Believe me, when Momma Sara hugs you, you know you have been hugged.

I dropped Jack off at police headquarters and returned to the office. Carol greeted me as I entered.

"Dr. Greene called while you were out and wants you to call him back as soon as possible. There are a couple of other calls, but they can wait. If Foster were here he could take care of them. I think they are about some equipment we are providing to one of the clients under contract."

I sat down in my chair, picked up the phone and dialed Sam. I got his receptionist but she said the doctor would like to speak to me and put me on hold. It seemed like forever but it was probably only a couple of minutes before Sam came on the line.

"Crane, I'm glad you called. Could you come by this afternoon sometime? I would like to discuss the results of the physicals I gave the boys last week."

"Sure, but couldn't you just tell me over the phone?"

"I would really like for you to come to the office. Can you make it at 3:30?"

"I'll be there, Sam."

This was not like Sam. All the other times I had taken Joel to him for the AIDS tests he always just gave me the results over the phone. The more I thought about it, the more worried I became.

CHAPTER 6

It was difficult for me to wait for my appointment with Sam. I couldn't concentrate on anything at the office so at around 2:30 I left the office and started for Sam's office. I knew whatever he had to tell me was not good. I was afraid it was Joel, but I also was not sure it wasn't one of the other boys. By the time I had driven to downtown and parked the car near his office, I was a basket case.

I walked into the office shortly before 3:15 hoping Sam would be available early. I was disappointed. He was running behind schedule and would not be able to see me for another half an hour. It was probably the longest half hour I have ever spent.

Finally, he finished with his last patient and I was ushered into the office. After the perfunctory greetings, I sat down in a chair in front of his desk and prepared myself for the worst, or at least I thought I had.

"Crane, the physicals for TJ, Chris, Larry and Lenny all are normal for their ages. The only thing I would suggest for them is a multi-vitamin daily," he said, as he picked up each of the files and briefly looked at each one.

"But, what about Joel? Is there something wrong with him?" I choked out my questions.

"There are some abnormalities in his blood that are very worrisome. He shows some signs of anemia which probably accounts for his shortness of breath. That's not the main concern, however. What worries me most is the number of immature lymphocytes. I noticed in his physical that his lymph nodes were slightly enlarged but not outside the normal range.

"I have consulted with Dr. Ahmad Darwish, a pediatric oncologist at Christus Santa Rosa. I had him look at the report and had the blood sample sent to him. He and I are in agreement that the results of the blood tests indicate a high probability that Joel has Acute Lymphoblastic Leukemia."

"Oh, my God! That can't be. It just can't be true," I sobbed. "He has endured too much already. Why?"

"I know, Crane. I have no explanation why this should happen to him. I have also become very fond of him over the past nine months. He has bravely faced all the things we have put him through without complaint.

"Now, because we have caught this early, there is an excellent chance it can be treated successfully. There is one more test we will want to run before we make the final diagnosis. It is not a pleasant one. We will want to take a sample of his bone marrow to confirm it."

"What is that? What do you have to do?" I asked trying to regain my composure.

"It's a bone marrow biopsy. During this test, a needle is inserted into a bone in the hip and a small amount of bone marrow is removed and examined under the microscope. That will enable us to determine what kind of leukemia he has, if indeed that is the case. There is some pain involved in this procedure. We try to eliminate as much as we can with a local anesthesia but this is not always completely successful.

"If, after the biopsy is examined, we confirm it is leukemia, we will probably order a spinal tap to determine if there are cancer cells present.

"Crane, I know this is an awful lot to take in at one time. The quicker we get the biopsy taken the quicker we can start the treatment plan," Sam concluded.

"Does that mean chemotherapy?" I asked, suddenly regaining my analytical mind.

"Yes, and depending on how advanced it is and, if the nervous system is involved, it could be quite protracted. In some cases radiation therapy is prescribed. There is also some testing going on with bone marrow transplants, but in my opinion, that is a last option."

"Where can he get the best treatment?"

"There are a couple of places. The most famous one is, of course, St. Jude Hospital in Memphis. The other one I would recommend is M.D. Anderson in Houston. Both have excellent reputations for treating children."

"When can we get the biopsy taken?"

"I have set up an appointment with Dr. Darwish for 8:30 tomorrow morning at Christus Santa Rosa. He will perform the biopsy and should be able to give you the results in about an hour. I have a number of articles on childhood leukemia I'm going to give you to read. There are a number of good sources for more information I will compile and give you. I'll drop them off at your house tomorrow, depending on the outcome of the test."

"Thanks, Sam," I said, wiping my eyes with my handkerchief. "What do I tell Joel?"

"For the time being, I would only tell him about the test tomorrow. That's going to be tough enough. If the results of the test are confirmatory, then he will need to be fully informed of the disease and the consequences of the treatment."

"God, I didn't know being a parent was going to be so hard," I said, getting up and taking the material Sam handed me.

"Are you going to be okay to drive home?" Sam asked. "Joel and those boys need you now more than ever. Please take care and drive safely."

"I will," I said, as I left the office.

The drive home was the longest I had ever experienced. I even had to stop once in Bulverde to wipe the tears out of my eyes and settle down enough so I could drive on home. As I neared the house I tried very hard to compose myself so that my appearance would not upset the boys.

They didn't seem to notice if, in fact, I was looking or acting differently. Hildy did notice something was different and asked me what was wrong. I put her off, telling her I would talk to her later.

"Joel, why don't you take your brothers into the family room and read them some more of the Robinson Crusoe book?" I suggested, after the supper dishes were cleared.

"Okay," he said. "Let's go get the book, TJ."

After I heard Joel begin reading to the others I turned to Hildy. "Dr. Greene called me to his office this afternoon. The news he gave me was not good. He believes Joel has a high probability of having leukemia."

"Oh, Jesus Lord, no! It can't be. It's just not possible," she sobbed.

"I have to take him in for another test tomorrow morning to confirm the diagnosis. I have to tell him tonight about the test without causing him too much stress. The only good news is that Sam says that because we found it early there is a good chance of it being treated effectively. There is hope for complete remission."

"Is there anything we can do?" she asked, dabbing at her tears with the hem of her apron.

"Pray for him and try to help keep his attitude positive. Having a positive attitude has been shown to enhance the outcome according to the literature

Sam gave me. Also I would appreciate it if you didn't tell anyone until we know for sure."

"Would you mind giving the boys their snack after while? There is some ice cream in the freezer and there are cookies in the cookie jar. I think I need to go to my room. This has been very unsettling. I just need some time to absorb all of this. Tell the boys I wasn't feeling well and I'll see them in the morning," she said, as she gave me a tight squeeze and then headed off to her apartment.

I went to check on the boys. Larry, Lenny and Chris were sprawled on the floor listening to Joel as he read. TJ was leaning against Joel as he did to me when I was reading. Joel looked up from the book when he noticed I had come into the room.

"Dad, this is harder to read out loud than when I read it to myself. The words are strange to say," he said.

"I know, son. Let me read it for a while and you can take a rest," I said, sitting down and taking the book from him.

He joined the three on the floor and TJ slipped under my arm as I started reading where Joel had left off. I continued to read to them for about another half an hour before I could see they were getting restless.

"Okay, that's enough for tonight. Why don't you go play with your new video games? I need to talk to Joel for a minute," I said to them.

After the four of them left, I motioned for Joel to join me on the couch.

"What's the matter, dad? Did I do something wrong?"

"No, son, you didn't do anything wrong. What I need to tell you is that you have to go see the doctor for another test. This is going to be different from all the others you've taken. The doctors want to take a sample of your bone marrow to see if it's okay. What that means is, they will insert a needle into your hip area about right here," I said, pointing to my hip. "Then they will withdraw the sample and analyze it. Do you have any questions?"

"Am I sick? Is that why I'm so tired all the time and have so many bruises?"

"That's what we want to find out, son. We have to be there early so I will get you up before the others so we can be there by 8:30. Now go play with your brothers. Hildy said you guys could have ice cream and cookies for your snack after while."

I put the boys to bed as usual and I followed almost immediately. That doesn't mean I was able to sleep. I tossed and turned and mulled over everything that had happened today. I don't think I got over a couple of hours of sleep when my alarm went off at six. After showering and shaving, I went to wake up Joel. To my surprise he was awake but still in bed.

"Time to get up, son. You wash up and I'll see if I can't find us something for breakfast," I said, giving him a hug. "Try not to wake your brothers."

I went to the kitchen and was just beginning to search for something I could fix us for breakfast when Hildy came in and took over. She quickly made us some oatmeal and toast. When Joel arrived, Hildy gave him a big hug.

We left for Christus Santa Rosa just after 7:30. Thankfully the traffic was not too heavy so we were able to get to the hospital in plenty of time for our appointment. I approached the reception desk and asked where I could find Dr. Darwish. The elderly black lady behind the desk began trying to explain the complicated directions to get to his office when a "candy striper" who was standing nearby volunteered to show us the way. It was a good thing because I would never have found the room from the directions that were given. I think hospitals are deliberately designed as mazes to confuse patients and visitors.

I thanked our guide as she led us to a room labeled ONCOLOGY with Dr. Darwish written below it.

"What does oncology mean?" Joel asked.

"Well, son, it means the study of abnormal cell growth."

"What's that?"

"It means like tumors and things."

"Do I have a tumor?"

"I don't know. Dr. Darwish should be able to tell us in an hour or so."

Thankfully, Dr. Darwish came in at that moment. He introduced himself to me and to Joel before settling down in a chair he pulled up so he was sitting right in front of us.

"Joel, has your dad explained to you what we're going to do today?"

"Yeah, he said you were going to stick a needle into my hip. Will it hurt?"

"I try to make it as painless as possible. Most people only feel a pinprick when we shoot in the painkiller. After that, all you should feel is the pressure as the needle goes into the bone. A few people do have some pain but it is usually not severe. I understand from Dr. Greene that you are a very brave boy. Do you have any questions?"

"Do I have a tumor?"

"Why do you ask that?"

"Dad said that oncology studied tumors."

"Well, that is part of what I do. There are other things an oncologist does. I look for cells that don't grow right and make people sick. That's what we are trying to find out with you. We want to know if there are any bad cells in your bones. Are you ready now?"

"I guess."

"May I stay with him while you take the biopsy?" I asked. Looking at Joel, I saw him nod his head.

"Yes, of course. It is usually less stressful if a parent is present. Now, if you'll both follow me we'll try to get this over with as soon as possible," he said, as he stood up and started toward the door.

I put my arm around Joel and we followed Dr. Darwish down the hall to another room with an examination table and all sorts of apparatus.

"Now, Joel, I want you to go behind that screen and remove your clothes and put on this gown. You may leave your stockings on, but remove all the rest of your things. When you're done, I want you to climb up on the table and we will get started."

Joel looked at me hesitantly, but when I squeezed his shoulder, he complied. He handed me his clothes as he came out from behind the screen. Dr. Darwish stepped out of the room while Joel was behind the screen. Joel had no more than got seated on the table when a middle-aged nurse entered the room carrying a tray with a small vial and what looked like a syringe inside a plastic package. After setting it down on a small side table, she opened a wall cabinet and removed a couple disinfectant swabs.

"Honey, I need for y'all to lie down on your left side so I can get your hip cleaned up," she drawled in her thick Texas accent.

Joel started to complain when she lifted his gown up and exposed his bare bottom. "It's all right, honey, I've seem more youngen's butts than y'all could shake a stick at."

For some reason, this struck Joel as funny and he started giggling. He giggled all the time the nurse swabbed the disinfectant on his hip. He only stopped when she filled the syringe with the anesthetic and injected it in two places in his upper and lower hip area. She covered the area with a large gauze pad and began picking up the used syringe and swabs.

Before leaving, the nurse said it would take about ten minutes before his hip would be completely deadened so we might as well make ourselves comfortable. I didn't think that was possible, but I tried to be calm for Joel's sake.

It seemed like an hour, but it was really only twelve minutes when Dr. Darwish returned with two young-looking men in white coats he introduced as residents and said they would be observing the procedure.

I went and stood by Joel's head as the three doctors gathered around the table. Dr. Darwish poked at the hip several times asking Joel if he could feel anything. When he was satisfied the area was sufficiently deadened, he took out the largest needle I think I have ever seen. I tried not to let my feeling of panic show on my face as he began probing Joel's hip for the right spot to insert the biopsy needle. I saw the needle start in, but had to look away. I looked into Joel's eyes and tried to exhibit a calm I did not feel. I held both of his hands in mine in case he felt any pain so he wouldn't try to grab for the doctors hands.

Joel gave a grunt as I heard the needle enter the bone. I could see the tears forming in his eyes.

"It's okay, son, it'll be over soon. You're doing fine. You're a very brave boy. I love you," I said, leaning down and kissing his forehead.

The procedure did not take that long but it was not over quickly enough for me. There were beads of sweat standing out on my forehead and I could feel sweat dripping down my back. I felt like I had run a mile. I was exhausted, and all I had done was hold Joel's hands.

Dr. Darwish put a small bandage over the spot where the needle had gone in before telling Joel he could get dressed with my help. The local anesthetic might make walking a little difficult for a while until it wore off. He said an orderly would be by shortly with a wheelchair is case we wanted to go to the snack bar. He would have the results in about 45 minutes and asked us to meet him in his office then.

The mention of a snack brought a sense of urgency to Joel's dressing. I was helping him with his shoes when the orderly arrived with the wheelchair. The young Mexican-American man offered to escort us to the snack bar. I thanked him and accepted his offer since I had no idea where it was.

Joel thought it was fun to ride in the chair, especially when Juan, our orderly, made sounds like a race car and took a route that bore a striking resemblance to a *gran prix* track. It was just the thing to brighten his and my spirits.

There were several other children in the snack bar with their parents. Some were in wheelchairs like Joel. Others were attached to IV bottles hanging from metal stands on wheels. Joel didn't seem to notice. He had his eyes fixed on the cinnamon rolls covered with white icing. He ate one and drank a pint carton of milk and then looked at me with that too familiar hungry look. He got another one.

Despite our circuitous route to the snack bar, I was able to retrace our path to Dr. Darwish's office. We had to wait a few minutes before he joined us. He looked at me and I knew the answer was not what I was hoping for.

"How would you like me to proceed? Do you want to talk to me alone or do you want Joel here as well?" he asked.

"Joel will stay," I said wrapping my arm around him and pulling him close.

"Very well then," he paused, looking at the folder in front of him. "I could give you the numbers but they wouldn't mean anything. It all boils down to one thing, the diagnosis is ALL (Acute Lymphoblastic Leukemia). I think Dr. Greene told you we would want to do another test if this were the results. We won't do that today. It will have to be done before any treatment is begun."

"Did he say I got leukemia?" Joel turned to me and asked.

"I'm afraid so, son," I said squeezing him even tighter.

"Am I gonna die?" His beautiful azure eyes looked into mine with the most fear I had seen in them since the whiskey incident just after he came to live with me.

"No way! I'm not going to let anything take my Joel away from me. Your brothers and I need you too much."

"Joel," Dr. Darwish spoke up, "we will have to begin a treatment program for you very quickly. However, with us finding your leukemia so early, I can almost guarantee we can put it into remission."

"I want the best treatment possible for him," I said. "I don't care what it costs. I'll take him anywhere at anytime to make sure he has the best available. I would be interested in your recommendation on where he can get that treatment."

"I only see two choices for his treatment. Dr. Greene, I'm sure, told you about St. Jude. They do fantastic things there. M.D. Anderson is also a great choice. They collaborate very closely with St. Jude and usually participate in the same clinical trials of new therapies. Their success rates are on par with St. Jude. Given that M.D. Anderson is only three hours away by car I would probably choose it. There would be less impact on your family being this close. Really, the choice is yours."

"When can we begin his treatment if we go to Anderson?" I asked.

"Before I came in here, I talked to a colleague there who is head of the oncology department. He has an opening he can see Joel tomorrow at three o'clock. After his evaluation he will probably admit Joel to the hospital to begin his treatment on Wednesday. If that is your choice, I will call him and confirm the appointment."

"How long will he have to be in the hospital?"

"That is hard to say. It all depends on the course of treatment selected. As a rough guess, I would say at least a month and then he would have to go back for a day or so every couple of weeks for a while. During the time he is not actually in the hospital he will also have to take some form of chemotherapy."

"Very well, let's do it. I will have Joel there at three tomorrow."

Dr. Darwish made the phone call while we waited. Everything was confirmed before we left. He gave me a couple of pain pills for Joel in case his hip began bothering him. I thanked him, gathered Joel up, and we headed for the car. Neither of us had much to say.

Joel was silent for most of the way home before he asked, "What's gonna happen to me? Do I have to go to the hospital?"

"I'll try to explain as much as I can to you when we get home. I want your brothers to hear about it too. Dr. Sam gave me some articles on leukemia yesterday and he said he would stop by on his way home tonight and bring some more. I know you have a lot of questions and I'll answer them if I can. If I don't know the answer we'll ask Dr. Sam when he gets there. To answer one of your questions now, yes, you will have to go to the hospital. I will be there with you."

It was almost lunch time by the time we got home. The other boys were full of questions as we walked in the back door. I tried to be forthright and at the same time not be too graphic about Joel's condition and his upcoming treatment. I was able to answer most of their questions but what helped the most was when Hildy announced lunch was ready. Becky Sue had sat quietly while I talked to the boys, but I could tell she was trying very hard to hold back the tears.

I elected to skip lunch and make some phone calls. The first was to a corporate apartment leasing company that ACC dealt with when we had staff living in Houston while they worked on projects. The apartments they rented were totally furnished except for food. I asked if they had two units available. I wanted a two bedroom and a three bedroom apartment. Thankfully, they had some available in a very nice complex with a pool and exercise room. Best of all, they were not too far from the Medical Center.

The second call was to a private jet service to see if I could charter a jet to take all of us to Houston tomorrow. When they asked how many passengers I told them to count on eight. I knew there would be seven for sure and if I could talk Becky Sue into going that would make eight.

The third call was to a limousine service in Houston to have them pick us up at Hobby airport and take us to the apartment. I would also need it to take Joel and me to the hospital. In order to feed the hungry hordes, Hildy would need to go to a market so she would need transportation.

The fourth call was to the office to tell them not to expect me back until I let them know. I told them the only way to get in touch with me for a while was to page me. As soon as I got a phone number in Houston I would let them know. I didn't share with them the reason I was going to be out of town; just that it was a family emergency.

After the last call I sat back trying to think what else I needed to do. Things were happening so fast I was sure I would forget something. Hildy came in carrying a sandwich and a glass of iced tea as I was sitting there.

"Here, eat this," she ordered, placing the plate and glass on my desk in from of me.

I knew better than to refuse.

"Sit down, Hildy," I said rubbing my eyes. "I need to let you know what is happening." I went on to describe the arrangements I had made. "I'm sorry if I were presumptuous in assuming you would travel to Houston with us. I think of you as a vital part of the family and the glue that holds us together."

"I would have been insulted if you didn't include me. Of course, I'll go with you. Are you going to ask Becky Sue if she will go?"

"Yes. What do you think? Will she be willing to go?"

"I'll get her," Hildy said getting up from her chair.

Shortly, she came back with Becky Sue in tow. When I explained the situation to Becky Sue, she was at first hesitant, but when I assured her she and Hildy would be sharing a two bedroom apartment, and I would be paying all of her expenses, she accepted.

Hildy and Becky Sue left to begin preparations for tomorrow's trip. The phone rang and I answered it. It was John asking to speak to Joel. He picked it up in the family room. John and Joel had become very good friends over the past six months. I never inquired into the details of their friendship. I relied on Joel's good judgment to keep it at an appropriate level.

"Dad," Joel said, sticking his head into the study. "Can I tell John about my leukemia?"

"If you want to, son. Make sure you tell him he can't catch it from you."

The rest of the day was a flurry of activity. Packing for five boys and making room for everything they wanted to take was an adventure. After looking at the mountain of stuff which didn't even include Hildy's or Becky Sue's luggage, I decided the plane could not hold it all. Since we were going to be gone for up to a month, I didn't want the boys to have to leave all of their toys behind. It was going to be upsetting enough for them. A courier service was the answer to our "stuff problem".

I contacted a service and arranged for them to pick up the majority of the baggage and have it delivered to our new temporary home by noon tomorrow. Becky Sue left to go home and pack her clothes.

Sam stopped by as promised and dropped off more reading material for me. After looking at some of it, I really didn't want to read any more. Much of the material was intended for medical professionals and was extremely graphic in its descriptions of treatments and consequences of various chemotherapy agents.

I convinced the boys to go to bed a little early, explaining we had a busy day tomorrow, and we had to get up early to get to the airport for our flight. This did not happen before they had their evening snack.

Before I went to bed, I called Eric and explained to him what was going on and asked him if he would stop by the house now and then to check on things. He was stunned by the news and readily agreed to look after things for me.

I went over my list one more time before I turned in. I noted that I had neglected to call Gerald and Carlos to let them know I would be out of town but that could wait. If they called the office Carol would let them know.

Exhaustion from the day's events had begun to take its toll as I slipped into bed. Laying there, my brave façade I had maintained throughout the day collapsed. My fear for the outcome of Joel's illness overwhelmed me, and I began sobbing uncontrollably. I could not bear to even consider the possibility of losing him. Tears streaming down my cheeks, I reached for the box of tissues I kept on the bedside table. Instead of finding the tissues my hand encountered a pajama-clad boy.

"Why are you crying dad?" Joel asked as he slipped into bed.

"Because I love you. I told you I would never let anything hurt you again, but I'm helpless to prevent what's happening to you now. I would do anything for it to be me that was sick instead of you."

"I know," he said, as he snuggled against me and promptly went to sleep.

I was not surprised a little later when TJ joined his brother in my bed.

CHAPTER 7

The bed seemed awfully crowded when my alarm went off. When my eyes were able to adjust to the morning light, I discovered the reason. Some time during the night Larry, Lenny and Chris joined us. My king size bed was overflowing with sleeping boys. I slipped out of bed trying not to wake any of them and went to take my shower. They were still sound asleep when I finished in the bathroom.

Slipping on a pair of slacks, polo shirt and sandals I went to the kitchen to see if Hildy was preparing breakfast. We didn't have to be at the airport in San Antonio until after nine.

Hildy had breakfast well under way when I got to the kitchen. I could see she had tears in her eyes. I went to her and without a word hugged her shoulder. She told me she needed about ten more minutes before she would be ready for the boys so I went to wake them. As I stood in the doorway watching my angels sleep I could hardly contain my pride in them and the love I had for them. But at the same time I cursed the disease that had the potential for taking one of my sons from me. Before this overwhelmed, me I started shaking the boys and telling them to get up and get ready for breakfast.

It didn't take long after I mentioned breakfast that they were up and off to their bathrooms to wash up. They did take just long enough to give me a hug before disappearing.

"Is Samson going to come with us?" Joel asked, as the boys finished eating.

"I'm sorry, son, but we can't have pets in the apartment where we will be living in Houston. I had forgotten about him in the rush to arrange everything for our trip. Do you think it would be all right if JR took care of him while we were gone?"

"I guess so. I wish Samson could come with me."

"I'll call Eric and see if it's okay with him if Samson can stay with them. I know JR likes Samson and would really like a dog of his own."

I hoped I would catch Eric before he left for the office. As luck would have it he was still there and agreed to keep Samson. When I heard him ask JR if he wanted to keep Samson, you could have heard the answer all the way from their house without the benefit of the telephone. Eric said he would have Mary Jane bring JR over in a few minutes to pick him up.

The goodbye scene with Samson was enough to tear your heart out. As each boy hugged Samson, he got his ear licked. Joel's goodbye was the longest as he tried to explain to Samson he would be back soon, and he was to behave for JR while we were gone. Samson looked into Joel's eyes as he received his instructions, and you would almost believe he understood what Joel said. Mary Jane and JR drove away with Samson looking back all the time they were in sight, there was not a dry eye in the group.

The van was stuffed by the time we got all eight of us inside plus what luggage would not fit on the roof luggage rack. We finally got started for the airport shortly after eight. Our plane was scheduled to leave San Antonio at 9:15 for the 53 minute flight to Houston's Hobby airport.

The boys were all excited about flying since none of them had ever been in a plane before. Becky Sue was a little nervous. She had never flown either which was surprising since she was nearly twenty-one. Hildy had only flown once and that was a long time ago, back when the planes were all propeller-driven. I knew they were all in for a treat.

I parked the van in the long-term parking lot and called the jet service to pick us up and transport us to the general aviation area and our plane. The boys had their noses glued to the windows of the van carrying us as they took in everything. Every plane they saw was a new cause for excitement. When the gate opened and we approached the plane that would take us to Houston, I thought the van would explode from their enthusiasm.

The van drove up to the jet and our driver got out, helped Hildy out of the van and then started unloading our luggage. The boys exited the van and stood transfixed at their surroundings.

Thankfully, our flight attendant stepped out of the plane and began ushering the awestruck boys up the steps into the plane. Hildy and Becky Sue followed, although I detected a little reluctance from Becky Sue. After seeing the luggage was stowed, I followed them into the plane's interior.

Captain Burleson greeted each of the boys and asked them if they would like to see into the cockpit. That was a foolish question as they all hollered their answer. So he took them two at a time into the cockpit and showed then the array of instruments. As they came back into the cabin area their mouths were literally open in amazement. Joel and TJ were first in with Chris and Becky Sue being the last.

Hildy and I saw they got into their seats with their seat belts fastened. Their eyes got as big as saucers when the pilot started the engines and the plane started to roll toward the runway. You could hear the intake of breaths when the plane began picking up speed as it raced down the runway. Once we were airborne, you could see the look of surprise when the landing gear retracted and there was a loud thump when the wheel well doors closed. After that, the smiles returned to their faces.

A few minutes later the captain announced over the speaker system that we were free to unfasten our seatbelts and move around the cabin. I don't think the boys even heard the announcement. Their noses were pressed against the windows trying to take everything in as we continued to gain altitude.

The flight attendant got their attention when he started through the aisle with donuts and cartons of milk for the boys and Becky Sue and coffee for Hildy and me. It must have been the excitement of everything that was happening, but about 15 minutes after we were airborne, TJ began to squirm in his seat.

"What's the matter, TJ?" I asked.

"I gotta go to the bathroom," he whispered.

"Come with me, I'll show you where it is."

"They got one on the plane?" he asked with surprise.

I led him to the small restroom and showed him how to flush the toilet and stood outside the door while he took care of business. When he finished, he ran back to the other boys and extolled the virtues of the in-flight facilities. This caused each of them to have to inspect and use the restroom whether they needed to or not.

It wasn't long before our captain announced that we were beginning our descent into Houston Hobby and for everyone to take their seats and fasten their seatbelts. Our flight attendant helped TJ get his fastened and made sure the others were buckled in as well.

The boys became saucer-eyed again as we made our descent and they looked out the windows and saw the tall buildings of downtown Houston. The thump of the wheel well opening startled them, as did the change in the engine noise the closer we got to the end of the runway. Our touchdown was smooth, but there was a collective "Ooooohhh" as the wheels touched the concrete.

It took a while to taxi from the end of the runway back to the terminal area where our pilot parked the aircraft. The limousine was waiting as we walked down the steps from the plane.

Becky Sue, who had been very quiet all through the flight, came up to me and said, "Crane, that was fantastic. I can't wait to tell Mary Jane and mom. Thank you!"

The ground crew removed our luggage from the plane and stowed it in the trunk of the limo. I shook hands with the pilot and co-pilot before I walked to the limo and got in.

"Wow! This sure is a big car," Joel said. There was agreement from the rest.

"It's called a 'stretch-limo' because they cut it in two and add several feet of car and then put it back together. That way it has room to hold all of us," I told him.

On the way to our apartments, I pointed out the Astrodome and Astroworld to the boys as we past them. Our apartment was in an area known as the Museum District, which was only a mile or so from M.D. Anderson. It didn't take us long to get there since Hobby was not too far from the apartments.

I was pleasantly surprised at the amount of room we had in the apartment. The three bedrooms were equipped with queen size beds. Two of the bedrooms shared an adjoining bathroom while the third bedroom had its own. The kitchen was well-equipped with everything you would need to fix meals. The only thing I saw that we might need was another couple of chairs for the table. There were only six and we would need at least eight. There was a large TV in the main living area plus another one in what would be my bedroom. All in all, it was going to be comfortable but not as spacious as home.

The driver had helped us carry our luggage from the limo to the apartments. When he finished, I told him we would need him back at noon so we could go somewhere to eat, and we would need a driver and a smaller car to take Hildy grocery shopping and to take Joel and me to the hospital.

We hadn't gotten our suitcases fully unpacked when the courier service arrived with the rest of our stuff. The closets were full by the time we got everything put away. I was hooking up the PlayStations to the TV's when our driver arrived to take us to lunch. The boys were ready to eat. It had been almost two hours since they had the donuts on the airplane.

I herded the boys into the limo followed by Hildy and Becky Sue. I told the driver to go to the nearest or most convenient Ninfa's. (Ninfa's is a famous Tex-

Mex chain of restaurants mainly in the Houston area.) He took us to the one on the southwest freeway. I had never been to this one but I was sure the food would be good. The boys loved Tex-Mex food so I knew they would be happy with my choice.

When we got there, the place was fairly crowded so we had to wait about ten minutes before we were seated. The aroma of all the food made the boys impatient. The chips and salsa started to disappear as soon as we sat down at the table. I wanted to order one of the Ninfaritas (Ninfa's version of a strong frozen margarita), but thought better of it because of the doctor's appointment later today. While we waited the boys watched the tortillas being made by two of the restaurant employees. They were fascinated at how quickly they could turn them out. We did manage to put away a good amount of food when it arrived.

It was almost two o'clock by the time we got back to the apartments. The boys wanted to go see the pool. I knew they wanted to go swimming but told them they had to wait an hour to let their lunches settle before Becky Sue could take them for a swim.

As the time for Joel's appointment approached, I became more and more nervous. I thought I knew what to expect but didn't know whether I was ready for it. Joel had been very much himself all day. If he was nervous, he didn't show it. I think I was nervous enough for both of us.

Our smaller car arrived at 2:30. Hildy decided to ride to the hospital with us and then have the car take her to do the grocery shopping. I would probably be at the hospital with Joel for quite a while. I didn't know if I would be able to force myself to leave him in the hospital by himself. I knew he was going to have to stay, but I hadn't worked out in my mind how I could be there with him and still be with his brothers. They needed me too.

Before we left, Joel took Chris and TJ aside and I heard him tell TJ he was not going to be able to sleep with him for a while and he wanted Chris to take his place. "I'm gonna be gone for a while and I don't want you to be lonely," he said, with tears in his eyes. "Chris will take good care of you. He promised he would. Didn't you, Chris?"

"Yes, Joel, I'll take good care of him. I promise," Chris said.

"I don't want you to go. Please don't go," TJ cried.

"I gotta go. They have to make me well again. You can come see me. Can't he, dad?" he asked, looking at me.

"Yes," was all I could get out.

Our driver dropped us off at the hospital and then took off with Hildy. The reception desk was very helpful and gave us a map of the hospital layout with

Dr. Kerner's office clearly marked on it. We arrived at his door a couple of minutes before our three o'clock appointment. His nurse greeted us as we entered the office. She told us to take a seat, the doctor would be right with us. She also handed me a clipboard with several pages of forms I needed to fill out. Joel sat beside me and read the forms along with me as I filled them out.

"Why do you need to fill out all that?" he asked.

"I don't know, son. It probably just gets stuck in some filing cabinet somewhere," I said, smiling.

I was working on the last form when Dr. Kerner arrived. He apologized for being late but said he had been responding to an emergency.

"Hi, there, I'm Dan Kerner and you must be Joel," he said, as he put out his hand to shake Joel's. "You're a fine-looking young man. We have to get you well and out of here as soon as we can. All right?"

"Yes, sir," Joel responded.

I could tell immediately that Dr. Kerner had a way with kids. He talked to Joel as an equal not as an adult to a kid. After the preliminaries were out of the way, he began telling Joel what was going to happen. He spoke directly to Joel. I was just an observer, although a very interested observer. He told him about taking a sample of his spinal fluid to see if there were any signs of leukemia in the central nervous system. He told Joel that if they didn't find anything there, that it would be a good sign and his treatment would be much simpler.

When he stopped and asked, "Do you have any questions, Joel?"

Joel paused a moment before he replied, "Am I gonna get well?"

"Son, if I were a betting man, I would bet on it. The odds are in your favor. Your leukemia was found early, you're still in good health and your dad can get you the very best of care."

Turning to me, Dr. Kerner said, "I see you requested a private room for Joel. Is that correct?"

"Yes, is there a problem?"

"No, no, it's just sometimes it is better to have someone he could share his experiences with while he is here. A private room can be a lonely place. I noted on the information I got from Dr. Greene that you have four other sons. Are they and Joel close?"

"Very close."

"Another argument for sharing a room. I have another patient about Joel's age who is going through the same thing. He has been here undergoing treatment for a little over a week now. His background is somewhat similar to Joel's also. I know you can afford a private room, and I won't object if that's what you want …"

I could tell by the way he trailed off that he really would object. "You're the doctor. I just want to make sure nothing is spared to make sure Joel gets the finest treatment available. I will spend whatever is necessary to help him get well."

"I think I'd like somebody, dad," Joel said quietly.

That was settled. Dr. Kerner got up and asked that we follow him. He led us up to the second floor and down the hall to a small examination room. We went through the same procedure we had gone through with Dr. Darwish. Joel got undressed, donned a hospital gown and got up on the table. This time Dr. Kerner swabbed the area of Joel's lower spine himself. The needle he removed from the packaging was not as large or menacing as the one used for the marrow biopsy but it was not small by any means.

"Now, Joel, I want you to curl up in a ball. Bring your knees up to your chest and hug them to your chest. You're going to feel a slight prick as the needle goes in, but it shouldn't last very long. I don't want you to move until I tell you. Okay?"

Joel did as he was instructed and only flinched slightly as the needle was inserted and the fluid withdrawn. God, I was so proud of him. All I could do was brush the hair from his forehead and kiss it. He was handling this a whole lot better than I was.

"Joel, you can get dressed and I'll show you to your room and then I'll explain what is going to happen next. You're doing great," Dr. Kerner said. He then left with the needle, but returned before Joel was dressed.

We followed the doctor down the hall to a room on the south side of the building. When we walked in there was a young boy in one of the beds and two middle-aged people, whom I assumed to be his parents, at his bedside. I placed the overnight bag with Joel's stuff which I had been toting around on the empty bed as Dr. Kerner started to introduce Joel to the other boy.

The boy's name was Tony Clausen and, as he said, "almost 12". The middle aged couple was introduced as Bill and Karen Boise. When I asked their relationship to Tony, they told me they were his foster parents. We chatted a few moments before Dr. Kerner started to tell Joel what was going to happen.

He started by showing Joel the IV in Tony's arm and said they would be placing a catheter in his arm just like it so they could feed the medicine into his veins. I noticed a frown appear on Joel's face, but he said nothing. He told Joel he wanted him to talk to Tony about his experiences to find out what the treatment is really like from a patient's view.

He then sent Joel into the bathroom to change into his pajamas. While Joel was in the bathroom another doctor arrived and showed Dr. Kerner a paper which he read for a moment before he looked at me with a smile.

"The preliminary examination of the spinal fluid showed no abnormalities. That's good. It simplifies the treatment options," he said taking out a pad and writing something on it before handing it to the individual who had brought the report.

Joel reappeared dressed in his pajamas. I took his clothes and hung them in the little closet. Dr. Kerner began explaining what was going to happen this evening.

"Soon one of the nurses will come in and insert the catheter. Then after you have had a light meal, one of them will come back and hook you up to all kinds of wires so we can monitor you for any reactions to the medicine we will start giving you through the IV. We'll also give you a mild sedative to help you sleep. The doses of medicine you will get tonight will be tests to see if you can tolerate the drugs before we start the full regimen. I will be back in to see you when you get the first dose of medicine."

I held Joel's right hand as the nurse put the catheter in his left forearm and attached an IV. She told us the IV had a mild sedative that would probably make him drowsy within an hour but probably not before his food arrived.

When it arrived, I was somewhat surprised that it looked quite good. It did not contain the quantity he was used to having. He ate it up and looked for more. I told him they didn't want too much food in his stomach because the medicine they were going to give him might make his stomach upset. He accepted the explanation, but, clearly, did not like it.

The nurse returned and taped a number of electrodes to Joel and then hooked them up to a monitor that was wheeled next to his bed.

It wasn't long after his food tray was taken away when Dr. Kerner returned with a resident to begin the treatment. Joel was beginning to feel sleepy as the resident hooked up a new IV. Dr. Kerner handed Joel a tablet and a cup of water and asked him to swallow it, which he did.

Turning to me, he said, "The IV contains a dilute chemotherapy agent that some patients have reactions to. That's why we aren't giving it full strength until we know how he'll react. If there is no untoward reaction by morning, we'll start him on the normal strength dose. From his medical records, I don't suspect there will be any problems, but there is always the possibility of anaphylactic reaction. I always error on the side of caution when beginning a patient's regimen."

I watched Joel intently for another half an hour or so before I saw he had drifted off to sleep. I decided this was a good time to go back to the apartment to let the others know what was happening.

Dr. Kerner was walking toward me as I left Joel's room. He stopped briefly to talk to Bill and Karen Boise. They had left a few moments before I did. As I approached the trio, I heard Bill say, "What are we going to do? Isn't there some way he can stay here?"

"Bill, we will just have to figure out how to get the money. We can't let him be transferred to Herman. They'd try to care for him, but they are so overcrowded with charity patients," Karen said, tears starting to run down her cheeks.

"Crane," Dr. Kerner acknowledged me as I stepped up to them. "I was just about to check on Joel."

"He was sleeping when I left just now and had been for maybe twenty minutes."

"Good, that's a good sign. I'll just slip in and check. He should be out for at least eight or ten hours if you need to get out of here for a while," he said, and started for the boys' room.

I caught up with the Boises who had departed when Dr. Kerner and I talked briefly. "I'm sorry we didn't get to talk much today. There are a lot of questions I have about what you've been going through and how you've managed to cope with the stress."

"I don't know if we've been doing a good job at that," Karen said. "We do try to keep up a brave front when we're with Tony, but it's getting harder to hide the strain this whole business has put on us."

"I wasn't trying to eavesdrop earlier," I began. "Ah … well … I couldn't help but overhear your conversation with the doctor. I didn't quite understand exactly what you were saying. Did I hear you correctly that Tony might have to be moved to another hospital?"

"Yes, but not if we can find a way to get the money to keep him here. You see the money the state provides is nearly exhausted and they don't pay for everything. We aren't rich people. We mortgaged our house and all that money is just about gone. Tony is like our own son and we will do everything we can to see he gets the best available treatment. Bill has to get back to work. His vacation is all used up. I just don't know what we're going to do."

By this time we had reached the front of the hospital. I hailed a cab and while I waited for it to pull up to the door, I asked, "Do you need a ride somewhere or do you have your car?"

"Thanks, but our motel is just over there on Old Spanish Trail. It's not that far. The walk lets us clear our heads. We appreciate the offer. I'm sure that we … at least Karen, will see you tomorrow. Good night," Bill said.

The moment I opened the front door of the apartment, I was surrounded by all four of the boys asking questions about Joel. I gave each of them an extra special hug and a kiss before I convinced them to let me into the apartment and close the door. I ushered them into the living room and we all sat down on the couch. It was barely big enough for the five of us and wouldn't have been if TJ hadn't climbed on my lap.

Hildy and Becky Sue joined us from the kitchen area where they had been cleaning up from the boys' evening snack. When everyone was settled, I explained what had happened at the hospital and what was happening to Joel. I tried not to be too graphic, but when they asked how they were putting the medicine into Joel's arm, I had to be a bit more descriptive. This caused TJ to turn his face into my neck, and I could feel the wetness of his tears.

"I wanna go see him," TJ sobbed.

"I know, son. I know," I said, rubbing his back. "If he's feeling okay tomorrow, I'll talk to the doctor to see if you can go see him tomorrow afternoon. Is that all right?"

He didn't answer, but I felt him nod his head.

"Can we go too?" Chris asked, which was quickly echoed by the twins. All I could do at that point was to shake my head.

After a few minutes of our cuddling, I said, "You guys need to get started getting ready for bed. Go take your showers. Chris, you and TJ can use the shower in my bedroom while Larry and Lenny use the other one."

"You look tired, Crane," Hildy said. "Why don't you go to bed too?"

"I will, but I need to fix a sandwich. I haven't eaten since lunch and I need to make some phone calls to let the office know how they can get in touch with me. This has been the most draining day of my life. Trying to be brave for Joel and feeling so inadequate has taken its toll on me."

"I'll fix you a sandwich before we go back to our apartment," Hildy said, getting up and heading for the kitchen. Becky Sue followed her and got a plate and glass from the cupboard.

Hildy and Becky Sue sat with me while I ate my sandwich, wanting to know all the details of Joel's treatment and the hospital and the boy in the room with him. It wasn't long before a fresh-smelling TJ approached and insinuated his way onto my lap.

"My, you smell good. Did Chris make sure you got all clean?"

"Yeah, but I miss Joel."

"I do too, but he has to stay at the hospital so he can get well."

"Why did he get sick?"

"Son, I wish I knew. He just did. Now I think it is time to get to bed. Say good night to Hildy and Becky Sue and then I'll tuck you in."

It was firsts all around. The first time since Chris joined our family that he and the twins had not shared a bed and the first time that Joel hadn't shared a bed with TJ. I wasn't sure if there would be much sleep tonight for the boys, but we went through the bedtime ritual anyway.

I called Gerald to let him know what was going on and how I could be reached. I discussed several other matters of a financial nature. Before I hung up, I apologized again for calling him at home so late. I also made a quick call to Carlos to see if there was anything new on the buyout. He said there wasn't, and as far as he knew, everything was on schedule for the end of next month.

I called the office and left a message for both Foster and Carol letting them know how to get in touch with me. I left a proviso that during the day, I could only be reached by pager.

Exhaustion finally overcame me and I collapsed into bed around ten o'clock.

I was not ready for the alarm to ring at six, but, if possible, I wanted to try to get to the hospital before Joel was awake. I thought it was important that I be there when he opened his eyes.

CHAPTER 8

❀

I rolled out of bed dreading the day ahead of me. I didn't expect that Hildy would be up but when I finished in the bathroom and prepared to leave for the hospital, she was there with coffee ready for me.

"If you'll wait a few minutes, I'll fix you a couple of eggs and sausage," she said brightly.

"Thanks, I don't know if I'll get anything to eat at the hospital. Joel's food looked good, but the quantity was not to his liking. I don't know about their cafeteria," I said.

"You know all the boys miss Joel and want to go see him."

"I know. I don't know what the visitor policy is, but I'll find out and see if they can go this afternoon. I assume you'll want to go also."

"Of course, I miss him desperately," she said, as the tears began to fall. "I just can't understand why he has to bear this cross. He has suffered enough. I pray every night he gets well. He has to!"

"Yes, it's all that I can do to keep from breaking down while I'm with him, but I don't dare let myself. So far he has been a lot braver than I could be under the circumstances."

Through her tears, Hildy dished up my eggs and sausage, then buttered my toast. The rest of breakfast was eaten in silence.

I left for the hospital a few minutes after seven. I was of two minds. Part of me wanted to get there as soon as possible, and the other part of me wanted to go back to the office and totally forget about what was happening. The responsible part of me won out. When I got to the street, the taxi I had called was waiting for me. If this continues, I would need to rent a car to get back and forth to the hospital and save the limousine for the rest of the family when we needed bigger accommodations.

Joel was still sleeping when I got to his room. I was thankful for that. However, it wasn't long before he woke up. He was still a little groggy from the sedative they had given him.

"Hi, dad," he mumbled. "Did you stay here all night?"

"No, son, I had to go tell your brothers how you were. They miss you very much."

"I miss them too. Is TJ okay?"

"Yes, but he wants to come see you. I'm going to ask the doctor if he and all your brothers can come this afternoon."

"I'm thirsty."

The water in his thermos carafe was barely cool but he didn't seem to mind. I kissed his forehead when I handed him the cup of water. His forehead felt warm as if he had a fever.

"How are you feeling this morning?" I asked, trying not to show concern.

"Okay, but my stomach feels kinda funny."

"Maybe you're just hungry."

As Joel and I were talking, Karen Boise walked into the room. She briefly acknowledged us and went directly to Tony's bedside. He appeared to still be sleeping. Joel and I had kept our conversations low in order not to awaken him. She leaned over the bed and kissed his cheek.

He stirred opening his eyes. "Hi, mom."

"Good morning, son. I love you," she responded.

"Me too," he murmured.

"How are you feeling this morning?"

"My stomach aches and my head hurts. I think I'm gonna throw up."

"That's okay, baby," Karen said reaching for tissues and the crescent shaped bowl on the nightstand.

She just barely made it in time before Tony began to vomit. There was very little that came up. He continued to have the dry heaves for another minute or so as Karen held him with one arm and the bowl in the other.

Joel watched all of this, his eyes getting wider the longer he watched. "Is that gonna happen to me?" he asked with fear and pleading in his eyes.

"It might, son. I hope not, but they can give you medicine to ease the stomach problems," I said. Turning to Karen, I asked if she wanted me to get the nurse. When she answered in the affirmative, I pushed the call button.

A nurse arrived shortly and approached Joel's bed. I told her that Tony was the one who needed the attention. After talking briefly with Karen and Tony she checked his chart and then left. She returned a couple of minutes later with a small white cup, which she handed to Tony along with a glass of water.

The breakfast trays arrived a short time later. The food on Joel's tray looked good, but again it was quite a bit less than what he would normally have had at home. There was a bowl with an individual serving of Wheaties and a carton each of skim milk and orange juice. Taking the cover off the dish revealed scrambled eggs, two pieces of bacon, toast and some grits.

"What's that, dad?" Joel said, pointing to the grits.

"Those are grits, son."

"It looks like paste. Hildy never makes that for our breakfast."

"Try it, you might like it."

Tentatively taking his fork, Joel scooped up a tiny bit of the grainy white material and gingerly brought it to his mouth. After touching it with the tip of his tongue and sniffing at it he put it in his mouth. I could hardly contain my amusement at his actions especially when he turned up his nose and made a sour face.

"Do people really eat that stuff?" he asked. "It tastes like stale popcorn flavored paste."

"Some people eat that every morning. I never liked it. That's why Hildy doesn't make it at home. If you don't want to eat it, you don't have to," I told him.

The rest of the breakfast disappeared quickly and he even took another look at the grits before deciding that, even though he was hungry, he was not that hungry.

"Dad, can I call John? He wanted me to come over to his house on Saturday, and I didn't get to tell him I wouldn't be able to."

"Sure, but let's wait until we know he is out of bed before you call. He probably hasn't had breakfast yet."

As we were talking a very large black orderly entered the room to remove the breakfast trays. He had to be over six foot four and must have weighed a good 275 pounds. "Good morning, good morning," he said brightly, looking directly at the boys and ignoring Karen and me. "And how are you fine young men this glorious morning?" Turning to Joel, he said, "You're new here. I'm Rodney. You'll see a lot of me."

"Hi Rodney, I'm Joel."

"Joel, I'm very pleased to meet you. If you ever need anything, you just ask for Rodney. Ain't that right Tony?"

"Yeah, he got me some ice cream on Tuesday—chocolate too," Tony responded with a giggle.

"Sssh! Somebody might hear." Rodney said, with a grin. "See you guys later." He picked up the breakfast trays and left the room, never once acknowledging Karen or me.

It was almost eight-thirty when Dr. Kerner arrived followed by a young man whom I assumed to be a resident. They first went to Tony's bed and pulled the curtain around the bed while they examined him. Maybe ten minutes later I heard Dr. Kerner say, "Well, Tony, today you don't have any medication scheduled, so if you want to go down to the lounge or TV room or go out to the grounds, it's okay. That is, as long as you're in your wheelchair and someone is with you. You're too weak to try and walk that far."

The curtain was pulled back and Dr. Kerner stepped over to Joel's bed. "Good morning, Joel. I'd like you to meet Dr. Barrow. He is going to be assisting me. This is Crane Johnson, Joel's father."

I stood and shook the new doctor's hand. Dr. Kerner drew the curtain around Joel's bed and began his examination. He concentrated on the lymph nodes under his arms, under his jaws and in his groin. He then began pressing on Joel's stomach. "Does this hurt?"

"No," Joel answered.

"Good, I don't find any significant enlargement of any of the lymph glands. Sometimes they enlarge when we start the chemotherapy. But then again, we haven't given you a full dose yet. That will come later this morning. Dr. Barrow will be back to administer the agent."

"Will it hurt?" Joel asked apprehensively.

"There might be some stinging around the place where the IV goes in your arm, but it shouldn't be too bad," Dr. Barrow answered.

"Will it make me sick like Tony and throw up?"

"Just to be on the safe side we'll give you something to calm your stomach. I'll be back later and we'll start your treatment," Dr. Barrow said, giving Joel's shoulder a squeeze.

Before the doctors left, I asked about whether the rest of the family could visit him this afternoon. At first, they didn't think it would be a good idea, but when they looked at Joel's pleading face, they relented and said they could come, but just for a little while.

"Can I call John now?"

"Sure, son," I said, and picked up the phone and handed it to him. "Dial 9 then 1830 and then John's number. Do you know what it is?"

"Yeah, I call it all the time."

"Okay, dad's going to get a cup of coffee so you can have some privacy. Don't talk too long. I'll be back in a little while." Turning to Karen, I said, "May I buy you a cup of coffee?"

"Thanks, I could use one. I didn't make any this morning because it was just me. Bill went back home last night so he could get ready to go to work this morning." Turning to Tony she explained she would be back in a few minutes. "Why don't you and Joel get better acquainted when he gets off the phone?"

We walked in silence part of the way to the cafeteria.

"I'm sorry that Bill and I unloaded our problems on you last night, but we're at the end of our rope. We love that boy," she said dabbing at her eyes. "We want to adopt him, but now …"

We arrived at the cafeteria and I pointed out an empty table and told her I would go get the coffee. I had to wait a moment while the two customers in front of me paid for their purchases which gave me time to check out what else the serving line had to offer. I spotted these huge blueberry muffins and I couldn't resist. I added two of them to the tray and several individual packets of butter. I figured if Karen didn't want it, I could always take it back to Joel.

She didn't refuse the muffin. They were delicious. I think they made it easier for us to talk. I have always believed good food paves the way for good conversation. She was able to answer a lot of my questions about the effects the chemotherapy was having on Tony. I hadn't noticed, but she told me Tony's hair was beginning to fall out and his stomach problems were becoming more frequent.

During our conversation, her handkerchief was always at the ready and frequently used. When I looked at my watch I noticed it had been a good half hour since we left the room. We agreed we needed to get back there.

Approaching the open door to the boys' room, we heard the sound of giggling boys. Joel was sitting on the edge of his bed facing Tony who had the head of his bed raised. They were talking and laughing like old friends.

"Hi, dad, Tony was telling me about this funny nurse that comes around. She wears a red clown's nose and does magic tricks."

"That's great. I'm glad you two are getting along. Did you talk to John?"

"Yeah, he didn't know what leukemia was and I tried to tell him, but his mom had to explain it to him. He was scared, but I told him the doctor said I was going to be okay. That's right, isn't it?"

"Yes, son, that's right," I said, and hugged him to me. "Has Dr. Barrow been back in?"

"No," he said.

He no more than got that out of his mouth when Dr. Barrow walked in with a nurse wheeling a cart.

"Hi, Joel, are you ready for your first treatment?" he asked.

"I ... I guess so," Joel responded.

"This is Nurse Sharon. She's going to start the IV drip to put the medicine into your vein. As Dr. Kerner said, you may feel a slight stinging in your arm as the medicine goes in. It usually goes away after a bit, but if it doesn't we can give you something to lessen it. Do you have any questions?"

Joel looked at me and shook his head. I took his hand as the nurse hung the IV on the stand and before she inserted the needle into the catheter and started the drip she made sure Joel's forearm was securely attached to the board designed to keep his arm straight. After she had adjusted the drip rate she handed Joel a small paper cup containing a white pill and poured him a glass of water.

"Dr. Barrow, are there any food restrictions while Joel is on chemo?" I asked.

"Well, he can eat pretty much anything. However, I would advise staying away from highly spiced foods because they might irritate his stomach. Nothing too greasy either. Anything that would normally upset his stomach would be a good thing to stay away from. Why?"

"Well, he usually consumes more food than he has been getting on his tray and I just wondered if it would be all right to bring him something from the cafeteria. The blueberry muffin I had there this morning, I'm sure he would have liked."

"I think something like that would be fine. But because of the possibility of stomach upset from the medicine, I wouldn't recommend that he stuff himself. It would be better if he ate several times a day instead of a lot all at once. The pill he just took is to help ease the nausea. It varies in effectiveness from patient to patient. We should know in a couple of hours whether it's working for him. I'll be back in after lunch to check on him," he said.

Rodney came in the room shortly after Dr. Barrow and the nurse left, pushing a wheelchair.

"Hey there, Tony, you ready to go for a ride. It's a beautiful day outside, but it's gonna get hot, hot, hot this afternoon. It's s'posed to be 95 in the shade and no shade."

He had both boys snickering as he prepared the chair for Tony and then lifted him from the bed into the chair. Rodney was a clown, but you could tell by the way he picked up Tony—as gently as a piece of fine china—that he loved kids. He made sure Tony was secure in the chair before he began pushing it.

"Let's go get some color in those cheeks, we can't have you looking like some snowball," Rodney said, as they left the room with Karen trailing them.

"He's funny," Joel said. "I like him."

The rest of the morning went by rather quickly. I had brought a book with me to read to Joel as he lay in bed. Tony joined our reading session when Rodney brought him back from his outdoor excursion. It was a Sherlock Holmes story, *A Study in Scarlet*. Joel had become fascinated by Doyle's quirky detective. I thoroughly enjoyed reading them again.

About an hour was all my voice would last before I had to give up, but I had to promise I would resume my reading tomorrow. I called the apartment to let Hildy know the other boys could come to the hospital this afternoon. I would come home for lunch and then we would all come back later. A call to the limo service confirmed a pickup at 1:30.

When Joel's lunch came, I got up to leave, telling him I would be back after lunch with his brothers in tow. There were no taxis at the front door as I exited so I had to wait a few minutes before one showed up. That made up my mind. I was going to rent a car to use until I brought one from home.

Hildy had prepared a mountain of sandwiches and a pot of vegetable soup for our lunch. To top it off she had baked a couple of apple pies which the boys insisted be served with large scoops of vanilla ice cream. I chose a small piece of pie without ice cream.

The limo arrived about a minute after we got to the parking lot of the apartment complex. When TJ saw the limo coming, he grabbed my hand and said, "Come on, dad, we gotta go see Joel. Hurry!"

"Hold on, son., We have to wait until the car stops before we can get in."

All the boys were excited as we drove to the hospital. Their seatbelts could hardly contain them. As we approached the hospital, I impressed on them that they had to stay with us and not run in the halls or be too loud. They all shook their heads indicating they understood. I just hoped they would remember.

We took the elevator to the second floor. As we stepped out of the elevator, TJ grabbed my hand. "Where's Joel?" he asked in a whisper.

"His room is down the hall and around the corner. You don't have to whisper, just don't yell or talk too loud. Some of the patients might be sleeping."

TJ never let go of my hand until we entered the room and he saw Joel. In a flash, he was at Joel's bedside and climbed into the bed with him before I could stop him.

"I missed you," TJ said and threw his arms around Joel and kissed his cheek. "I want you to come home. I don't want you here." At that, TJ broke down and sobbed uncontrollably.

Larry, Lenny and Chris had, by that time, crowded around Joel's bed and were trying to touch him and grab on to his hand. Hildy was trying very hard to keep from crying. Seeing Joel lying there with the IV in his arm was almost more than she could stand. Becky Sue was somewhat less affected.

Joel cuddled TJ in his one free arm. "I want to come home too, TJ, but they gotta get me well first. I miss you. I miss everybody. But you can come to see me every day if you want to."

Hildy approached the bed from the other side, the one with the IV stand. She brushed the hair back off of Joel's forehead before leaning down and kissing him lightly. "How are you feeling, Joel?"

"Okay, I guess. My stomach feels funny and my arm where that needle thing is feels like a mosquito bit me."

"Your dad said you didn't think you were getting enough to eat so I sneaked a sandwich and a piece of apple pie in. Do you want to eat it now?" Hildy said as she opened her large purse and took out the napkin-wrapped sandwich and a foil package containing the big slice of pie.

"Oh, yeah! Lunch was okay, but it was awful small," Joel said.

Kissing TJ on the forehead, Joel disengaged his one good arm and took the sandwich from Hildy and began eating it. TJ moved himself so he was positioned with his head on Joel's chest, leaving Joel barely enough room to get the sandwich to his mouth. But he managed.

While Joel was eating, I guided Larry, Lenny and Chris to Tony's bed and introduced the three of them to him. They hit it off right away and within minutes were gabbing away like old friends.

I heard Tony tell my boys, "I wish I knew where my brother Benny was. He went someplace else when I came to live with mom and dad. He was eight. He is nine now. I wish he could live with me."

The boys would alternate between Tony, who was becoming their new friend, and Joel. TJ stayed snuggled up against Joel.

Dr. Kerner was surprised when he came in to check on Joel and found two people in the bed, but took it in stride. "Hi there, young man, I'm Dr. Dan. What's your name?"

"This is my little brother TJ. Say, 'Hi', TJ."

"Hi," came a barely audible response.

"I'll tell you what, TJ. I need to examine your brother. If you will just move over a little so I can listen to his heart and check him out, I'll be done in just a minute."

TJ looked into Joel's eyes and getting a nod from him scooted over to the side of the bed but watched closely as the doctor went through the exam. Noticing the piece of pie Hildy had placed on Joel's table, he said, "Oh, that pie looks good. Do you know what would make it even better? Some of that frozen yogurt they serve in the cafeteria."

That got the attention of the six young men in the room. "Can we get Joel some of that stuff that Dr. Dan said?" TJ asked.

"Sure, if Dr. Dan says it's okay, we'll all get some," I said, turning to Karen. "Would you and Tony like to join us?"

She agreed, but then it dawned on me we would need to get a couple of wheelchairs for Joel and Tony. When I mentioned it to Dr. Kerner he said it would be no problem. He would see if Rodney could bring a couple and help us to the cafeteria.

The IV had nearly finished when Dr. Kerner had come in. He had removed it from Joel's catheter after the exam so he was free to move about more freely.

I was getting Joel's robe and slippers out of the wardrobe when Rodney came in pushing one wheelchair and pulling the other. "Good heavens, they're multiplying," he said. "Where did all you guys come from?"

"Rodney, they're my brothers," Joel said. "This is TJ and the twins are Larry and Lenny and the one over by Tony's bed is Chris."

"My, what a fine looking bunch of boys. Are y'all ready to go?"

I helped TJ out of the bed and then guided Joel into the wheelchair. TJ stared at Joel in the chair. "Do you gotta sit in that thing?" he asked.

"Yeah, they don't want me to walk around. The medicine can make me dizzy," Joel said. "You want to ride with me?"

There was no hesitating on TJ's part. He immediately jumped up on Joel's lap. If he had smiled any more he would have injured his face. Joel wrapped his unencumbered right arm around TJ to keep him from falling out of the chair and also to keep him from wiggling around. I turned the chair around and started the procession of the Johnson clan out of the room and toward the cafeteria. Rodney pushed Tony and Karen followed close behind. We were quite a crew, all eleven of us heading down the hall.

Hildy had thoughtfully picked up Joel's piece of pie and brought it along. When we got to the cafeteria we found a large round table that would seat all six of the boys and a smaller square one next to it that would seat the four adults. Rodney had to go about his duties and was not able to join us.

Becky Sue and I went to get the frozen yogurt after finding out what flavor the boys wanted. Making a decision from the three flavors, vanilla, chocolate and strawberry was a major undertaking. When I saw it was going to tax their brains to the maximum I suggested we get each one a little bit of each flavor. That met with approval from all of them. I didn't tell them there were toppings they could have on the yogurt. I didn't want them to have a meltdown.

All the boys were having a great time when we returned to the table with their yogurt. They were all talking and laughing at the same time. It didn't seem that anyone was listening. That all stopped when the yogurt was passed out and the spoons began making round trips between bowls and mouths.

Karen's eyes were moist as I placed the adults' yogurt on our table. "He hasn't been this happy since he came to live with us. He misses his little brother all the time. They won't tell us where he is so we can even take Tony to visit him. I wish we could adopt them both but CPS told us we couldn't qualify because Bill doesn't make enough money. They may not even let us adopt Tony." With that, the tears really began to flow down her cheeks.

"Look, Karen, I know of a foundation that is set up to handle just the kind of situation you describe. It provides yearly grants for good people who want to adopt but don't have the financial resources to qualify. The grants continue until the adoptee finishes school provided it's accomplished within a reasonable time. Let me have them contact you to see if they can help out," I said, trying not to let on it was my foundation that would be contacting her.

"Oh, yes, please. That would be wonderful," she said, drying her eyes.

I had convinced TJ to sit in his own chair instead of sitting on Joel's lap while they ate the frozen yogurt. He chose to sit on a chair between Tony and Joel. As they were finishing their treat, I saw TJ looking at Tony with a strange look in his eye. Finally his curiosity got the better of him, and he asked, "Why do you have spots with no hair?"

Tony turned to TJ, his face beginning to redden, "The medicine does that. Dr. Dan said it all would fall out."

"Oh," TJ said, looking even more confused. Turning back to Joel, "Is your hair gonna fall out, too?"

There was silence as the other boys sat there, wide-eyed, waiting for Joel to answer.

"Yeah, that's what the doctor says."

We stayed in the cafeteria for another twenty minutes or so before it became apparent that Tony was beginning to tire. Becky Sue and I cleaned up the tables before I told the boys it was time to go back to the room.

"Can we push Joel's wheelchair?" Lenny asked.

"Yeah," Chris and Larry chimed in.

TJ had already resumed his place on Joel's lap. "Well, I guess you could. How about if you take turns? Maybe someone could push Tony also."

"I will!" Chris volunteered.

Once we got the two wheelchairs out into the hall we let the boys begin pushing them. Larry and Lenny each had a handle of Joel's chair while Chris pushed Tony. Joel's chair was heavier due to TJ's added weight.

Back in the room, I called the limo driver and told him we would need the car in about fifteen minutes. I thought that would give the boys enough time to say their goodbyes to Joel. TJ had climbed back in bed with Joel and didn't want to leave. I finally convinced him that Joel had to have another treatment tonight and that he couldn't stay. He wasn't happy about it but gave in reluctantly.

One by one the boys took turns giving their brother a hug. Then to my surprise they did the same to Tony. I think it surprised him also. I know it did Karen.

I walked our family down to the front door and helped everyone get into the limo and saw that their seatbelts were fastened, gave them all a hug and told them I would be back to the apartment later. Becky Sue was going to give them all a swimming lesson before supper.

When I returned to the room, Tony was crying and being comforted by his mother. I asked Joel what happened. He told me Tony was sad because he hadn't seen his brother in a long time. I guess seeing all of my gang and getting hugs from the boys was too much. It had surfaced old memories of happier times.

I made a mental note to call Darcie and Jack when I got back to the apartment.

CHAPTER 9

Although there were two TV's in the room, one for each bed, I don't think either one of them had been turned on while I was there. Joel hardly ever watched television unless it was a special program we watched as a family. The boys used their TV's for the video games. I guess Tony was not a TV watcher either.

After Tony had calmed down, I asked him and Joel if they wanted me to read another chapter or two of Sherlock Holmes. That met with instant agreement, so I took out the book and started reading. By the time I had read three chapters I was just about out of voice. I was saved by their food trays arriving.

About ten minutes before seven o'clock Dr. Barrow and Nurse Sharon returned to give Joel his second dose of chemo. The IV bag was hung on the stand and the needle inserted into the catheter and the drip adjusted. I wanted to get up and run out of the room but knew I couldn't. Joel on the other hand was calm and accepted the IV so nonchalantly my heart nearly burst with pride. I didn't want any of this to be true. I wanted to wake up from this terrible nightmare and for everything to be back the way it was.

"This medicine can sometimes cause sleeplessness so we are going to give you a mild sedative to help you sleep," Dr. Barrow told Joel as he handed him a small paper cup with a couple of pink tablets in it. "These pills won't knock you out. They will only let you sleep."

When Dr. Barrow left I asked Joel if he would like to watch TV. He just shrugged. I turned it on anyway because I knew there was a PBS program about Tom Sawyer and Huckleberry Finn that he would enjoy. The program was just beginning when I turned the TV on and switched to the correct channel. It didn't take him long to realize what the program was and his interest was immediate.

Tony saw what was on Joel's TV and asked his mother to give him the remote so he could watch the program as well. The TV remotes also had the speaker built in as part of it so the sound could be isolated to the bed of the person watching.

Before long both boys were totally engrossed in the program. I decided this was as good an opportunity as any to tell Joel I would be late coming to see him tomorrow because I planned to fly back to San Antonio so I could bring the van back to Houston. It would probably be ten o'clock or so before I would be able to visit him.

"I'll see if Hildy can come early after she has given your brothers their breakfast," I told him, as I leaned over and kissed his forehead. "I love you, son."

"I love you too, dad. Can TJ come back tomorrow?"

"Yes, I'll bring all of your brothers again tomorrow afternoon."

With that, I left, but not before saying goodbye to Tony and Karen. On the way out of the hospital, I called the airline to see if I could get a seat on the 9:30 flight to San Antonio. They said there were two first class seats available so I booked one.

I caught a taxi to the apartment. When I got there I confirmed that Hildy would spend the night in the apartment with the boys while I was gone. TJ was not happy that I would not be there all night, but after I assured him I would be back tomorrow morning, he acquiesced reluctantly.

Jack answered the phone when I called. "How's Joel?" were the first words out of his mouth when he knew who was calling.

"He's doing okay. We won't know anything for sure for about two weeks. If he is responding to the treatments by the end of that time then a cure is pretty well certain. We have our fingers crossed."

"Be sure to keep us informed. That little guy means a lot to all of us."

"I will, Jack. I need to ask you for a favor and I don't know if it is really proper, but I'm going to ask anyway …"

"Go ahead, Crane. You know I'll tell you to get lost if it's something I'm uncomfortable doing."

"I want you to use your influence to try to find the whereabouts of a nine year old boy."

"Good God, Crane. You're not going to take in another one, are you?"

"No," I laughed. "His brother Tony is in the hospital room with Joel. CPS won't let Tony's foster parents know where his brother has been placed. Could you check around with your contacts to see if they have any information on a Benny Clausen? His brother Tony and his foster parents live in Fort Bend County so the greater Houston area is probably where the child is. These two boys are potential candidates for the foundation I'm setting up. If you can't find out anything, I'll understand. But if you decide to set up your own private investigation business, then this will be your first assignment."

"Crane, I'll do what I can. I have a few contacts in HPD (Houston Police Department) I can check with. One of them works in the juvenile division. He is probably my best hope of getting information. More than likely, I won't be able to find anything out this weekend. I'll start beating the bushes first thing on Monday."

"Thanks, Jack, I knew I could count on you," I told him, and then, before hanging up, gave him the number at the apartment.

My next call was to Darcie. Unfortunately, she was not in. She was probably out with Mel. I would have to call her again tomorrow.

Hildy insisted on fixing me something to eat after she learned I had not had anything to eat since our foray to the cafeteria this afternoon for frozen yogurt. I quickly packed my shaving kit and decided I didn't really need to pack anything else since I would be spending the night at home and had plenty of clothes there I could change into.

By the time I left the apartment it was nearly eight o'clock. The trip to Houston Intercontinental took nearly an hour. The taxi dropped me off in front of the Continental Airlines terminal so I didn't have far to walk to the ticket counter. As the first class line was not busy I was able to get ticketed and off to the gate in only a few minutes. The plane was just beginning the boarding process as I got to the gate after passing through the security checkpoint.

The flight was quick and uneventful. It took me almost as long to get from the plane to the van as the flight took. It was midnight before I pressed the button to open the gate to the property. The house seemed so empty as I walked in the back door. This would be the first time I had been alone in the house since that first night Joel came home with me. "God, I miss those boys," I muttered to myself, as I prepared for bed.

Five AM came way too early but I wanted to get on the road by six. There wasn't anything to eat in the house so I decided to stop at McDonalds or Burger King to get something on the way. How they have the nerve to call what

I bought coffee is beyond my comprehension. The only thing it had going for it was that it was hot.

I regretted my early start shortly after I turned on to I-10 at Seguin. The freeway heads in a direction just north of due east which put the morning sun directly in my face. Determined to get back to my boys, I flipped down the visor and set the speed control at 75 mph and tried to make the best of it. The trip from Seguin to Houston would take about two and a half hours of sheer boredom. The towns are widely spaced and very few of them are within sight of the freeway. The only breaks in the monotonous scenery were the occasional exits with the obligatory gasoline station or Dairy Queen.

I was glad when the outskirts of Katy came into view. It meant I was almost there. The worst part of the drive was to come. Even though it was Saturday, the Houston traffic was miserable. It was made even worse because of the never-ending road construction once I got past Highway 6. It took me just under an hour to get from the west side of Houston to the apartment.

My route to the apartment took me past the complex's swimming pool. I could see a number of people in the pool, but I wasn't able to tell if any of them were my boys. That didn't last long. Before I had my seatbelt unbuckled after parking the van, there were four dripping wet boys trying to get my door open.

I was nearly knocked over backwards as I stepped out of the van when TJ jumped up, wrapping his arms around my neck. The others surrounded me and hugged us both. I was getting soaked but I couldn't have been happier.

"I missed you, dad," TJ said into my ear, as he hugged my neck even tighter and wrapped his legs around my waist.

"I missed you too, little one. I missed all of you like mad," I responded. "Let's go into the house. Dad has to change his clothes and then go to the hospital."

"Can we go too?" Chris asked.

"I'll take you guys to see Joel this afternoon."

I carried TJ to the apartment. He didn't want to be put down even after we got inside so I sat down on the couch and held him for a few more minutes. That few minutes of cuddling seemed to help TJ. It certainly did wonders for me.

When I got to the hospital, I found Hildy reading the Sherlock Holmes book to Joel and Tony. Joel was so engrossed in what Hildy was reading he didn't notice me standing in the doorway for almost a minute.

"Hi dad," he said, when he saw me. "How long have you been there?"

"Oh, just a minute, I didn't want to interrupt Hildy's reading. How are you feeling today?" I asked.

"Pretty good, I got to take a bath this morning. They put this plastic bag on my arm so I wouldn't get this needle thing wet," he said pointing to the catheter. "Hildy brought me some clean pajamas, too."

"Thanks, Hildy, I don't know what we would do without you looking after us," I told her.

Hildy stayed a few more minutes before she kissed Joel and headed back to the apartment. She hadn't been gone long when Dr. Barrow and Dr. Kerner arrived for their morning rounds. They went first to Tony's bed and pulled the curtain. I was talking to Joel so I wasn't paying any attention to what was happening on the other side of the room. That is until I heard Karen say, "Oh, my God, that's wonderful! But who? Why? When did this happen?"

A few minutes later the two doctors approached Joel's bed. After greeting us both they pulled the curtain around Joel's bed and began their examination. After poking and prodding him and taking his temperature and blood pressure they seemed to be satisfied.

"He has a slight fever. Nothing to worry about but we will give him some Tylenol to bring it down," Dr. Barrow said turning to me.

"Joel," Dr. Kerner started, "your next treatment will be an injection into your behind or thigh. The choice is yours. It has to be given in one of your larger muscles. Dr. Barrow will be back around four o'clock to give it to you."

Dr. Barrow was busy writing on Joel's chart while this was going on.

Before pulling back the curtain, Dr. Kerner approached me and extended his hand, mouthing the words, "Thank you," and nodded toward Tony's bed.

"It's my pleasure," I said quietly.

Before long the lunch trays arrived. The food looked good. There was meatloaf, macaroni and cheese, green beans and a bread roll. Along with milk, there was some pudding that looked like butterscotch. It disappeared quickly from Joel's tray. I think he would have picked the plate up and licked it if I hadn't been there.

"Are you still hungry?" I asked.

"Yeah, a little," he answered sheepishly.

"Well, maybe we can go to the cafeteria again this afternoon when your brothers get here," I said.

Bill walked in as I was about to get up to go get the rest of the boys. He waved at us as he made a beeline for Tony's bed.

"Hi dad," Tony said, as his face lit up with a smile that would melt even the coldest heart.

"How are you, son?" Bill asked, as he engulfed Tony in a bear hug. "I missed you so much."

Turning to Karen he gave her a hug and a kiss. "Bill, the most wonderful thing has happened. Dr. Kerner said he has gotten a grant from an anonymous donor to pay for all of Tony's hospital bills. Isn't that fantastic?"

"Oh, babe, that's wonderful. When did you find this out?"

"About an hour ago, I guess. It was when he came in to check on Tony," Karen said dabbing at her eyes.

When I got up to say my goodbyes to Joel he looked at me, then at Tony and then back at me with a quizzical look in his eyes. "Did you …" he whispered.

I put my finger to my lips to indicate he was not say anything.

He opened his arms indicating he wanted a hug. I obliged. "I love you, dad. You're the best. Thanks!" he said in a low voice.

It was nice to have the van so I didn't have to wait on a taxi. I rushed home to give the boys some of my time before we went back to the hospital. Everyone had finished their lunches by the time I arrived. When Hildy found out I had not eaten, she immediately began scurrying around the kitchen to fix me something. While she did, I took the opportunity to call Darcie. Thank goodness she was in this time.

After we got the formalities out of the way and the condition of Joel, I asked her, "Have you given any more thought on my offer for you to run the foundation I'm going to set up?"

"Yes, Mel and I have discussed it at length. Although he would still like for me to stay at home and not work, he knows I wouldn't be happy just being a housewife. So I intend to take you up on your offer. I think it's a fantastic idea and I want to be part of it."

"Great! Now I want to ask you a favor. First of all, do you have any contacts in the CPS offices in the Houston area?"

"I know several people who work there, why?"

"I would like for you to find out any information you can on two foster children. Their names are Tony and Benny Clausen. Tony is 12 and Benny is 9. I think they may be the first candidates for the foundation. Tony is in the room with Joel so I pretty much know his situation. I don't know where Benny is or under what conditions he's living. Tony's CPS case worker won't reveal where Benny is. This is causing Tony a lot of stress which he doesn't need right now."

"Sure, I'll do what I can. I'll call a girlfriend who works there. I want to see if she can come to my wedding anyway, so it gives me a reason to call her right away. We went to college together and were in the same sorority. How can I get in touch with you?"

I gave Darcie the phone number at the apartment just as Hildy placed my lunch in front of me. I ate the meal quickly and then rounded up the boys to go to the hospital. TJ was standing by the door waiting for us to leave.

It was nice to have the van available for the trip to the hospital. It might not be as luxurious as the limo but it sure gave us more flexibility. I had to restrain TJ to keep him from running to the hospital after I had parked the van.

"Hold on, TJ, I don't want you to get run over by a car. You might end up in the hospital too," I said, as I grabbed his hand.

"But dad, we gotta see Joel!" he said, with a pleading look in those beautiful blue-green eyes all the boys except Chris had. "Hurry!"

There was a crowd waiting for the elevator so we elected to walk up the stairs. When we got to the top of the stairs, TJ recognized where we were and began dragging me toward Joel's room. As we turned the corner of the corridor where Joel's room was, TJ let go of my hand and ran as quickly as his little legs would carry him down the hall and into the room. By the time the rest of us arrived, TJ was in the bed with Joel, just as he had been the day before. Hildy, Becky Sue and I stood back and let the boys say their hellos and get questions about how Joel felt out of the way.

Hildy was the first to approach. She leaned over the bed and kissed Joel on the forehead. Stepping back from the bed she opened her big purse and brought out a large plastic bag full of peanut butter cookies. "Do you think you could eat a peanut butter cookie or two?" she said with a giggle in her voice. "Crane, do you think you could get these boys some milk from the cafeteria?"

"I think I can manage that. Becky Sue will you come with me to help carry it?" I asked. "Tony, would you like some too?"

He looked at his mom and when she nodded, he said, "Yes sir, I like peanut butter cookies."

It didn't take us long to get six pints of milk, but despite that quite a few cookies had disappeared by the time we got back. The twins and Chris split their time between Joel's bed and Tony's bed.

Bill came over to me and we started talking. There was so much confusion in the room we stepped outside the door so we could talk at normal volume. "It makes Tony happy when your twins come to see Joel. His brother would be just their age. It also makes him sad when they leave. He misses his brother so much. I think it's downright cruel for CPS to keep them apart."

"Look, Bill, I don't want to interfere but I have a friend in the San Antonio Police Department and also a good friend who used to work with CPS. I've asked them to see if they can find out any information about Benny. I've had my problems with CPS and if there is anything I can do to make them live up to their responsibilities to care for kids, I'll do it. I can't promise they'll have any success, but it won't be for not trying. Anything you can tell me about the circumstances of Tony and his brother would be helpful."

I jotted down a few notes as Bill told me all he knew about Tony and Benny's background. It wasn't much but I would pass it along to Jack and Darcie. It couldn't hurt. By the time Bill and I stepped back into the room all the cookies were gone, but the boys were still having as good a time as they could have under the circumstances. Tony and Joel were both sitting on the sides of their beds. TJ was glued to Joel's side. Larry and Lenny had taken positions beside Tony on his bed and Chris took a position beside Joel on his bed.

Hildy, Becky Sue and Karen had retreated to a corner of the room and were having an animated conversation about something or other.

"Hey, guys, how would you like to get out of the room for awhile? It's such a nice day! Why don't we go out to the gardens?" I asked the boys.

That got an immediate positive response from all of the boys. I stepped out and down the hall to the nurses' station to see if I could get two wheelchairs for Joel and Tony. The large heavy-set black nurse wearing a nametag that said "Charlene" promised she would have an orderly bring them to the room in a few minutes.

Shortly, a young man arrived with both wheelchairs. Joel had decided it was going to be too hot to wear his robe. He didn't care if people saw him in his pajamas so he only put on his slippers in preparation to go outside. Tony said if Joel wasn't going to wear a robe then he wouldn't either.

TJ decided he would ride in Joel's chair again today. As we all got onto the elevator, I was glad it was made to haul gurneys because the twelve of us with the two wheelchairs just about filled it up.

The landscaped garden area for the hospital was immaculately maintained and although the azalea season was over there were still a number of blooming plants. There were several benches scattered along the wide paths that wound through the area.

"Dad," Lenny whispered to me, "can I ride in the chair?"

"Well, why don't you ask Joel if he'd like to sit on the bench for awhile? Then you guys can take turns riding in it. Will that work?" I asked.

I knew Joel could never turn down a request from his brothers so he took a seat on the bench next to me with TJ at his side while the other boys took turns pushing each other around the paths. They were having a great time but all too soon it was getting close to time for Joel to have his next treatment. Reluctantly, we all went back to the room.

When we got back to the room I gave the keys to the van to Hildy and told her either she or Becky Sue could drive it to the apartment. I would take a taxi later tonight. The boys began saying their goodbyes to Joel and Tony, each getting and giving a hug. Even Karen and Bill got their share of hugs. There were tears in TJ's eyes as he left the room looking back as long as he could to see and wave to Joel.

Karen was a little misty-eyed when the troops left. "Crane, you are an extremely fortunate man to have such wonderful sons. I love this young man with all my heart," she said, looking at Tony, "but I don't think I could cope with five active boys."

"I couldn't if it weren't for Hildy. She is an amazing woman. But I do agree the boys are definitely wonderful," I said, giving Joel's shoulder a squeeze.

Joel had laid back on the bed. I guess the boys visit and the excursion outside had worn him out. I noticed Tony was having a hard time keeping his eyes open also. Soon both boys were resting peacefully. Bill, Karen and I continued to talk quietly until Dr. Barrow and a nurse came in to give Joel his next batch of chemotherapy.

I gently shook Joel to wake him. He looked up at me with sleepy eyes. I explained to him it was time for his treatment. He just muttered an okay and closed his eyes as if to go back to sleep.

"Where do you want the injection, Joel?" Dr. Barrow asked.

"Um, I think in my leg so if it gets sore I won't have to lay on it," he said, waking up.

"Good choice, smart boy," Dr. Barrow said.

The nurse had pulled the curtain around Joel's bed while this conversation was taking place.

"Now Joel, I need for you to lower your pajama bottoms so I can get to your leg. Nurse Carter is going to disinfect it. It will probably feel kind of cool," Dr. Barrow said.

Without hesitation Joel shoved his pajama bottoms down. I was surprised until I saw he was wearing a pair of briefs under them.

"Good thinking," I said, grinning at him, causing him to giggle.

The nurse began scrubbing the thigh with first what smelled like alcohol and then with what looked like iodine. While she did this Dr. Barrow explained, "The injection will go into a group of muscles called quadriceps and specifically into the *Vastus Lateralis* which is the muscle that runs down the side of the thigh. We have to inject about 20cc and we have to do it slowly. It will take several minutes before it is all injected. During that time I need you to lie very still. You will probably feel some stinging where the medicine goes in, but it shouldn't be too bad. Are you ready?"

Joel looked at me and reached out his hand and grabbed mine. "Yes, sir," was his only reply.

I saw him wince as the needle was inserted into the muscle of his leg and felt his hand squeeze mine more tightly. I turned to watch the medicine being slowly injected. I was both fascinated and horrified as I watched.

Suddenly Joel grabbed my hand and pulled it towards him and at the same time grabbed his throat with the other. There was a look of abject fear in his eyes that will haunt me until the day I die. A struggling gasp came from his throat.

"Doc, there's something wrong! He can't breathe! He needs help!" I yelled.

The next few minutes were a blur. I heard him say something about epinephrine and code blue and intubate and a lot of people rushing in the room and being pushed unceremoniously out of the way. I watched in horror as the fear in Joel's eyes turned from fear to sheer panic and then blank as he passed out.

The next thing I remember was Dr. Barrow saying "Let's move. We have to get him to ICU, stat!"

With that, Joel's bed was wheeled out of the room and down the hall and around several corners to the ICU. I was following in a daze. I couldn't believe this was happening. Just a few minutes ago he was lying there holding my hand and now … I couldn't let myself think anything bad would happen to him.

I was stopped at the door to ICU by one of the nurses. I just stood there staring at the closed doors not really comprehending what was going on. "Why don't you come over here and sit down?" she asked, taking my arm and leading me to a small room equipped with chairs and a couch. "As soon as the doctors know anything, we will let you know."

I sat there like a zombie, not feeling for several minutes. All at once it hit me that there was a real possibility I was going to lose Joel. I completely lost it. I broke down and wept uncontrollably for maybe ten minutes. I wanted to do something but I couldn't think of anything I could do that would help the situation. I got up and started walking. I didn't have a destination, I just had to walk. I passed a restroom and went in and bathed my face in cold water then I took off walking again. I must have walked every corridor on the floor at least once.

Passing one door I stopped. It was a door into a chapel. I hesitated and then went in. It was deserted. It was a small chapel with just three pews on each side of the aisle and a modest pulpit in front. I don't know why I went in there. I am not a religious person. I guess I thought it wouldn't hurt to ask for help.

Sitting down in the last pew I gathered my thoughts. It had been a long time since I had prayed, but if there was a God he would know that already. "God, I am begging You to let my son Joel recover. He is the kindest, gentlest, most loving boy there could ever be. He has been tested more than any child deserves to be. I would gladly trade places with him if it were possible. He has so much to offer. Please don't take my son away from me and from his brothers."

I sat there for a few more minutes before getting up and making my way back to the ICU waiting room. I had barely settled into my chair when Dr. Barrow entered the room.

CHAPTER 10

I was so deep in my own thoughts I didn't notice Dr. Barrow until he placed his hand on my shoulder. I jumped as if I'd been shot.
"He's okay, isn't he? My Joel is okay, right?"
"Yes, he's okay. He's not out of danger yet, but he's stable."
"May I see him?"
"Yes, but he's sedated and won't know you're there. We will keep him in ICU overnight and possibly all day tomorrow depending on his condition. He has a breathing tube so he wouldn't be able to speak even if he were awake."
"What happened? Why did this happen?"
"The simple explanation is, he had an allergic reaction to the chemo. It's called "anaphylactic shock". This is not common with the medicine that was being used, particularly when it is injected into a muscle. The reaction is much more common when it is used intravenously. You have got to realize these agents are in reality poisons. We are trying to kill the cancer cells. These agents act most aggressively on the rapidly growing cells or those cells which divide the fastest."
"May we go see him now?"
"Sure, let's get you all fixed up with a gown and mask and so forth. You can only spend a few minutes with him. Don't be alarmed by all of the equipment he's hooked up to. It's there to make sure he doesn't have a relapse and to make sure he recovers fully from the reaction."
I followed Dr. Barrow to a small room next to the ICU where I was outfitted with sterile garments, booties and mask. I was then led into the ICU. There were three other beds besides Joel's that were occupied all surrounded by

machines and tubes and wires that went every which way. As we approached Joel's bed my knees started going weak and my heart started beating faster.

Joel was hooked up to the same array of machines I had seen around the other patients' beds. There was barely room for me to reach the side of his bed. I gently took hold of his hand which felt cool to my touch.

"Why does his hand feel so cold?" I asked.

"The temperature in here is kept very cool. It's kept that way for various reasons," Dr. Barrow answered.

I rubbed Joel's hand as I leaned over and kissed his forehead through the mask covering my nose and mouth. "Dad's here, son. I love you."

He looked so pale and helpless just lying there in that bed with all the stuff hooked up to him beeping and whirring and whooshing. Tears started to run down my cheeks soaking my mask. "Why? Why must you suffer when all you deserve is to be healthy and a normal happy boy? You never hurt anyone. Please get well. Your brothers need you. TJ needs you. I need you. You have made my life so much better just because you came into it."

Dr. Barrow placed his hand on my back and indicated it was time to go. I followed him and placed my gown in the receptacle he showed me. Before I started back to Joel's room, I got assurances I would be notified if there were any changes to Joel's condition.

On my way back to the room, I started thinking about how I would tell the boys or if I should tell the boys about what had happened to Joel. I was undecided. Part of me thought they had a right to know their brother had a problem and another part thought it would only cause unnecessary worry for them.

When I got to the room, Bill and Karen were still there with Tony. As soon as I stepped inside, they immediately bombarded me with questions about Joel's condition. I reassured them, as best I could, and tried to reassure myself at the same time.

"Our prayers are with you and Joel and, of course, his brothers. Tony has gotten very attached to the twins," Karen said, as she gave me a friendly hug.

"Thanks," was all I could say. I shook hands with Bill, waved goodbye to Tony, picked up my stuff and hurried out the door. I still hadn't decided what I was going to tell the boys.

I reached for my car keys and when I didn't find them I panicked. "Where the heck did I put those keys?" It took me several minutes of searching through everything I had with me before it dawned on me that I had sent the van home with the rest of the family earlier. It seemed like an eon ago but in reality it had only been a few hours. I didn't even know what time it was. When I reached the front door of the hospital I saw the sun was just beginning to set so it had to be around eight. I looked at my watch and it showed 8:17.

The taxi let me out in front of the apartment. I slowly made my way to the door and inserted my keys. I had no more than got the door open when my arms were full of boys. They each got a special hug and kiss as I made my way into the apartment.

"Daddy, we got to go to the zoo on the way home," TJ said, in his excited high-pitched voice. "There were lions and tigers and elephants and ostrics and monkeys and snakes and all kinds of animals. It was fun. Can we go again? Please?"

"I'm sure you can and didn't you mean ostriches?" I said, ruffling his hair.

"And there is a train in the park and we got to ride it," Chris said.

Not to be left out, Larry said, "There was this bird that had a great big tail. It was blue and green and it looked like it had eyes on the feathers. It was pretty."

"Oh yeah, that was a peacock," I said.

"They even had a porcupine and a llama," Lenny added. "And a eagle."

"That's great, guys. Have you had your snack yet?"

"No," was the unanimous response.

"Well, let's go see if Hildy has anything for you to eat."

Hildy gave me a worried look as she saw my face. "Have you had anything to eat?" she asked. "We had Kentucky Fried Chicken for supper. I didn't have time to prepare anything since we took the boys to the zoo. I saved back a couple of pieces in case you didn't eat at the hospital."

"Thanks, a piece of cold chicken and glass of milk sounds great right now," I answered.

"Okay, boys, we have ice cream for your snack. Take your seats and I'll bring your bowls. There is some chocolate syrup to put on it if you want," Hildy said, stepping out of the way of the thundering herd of boys heading for the table.

Soon the only sounds in the room were spoons scraping bowls as nearly a half-gallon of ice cream disappeared in record time. There was just enough left for me to have a small bowl.

"Okay, guys, as soon as you put the dishes in the dishwasher, go get your showers taken and brush your teeth. Then we need to have a family meeting," I told them, barely able to keep my voice from cracking.

As they rushed off to the bathrooms to shower, I motioned for Hildy and Becky Sue to sit down at the table.

"What's wrong, Crane? I noticed you looked upset when you came in. Is Joel all right? Oh, God, please!" Hildy pleaded.

"Not exactly," I said, and then went on to explain the events of the afternoon. By the time I was finished, Hildy was in tears as was Becky Sue. Although I tried to put it in as positive a light as I could, I was not too successful. How do you put a positive light on a train wreck in your life?

Soon four freshly scrubbed boys bounded into the living room. Hildy and Becky Sue busied themselves in the kitchen. Patting the couch beside me indicating I wanted them to sit next to me, I picked up TJ and placed him on my lap.

"Look, guys, I know you just saw Joel this afternoon and he was fine. He was happy to see you. After you left and were at the zoo, the doctors gave him some more medicine. Joel had an allergic reaction to the medicine and is now very sick. Do you understand?"

"What's 'lergic?" TJ asked.

"You know when a mosquito bites you how you get a bump and it itches, that's like a little allergic reaction. Well Joel's allergic reaction was in his throat and windpipe. It made his throat swell so much he couldn't breathe for a while until they gave him some special medicine. Now he is in a special place in the hospital where they put people who are very sick."

"Can he breathe now?" Chris asked.

"Yes, he can now. The doctor put a tube in his throat so he could breathe."

"Can we go see him?" Lenny asked.

"Probably not, son, we will just have to see how he is tomorrow. If they bring him back to his room then you may be able to see him. He's still really sick."

"I wanna see Joel," TJ cried, burying his face in my chest.

"I know, I know," I said, rubbing his back.

I wrapped my arms around all four of the boys and we sat there for several minutes just comforting each other without saying a word.

"Time for bed," I said. "I'll be in to say good night in a few minutes. Let's go!"

While the boys headed for bed I went and talked to Hildy and told her I would be leaving for the hospital by seven. I wanted to be there in case he woke up.

Then I went in and tucked the boys into bed. I gave each of them an extra hug and kiss before I went into my own bedroom. I brushed my teeth and slipped on my pajama bottoms before getting into bed. I knew it was going to be a long night. My mind was racing with all of the possibilities. Sleep would not come easy tonight. I tossed and turned for several hours with no sleep on the horizon.

I heard my bedroom door opening slowly and then the sound of little feet padding across the carpet. I knew it was TJ. This visit was not unexpected. As he slipped under the sheet I turned over and drew him to me.

"I'm scared, daddy. I want Joel to come home. Why can't he come home? I miss him," my little angel sobbed.

"I wish he could come home too, pumpkin. The doctors have to get him well before he can come home. We want Joel to get well so he can be with us for a long time," I said.

"But I still miss him," TJ said, as he snuggled up against me. It wasn't long before his breathing showed the pattern of sleep.

The last time I looked at the clock it was about ten minutes before two. That didn't stop the alarm from going off at six. I quickly shut it off before it woke TJ. I looked over at my sleeping angel and kissed him lightly on the forehead. As I got out of bed I noticed another lump in the bed on the other side of TJ. When I looked closely, I could tell it was Chris. I kissed his forehead also before going to take my shower.

I checked on my other two angels before going to the kitchen to grab something to eat. I should have known Hildy would be there, but it surprised me none the less. When she saw me she walked up and hugged me.

"I prayed for Joel last night," she said, dabbing at her eyes with her apron. "I just know he will be all right."

"I hope you're right. I can't imagine my life without him. He's such a special boy."

I called a taxi to pick me up at seven and then ate the breakfast Hildy had prepared for me. I planned to leave the van for the family in case they wanted to go back to the zoo or one of the museums in the area. I don't even remember what she had fixed for my breakfast. My mind was a million miles away, trying not to think of the worst things that could happen to Joel.

As I was waiting for the taxi to arrive I noticed a young black male who looked maybe 14 or 15 sitting on the ground with his back against one of the walls of the apartment. It seemed strange but the taxi came before I could give it much thought.

I stopped by Joel's room first, just to make sure they hadn't brought him back from ICU. Tony was still sleeping and Karen had not yet arrived. Joel was not there so I continued to ICU. The closer I got the more it felt like I was walking in molasses. I wanted to get there quickly but my feet were not cooperating. I did finally make it to the nurses' station outside the ICU.

"Good morning, I'm Crane Johnson. My son Joel is in there. Could you tell me how he is?" I asked the attractive nurse sitting at the desk.

"Good morning, Mr. Johnson, Dr. Kerner and Dr. Barrow are in there with him now. Your son's vital signs all look normal according to the monitors here at the station. If you'd like to wait, I'll tell the doctors you're here when they come out. They have been with him for about ten minutes so it shouldn't be long. There is a coffee pot in the waiting room if you would like a cup," she responded brightly.

"Thanks," I said, as I turned toward the waiting room. I sat down and picked up a three-year-old copy of *Newsweek* thumbing through it without even seeing what was on the page in front of me. I don't know how many times I flipped through the magazine before Dr. Kerner came in and sat down beside me.

He held up his hand as I started to ask questions. "Before you ask anything, Joel is fine. We removed the breathing tube and he's breathing on his own. We still have him on oxygen but that's just a precaution. If there are no further complications we'll take him back to his room by around noon."

"Can he have visitors?"

"Yes, but I would like for you to limit it to one or two visitors besides yourself. This has been a shock to his system and he'll be weak for a few days before he's back to normal. He'll be able to talk but his throat will be sore and his voice will be very hoarse. Just don't let him talk too much. I'll give him some lozenges that'll help the soreness, but they won't completely eliminate it."

"Thanks Dr. Kerner, is it possible to see him now?" I asked.

"Yes, but only for a few minutes. He is still groggy and not quite awake yet. He may not even know you're there," he said.

"That's okay, I need to see him."

I went through the same ritual as before getting all outfitted for the ICU. I approached Joel's bed tentatively, not knowing what to expect. His eyes were half open but glazed. As I took hold of his hand, he turned his head toward me. There was no recognition in his eyes.

"It's dad, Joel. How are you feeling?"

"Not too good," he said in a raspy whisper. "My throat hurts and I'm cold."

I looked around for a blanket and found one on the foot of his bed. Grabbing it, I spread it over him.

"What happened? Why am I here?"

"You had a bad reaction to the medicine. Don't talk too much they had to put a breathing tube down your throat. That's why it's sore." I leaned over and again kissed him through the mask.

"How's TJ?"

"He wants to come see you, but he can't until you get back to your room."

Dr. Kerner came up and placed his hand on my shoulder indicating it was time for me to go. I squeezed Joel's hand and started to leave.

"I'm hungry," Joel rasped.

"I'm glad," Dr. Kerner said. "I'll have them send up some soft food so it won't irritate your throat."

As we walked out, Dr. Kerner said, "Having an appetite is a good thing. He hasn't eaten anything since yesterday noon so I'm sure he needs something to eat. I'll order a high calorie drink for him to go along with his breakfast."

"No grits, though. He's like me; he doesn't like them," I laughed.

"Okay, we will continue to monitor him, but if he continues to improve I'm sure we can have him back in his room by noon. I want to run one more blood test before we release him from ICU."

I decided since I wouldn't be able to see Joel again until he got back to his room, I would go back to the apartment and spend some time with my other sons. I had been guilty of neglecting them since Joel had been in the hospital and although I think they understood, I'm sure they didn't like it. I grabbed a taxi and headed back to the apartment.

Hildy had a worried look on her face when I walked in. "He's all right," I said. The relief showed on her face.

"Daddy, when can we go see Joel?" TJ asked.

I explained we could go this afternoon but only a couple of them could go in to see him at a time. That seemed to satisfy them that they at least were going to get to see their brother.

"That guy looks so sad," Chris said.

"What guy, Chris?" I asked.

"That guy sitting over there against the wall. He's been there since last night. I saw him," he replied.

"Let me see," I said. "Oh, I saw him there earlier when I left for the hospital. Do you want to go see why he's so sad?"

"Yeah," Chris said, and got agreement from all the other boys.

"Okay, get your shoes on and we will go for a walk. We don't want to scare him so we will walk around a bit first."

We walked around the apartment complex for about five minutes before we rounded the corner of the building where he was sitting.

"Hi, Chris said you've been sitting there since last night. Is something wrong?" I asked.

"None of your damn business," he retorted.

"You're right it isn't any of my business, but if you need some help maybe I can."

"Why would you want to help me? You don't know me."

"Call it a hobby. As I said, if you need help just give me the word."

"My dad kicked me out," he said sullenly.

"That's too bad. Are you hungry?"

"Don't you want to know why he kicked me out?"

"Not unless you want to tell me. By the way, my name is Crane and these are my sons Chris, Larry, Lenny and the little one here is TJ. Do you have a name?"

"Bran."

"I'm glad to meet you Bran. You didn't answer my question. Are you hungry?"

"Yeah, I haven't eaten since yesterday morning. What's it to you?"

Chris went up to Bran, sat down beside him and began whispering in his ear. Bran got a funny look on his face before he said, "No shit?"

"I don't know what Chris told you, but if you want to come with us we'll get you something to eat and then try to decide what to do next."

I noticed he winced as he got up and walked slightly hunched over as we made our way to our apartment.

"Hildy," I started, "this young man is hungry. He hasn't had anything to eat since yesterday morning. Do you think you could get him something to eat?"

"Of course," she said. "Will one of you boys show him where to get washed up. And you might wash your hands also if you want a snack."

The room cleared in a flash as they herded Bran to the bathroom to wash.

"What are you getting yourself into now?" Hildy asked.

"I don't know. I just think the kid needs some temporary help is all. It seems his dad kicked him out."

A few minutes later and with the help of the microwave Hildy had a complete hot meal ready for our guest. Hildy put his plate at the end of the table with the other boys on the sides. He sat down, took his napkin and placed it on his lap. He closed his eyes, mumbled a few words and then crossed himself.

The boys looked at him as he did all of this. They had this quizzical look on their faces and I knew they were dying to ask why he did that. I guess they had never been around Catholics much. I think most of our friends were either Baptist or Methodists.

Bran quickly finished the plate Hildy had fixed for him. Hildy began dishing out second helpings to his dazzling smile. The second helpings disappeared almost as quickly.

"Would you like some fruit cocktail and whipped cream like the boys had?" Hildy asked.

"Yes, ma'am," he said enthusiastically.

The boys and I had already eaten our dessert. I skipped the whipped cream and had a small bowl of fruit cocktail. After he had finished and the dishes were removed, I asked, "Why did your dad kick you out of the house?"

"What the hell do you want to know for? So you can throw me out too?"

Hildy reached around in front of Bran and grabbed a bunch of his shirt. "Now you listen to me, young man. When you are in this house you will keep a civil tongue in your head. There will be no swearing as long as I'm around. Now, Crane asked you a question. I suggest you answer him in a civil manner. I know you have better manners than that," she said looking him straight in the eye.

The expression on his face was almost comical. Hildy had been so mothering that the change in her demeanor took him totally by surprise.

"Y ... yes ma'am," he said, totally cowed by what had just happened. Then looking at me, he said, "It's kinda personal. Can we talk alone?"

"Sure, let's go for a walk," I said getting up from the table. "You boys stay here while I talk to Bran."

We walked in silence for a few minutes before he began to open up. "My dad hates me. He says I'm no good, that I'm a disgrace to the family."

There were tears in the corners of his eyes as I looked at him. "Why would he say a thing like that? You appear to have good manners except for your tendency to use profanity."

"Is she your mom?"

"No, Hildy is our cook, housekeeper, nanny for the boys and is their surrogate grandmother. She is not a lady to mess with as you just learned."

"Does she hit people?"

"No, she would never do that."

"I wish my dad didn't," he almost whispered.

"How does he hit you?"

"With his fist or his belt or whatever he can get his hands on. He never hits me where people could see. I'll show you," he said, lifting his shirt tail up over his ribs.

His skin color was more honey brown than black probably indicating mixed race. The bruises were clearly visible on the sides of his ribcage and when he turned around his back was bruised as well. There didn't appear to be any lacerations of the skin, but it was apparent from the various stages the bruises were in that he had been beaten for some time.

"How long has this been going on?" I asked.

"A couple of weeks," he said, looking at the ground after pulling down his shirt.

"Okay, we have been skirting the issue for quite a while now. Why don't you tell me why your dad does this and why he kicked you out of the house?"

"I might as well. You'll probably kick me out too. He found out I was gay. There, are you satisfied? You hate me too, don't you?" he said, as the tears began to fall.

I didn't answer. I simply wrapped my arms around him and hugged him. After a few minutes, his sobbing subsided enough for him to look up at me. "Why did you do that?"

"I guess because you needed to be comforted. I could never hate you for what you are. I know you didn't choose to be gay and you would probably give almost anything to be normal. So you're gay, big deal! That doesn't give your dad the right to beat you. No one deserves that.

"Now, where do you live? I think we need to have a talk with your father."

Bran lived in the same apartment complex we did, but in a building several over from where ours was.

The meeting with Bran's father was neither pleasant nor successful. His attitude toward gays was unbending and vehement. I thought for a minute he was going to strike me but I guess he came to his senses long enough to realize my six-inch height advantage and much fitter physique put him at a distinct disadvantage. The confrontation ended with Bran's clothes and belongings being tossed out the front door. There were not that many, so between the two of us we were able to carry them all back to my apartment.

Hildy and Becky Sue gave me strange looks as we entered with Bran's stuff. I suggested that Becky Sue take the boys to the swimming pool for their swimming lesson while I tried to sort out what to do about Bran. I noticed he had a pair of trunks in his belongings so he could go also.

While they were gone I explained the situation to Hildy. "You know I hate to do this, but I think the best thing we can do is to call CPS. I simply cannot take on raising another boy. If it weren't for Joel's illness I might think differently but I'm not able to spend enough time with the other four, let alone adding another one."

I called the weekend number for CPS and explained the situation to them as best I could. The man I talked to on the phone seemed very sympathetic which was encouraging. He said someone would come by to assess the situation in about an hour.

CHAPTER 11

While waiting for the CPS case worker to arrive, the phone rang. When I answered it, Eric was on the line. He said JR and he had driven to Houston and wondered if it was all right to stop by and see the boys. I naturally agreed and gave him directions to the apartment complex. Since he had lived in Houston, he was familiar with the area where the apartments were located. He said they would be here in about fifteen minutes since they were just passing the Galleria on the West Loop.

I'm glad he was used to driving in Houston traffic. There was no way I would drive and use a cell phone with all the crazy drivers on the freeways.

It was nearing eleven o'clock and I wanted to be back at the hospital by around noon to see if Joel had been returned to his room. Too much was going on and I was in danger of losing track of everything when the doorbell rang. When I answered it, a young man who looked to be in his mid-twenties was standing there.

"Hello, my name is Chad Dinkens with CPS. Are you the person who called about a Bran LeBeau?" he asked.

"Yes, please come in. I'll go get Bran," I said showing Chad into the family room.

"I would rather talk to you for a moment before I see the boy. I need to gather a little more information if you have any."

"Well, there's not a lot I can tell you. My first contact with Bran was about two and a half hours ago," I stated, before reciting everything I knew about him. It only took a couple of minutes to tell the story.

"Is there someplace private where I may talk to Bran?"

"Just a moment," I said, going to the kitchen to ask Hildy if Chad could use her apartment to talk to Bran. I knew she wouldn't mind but wanted to ask her anyway.

She agreed, so I showed Chad to the other apartment and went to get Bran. The boys were having a great time playing in the pool with Becky Sue when I arrived. I motioned for Bran to come to me.

"Is something the matter?" he asked.

"No, there's a man here from Social Services who would like to talk to you. Here's a towel. Dry off and come with me, please."

He complied and we started to walk the half a block back to the apartment. We were just about to cross the driveway to the apartment when Eric and JR arrived in their car. They pulled into a parking spot and began to get out of the car when I saw they had another passenger with them, causing me to smile. I stopped long enough to greet them and briefly introduce Bran. Telling them I would be right back, I continued to Hildy's apartment with Bran. It only took a minute and I was back to give them a warmer welcome.

I gave JR a big hug and then did the same to Eric.

"What brings you guys to Houston?" I asked.

"A couple of reasons," Eric said. "First, we wanted to see Joel, if possible, and second, Samson is pining for his family. He won't eat. All he does is mope around all day long. He lays at JR's feet and moans."

"Come here, Samson. Let's go find your boys," I said, grabbing hold of his leash. "The boys are at the pool."

We walked back toward the pool with Samson pulling at the leash. We got almost to the gate leading into the pool when the boys spotted us coming. There was a sign saying animals were not allowed in the pool area but it didn't matter, we never made it that far. Four very wet boys descended on us and were greeted by one very happy dog. I think they were wetter after their greeting than when they got out of the pool from the licking they got from Samson.

After Samson had been properly greeted, the boys turned to JR and Eric, each getting enthusiastic greetings. Becky Sue also got a greeting from Samson but not as wet. As my boys and JR got caught up on the four days they hadn't seen each other, Eric and I did the same.

"What's the story with that kid, Bran?" Eric asked.

I briefly explained what little I knew about the situation, leaving out the part about Bran saying he was gay. "He's talking to a caseworker from CPS right now. I don't know what the outcome is going to be. He has no place to go. As far as I know there are no close relatives in the state who could take him. I really feel for the kid, but I don't think I could take on any more responsibilities right at the moment. Hey, maybe you should take him," I chuckled.

"Whoa! Let's not get carried away. Sometimes I think JR is too much to handle. But, you know that kid did look vaguely familiar. What is his last name?" he asked.

"LeBeau."

"I wonder if he is related to the LeBeau who worked for me as a network technician a couple of years back. His first name escapes me at the moment, but he was a black man and as I recall fairly short maybe five-six or seven. I had to fire him because of his foul mouth around my clients. Some of them refused to allow him on their sites."

"That sounds a lot like Bran's dad. We only had one very unpleasant meeting but this guy's name was Harry …"

"I'll bet that's him," Eric interrupted. "Now I remember, his name was Harrison but everyone called him Harry. I never met his son. I only saw pictures of his wife and kid on his desk. Did you meet his wife?"

"No, I didn't see a wife when I went to the apartment with Bran and he didn't mention his mother when I talked to him," I said. "I hate to run, but I need to get to the hospital to see if Joel is out of ICU yet."

"Wh … What's the matter? Why is Joel in ICU?" Eric sputtered.

"Oh God, I guess you haven't heard. Joel had an allergic reaction to one of his medicines and went into shock. They told me he might be released back to his room around noon and I need to be there when he get back."

"Ah, I see. Is there anything I can do?"

"I don't think so, Eric. Thanks for asking. Wait, maybe there is. Could you drop me off at the hospital?"

"Sure, no problem. Will we be able to see Joel today?"

"I don't know. Dr. Kerner said he didn't want more than one or two visitors for him at any one time after he got back to the room." Then turning to the boys I said "Come on, guys, go jump in the shower and get ready for some lunch. Dad has to go to the hospital soon."

"Can Samson come in the house?" TJ asked.

"Yeah, I guess but only for a little while. We are not supposed to have pets in the apartment."

We all headed for the apartment to get cleaned up for lunch. I just assumed Eric and JR would stay so I headed to the kitchen to tell Hildy. I then went into the bedroom and changed clothes getting ready to go to the hospital. I could hear the boys laughing and carrying on in the shower as I changed.

I asked Eric where he and JR were going to stay while they were in town, when I returned to the family room.

"We stay with my parents when we come to town. It gives JR a chance to be spoiled by his grandparents, as if he isn't spoiled enough by me," he laughed, tousling JR's hair.

"Aw, dad," JR complained, "I just combed my hair."

Just then the doorbell rang. When I answered it, Chad was standing there with Bran.

"Mr. Johnson, I wanted to thank you for calling us so we can help this young man," he said.

"What's going to happen to him?" I asked.

"For the weekend he'll be going to a shelter. The first of the week he'll be processed into the system and then we'll begin a search for a foster family for him. That usually takes from two weeks to a month to locate him a proper family to live with."

All this time, Bran was standing there looking down at his shoes, not saying anything.

"You mean he may spend up to a month in a so-called 'shelter'? That's not acceptable! From what I've heard about these shelters, all they do is shelter the public from what is going on in there. Eric, do you know any foster homes in the area that might be willing to take an emergency placement?"

"I know of one. Let me make a phone call and I'll check to see if they are agreeable," Eric said, and headed to my bedroom to make the call in private.

My four freshly scrubbed boys emerged from their bedroom and joined us in the family room bringing Samson with them.

"Hi, Bran," TJ said. "Did you see our dog? His name is Samson."

Bran knelt down as Samson approached and Bran began scratching him behind the ears.

"He likes you," TJ said to Bran.

"I like him too," Bran said. "I never had a dog."

"I have a family that will take emergency placement of Bran," Eric announced as he returned to the room. "They are licensed to have up to six foster children and at the moment they don't have any. Chad, I know you can make the placement because my sister worked for CPS."

"I'd have to confirm that information. Who are these people and where do they live?"

"They live out in Hedwig Village and their names are Ethel and Alan Levin," Eric said with a smile. "They're my parents."

"I'll need to confirm the information," Chad said as he walked to the phone and made a call to CPS. Within a few minutes he returned. "The information you provided was correct. I'll have to inspect the residence before I could leave Bran there, but if everything checks out, I think it's a viable option for him."

"Good, I'll call mom and dad and let them know you're coming," Eric said.

When Eric came back he gave the address to Chad before he left with Bran. Chris and JR helped Bran take his clothes and things to Chad's car.

"I've got to get to the hospital. You guys stay here and be good for Hildy and Becky Sue. If the doctor says you can see Joel, I'll come back and take you to the hospital. Give me a hug and then go eat your lunch."

Eric and I left for the hospital. Most of our conversation centered on Bran and why a father would kick his son out of the house. Although I didn't really think it was my business to tell Eric that Bran told me he was gay, I told him anyway. I figured his parents had a right to know in case they had a problem with it. I was relieved when Eric assured me they would not be freaked out.

"When I came out to them, they just looked at me and asked me why it had taken me so long to realize it. It seemed they had suspected since I had been in high school," he said.

Eric let me out at the hospital entrance and I made my way to Joel's room as quickly as I could. It was getting very close to noon and I was hoping I would get there before he did. As it turned out they were wheeling Joel down the hall on a gurney when I rounded the corner of the hallway to his room. I rushed to his room to be there when they lifted him from the gurney to his bed. He looked so pale and fragile, my heart nearly broke.

"How are you feeling, son?" I asked as I took hold of his hand and leaned over and kissed his forehead.

"Not too good," he whispered in his raspy voice. "I'm kinda hungry."

Dr. Barrow walked in as we were talking. After we got the formal amenities out of the way, I said to him, "Joel says he is hungry. Has he been able to eat anything?"

"I have ordered a tray for him which should be here very shortly. He hasn't had anything since breakfast so I'm sure he's starved," Dr. Barrow chuckled.

Before he had finished his examination of Joel, the lunch tray arrived. It was quickly devoured by Joel. I think he liked the cup of chocolate ice cream the best because it soothed his throat.

While Joel ate, I asked Dr. Barrow about visitors and was told Joel could have a couple of visitors at a time, but they were not to stay too long and tire Joel out. I also asked when he would be able to go outside in his wheelchair. He indicated that if Joel continued to improve from the reaction, he might be able to go out tomorrow afternoon.

I talked with Joel for about an hour after Dr. Barrow left. I explained that Eric and JR had come to town and wanted to come see him this afternoon. I also told him about Bran. The more I talked about Bran, the sadder Joel's expression became.

"What's going to happen to him, dad?"

"I don't know, son. For the time being he's going to be living with Eric's mom and dad. I don't know what's going to happen to him after that. We'll just have to wait and see."

I picked up the phone and called the apartment to let them know Joel could have visitors and I would be home shortly to get them. Eric came on the line and suggested he load everyone into the van and drive it to the hospital thus saving me an unnecessary trip. I thought that was a wonderful idea, it would give me more time to spend with Joel. I told him I would meet everyone in the lobby in about twenty minutes.

I had to wait several minutes for the boys to arrive. It seemed the parking garage was nearly full and Eric had to park the van farther away. As soon as I saw them I knew who was going to be first to visit Joel. TJ could barely be restrained.

"Guys, listen to dad. Only two of you can go in at a time so a couple of you will have to stay in the waiting room while the others go in to see Joel. I think TJ wants to go first, so who wants to go with him?"

Chris was selected to go with TJ. I escorted everyone else to the second floor waiting room and then started toward Joel's room with TJ pulling on my arm. As we approached Joel's door, TJ again released my hand and bolted into the room and climbed over the guardrails on the bed. When Chris and I entered the room he had wrapped himself around Joel and was crying on his shoulder.

"I was so scared when dad said you were really sick," he sobbed. "I want you to come home. I don't want you to be sick."

Chris had approached the bed from the other side and had reached through the guardrails and was patting Joel on his shoulder. He couldn't get close enough to give him a kiss like he would ordinarily have done.

We had only been in the room a couple of minutes when a stern-faced nurse walked in. Looking at Joel's chart she announced in her best authoritarian voice, "There are only supposed to be two visitors at a time for this patient. One of you will have to leave. And what is that kid doing in the bed with him? Get him out of there immediately."

"Nurse ..." I started, looking at her nametag. "Nurse Grantham, may I see you in the hall please? You boys stay right there."

Taking her by the elbow, I gently but firmly led her out the door and closed it behind us. "Now, Nurse Grantham, Dr. Barrow told me I could bring Joel's brothers in to visit him two at a time and that is what I plan on doing. I don't care what the chart says, that's what I'm going to do. Their visits do more for his mental well being than all the medicine this hospital has."

"But ..." she sputtered, but realized from the tone of my voice I was determined to have my way. "Okay, but that kid has got to get off the bed."

"We'll see. What difference does it make?"

"It's against hospital policy to have two people in a bed," she said smugly.

"Lighten up a little. What harm is he doing? None! He's comforting his brother in the best way he knows how. It comforts both of them. Dr. Kerner doesn't seem to have a problem with it, so why should you? I respect that you are trying to enforce hospital policy, but my only concern is for my son's, all my sons', health and well being. If that means breaking hospital rules, then so be it," I said and turned and re-entered the room leaving her standing there, staring daggers at my back.

"I hope you gave her what for," Karen said, as I stepped back into the room. "She's the nastiest nurse on the floor. She's hassled Bill and I for things we've done. I don't think she cares a whit about her patients, just the bloody hospital rules."

"Well, I hope she won't bother us any more," I said, returning to Joel's bedside.

Chris was telling Joel all the things that had happened to them since yesterday afternoon. You would have thought they hadn't seen each other for days if not weeks. At least he was doing all the talking and all Joel had to do was nod or give a grunt at the appropriate times. I let them talk a few more minutes before I suggested they let the twins come see Joel. Chris was not happy but agreed to leave. TJ was having none of that. He just clung tighter to Joel and the tears started welling up in his eyes.

"Why am I such a softie?" I asked myself, and agreed to let TJ stay a little longer. I took Chris to the waiting room and got the twins and led them to the room. I intended to persuade TJ to leave so we wouldn't be violating Dr. Barrow's orders. That didn't work.

"I'll be in deep kimchi if Nurse Grantham comes back, but what the heck," I muttered.

I didn't think I spoke loud enough for anyone to hear so it surprised me when Karen said, "If she does, one of the twins can visit Tony."

"Oh … Thanks, I didn't think you could hear that," I said, looking up with an embarrassed smile. "I'm sure they want to talk to him too." I was right. Larry and Lenny split their time between the two beds. It gave them both a chance to talk to someone at the same time.

Hildy and Becky Sue were the next two to visit Joel. I stayed in the waiting room while they visited. I didn't want to leave Eric with the responsibility for watching my three as well as his son. JR was awfully quiet as we sat in the waiting room. He seemed very uncomfortable. When I asked Eric about, it he said JR had never been in a hospital and really didn't know what to think. JR said it smelled funny.

Last to visit Joel were Eric and JR. While they were visiting Joel I took the other boys to the cafeteria to get them something to snack on. It had been a couple of hours since they had eaten. This time they wanted the frozen yogurt but they wanted chocolate syrup and nuts on it. After I got the boys settled with their snack, I left them with Hildy and Becky Sue and fixed a couple more of the sundaes before heading to Joel's room.

I didn't think until I was almost to the room that I hadn't brought a sundae for JR. As I entered the room I said, "Sorry, JR, I didn't bring you a sundae but if you want to go to the cafeteria you can join the other boys. I'm sure your dad will buy you one."

I raised the head of Joel's bed so he was in a more upright position before I handed TJ and him their treats. JR took one look at the sundaes and began tugging his dad toward the door. I gave Eric directions to the cafeteria as he was being pulled out the door.

Then it hit me. Not only had I not brought anything for JR, but I had also neglected to get something for Tony. "Oh, Tony, I'm sorry for my bad manners, I should have brought you some yogurt, too. Bill, if you will go get him some, I will pay for it."

"Thanks, Crane, but we were about ready to take Tony out for a little ride around in his wheelchair. I think it would be a good idea to go to the cafeteria so he has a chance to talk to your sons again."

I hadn't noticed the wheelchair sitting in the corner of the room until Bill mentioned they were going for a ride. Karen pushed the chair up beside the bed and Bill lifted Tony with great tenderness into it.

A half an hour later Bill and Karen were back, wheeling Tony, who looked absolutely exhausted. "I think we overdid it with Tony today. He was having so much fun talking to your boys we didn't notice he was getting so tired," Bill said. "You're blessed, Crane. Your sons are so friendly. They treated Tony like he was one of their brothers."

"Thanks, Bill, they're good kids," I said, before turning to TJ. "I'm going to go get your brothers and then we need to go back to the apartment and let Joel rest also."

TJ shook his head indicating he didn't want to leave. I just nodded my head yes and went to get the others.

I found the rest of the clan still in the cafeteria. At least they weren't still eating. I gathered them up and we headed back to Joel's room. I told the boys they could go in one at a time to say a quick goodbye to their brother. The rest of us stayed outside the door while each one went in and climbed up on the bottom bar on the guardrail and gave Joel a kiss. Hildy and JR also made the trip. When all were finished, I entered the room and told TJ it was time to go.

"No! I don't want to go," he said, sticking out his lower lip.

"Yes, son, we need to let Joel have some rest. You can come back tomorrow," I said reaching over the guardrail to lift him out of the bed.

"No, I wanna stay with Joel."

Joel looked into TJ's eyes and said in his still-raspy voice, "You have to go with dad. I love you, TJ, but you have to go."

"Come on, give your brother a hug and a kiss and then let's go. Everyone is waiting," I said, lifting TJ out of the bed after he got and gave a hug and kiss.

TJ started crying loudly like his heart was broken as I carried him out of the room to join the rest of the family. He cried all the way to the van and all the way back to the apartment. No one could console him or get him to stop crying.

When we got to the apartment I carried my still sobbing son into the family room and sat down on the couch with him on my lap.

"TJ, I know you miss Joel very much but he has to stay at the hospital to get well. I would like nothing better than to have him come home with us back to Canyon Lake."

"I don't like you! I don't want you to be my daddy no more!" With that, he tore out of my arms, ran to his bedroom and slammed the door.

It was as if a knife had been thrust through my heart when I heard those words he uttered. I sat there in total shock as were the other boys who had been sitting around us. For what seemed like an hour, I couldn't catch my breath.

I saw Hildy heading for TJ's room, "No Hildy, I'll handle it in my own way. Don't scold him."

Hugging the rest of the boys, I left the apartment and returned to the hospital.

"What's the matter, dad?" Joel asked, after I had been there a little while. "Is something wrong?"

"Nothing for you to worry about, son. It's just that TJ was so upset about having to go home today. I worry about him."

"Me too. I always tried to be there to protect him and now I can't."

We sat there in silence for quite some time with our own thoughts until Dr. Kerner came in for his evening rounds. He went first to Tony and checked him out before coming to Joel.

"How are you doing this evening, Joel?" Dr. Kerner asked.

"A little better, I'm still kinda dizzy when I sit up."

"That's to be expected. Have you been able to eat anything today?"

"Yeah, but my throat still hurts a bunch."

"That should go away in a day or two but I'll prescribe some Tylenol so you'll be able to sleep without pain. Tomorrow you have another treatment. Not the kind that made you sick, but one through your catheter. This one will take a good four hours to complete so you'll have to stay in bed all that time. I'll have an orderly come help you take a bath after breakfast and we'll start the treatment right after that. Does that sound okay?"

"Yeah, I guess. Can't I take a bath by myself?"

"Sure, the orderly will just make sure you don't fall and hurt yourself. You may still be a little dizzy tomorrow morning."

I stayed until Joel's pain relievers were delivered and then gave him a kiss and hug before I left. Walking to the van, I remembered I hadn't eaten since breakfast. I hoped Hildy had some leftovers so I could get something quick to eat.

The boys were in the shower getting ready for bed when I got back to the apartment. Hildy was able to rustle me up a substantial meal in very short order. She even insisted I eat the large piece of blueberry pie with a dollop of whip cream on top. I didn't have the strength to argue and really didn't want to.

I went to tuck the boys in bed as always. When I got to TJ he turned his back to me so I kissed the back of his head and told him I loved him. My heart felt like lead in my chest. I struggled to breathe and to keep from crying as I walked quickly to my bedroom. I went through the motions of preparing for bed as though I were a zombie.

Sleep refused to come. I wondered how I was going to resolve the problem of TJ's first defiance of me. I could understand his distress of being separated from Joel. I realized it was his strong emotional bond to Joel that caused him to act this way, but I still couldn't allow him to continue in his defiance.

I considered every course of action I could think of and rejected all of them. I guess I'll have to have a talk with Dr. Adams if this continues. I looked at the clock, it said fifteen minutes before three and I hadn't been to sleep. A few minutes later I heard the faint sound of a door being opened. I lay there not making a sound. A moment later I felt someone climb into bed with me and then snuggle up against my back.

Slowly I turned over so I was facing my snuggler. I was not too surprised when I saw it was TJ.

"Are you okay, son?"

"Um … Do you hate me?"

"Oh, no, I could never hate you. I love you so much, even when you're naughty. You are my little TJ."

"I'm sorry, daddy. I'm sorry."

"I know son. Now go to sleep. It's late. I love you," I said kissing his forehead. This time he did not turn away. He was asleep in less than five minutes and I was not far behind.

CHAPTER 12

I awoke with a start Sunday morning. When I opened my eyes TJ was staring down at my face. He was only inches away.

"Good morning, son."

"Do you still like me?" he asked hesitantly.

"No, I don't like you," I started, and saw his face fall. "I love you."

His eyes brighten when he heard that. He moved closer and kissed me on the tip of my nose. "I love you, too. I didn't mean what I said yesterday," he said, laying his head on my shoulder and slipping his arms around my neck.

"I know you didn't. We all say things we don't mean sometimes when we're angry. Now why don't you go wash your face and hands? I'll bet Hildy is fixing breakfast. Are you hungry?"

"Yeah," he giggled. "Your whiskers tickle."

"Dad's got to shave and shower and then I'll eat breakfast with you," I said giving him another squeeze.

He hopped out of bed and ran for his bedroom to get cleaned up. I made my way to the shower in a more leisurely manner. It only took me a few minutes for a quick shower and shave before I was able to head for the kitchen and breakfast.

As I was about to enter the kitchen area, I could see Hildy sitting on a chair with TJ on her lap.

"I love you, grandma Hildy," TJ said hugging her neck.

"Oh, my," Hildy choked. "I love you too, baby. You know you were naughty yesterday, don't you?"

"Uh huh," he murmured.

"Have you told your dad that you're sorry?"

"Uh huh. He said he loved me. He really did."

"That's good, baby. I know he loves you. Now then, what do you want for breakfast?"

"Pancakes!"

"Okay, hop down and I'll fix us some pancakes."

"That sounds good to me," I said, walking into the kitchen. "Why don't you go wake up your brothers and have them get ready for breakfast."

"Okay," he said, jumping down from Hildy's lap and making a beeline for the bedrooms.

"You all right with his conduct yesterday?" Hildy asked.

"Yes, he was just angry. Angry that Joel is sick. Angry that he doesn't understand why Joel can't come home. Angry that he can't be with Joel more of the time. He struck out at someone he loved, whom he knew wouldn't strike back. I can't tell you how much what he said hurt. I knew he didn't really mean it, but it still hurt. He crawled in bed with me early this morning seeking comfort. I love all of the boys with all my heart but I must admit he has a special place in my heart."

"I know what you mean, Crane. He does insinuate himself into your heart," she said, as she began preparing the pancakes.

It was a good thing the stove in the apartment was equipped with a griddle that allowed her to fix six pancakes at a time or she would never had been able to keep up with the hungry horde that was about to descend on the breakfast table in a few minutes. TJ was the first to sit down while he waited impatiently for his brothers. Ordinarily Hildy insisted everyone be seated before anyone was served, but she made an exception this time and gave TJ a couple of pancakes to keep him from fidgeting.

"These are good, but they taste different. How come?" TJ asked.

"That's because we don't have any pure maple syrup, honey," Hildy responded. "I didn't pack it and the store didn't have any when I went shopping."

"Oh, that's okay," he answered taking another bite, dripping syrup down his chin.

Becky Sue arrived almost simultaneously with the twins and Chris. I enjoyed a cup of coffee while everyone else dug into the stack of pancakes Hildy had ready. She wasn't foolish enough to think the stack would last, so she busied herself with trying to stay ahead of their appetites and out of the way of their knives and forks.

I had just poured my second cup of coffee when the phone rang.

"Good morning, Eric," I said. "How is everything with Bran this morning? Has he settled in all right?"

"He is doing just fine. He's had a ball playing with Samson. I think it was good for Samson too. Between JR and Bran, I think they wore the poor dog out. He was a tired but happy dog last night."

"So I guess JR and Bran are getting along fine then?"

"Yes, so far they've been having a great time," Eric said. "What I called you for this early in the morning was to find out if the boys would like to go to Astroworld with us this afternoon? I'm taking Bran and JR. We plan to get there around one o'clock and spend the entire afternoon."

"Well, I don't know. I was thinking about seeing if Dr. Kerner or Dr. Barrow would let Joel go to the park area at the hospital so he could see Samson. I know Joel has a treatment today that should last several hours so I don't know if he will be allowed to leave the room. Let me call you back after I get to the hospital and see what they say. I'm sure the boys would love to go if they can't see their brother," I said.

We talked for a few more minutes before hanging up. I needed to get to the hospital to see Joel. I knew he wasn't looking forward to having the orderly help him take a bath, even if it were Rodney, whom he liked.

I got four very sticky kisses as I said goodbye to the boys telling them to behave themselves and I would be back around noon. I took the van knowing the family was not going to be going anywhere this morning. Hildy would be going to church, but it was only a block and a half away so I'm sure she would be able to walk there.

Joel had just finished his breakfast as I walked into his room. He and Tony were talking but stopped when I walked in the room. I gave Joel a hug and a kiss on the forehead before I walked to Tony's bedside and gave him a hug also. He was a little surprised but hugged me back. Neither Karen nor Bill had arrived to visit Tony yet.

"Do you want to go get a bath taken?" I asked Joel. "Hildy sent some clean pajamas for you to wear."

"Yeah, I gotta get something to wrap around my arm so I don't get this thing all wet. Last time they gave me some plastic stuff to wrap it."

"I'll call a nurse and get something for you," I said, and buzzed the nurses' station.

I told the nurse what we wanted and then went into the bathroom to begin drawing the water for Joel's bath. I hoped the nurse would be there by the time

I had the bath ready. Thankfully, we only had to wait a minute or so before she arrived. She quickly covered the IV shunt so it wouldn't get wet.

I helped Joel out of bed and steadied him as he walked to the bathroom. He wasn't too unsteady but I didn't want him to have any chance of falling. I gave him some privacy while he used the toilet and then helped him into the tub. I left him to bathe himself but told him to call when he finished so I could make sure he didn't fall in the tub.

I talked to Tony for a few minutes before Karen and Bill arrived. Tony seemed to have a slight cold as I talked to him and I mentioned it to Karen. She seemed to take it very seriously. It took me a few moments before I remembered the chemotherapy the boys were receiving in addition to killing the cancer cells also killed the cells that helped to fight infections.

I was distracted by Joel calling me to come help him out of the tub. He dried off and got into his clean pajamas. I still stayed close to him in case he got dizzy, but he made it back to bed without any problems.

It was about ten minutes later that an orderly came in to help give Joel his bath. When he was informed Joel had already bathed, he responded, "That's great. I've been running behind all morning. Maybe this'll help me catch up. One of the other orderlies called in sick this morning so we're short-handed. Call if you need anything." And with that, he left for his next patient.

At ten o'clock Dr. Barrow arrived with a nurse to begin Joel's chemotherapy. He informed us the treatment would take a total of about five hours. There would be two IV's, each one taking approximately two and a half hours. The medication they were going to give him would probably make him very drowsy for the rest of the day. That answered my question about taking him out to see Samson this afternoon.

"Will he be able to have visitors this evening?" I asked.

"He should be alert enough to have visitors after his supper, say around seven o'clock. I wouldn't recommend they stay too long. This particular medication makes the patient feel very weak. He'll feel a lot more alert tomorrow," Dr. Barrow said.

All this while, the nurse had been hooking up sensors to Joel's chest and talking to him quietly.

Dr. Barrow saw me looking at what the nurse was doing and explained, "This is just a precaution. The reactions to this medication are extremely rare, but with his reaction to the last intra-muscular injection, we don't want to take any chances. Are you going to be around for a while?"

"Yes, I'm going to be here for about another hour. I have to give the boys' nanny some time off. The poor girl didn't know what she was getting herself into when she took the job," I chuckled.

"Good, monitor his reactions for a while. I'm sure everything will be all right," he said. He then went over to the nurse and began adjusting the drip speed on the IV.

When Dr. Barrow finished with Joel he went over to Tony's bed and began examining him after pulling the curtain. I told Joel what Eric had suggested that the rest of the boys do today. His face showed disappointment that he would not be able to go with them but he understood.

"When you get well, I promise I will take you wherever you want to go. You just name it," I said, feeling guilty that we would be enjoying ourselves while he was stuck here in the hospital.

After a while he seemed to drift off to sleep so I took the opportunity to call Eric and tell him we would be going to Astroworld with him. Then I remembered I had not mentioned anything to Hildy, Becky Sue or the boys, so I made a quick call to inform them. I reached Becky Sue; Hildy had not yet returned from church. I told her she needn't come with us this afternoon if she wanted some time for herself but she insisted, saying she had never been to Astroworld.

Making sure Joel was sleeping, I kissed him lightly on the forehead and quietly left for the apartment.

Hildy had returned by the time I got back. When I explained to her what was going to happen she said she would go to the hospital and sit with Joel. She didn't think she was up to traipsing around a theme park all afternoon in the hot Texas summer sun.

Eric, JR and Bran arrived shortly after we had eaten a light lunch. I was sure there would be plenty of opportunities for the boys to eat at the park. We all jumped in the van and headed off to the Astrodome, dropping Hildy off at the hospital on the way.

"Why are we parking here?" Chris asked. "Isn't Astroworld over there on the other side of the highway?"

"Yes, it's over there across Loop 610 but the parking for it is here in the Astrodome parking lot. There is a foot bridge over the road. We can walk over or we can get on that trolley and it will carry us to the gate. What do you want to do? Walk or ride?" Eric asked.

It took a minute or so but finally everyone agreed they wanted to walk so they could look down at the cars on the highway. By the time we got to the entrance to the park, I think they regretted their choice. It was a long walk on hot concrete with no shade. The excitement as we entered the park with all the rides spread out in front of us seemed to quickly revive them

It had been a long time since I had been to a theme park and they certainly had changed since then. The one ride I always enjoyed was a wooden rollercoaster. I know there are more modern ones. Ones that go faster and do all sort of outrageous things, but the feel of the old wooden structure coasters has always held that indefinable attraction. The *Texas Cyclone* was one of the best in the southwest. The ride only lasted a little over two minutes but it was a fantastic two minutes.

We rode on all the rides the boys wanted to and more than I wanted. There were some TJ couldn't ride on because he wasn't tall enough. Those usually coincided with the ones Becky Sue volunteered to stay with TJ while the rest of us risked life and limb. An interesting new ride, just installed this year, was the *Mayan Mindbender*. It was unique because it was an indoor rollercoaster and a lot of the ride was in the dark. I still liked the *Texas Cyclone* better.

Bran was a perfect little gentleman all the time at the park. I never heard him utter a single profanity the whole afternoon. He and JR were constantly together on the rides wherever possible. Bran had a great sense of humor. He had the rest of the boys in stitches most of the afternoon. He also appeared to be a bright young man. All in all, he was a welcome addition to our outing.

Larry and Lenny were absolutely fearless when it came to the rides. They loved the thrill when the rollercoaster made the big drops that caused me to lose my breath. They begged to go on it over and over. Now I loved the rollercoaster, but twice was enough for me and my lunch.

One of the good things about the park was when you got tired you could sit at covered tables which had cooled air flowing out of vents overhead. In the heat and humidity of late May Texas afternoons, it was a godsend. We bribed the boys to sit for a while by letting them eat a shameful amount of junk food.

By five o'clock everyone was dragging. No one complained too loudly when Eric and I suggested we head for home. This time we took the little trolley which dropped us off very close to the van. TJ was nearly asleep by the time we got to the van.

We left the Astrodome parking lot and headed to the hospital. I wanted to pick up Hildy on the way back to the apartment. Eric suggested when we got to the hospital that he stay with the boys while I went in to fetch Hildy. Everyone except TJ found this to be acceptable. He insisted he wanted to go in with me. I didn't resist too much, so the two of us took off for Joel's room.

As we approached the room I said, "Son, Joel may be asleep when we get in there. If he is I don't want you to wake him."

"Okay," he said, looking up at me and nodding his head.

This time, instead of running into the room and climbing up into bed with Joel, TJ walked along side of me as we entered the room. Joel appeared to be sleeping. Hildy was sitting by his bed reading her Bible.

"Is Joel sleeping?" TJ whispered to her.

"Yes," she answered quietly. "He has been sleeping most of the afternoon. How did you like Astroworld, little one?"

"It was lotsa fun. But I got tired. We rode on this one that went down this slide and splashed into the water and I got all wet. It felt good," TJ bubbled.

"All right son, let's go home and have supper. We can come back to see your brother after we eat. He should be awake by then. How about if we order some pizza? Does that sound good?"

"Oh yeah! Can we have one with that round meat on it?" he asked.

"You mean pepperoni?"

"Uh huh," he said, walking up to Joel's bedside and patting Joel's hand.

As soon as we got back to the apartment I checked the Yellow Pages for the nearest Domino's. With Eric and his crew we had ten to feed. I thought three large pizzas would be enough but to be safe I added another medium to the mix along with four orders of breadsticks. It turned out it was a good idea. By the time we finished eating there were only two slices of pizza left and no breadsticks.

"Can we go see Joel now?" TJ asked as the last of the pizza boxes was placed in the garbage can.

"We still have guests, son," I answered. "In a little bit."

"Crane, it's been a fun day, but I have to get back to Canyon Lake. Some of us have to work tomorrow," he said, barely able to keep the smirk off his face.

"Yeah, it's a tough life, but someone has to do it," I laughed.

"Look, JR is going to be spending the week with my folks so why don't you bring the boys out there to visit. Samson is going to be staying also and I know he would like it. Mom and dad have a big back yard where the boys could play with him."

"That sounds great. It'll give the boys a chance to get out of the apartment for a while and getting to play with Samson is a bonus. Write down the directions and your folks' phone number."

"JR, Bran, say goodbye to your friends, I need to get on the road back home," Eric said.

Bran stood back while JR was hugged by my four, then they approached him and gave him hugs also. JR grabbed Bran's hand and led him into the kitchen where they both got a hug from Hildy. A smiling Bran left the apartment with JR and Eric.

"Why don't you go jump in the shower and clean up a bit before we go see Joel. A couple of you can use the shower in my bedroom," I said to a disappearing bunch of boys.

It was about twenty minutes after seven when we got to Joel's room. He was being examined by Dr. Barrow. TJ stood at the side of the bed looking from Joel to Dr. Barrow and back again.

"Well, aren't you going to climb up and greet your brother?" Dr. Barrow said to TJ.

With a grin and a giggle, TJ was in bed beside his brother in a flash giving him a hug and kiss on the cheek. Each of the other boys hopped up on the bottom bar of the side rails so they could get close enough to give their brother at least a partial hug.

"How's he doing, doc?" I asked.

"Very well, he tolerated the treatment with no difficulties which is encouraging. It will be another week before we have a good feel for the long term and whether we will have to resort to more aggressive treatment options. That is something I don't want to worry about at the moment."

In the confusion of all the boys and I entering the room, I had not even acknowledged Bill and Karen who were sitting beside Tony's bed. While the boys were telling Joel of their afternoon adventure, all of them seemingly talking at once, I went to talk to Bill and Karen. As I walked over I noticed Tony was wearing a surgical mask.

I guess my quizzical look was enough. "Dr. Kerner said that for the next several weeks it would be better if Tony wore the mask to help prevent him contracting any disease from us or any other visitor. His immune system has become so weak that any infection could be very serious. So for a while he's our little bandit," Karen said, looking at Tony with a big smile on her face.

"Aw, mom, I don't even have a gun," he giggled through his mask.

We chatted for a few minutes before Bill said he had to get back to the motel and gather up his stuff and head for home. He had to be at work early tomorrow morning.

"Bill, don't forget to pay the motel bill before you leave. They asked me about it today and I forgot to mention it," Karen said.

"Okay, I'll take care of it," he said, giving her a kiss. He then turned to Tony and gave him a bear hug and a kiss on the forehead. "You be a good boy. I'll telephone you during the week. I love you son."

"I love you too, dad. I'll miss you," Tony said.

Bill walked quickly out the door. I could see the glint of tears in his eyes as he left.

"Karen, it is none of my business, but have you considered living at the Ronald McDonald House? It is not that far away and it wouldn't cost you anything."

"No, I didn't think we would be eligible since we are only foster parents. That would be a great help. Paying the motel bill and all the expenses of a house, too, is a bit much. I know where that place is. Bill and I have walked by there but I never thought about stopping. Maybe I'll stop by there tomorrow and see what they say. Thanks."

"I'm hungry, dad," Joel said from across the room. "I didn't get any lunch 'cause I slept through it and supper was kinda small."

"Let me go see if the snack bar or cafeteria is open. Chris, would you come help me? I'm sure everyone will want something. It's been at least an hour since we had pizza."

The snack bar was about to close when we got there but we were still able to get six paper bowls filled with chocolate frozen yogurt which Chris insisted on topping with more chocolate syrup and chopped nuts. Chris carried two and I carried the other four bowls back to the room. We made it back without mishap.

I apologized to Karen that I hadn't brought any for her but I didn't think we could have carried any more. Tony did get one of the sundaes. He removed his mask long enough to enjoy it.

After everyone had enjoyed their treats it was getting time to go back to the apartment.

"Okay, guys, it's time to go. Everybody say goodnight. You can come back tomorrow," I told them.

For what seemed like the next ten minutes everyone made their goodbyes to both Joel and Tony each getting and giving hugs. I let Joel know I would be in late tomorrow because I needed to call the office and take care of some business first thing in the morning.

"That's okay, dad. Would you leave the Sherlock Holmes book? Maybe I can get some of it read. Dr. Barrow said I didn't have any chemo tomorrow," he said.

I gave him a hug and a kiss and then herded the others out of the room. At least we didn't have a scene with TJ tonight. He looked like he could fall asleep at any moment. Astroworld had worn him out. I thought all of us would be able to sleep well tonight.

Even though it was barely dark when we got back to the apartment, nobody complained when I told them to change into their pajamas, brush their teeth and get into bed. TJ was asleep when I went to tuck them in. The rest were not far from it.

I awoke to the smell of freshly brewed coffee. That meant Hildy was getting ready to prepare breakfast. I quickly took care of my morning duties and then headed for the kitchen for a cup of coffee. I told Hildy the boys would probably sleep in a little this morning so she could delay starting breakfast for a while.

It was almost half past eight when Larry and Lenny descended on the kitchen and were soon followed by Chris and TJ. All of them were still in their pajamas. Hildy and I got our morning hugs before they pulled up to the breakfast table. It seemed Becky Sue was feeling the effects of our theme park visit also. She hadn't shown up for breakfast and presumably was still sleeping.

I called my office to check on things when I felt Foster would be in. I talked first to Carol to see if I had any messages I had to handle personally. Having been assured there was nothing pressing that needed my attention she forwarded my call to Foster.

For the next half hour we discussed the status of our projects and the status from his viewpoint of the sale of the business. I felt reassured he did not see any stumbling blocks that would prevent the sale from going through.

Next I had the operator set up a three-way call with Carlos and Gerald to see if they had any information that would cause the sale to be sidetracked. Again they saw nothing from either the legal or financial aspects that would put up a roadblock.

I was about finished organizing my notes of the phone calls when the phone rang. It startled me because I was not expecting anyone to call this early. It was Jack.

"Good morning, Jack," I said. "What gets you up this early? I didn't think detectives got to work before noon."

"Hey, be nice or I won't tell you what I've found out about the kid you were interested in finding ... ah ... let's see ... Benny Clausen."

"Okay, okay!"

"It seems from what my friend Casey says both of the boys have come in contact with the juvenile division. Apparently their only crimes were to run away from home and be truant from school. His information is that they ran away at least twice over the past couple of years. He did not personally handle the cases. His information comes from another officer in the HPD. He knows both of the boys were turned over to CPS because of suspected abuse in the home."

"Does he have any information on where Benny is now?"

"No, once the kids were turned over to CPS the police didn't have any reason to stay involved since no apparent crime was involved."

"Thanks, Jack. If you find out anything else, please let me know."

After I hung up, I decided to make one more call before I went to the hospital. I wasn't sure I would be able to get Darcie on the phone, but dialed her number anyway.

"Hello, Darcie," I said, when she answered. "This is Crane. How are you this morning?"

"Crane, I'm glad you called. I talked to Cindi last night. She had gone to New Orleans and just got back yesterday afternoon. Oh … you don't care about that. Anyway, Cindi is my girlfriend who works with CPS there in Houston.

"I'm afraid the information she gave me is not what you had hoped for. The reason Tony's caseworker didn't want to tell his foster parents where Benny was is she doesn't know …"

"What?" I shouted, much louder than I had intended.

"It appears the people who were looking after Benny have moved and taken him with them. At least they are not living at their old address and CPS doesn't know where they are."

CHAPTER 13

"How long have Benny and his foster family been missing?" I asked Darcie.

"That's hard to say. It seems the caseworker has been submitting regular reports on Benny for the last six or so months. However, when the supervisor did a spot check on her cases he found she had not been visiting her cases and had been fabricating the reports. They have been able to determine the caseworker had not seen Benny for at least four months. So, sometime in the last four months the family has moved," Darcie concluded.

"What are they going to do to find the family?"

"I hate to say this but my guess is they will check with the post office to see if a change of address has been submitted. If the family didn't submit one, they will probably wait to see if they contact CPS. If that doesn't happen then they will just hold the file open and probably forget it."

"Isn't there any way we can force them to put forth more effort to find Benny?" I asked.

"Not really. If you try to interfere they will stonewall and you'll get nowhere. However, there are a couple of things you could try. You could contact the *Houston Chronicle* and see if they are interested in publishing a story about a missing boy. They may or may not be interested. Another avenue is to see if you can get Marvin Zindler interested. He was made famous in that play and movie *The Best Little Whorehouse in Texas*. He works for a TV station there in Houston and is famous or infamous for getting results and embarrassing officials."

"What happened to Benny's caseworker?"

"According to Cindi, the only thing that happened was the caseworker got a verbal reprimand. The really irritating thing is, this is the third time she has been reprimanded for the same type of thing."

"That's unbelievable! How could they overlook such incompetence?" I asked.

"Well, again according to Cindi, the woman's husband is a big shot in the Harris County Democratic Party and also has a lot of influence in Austin. There is talk he will either run for mayor or county commissioner. Nobody wants to get on his bad side even though his wife, is as Cindi said, 'a lazy bitch who should have been fired years ago.'"

I gathered more information from Darcie about Benny's caseworker and also the number of her friend Cindi, in case I wanted even more information.

After I hung up the phone, I went to say goodbye to the boys before I left for the hospital. Becky Sue had arrived while I was on the phone. She was talking to the boys when I entered the kitchen. She was telling them she would be giving them another swimming lesson after their breakfasts had settled. That reminded me I had been very negligent in doing my laps in the pool since Joel was hospitalized.

It was after ten when I got to the hospital. I met Dr. Kerner in the hall as I got off the elevator. He updated me on Joel's condition indicating he seemed to be recovering nicely from the reaction.

"Is it okay to take him outside for a while this afternoon?" I asked, before we parted.

"I think that would be okay for a little while. Just make sure he doesn't get too tired. A half an hour or so would probably do him good," Dr. Kerner replied.

I thanked him and then made my way to Joel's room. He was sitting on the side of his bed facing Tony. They were having an animated conversation about their schools.

"Hi, dad," Joel said, when he saw me standing there. "Tony was telling me about one of his funny teachers. He wears real baggy pants with suspenders and wide ties like a clown, and he wears black and white tennis shoes."

"That is a little strange," I said, giving Joel a hug and kiss on the forehead. "Dr. Kerner said you could go outside this afternoon for a while. Would you like that?"

"Yeah. Can Tony go, too?"

"If his mom says it is all right, he can," I said, looking over to Karen.

"Dr. Kerner said he needed to get out of bed once in a while so I think that would be fine. But, I need to get something to cover his head," Karen said.

I thought that was strange until I looked closer at Tony. His hair was definitely falling out now. "Oh, I see. I guess I need to think about that for Joel, too."

"Dr. Kerner said all my hair will fall out in the next couple of days," Tony added, through his surgical mask and then with a giggle, "At least I won't have to get a haircut."

After things settled down, Joel asked if I would read some more of the Sherlock Holmes book. He said it was more fun when I read it.

I opened the book to the place where Joel had marked it. We had nearly finished the book. Only three chapters remained to be read.

THE COUNTRY OF THE SAINTS
Chapter 5
THE AVENGING ANGELS
ALL night their course lay through intricate defiles and over irregular and rock-strewn paths. More than once they lost their way, but Hope's intimate knowledge of the mountains enabled them to regain the track once more. When morning broke, a scene of marvellous though savage beauty lay before them. In every direction the great snow-capped peaks hemmed them in, peeping over each other's shoulders to the far horizon. So steep were the rocky banks on either side of them that the larch and the pine seemed to be suspended over their heads, and to need only a gust of wind to come hurtling down upon them. Nor was the fear entirely an illusion, for the barren valley was thickly strewn with trees and boulders which had fallen in a similar manner. Even as they passed, a great rock came thundering down with a hoarse rattle which woke the echoes in the silent gorges, and startled the weary horses into a gallop.[1]

I read the rest of the book before an orderly brought the boys their lunch. My voice had just about given out as I read the last few lines. Joel asked me what the last couple of lines meant, but I had to tell him I didn't know Latin, so I couldn't translate it for him.

"Will you bring another book?" he asked.

"Sure, what do you want me to bring? I only brought a few books with us," I said.

"I don't care. I like to read everything."

"Okay, I'll bring a book and your brothers when I come back about two o'clock. You eat your lunch and I'll see you then." I gave him a hug and said goodbye to Karen and Tony before leaving.

On the way to the van I called Eric's parents and told them I would be out to pick up Samson in a little while. I told Ethel, if they didn't mind, I would take JR and Bran to visit Joel saying I had to bring Samson back anyway. She hesitated for a moment before agreeing. She said it would give her time to go to the grocery store. She had forgotten how much two young boys could eat.

I drove directly from the hospital to the Levin's house. I should have known it would take me a while to get across town during the noon traffic rush. I did finally make it. Bran and JR were ready as was Samson. He nearly jerked the leash out of JR's hands when he saw the van drive up. I went inside and introduced myself to Eric's parents. They said they had heard all about me from both Darcie and Eric. I was impressed with the way they were already interacting with Bran. They treated him the same way they treated their own grandson.

After we exchanged pleasantries, I loaded the boys and Samson into the van and headed back to the apartment. Bran sat in the front passenger seat while JR and Samson sat in the seats behind us. I should say JR sat in the seat. Samson was so worked up it was all JR could do to restrain him. I'm sure he could pick up the scent of the boys in the van.

Samson went wild when he saw his boys waiting for him at the apartment. After giving each one of them an enthusiastic welcome he began looking around, searching for something. He would keep coming back to the boys and going from one to the next and then he would go searching again.

I patted him on the head and said, "Don't worry boy, you'll get to see Joel soon."

At hearing Joel's name he gave a loud bark.

"I think we had better go before we get kicked out of the apartment for having a dog," I smirked.

I received no resistance from the boys. They were out of the apartment almost before I could grab another book to take to Joel. I had given Becky Sue the afternoon off while I took the boys to the hospital. She left the same time we did, but her destination was the Houston Museum of Fine Arts which was only four blocks away. I offered to drop her off in the van but she elected to walk.

When we arrived at the hospital, I escorted all six of the boys along with Samson and Hildy to the garden area outside the hospital building. I was not surprised when TJ insisted on going with me to get Joel.

Joel was already sitting in a wheelchair when we got to his room. TJ immediately hopped up on his lap and hugged his brother tightly around the neck. I placed the book on the side table before I leaned over and gave Joel a kiss on the top of his head.

When I looked over, Tony was also in his wheelchair ready to go out as well. I noticed Karen had gotten him an Astro's baseball cap to cover his now balding head.

"Well, if you guys are ready to go, the rest of the gang is waiting for us outside," I said, grabbing onto the handles of Joel's wheelchair and starting out the door, with TJ still sitting on Joel's lap.

Karen and Tony followed us as we headed for the elevator.

"Nice hat there, Tony. Did your mom get that for you?" I asked, as we waited for the elevator to arrive on our floor.

"Yeah, isn't it neat?" he replied.

"Can I get one too, dad?" Joel asked.

"I don't know why not. I'll bet your brothers would like one too. How about it, TJ?"

"If Joel gets one, I want one," TJ answered.

"Five Astro ball caps coming up."

I hadn't told Joel we planned to bring Samson to see him. I'm not even sure if he knew Samson was in town. However, when we got out in the garden where I had left everyone he soon learned of his presence. Samson jerked the leash out of Lenny's hand and raced the twenty or so yards between him and Joel's wheelchair. He leaped the last couple of yards and landed in their laps. He was immediately hugged by both of them and they received a happy tongue licking.

"Oh, Samson, I missed you so much. It's so good to see you," Joel said, as he held Samson's face and looked him straight in the eyes. "Tony, ... Tony, come here. This is my dog, Samson."

Karen wheeled Tony up beside Joel's chair so he could pet Samson. Samson lifted his paw as if to shake hands with him.

"Why are you wearing a mask?" TJ asked Tony.

By this time all the rest of the family had gathered around to hear Tony explain why he had to wear a surgical mask.

"Son," I said to Joel, "this young man is Bran LeBeau. He is staying with JR's grandparents for a while."

Joel and Bran seemed to hit it off right away and were talking like old friends within a few minutes. Tony joined in and before long all of them were having a great time. However, it didn't take too long before it became apparent that Tony was getting tired. Karen noticed it and although Tony protested mildly she began wheeling him back toward the hospital.

"Samson, I love you, boy. but you're awful hot on my lap," Joel said, as he carefully urged Sampson off his lap. Although he was off Joel's lap he didn't move far away. He was always within reach of Joel's petting hand.

I let the boys and Samson enjoy themselves while Hildy and I chatted. While we were sitting on a bench under a live oak tree my cell phone rang. When I answered, it was my secretary Carol. She asked if it would be possible for me to come to the office tomorrow to meet with William Weller. It seemed he was going to be in town on Tuesday and wanted to meet with the major players in my organization to get a progress update on the sale from our side and provide one from their side. I told her to go ahead and set up the meeting. I would be in the office by nine.

After about an hour I could tell Joel was starting to get fatigued so I told the boys to say their goodbyes to their brother. I asked Hildy to remain with the troops while I took Joel back to his room. The goodbye between Joel and Samson was emotional. He had remained at Joel's side all the time and didn't want Joel to leave but after a hug and some ear scratching he consented to stay behind with the rest of the boys. That is except for TJ who resumed his position on Joel's lap for the trip back to the room.

When we got there I told Joel I had to go back to the office tomorrow and wouldn't be able to visit him until in the evening. I planned to fly back to San Antonio tonight and then take the afternoon plane back to Houston.

"That's okay, dad. I know you gotta work sometime."

"You know something?"

"What?"

"You are one great kid," I told him. "I love you and your brothers so much it makes me wonder what I ever did to deserve you guys."

"I know. It's 'cause you got a good heart," Joel said, holding his arms out for a hug. It ended in a three-way with TJ joining in.

"Okay, TJ, it's time for us to go and let your brother rest. We'll come back to see him tomorrow evening when I get back in town."

We just started out of the room after saying goodbye to Tony and Karen when Dr. Barrow came in.

"Mr. Johnson, I'm glad I caught you. We are going to start a new series of chemotherapy treatments for Joel tomorrow. This will be a series of oral and intravenous medications that will go on for two days. During that time we would recommend he have a minimum of visitors. The medications can cause a number of side effects. None of which is life threatening but can make him nauseous and sometimes causes diarrhea. All in all it is one of the most unpleasant of the treatments he will undergo."

"Should I be here with him? I'm supposed to have an important meeting in San Antonio tomorrow morning, but if necessary I will cancel it."

"I don't think that will be necessary," Dr. Barrow said.

"Crane," Karen interrupted, "I'll be here in case he needs someone. I went through this with Tony and know sort of what to expect."

"Oh, thanks, Karen," I said. "That would be great. Thank you." I realized how fortunate we were that I allowed Dr. Kerner to convince me to put Joel in a semi-private room. Meeting Karen, Bill and Tony was a blessing in this unfortunate situation.

We stayed a few more minutes before TJ and I left to get the other boys and Hildy. I had nearly forgotten we had to drive all the way across town to drop off JR and Bran. I made a quick call to the Levin's to see if they were home. I didn't want to get there and them not be there. Thankfully, they were home so we took off for Hedwig Village, the six boys, Hildy and I and one dog in a van.

Samson was not happy when we let him out of the van and the boys didn't get out with him. Bran and JR talked to him and petted him and finally he calmed down but barked constantly as long as we could see him as we left in the van.

Something had been nagging at the back of my mind since I talked to Darcie this morning. The idea of contacting the newspaper or this Marvin Zindler character had some appeal, but it could take too long before they could develop the story and get it on the air or in print. I wanted Benny to be found now. Then I wanted CPS to get their noses rubbed in the mess. I decided to call Collin Cupp with Independent Investigators. He was the man I used to dig up the dirt on the Reverend Fullwell.

When we got home Hildy took the boys into the kitchen to get them a snack to tide them over until supper while I went to call Collin. I was lucky. He was in the office when I called. I explained to him what I wanted done and gave him Darcie's friend Cindi's information assuring him she would cooperate with the investigation. When he asked what priority I wanted them to place on it, I answered that I wanted the boy found as quickly as possible. They were to spare no resources to find him. He was to call me day or night when they located Benny.

Next I called Continental Airlines to see if I could get a flight to San Antonio this evening. They had one leaving Houston Intercontinental at 7:48 so I booked a seat on it and a return flight at 3:31 tomorrow afternoon. Then I went to tell the boys I would be leaving but would be back tomorrow.

Becky Sue had returned while I was on the phone and had joined the boys in enjoying ice cream sundaes. She was telling the boys about all the great art work she had seen today at the museum. The boys were more interested in the ice cream but at least they didn't interrupt her.

I asked Hildy if she would mind staying with the boys in the apartment again tonight. She agreed, as I knew she would.

"Hildy, I don't know what I would do without you. You bring sanity to this asylum. I thank you," I said, giving her a hug before heading for the bedroom to pack my shaving kit and personal items I would need. I also called a taxi to pick me up in twenty minutes.

The house seemed like a morgue when I got there. I turned on the TV just to have some noise. It was always so full of life when the boys were here. It was all I could do to make myself stay. I hadn't eaten before I left Houston and the flight was so short that no meal was served. I didn't have the forethought to stop on the way home to get something to eat so I was left to scrounge around to find something to eat. There was nothing fresh but I was able to find a frozen pizza which would have to do. I preheated the oven while I changed into my swim trunks. The pizza would take 55 minutes to bake since it was one of those deep dish ones. That would give me time to get in some laps in the pool that I had been neglecting.

After about twenty minutes in the pool I was hurting. How I wished everything was back to the way it was before Joel's illness. I would be getting up in the mornings and doing my laps with Chris joining me on occasion. But it was not to be. The emotions I had been suppressing since Joel's leukemia was diagnosed came flooding to the surface. I sat on the side of the pool and just sobbed uncontrollably. The only thing that snapped me out of my depression was the buzzer of the timer telling me my pizza should be done.

Mechanically I got up and went into the house. I was a bit ashamed that I allowed myself to give in to the depression that I felt. I was just glad the boys were not here to witness it. I ate the pizza barely tasting or enjoying it. I ate because I needed food. As soon as I had my fill I cleaned up my mess and went directly to bed.

I got to the office just before nine Tuesday morning. The first thing I did, after greeting Carol and getting a cup of coffee, was to call Joel. The phone rang several times and I was getting worried but then Joel answered it.

"Hi, son, it's dad."

"Hi, dad."

"How are you feeling?"

"Oh, pretty good. They gave me the pills a few minutes ago. There was four of them and they were big and I couldn't chew them. I had to swallow them. I drank a whole glass of water to get 'em down."

"Have they started the IV yet?"

"No, not yet, Dr. Kerner said they'd be back in a while for it."

"Did they give you anything to calm your stomach?"

"Yeah, I forgot. They gave me a cup full of this thick white stuff that tasted like peppermint chalk. It made my mouth taste nasty."

"Okay, son, dad's got to go. I love you and I'll see you tonight. Bye!"

"Bye, dad, I love you too."

The meeting with Weller was scheduled for ten o'clock. I had used the time between when I got off the phone with Joel and the meeting to catch up on the mountain of paper work on my desk. I had gotten through maybe two-thirds of it when Carol told me everyone was assembled in the conference room.

To say the meeting was boring would be an understatement. Foster was first to give a complete status update on the ten current projects we had on the table. He was followed by Gerald and then Carlos from our side. Weller made a few remarks before he turned it over to his financial person and then to his legal eagle. There was nothing discussed in the meeting I had not already heard and I had been out of the office for some days now. I sometimes think businesses have meetings just to have meetings. I guess that's why I'm such a fan of the *Dilbert* cartoons. Scott Adams has a way of capturing the idiosyncrasies and idiocies of the business world.

The meeting droned on and on. It was approaching two o'clock when I announced I had a plane to catch so I could get to the hospital to see my son. The meeting broke up within minutes. I think all it needed was an excuse to end.

I grabbed up my things, jumped into the BMW and sped off to the airport. One advantage of flying first class is the wait for check-in is minimal. I got to the gate with about fifteen minutes to spare before takeoff. First class had already loaded, but I was allowed to board immediately.

I was just getting settled when my cell phone rang. They hadn't told us to turn off all electronic equipment yet. I didn't know whom to expect on the phone, so I answered it with a great deal of apprehension hoping it was not the hospital.

"Mr. Johnson, it's Collin Cupp. I have some news for you. We have located Benny Clausen."

"Mr. Cupp that's fantastic news! Where is he?"

"I'm sorry to say he's in Piedras Negras, Mexico."

"How in the world did you find him so quickly if they took him out of the country?"

"It's a long story but the short version is once we had talked to that Cindi you referred us to everything dropped into place. We were conducting another investigation into a couple who were scamming old people out of money and it turned out Benny's foster parents were that couple. They were using him as bait for the scam. That's not important, but what is important is there is evidence of them abusing him."

"How do we get him back into the US?"

"The legal route could take months if not years to work through both the American and Mexican courts. But there are other ways…"

"Look, I'm on a plane that is about to take off for Houston. I'll give you a call in about an hour and a half and we can discuss the other ways. The stewardess is giving me nasty looks to shut off my phone. Bye."

CHAPTER 14

The flight seemed to take forever before we landed in Houston. It was only 4:30 but I knew it would take me as long to travel from Houston Intercontinental Airport to the apartment as it did to fly from San Antonio to Houston. Since I didn't have any luggage except for my shaving kit it didn't take me long to get to the taxi stand and hop in one. I wanted to call Collin back immediately but I also wanted some privacy when I did. I had the distinct impression the "other ways" he mentioned to bring Benny back to the States might not be totally legitimate. If that was the case, I didn't want any witnesses to the conversation. Besides I needed to see my sons. It was going on twenty-four hours since I had seen them.

The rush hour traffic was an absolute nightmare and we were going against the traffic. The closer we got to the apartment the more excited I became. I paid the taxi driver and rushed into the apartment expecting to see the boys but there was nobody there. I looked in every room and then went outside and walked to the pool. Still no one was there. Although I hadn't called to tell them what time I was going to be back, I just assumed they would be there waiting for me.

I walked back to the apartment and went to change my clothes in the bedroom. I was really feeling low and I guess feeling sorry for myself. The TV didn't help. It was just noise. When I heard the door to the apartment open I leaped to my feet and literally ran to see who it was.

Hildy entered first followed by the boys and Becky Sue brought up the rear.

"Hi, dad," TJ said, as he jumped up into my arms. "I missed you."

"Me too, kiddo," I said as I gave him a big hug and a kiss.

"We did too," Larry and Lenny said in unison before they got their hugs.

Chris just pushed into our group hug and said, "Uh huh."

"Where've you guys been?" I asked after everything settled down.

"We went to the park again," Chris said. "It's a neat place."

"Yeah and I got to ride the train again too," TJ added.

"That's great! Are you guys hungry? As if I didn't know," I asked.

My question was answered in the affirmative, unanimously, as expected.

"Hildy, if you don't have anything planned for supper, why don't we all go over to the Wendy's and get hamburgers for the boys. We haven't eaten out in a while and it will give you a chance to rest. Afterwards, we can go to the hospital and see Joel," I said before turning to the boys. "You guys run to the bathroom and wash up. Dad has to make a phone call and then we'll go."

"Crane, you haven't forgotten that Joel's birthday is this Saturday, have you?" Hildy asked, after the boys had disappeared.

"I knew it was coming up, but I hardly know what today's date is anymore. I guess I need to take the boys shopping sometime. Maybe we could go to the Galleria after we visit Joel. I think the boys might find some interesting things to see there as well as find something for Joel's birthday. On second thought, I think I'm too tired to go shopping tonight. The rushing around and the flight has taken its toll on me."

The phone call to Collin was disturbing. He outlined a number of alternatives that could be pursued to get Benny back in the US. Each one of them had an element of danger and was of dubious legality. He said he needed more time to assess the situation in Mexico before he could recommend a plan that would have the best chance of success and the least amount of danger to Benny and the people involved in the operation. He rang off saying he would get back to me when he had put together the best plan.

The boys thought Wendy's was a great idea. With Hildy's great home cooked meals they didn't get to eat out all that often so they always thought it was a treat to do so. We piled into the van and took off for our fast food feast.

After a mountain of cheeseburgers, French fries and those frozen chocolate concoctions called "Frostys", the boys seemed to be full. At least they slowed down.

"Dad, can we take Joel a Frosty?" TJ asked.

"I think that is a good idea. Shall we get him a small one or a big one?"

"A big one! If he don't eat it all, I can help."

"I bet you could," I laughed.

The hospital wasn't that far away so the Frosty didn't melt too much before we arrived at Joel's room. He appeared to be sleeping when we arrived, but that didn't last too long when TJ climbed into the bed with him and gave him a kiss on the cheek.

"Hi, TJ," Joel said sleepily. "Hi guys, hi Hildy, Becky Sue."

"Careful, TJ, Joel still has that tube going into his arm," I said. "How are you feeling son?"

"Okay, but that stuff makes me dizzy," he said pointing to the IV.

"Well, you just rest," I said, leaning over TJ to give Joel a kiss. "TJ thought it would be a good idea to bring you a Frosty. He said if you couldn't eat it all he would help you."

"That'll feel good. My throat is still a little sore. I'll save some for you, TJ."

"TJ, you hold it for your brother so he can eat it. Don't spill it."

All this time Larry, Lenny and Chris had been crowded around the bed trying to get as close to their brother as they could. Even Hildy and Becky Sue had approached the bed.

I left the boys to enjoy each other and went to say hello to Tony and Karen. "I want to thank you for standing by for Joel today while I was away, Karen. It looks like he is taking the treatment very well."

"No problem, Crane. I was going to be here anyway and I thought I knew what to expect. He did fine," she said.

"Well, I appreciate it, none the less. And Tony, how are you feeling today?"

"Okay, I guess. I still have to wear this mask and my hair is almost all gone," he said removing his baseball cap.

"I see. Joel is going to start losing his hair pretty soon also, so you won't be alone."

As we were talking, the twins came over and began talking to Tony. "Karen, why don't we step outside? There are some things I want to discuss with you."

I don't think anyone noticed us leave the room. Once outside the door, I began to tell Karen everything I knew about Benny and his current status. I didn't tell her we were talking about a rescue of him only that we were pursuing all avenues to see he was returned to the States. By the time I finished telling her what I knew, her eyes were filled with tears.

"How could that woman, Mrs. Venisti, let that happen to that boy? Why wouldn't she let us have Benny too? She's cold and unfeeling just like that blankety-blank, power-hungry husband of hers," she sobbed.

That was as close to profanity as I had heard from Karen's mouth. "I'm afraid I don't know Mr. Venisti except by what I have heard. I do understand he is not one to be messed with. They say, in not too flattering terms, that he is a holdover from Houston's corrupt political past of the sixties and seventies when city and county governments and their bureaucracies were for sale to the highest bidder. Where the easiest path to becoming a millionaire was to become the County Judge."

"How did people like that get a foster child, anyway?" Karen asked.

I didn't have an answer. All I could do was shake my head.

After Karen dried her eyes we went back into the room. TJ was helping Joel finish the last of his Frosty while the other boys looked on in envy. I took one look at TJ and headed for the bathroom to get a washcloth to erase the chocolate beard and moustache he was now wearing. When Hildy saw me coming out of the bathroom with it, she held out her hand and I gave it to her.

"That tickles," TJ giggled, as she washed his face and hands with the wet cloth and then started on Joel.

Dr. Barrow came in as Hildy was finishing cleaning up the two. "It looks like I'm too late," he said, looking at the empty Frosty container.

"Yeah, TJ ate it all," Joel said, laughing.

"Well, TJ, if you'll just slide over a little so I can examine your brother I'll get out of your way in a hurry," Dr. Barrow said, adjusting his stethoscope.

He took Joel's temperature, checked his pulse, listened to his lungs and heart and felt the major lymph nodes before announcing, "Everything looks pretty good. I'm going to remove the IV for the night, but you'll have another one tomorrow morning and then you'll have a couple of days before we start another round of treatment."

I walked Dr. Barrow out, after he had examined Tony. When we were outside the door I told him Joel's birthday was Saturday and we wanted to do something for him. I wanted to know if his treatment schedule would interfere with anything we might plan.

After consulting his chart, he said Joel had no treatment scheduled for that day. He did advise that we not plan anything too tiring and to consider foods or treats that would not be irritating to his stomach. Other than that, he didn't see any reason why we couldn't have a small party.

I went back in and rounded up the boys telling them we had to go and to say their goodbyes. This turned into quite a production with the four boys all crowding around Joel to give him a hug and kiss followed by Hildy and Becky Sue and then me all taking our turns. Then the process was repeated with Tony and Karen receiving hugs from the boys.

On the way home, I explained to them we would like to have a small birthday party for Joel on Saturday and would like them to think about what they would like to do, realizing that Joel had to stay in the hospital.

"Can we have a cake? He likes chocolate," Lenny said, and then with a giggle, "Me too."

"Of course we can have a cake," Hildy said. "I'll bake a big one so we can all have big pieces."

"And some ice cream and candles on the cake like you did, dad?" Chris asked.

"Yeah, he'll have thirteen candles on his cake," I answered.

As we drove into the apartment complex, TJ asked, "Can we have a snack now?"

"TJ! You just finished helping Joel finish his Frosty. You can't be hungry already," I exclaimed.

"Crane, that has been almost an hour you know," Hildy chuckled. "All right boys, how about some fruit? I think you have had enough junk food for one night. I have bananas and some white grapes."

That seemed to satisfy them. I guess they realized fruit was their only option tonight. When Hildy spoke there was no use arguing for something else.

While the boys snacked I went into my bedroom and changed into a pair of shorts and a tee shirt. TJ was trying to demolish a large bunch of grapes when I returned to the kitchen.

"Dad, you want some grapes?" he asked.

"No thank you, son. Dad's eaten more calories today than he should have."

"What's a cowory?"

"Cal-o-ree. That is something that can make me fat if I eat too much or the wrong kind of food."

"Will it make me fat, too?"

"It could if you didn't get a lot of exercise like your swimming. By the way, how are you doing with your swimming lessons?"

"I can swim all the way 'cross the pool and Becky Sue taught me how to float," TJ said proudly.

"That's great!" I said, patting him on the shoulder.

"We can swim across the long way of the pool four times. Can't we, Lenny?" Larry volunteered.

"Wow! You two are doing great too. Chris, I know you could swim well before. Have you learned anything new?"

"Yeah, she's teaching me to do the backstroke. I like that, but it's hard to keep straight. Also the butterfly, but that's hard. It makes me really tired," Chris answered.

"I'm impressed with all of you. If I don't watch out you'll be swimming better than I do in no time.

"Now I think it is time to get a shower, brush your teeth and get ready for bed. Tomorrow we are going to go shopping for birthday presents for Joel. I know you'll like where we're going."

The boys went off to take their showers, and I went into the living room to read the morning paper. I hadn't had a chance to read it earlier. I had just settled onto the couch when the phone rang. I didn't know who it could be calling at this time of the day.

"Hello," I said as I picked up the phone.

"Mr. Johnson? This is Collin Cupp. Sorry to disturb you this late but I thought you would be interested in some news I just learned about Benny Clausen."

"No problem, Mr. Cupp. What have you learned?"

"I talked to a friend in the Juvenile Division in the HPD, Lt. Casey Bowser, and told him we had located the Bensons and Benny Clausen. He was most interested when I told him they had taken a foster child out of the state without CPS's knowledge or permission. It seems that is a no-no, but when I told him they had taken him out of the country, he was really interested. That is against the law. To make a long story short he has gotten a warrant issued for their arrest if they ever come back across the border."

"What good does that do for us in getting Benny back into Texas?"

"It means the foster care placement of Benny has been automatically revoked. It also means if we're able to rescue him we're not liable for interfering with the custody of a minor. That's one obstacle out of the way. The next one is to get CPS to agree to allow Benny to be placed in a foster home we approve of instead of being placed in the 'loving' hands of CPS."

"How can we manage that?"

"I have received some preliminary information on how and why the Bensons were able to get Benny placed with them. Now I must stress that this information is only preliminary and needs to be verified, but it seems there was some money that changed hands. It looks like a $5000 contribution was made to Richard Venisti's campaign fund and the Benson's were granted an unrestricted foster parent license two days later. We cannot show a direct *quid pro quo* but it looks mighty suspicious when the caseworker who made it all possible was his wife.

"I think that gives us some 'political' leverage with CPS in case you ever wanted to go public with the information."

"Yeah, I think it does. There is only one small problem, a nine year old boy in Mexico. How are we going to get him out?"

"We are working on that. It will happen soon. That's all I can say right now. Oh, by the way that Lt. Bowser I talked to said a friend of his in the San Antonio Police Department had also asked about Benny."

"That's my friend, Jack Hogan," I said, and then explained how that had come about. Before I had finished talking, I had a fresh-smelling six year old snuggled up on my lap. "Thanks Collin, I have to run. I need to tuck my sons into bed. Call me if you get any more information."

I got the boys all settled in bed before I went back to the living room to finish reading the paper. It wasn't long before I started getting drowsy and decided to go to bed as well.

I don't know how long I had been asleep, but I knew it wasn't time to get up when I heard a little voice say, "Dad! Dad, wake up!"

I sat bolt upright in bed, hoping it was a dream. It wasn't. I could see in the moonlight streaming through the bedroom window. It was one of the twins standing beside my bed.

"What's the matter, son? Are you sick?" I asked, as the cobwebs started clearing from my brain.

"No, Lenny had a bad dream and is crying. Can you come?" Larry said, as he grabbed my hand and started pulling on it.

"Sure," I said, throwing off the covers and following Larry to their bedroom.

Lenny was on the bed curled up in a ball sobbing like his heart was broken.

I sat down on the bed and drew him to me, pulling him gently until he was on my lap. I began stroking his back and kissed the top of his head. "It's all right now. Dad's here. Nothing is going to hurt you now. It's okay."

We sat that way for maybe ten minutes before he stopped sobbing and only sniffled once in a while. Larry had been sitting there the whole while watching his brother with obvious concern on his face.

"Lenny, can you tell dad what frightened you. Your brother said you had a bad dream. Is that right?"

I felt his head nod against my bare chest. He turned more toward me and then wrapped his arms around my chest. Then in a voice that was barely audible he started to describe his dream.

"I went in this room and Joel was sleeping in a box like momma was in … I tried to wake him up. I shook him and shook him but he wouldn't wake up …"

He started sobbing again. A minute or so later he spoke again, "Then a man came and shut the box and pushed it out the door, and he wouldn't let me go with them. He told me Joel couldn't play with me no more."

"It was just a bad dream. Joel will be out of the hospital in a few weeks and he will be able to play with you again. Why don't you guys come sleep in my bed the rest of the night? Okay?"

Getting agreement from both of them, I picked up Lenny and carried him into my room and placed him on the bed. Larry followed us and climbed in beside his brother and put his arms around him. I went around to the other side of the bed, got in and pulled up the covers after giving them both another kiss on the head.

With all these boys have been through it's a wonder they haven't had more nightmares. The only other one I can remember is the one TJ had after he fell in the lake. That still is not much consolation when one of your kids is hurting.

It didn't take long for the twins to fall asleep but it eluded me for about an hour or so. When I woke up I felt Lenny's warm body snuggled up against me sleeping peacefully as if nothing had happened. I hated leaving the comfort of the bed, but I knew we had a lot to do today.

I was sitting at the kitchen table reading the paper and drinking my last cup of coffee when Larry and Lenny walked sleepily into the kitchen. I didn't know whether to bring up last night's incident or to let it pass. I gave each of them a hug. When it was Lenny's turn I ventured, "How are you feeling this morning?"

He gave me a quizzical look and just said, "Okay."

Well I guess that just goes to show the resiliency of youth. It wasn't long before Chris and TJ showed up and received their morning hugs as well. TJ crawled up on my lap and with his back against my chest, raised his arms above his head and wrapped them around the back of my neck. I reached around him and started tickling his stomach which sent him into a fit of giggles.

"Don't, dad. That tickles," he said, between giggles.

"I love you, little one," I responded, kissing him on the top of the head.

Seeing my half-empty coffee cup on the table he picked it up and took a sip. "Yuck! That tastes bad."

"Good, you're too young to drink coffee," I said, giving him another squeeze.

Shortly I headed off for the hospital to check on Joel. On the way I decided to stop off at a convenience store to pick up some nutrition bars for Joel to snack on. Although he never really complained, he did frequently mention the meal portions were 'kinda small'. I picked up a dozen and continued on to the hospital.

Dr. Kerner and his nurse were leaving Joel's room as I approached. "Good morning, doctor," I said.

"Ah, Mr. Johnson, we have just now started your son's IV. As the one did yesterday, this one will probably cause him to be a little dizzy. I wouldn't recommend he get out of bed without help and only then if it's absolutely necessary. He'll probably sleep most of the day. He's doing fine. I have every reason to believe he will go into full remission, but only time will tell."

"Thanks, doctor," I said, and went in the room.

"Hi, dad," Joel said, as I walked in.

I walked over to him and gave him a tight squeeze and a kiss. "I brought you something to snack on if you get hungry. I got some for Tony too. If you like them, I'll get some more. There are chocolate and coconut and granola and fruit."

"Can I have one now? They had grits again ..."

"Sure, take your pick. Tony would you like one also?"

"Yes, thank you, Mr. Johnson," Tony said grinning. "I don't like grits either."

"That's very kind of you, Crane," Karen said.

I sat down beside Joel's bed and we talked for a while until I noticed he was about to fall asleep. When I was certain he was asleep I decided to slip out and make a couple of phone calls. Digging out my address book, I found Cindi's number and called her hoping that she would be in the office. Luck was with me when she answered the phone.

"Cindi Sessions, how may I help you?"

"Cindi, my name is Crane Johnson. I think you know a friend of mine, Darcie Levin."

"Yes, Mr. Johnson, Darcie told me about you when we talked last weekend. It's about that boy Benny Clausen, isn't it?"

"You're right ... I'm going to ask you if something is possible and I don't know just how to go about it. I guess just straight out. Can you get Benny Clausen's case transferred to your care?"

"I might be able to, I really don't know. Why?"

"If necessary, I can give you any ammunition you need to make it happen, but I would rather do it nicely."

"Isn't this all a little moot? We don't even know where Benny is at the moment."

"That's not entirely true. That's all I want to say about it right now. The less you know, the less likely you are to get burned if anything goes wrong. Let me just say I have information that Benny has been abused by his current foster family."

"Look, I'll do what I can. I know the director's in his office. I'll try to get in to see him. He's the only one who can authorize switching a case to a different caseworker. Let me call you back after I've seen him."

"Thanks, Cindi, I appreciate what you're doing."

I then called the office to see how things were going and to see if there was anything that needed my attention. Carol and Foster both said everything was under control, and they would call me if there was anything I needed to take care of.

Joel was still asleep when I re-entered the room. I chatted with Karen and Tony until Dr. Kerner returned with another round of chemotherapy for Tony. It wasn't long before Rodney came in carrying the boys' lunch trays. I shook Joel gently to wake him up. The last thing he needed was to miss a meal.

Even though he was sleepy, the smell of food soon got his attention. The meal looked surprisingly good. This time the tray contained slices of roast beef, mashed potatoes with gravy, corn and a bread roll with butter. There was a carton of milk that Joel asked me to open for him since one arm was out of commission, due to the IV. For dessert he had sliced peaches and a small cup of ice cream. Although he only had the use of one hand, the meal disappeared rather quickly.

After he finished, he asked, "Can you take me to the bathroom? I don't like using that bedpan."

"Sure. Can you walk or do you want me to put you in the wheelchair?"

"I can walk if you hold me."

I lowered the rails on the side of the bed where the IV stand was and helped him to stand up. I wrapped my left arm around his waist and pushed the IV stand ahead of us with the other. Joel wrapped his right arm around my waist and off we went. It wasn't but a few steps to the bathroom but it was a major undertaking. After getting him situated, I left to give him some privacy.

Shortly, I heard him call out for me, and we started the process over again except in reverse. It wasn't long after I got him back in bed that he was asleep. I kissed him lightly on the forehead before leaving for the apartment.

Our trip to the Galleria was an experience. The boys were in awe. The place is huge with multiple levels and almost everything imaginable for sale. One of the first stops we made was to the sports memorabilia shop.

"Hey, guys, I said I would buy you an Astro baseball hat but I forgot you already have one. So, what would you like instead? A Spurs cap? Or maybe a Rockets cap or an Oilers? Look around, they have all kinds to choose from."

After much discussion and trying on of hats, the decision was finally made. They wanted the San Antonio Spurs hat. I also bought one for JR and a Houston Rockets cap for Tony and Bran.

With all the stores, it was difficult to decide which ones to go to in order to find birthday presents for Joel. But after about an hour each of the boys had selected the present they wanted to give him. I hadn't found one but I still had a couple of days to decide what to give.

"Let's go get a snack and then I want to show you something," I told them. I don't think they heard anything except snack. We quickly made our way to the food court. Again there was a dizzying array of things to choose from, making their decisions difficult.

I decided they had made enough decisions for the day so I had them sit with Hildy while Becky Sue and I went to different counters to make our purchases. She bought seven of these really large chocolate chip cookies and I got the same number of cups of frozen yogurt. Our choices of snacks seemed to satisfy the troops. At least we didn't hear any complaints as the snacks disappeared.

When they were finished and Hildy had made sure all their faces were clean, I led them to the lower level of the mall. In front of us was an ice skating rink with only a few skaters using it.

"Doesn't that look like fun?" I asked them.

"Yeah," came the responses and several heads nodded as they stared at the skaters.

"Do you want to try it?"

Again, I saw all heads nod in unison.

"Okay, follow me, and we'll rent some skates. Hildy, Becky Sue, do you want to try it too?"

"Crane, I haven't been on ice skates for twenty years. My husband and I used to go to the old rink out on Broadway in San Antonio. The place burned down shortly after my husband died," she answered. "I could probably still stand up on them."

"I think I'll just watch. I was never very good on roller skates even," Becky Sue said, suppressing a giggle.

"All right, you can watch our packages while we make fools of ourselves," I said, handing her the packages I had been carrying.

I had learned to ice skate while attending prep school in the Northeast, but, like Hildy, I hadn't been on them in close to ten years. We strapped on our rented skates and then I had the boys try to stand up on them before we tried it on the ice. TJ was doing pretty good. His ankles were a little wobbly but not bad. The twins were doing okay, but I could foresee them polishing the ice a lot. Chris was having the most problems. While I was working with the boys, Hildy went out and circled the ice.

"Look, dad, look at Hildy. She's really skating," Chris said in amazement.

We all stood there with our mouths open, not believing the sight we were witnessing. Hildy was skating like a pro. She skated forward and backward, made circles and figure eights before skating over to us and spraying ice crystals on us as she stopped.

"Yeah, you can stand up on them all right," I said, in admiration.

For the next hour Hildy and I worked with the boys showing them some of the basics of skating. One of the most important lessons was how to get up when you fell down. TJ was able to skate by himself a little bit. He didn't break any speed records, but he also didn't break any bones. Larry and Lenny did all right as long as they were hanging on to the side of the rink and sometimes when they held on to each other. Most of the time they sat on the ice, giggling and trying to get up.

Chris was another matter. The only way he could stand up on the ice was if Hildy or I were holding him. He still had fun. At least he was giggling most of the time.

At the end of the hour they were all pretty much worn out and didn't complain when I told them it was time to go back to the apartment.

"Can we go see Joel tonight?" TJ asked, as we entered the apartment.

"Right after supper," I said. "Go wash your hands and faces and get ready for supper."

I sat down in the lounge chair to rest my weary backside which had kissed the ice more times than I wanted to think about or admit. I had just gotten comfortable when the phone rang. I struggled out of the chair and answered it.

It was Cindi Sessions. "Cindi, it's good of you to call back. I hope you have good news for me or rather for Benny."

"Yes, I do. I think the director was looking for a way to relieve Betty Venisti of the case and when I volunteered he jumped at the chance. I still don't see what good it is for me to be Benny's caseworker."

"Cindi, can you make a placement of Benny to another family even though you don't know where he is?"

"I don't know. I guess I can. I never had anyone ask me that before. The family would have to be licensed or I couldn't do it though."

"Thanks, I know this all sounds a little strange to you but believe me it is all on the up and up. I will call you as soon as I have Benny's new foster family lined up. I appreciate you going out on a limb like this for a stranger you've never met."

"Well, Darcie warned me you were a crazy bachelor who had a heart of gold and five adopted sons. That's good enough for me. I'll be waiting for your call."

Before she hung up the phone, she gave me her cell phone and home numbers just in case.

I made a quick call to the Levins to see if they would be willing to take another placement of a foster child. When I explained Benny's circumstances they immediately agreed to take him if it was possible to get him back into the country.

After a marvelous meal of broiled red snapper, we went to visit Joel and take him and Tony their caps. The other boys strutted into the room wearing their own caps and made a big deal out of presenting the caps to Joel and Tony. Tony thanked us for getting him the Rockets cap instead of the Spurs one. It seemed that Akeem Olajuwon, the Rockets' center, was his favorite basketball player.

It didn't take long for Joel to show signs of being tired. Even though he had slept most of the day the chemotherapy was really sapping his strength. It took a while for all the goodbyes to be said. The boys were a little reluctant to cut their visit so short even though they could see their brother could hardly keep his eyes open.

TJ crawled up on my lap when we got home. He didn't say anything. He just sat there with his head on my chest. Every once in a while he would let out a big sigh.

"Is there something wrong, son?"

"Um," was the only response I got from him.

After a few minutes, I asked him again.

In a voice barely above a whisper he said, "I wish Joel wasn't sick. I miss him a bunch."

"I know you do. I do too, so do your brothers. Hildy misses him too. Everybody misses him. But it's still going to be a few weeks before we can all go home together again. Now, why don't you go get your shower taken and get ready for bed? I'll be in to tuck you in after while," I said, and kissed the top of his head.

I called Cindi at her home number and told her the Levins were willing to take in Benny. She said she had talked to Chad Dinkens when he placed Bran LeBeau with them so she was not entirely unfamiliar with them. She said she would fill out all the necessary paperwork in the morning that would make the Levins the legal foster parents for Benny.

When I heard the showers shut off, I gave the boys a few minutes and then went to tuck them in. This was a ritual I thoroughly enjoyed each evening. No matter what the day's events were, spending a few minutes with my sons and assuring myself of their safety made all my troubles disappear in the glow of the love I felt for them and the love I received in return.

After seeing to the boys, I decided to read a couple of chapters in a book I had been trying to read over the past week and a half. I settled down in the lounge chair and was just getting completely immersed in the story when the phone rang.

"Who the devil could that be at this time of night?" I muttered to myself.

"Hello," I said.

"He's out. We got him."

"Collin, is that you?"

"Yes," he answered.

"You mean that you have Benny and he's in Texas?"

"That's right. One of my operatives called me less than five minutes ago. They were in Eagle Pass and heading for Houston. Benny is fine. A little scared, but he is doing fine. They should be in Houston by morning. Where do you want us to take him?"

I gave him the Levins' address and said I would contact them to let them know to expect their new foster son in the morning.

After I called the Levins, I decided I had enough excitement for one day and headed off to bed with a smile on my face.

CHAPTER 15

Thursday morning I was awakened by a loud clap of thunder. I jumped out of bed and went to check on the boys to see if they were awakened by it also. Thankfully, they had slept through it somehow. Although it was a little early I decided to take my shower and get ready for the day.

Hildy was in the kitchen when I finished in the bathroom. I could smell the coffee brewing before I even opened the bedroom door.

"Something smells good," I said to her as I walked into the kitchen. "What do you have in the oven?"

"Blueberry muffins," she replied. "The store had some nice looking fresh blueberries when I went shopping the other day. I hadn't made any for awhile so I thought the boys would enjoy them."

"Me too! I love blueberry muffins. I hope you have butter to put on them."

"Of course! You can't eat blueberry muffins without real butter."

The muffins were not quite finished baking when Chris and TJ appeared, closely followed by Larry and Lenny, all still in their pajamas.

"Did you boys wash your hands?" Hildy asked. That got an immediate response from them as they turned and rushed back to the bathrooms.

The suitably cleansed boys arrived back in the kitchen as the muffins were being removed from the oven. After hugs were received and given all around, they settled themselves into their chairs at the table. Hildy began dishing up the scrambled eggs, bacon and hash browns for each of the boys. A large basket of muffins was placed in the center of the table.

"Those smell yummy," TJ said, grinning at Hildy.

"Yeah," chimed in the other three.

I managed to get one of the muffins and spread a generous portion of butter on both halves of it. "Hildy, these are terrific. I have never tasted better."

After finishing my muffin and coffee I looked out the window and saw the rain still pouring down. It looked like one of those Houston days where it would rain all day without letup. I just hoped the streets didn't flood. I had been in Houston some years back when there was a heavy rain and some of the streets around the Medical Center had flooded. I didn't want anything to prevent me from getting to see my son.

At around nine o'clock I decided to call the Levins to see if Benny had arrived. The phone rang several times before it was answered.

"Good morning, this is Crane Johnson. I was wondering if Benny had arrived yet."

"Oh, Crane, I'm glad you called. Benny arrived about two hours ago. The poor kid is scared to death. The Bensons had literally starved the boy as part of their scam to get money from people to pay for bogus medical treatment for him. They told people he had cancer and needed an operation to save his life. His head's been shaved. It just breaks your heart the way he has been treated," Alan Levin said.

"Is he all right? Does he need medical care?"

"I've called a doctor friend who said he would take a look at Benny at ten o'clock. Ethel is feeding him some oatmeal right now. He looks like he's afraid to eat, like he thinks he'll be punished if he does eat it."

"Let me know if he needs specialized help. I have a vested interest in him and want him to be well taken care of," I told him.

"I think he'll be all right physically. He just needs to put on the weight he's lost. What's been done to him psychologically may take longer to heal. Getting to see his brother again will probably go a long way in helping him to recover. I think that can wait a day or two until he is comfortable in his new surroundings and begins eating normally."

"Alan, I want to thank you and your wife for taking in Benny and, for that matter, Bran. It's good to know there are still people who care what happens to kids in trouble."

"Crane, no thanks are necessary. Ethel and I have become very attached to Bran in the short time he's been here. I guess we didn't realize how much we missed having kids in the house until he came to us. And having our grandson here for a week also has been a great help. JR and Bran have really hit it off. I know he is going to miss JR when he goes back to Canyon Lake."

"Let me know what the doctor says about Benny. I would like to reunite him with Tony as soon as he says it's okay."

"I will. That Cindi Sessions is supposed to be here shortly to check on Benny. I hope she gets here before we have to leave for the doctor's office. I'll call you after we get back from there."

"Thanks, goodbye," I said, hanging up the phone.

Grabbing my umbrella, I bade the boys goodbye and headed out the door. I had decided what I was going to give Joel for his birthday, so on my way to the hospital I stopped off at the shop and told them exactly what I wanted. They said they would have it ready for me around one o'clock and I could pick it up then.

When I entered Joel's room a nurse was trying to convince him she was going to give him a sponge bath and he was not having any part of it. It was all I could do to suppress a chuckle.

"Nurse, I'm Joel's dad. If it is all right with you I'll see he gets bathed. Now, if you will provide something to cover his IV, I'll see to everything else."

"Thanks, dad," Joel said as the nurse left the room. "It's kinda embarrassing."

"I know, son. Are you going to sit in the tub or are you going to try to stand for a shower?"

"I think I'll have to sit down. I'm still a little dizzy and feel kinda weak."

"I'll start running your bath then," I said, heading to the bathroom.

The nurse returned with the plastic wrap for Joel's arm and I assisted him into the bathroom and the tub. "Give me a shout when you finish and I'll help you get out of the tub."

While Joel was enjoying his bath, I spent the time talking to Tony and Karen. I was very happy for him when Karen told me Dr. Kerner had said the results of Tony's latest blood tests show an excellent response to the chemotherapy. Although he was not completely out of the woods yet, Dr. Kerner said he was better than 90% certain a complete remission was possible. He would still have to undergo long term treatment, but if everything continued as it were he would be able to go home in a couple of weeks.

"I'm done, dad," Joel said from the bathroom.

I grabbed the towel as I entered and wrapped it around him then helped him out of the tub.

"My hair is coming out," Joel said with a frown.

I looked closely at his scalp and sure enough there were spots where the hair was definitely thinning. "Well, we knew it was going to happen. It just means the chemotherapy is working. I know you might feel embarrassed about it but whether you have hair or are bald, your brothers and Hildy and I all love you just the same."

I steadied him as he slipped on the clean pair of pajamas Hildy had sent for him.

"Dad, can I call John?"

"Of course you may. Do you remember all the numbers you have to dial?"

"Yeah, I wrote them down on my tablet."

I handed Joel the telephone after I helped him back into his bed.

"Karen, may I buy you a cup of coffee? I have something I would like to discuss with you."

She looked at me quizzically but got out of her chair and followed me out the door. "What is it, Crane?"

"Let's wait until we get to the cafeteria," I said.

I went through the serving line while Karen sat at a table waiting for me to bring the coffee. I set the cups on the table before I began. "Karen, I have some news about Benny …"

"What is it? Tell me, please!" she interrupted.

"He's okay. He is in Houston. I'm not sure how it happened exactly, but he was rescued and, I assume, smuggled across the Mexican border and brought to Houston. He's been placed with a foster home. He's being well taken care of."

"Oh, thank God!" she exclaimed and buried her face in her hands. "I can't wait to tell Tony. He has been so worried about his brother."

"That's up to you but it might be a few days before he would be able to see him. The Bensons, who were his former foster parents, starved and abused him. He should be at the doctor's office right now to see if he has any serious problems. His new foster parents are the parents of a couple good friends of mine. I know they will take good care of him. It might cause Tony more agitation knowing Benny is in town and not being able to see him than if you waited to tell him."

"Crane, you're right, of course. When do you think he might be able to see him?"

"That all depends on what the doctor's report is. If he finds nothing seriously wrong with him it shouldn't be but a day or two. From what I have been told he needs to get some nourishment and some loving. He'll get both of those things from the Levins. He'll also have a couple of young boys to play with. Their eight-year-old grandson is with them this week and they also have a teenage foster son."

Karen dried her eyes as we headed back to the boys' room. "Please let me know anything you find out about Benny. I want to tell Bill everything I can when I talk to him tonight. I know he feels the same way I do about that boy."

"By the way, we plan to have a little birthday party for Joel this Saturday. I have a small conference room spoken for where we can all get together. Please don't think you have to buy a gift for him. He will get more than enough presents from his brothers and the rest of his friends. We want you all there because Tony has been a good role model for Joel in the way he has accepted his treatment. It's made Joel feel more secure despite the horrendous things both the boys have had to go through. I know Joel feels very close to Tony. All my boys are fond of Tony."

Joel was still on the phone to John when we entered the boys' room. When he saw us, he started to wind up his conversation. "I hope I can come home in about two or three weeks, and then you can come over to our house. I miss you. I wish I could play on the soccer team with you. Maybe next year I can. Bye," Joel said, and hung up the phone.

I saw that he was upset so I sat down on the side of his bed, gathered him in my arms and hugged him. "I know being sick is a real bummer. I wish this never happened to you, but it did. We don't like it, but we have to deal with it the best way we can. I know you miss John. He is a good friend to you. Maybe he can come see you one of these days." I continued to hold him for several minutes.

"Thanks, dad," Joel said. "Sometimes it gets to me. I wonder, 'Why me?'. I know there's no answer. It just seems so unfair."

"I know, son. I know."

I stayed and talked with Joel until his lunch was brought in by Rodney. Rodney was his usual jovial self. His light-hearted attitude was infectious and soon both boys were smiling and giggling at his antics.

I opened the carton of milk for Joel and made sure he would be able to eat all of his lunch before I left to pick up his birthday present. I told Joel I would be back with his brothers this evening. I felt I should spend some time with his brothers this afternoon. I also wanted to find out about Benny from Alan. Thankfully, the rain had stopped before I left the hospital.

The news about Benny was mostly good. His main problem was malnutrition. He had suffered some bruising and a few scrapes but overall he was in pretty good condition physically. His mental condition on the other hand was less positive. He was very nervous and was fearful of nearly everyone. The only one whom he seemed to be able to trust was Mrs. Levin. He clung to her like he expected her to desert him. Ethel was the perfect grandmother type. She was a woman who could best be described as a little on the plump side. All Benny seemed to want to do was to sit on her ample lap and be hugged which she did with relish. Alan related all of this when I talked to him on the phone.

I made another call to Collin Cupp to find out just how they had managed to get Benny out of Mexico so quickly. After we exchanged pleasantries he began to relate how it all happened.

"As you know we'd traced the Bensons to Piedras Negras, Mexico, because of another investigation we had ongoing. Two of my investigators were observing their activities. We decided the best way to carry out the rescue was the direct approach. The investigators simply contacted the Bensons and laid out the information we had gathered and then came the big lie. They told them the Mexican state of Coahuila de Zaragoza had issued an order for their arrest and the investigators would assist them in making an escape on the condition they, the Bensons, provide a complete statement detailing their arrangement with Venisti and his wife and also hand over the boy to the investigators. They readily agreed. I guess the thoughts of a Mexican prison were not pleasant ones.

"Anyway, we were able to get a video-taped confession of their deal to exchange a $5000 'contribution' to Venisti's campaign for them getting a foster child so they could run their scam. Whether the Venistis were aware of their plans for the boy is an open question. They also admitted their abuse of Benny."

"Where are the Bensons now?" I asked.

"They are still under observation by my investigators. They have moved to Ciudad Juarez, Mexico. That's not too far from El Paso," Collin replied.

"Okay, how did you get Benny out of Mexico?" I asked.

"That took a lot of coordination. We had contracted a small plane in the border town of Eagle Pass from a gentleman whose reputation and occupation were, to say the least, suspect. He agreed to fly into Mexico and pick up a passenger. On the Mexican side of the border it required we make certain payments to the police and to the operator of a small landing strip where our plane was to land. One of our female investigators accompanied the pilot on his low level flight across the border to pick up Benny. Everything went smoothly until the plane was on its return to Eagle Pass. Just as they were crossing the Rio Grande they sighted a border patrol spotter plane. Janie, our investigator in the plane, said she thought she was going to 'lose her lunch' several times as the pilot took evasive actions to lose the spotter plane. The plane she was in was running without lights and it was nearly dark out. The pilot darted in and out of clouds, dove nearly straight down, circled back and took sharp turns that Janie said she was sure would tear the wings off the plane. But in the long run they did manage to evade the border patrol and land at a remote strip where we had a car waiting. The pilot of the plane had surely done this all before since it didn't seem to faze him one bit."

"I can see why Benny may be a little frightened from his experience," I chuckled. "Collin, I want to thank you for your agency's excellent work in the quick recovery of Benny. Send your bill to my accountant and send me a copy of the video tape. I have plans for it."

After talking to Collin, I called the office and talked to Foster to see how things were going. I was both relieved and disappointed that my presence was not necessary. I was winding up my conversation with Foster when Eric came on the line. He told me he would be driving down to Houston on Saturday morning to pick up JR. I told him about the birthday party we were going to have for Joel on Saturday afternoon and asked him if he would do me a favor. He agreed, so I told him what I wanted him to do.

I made a couple more telephone calls to firm up the preparations for the party and then went to see what the boys wanted to do this afternoon. I found them at the kitchen table where Chris and Becky Sue were trying to teach the others the game of 'Old Maid'. From appearances Larry and Lenny were learning quickly. However, TJ was another matter. He was more interested in making patterns with his cards on the table.

I don't know where they got the deck of cards. Becky Sue must have brought them because I didn't think we had any in the house.

"Hi, guys, are you having fun?"

"Yeah, dad, but TJ won't play right," Chris complained.

"Well, he might be a little young to play 'Old Maid'. Maybe we can find some other card game he could learn. What would you guys like to do this afternoon?"

"Can we go to a ball game?" Lenny asked.

"Yeah!" both Chris and Larry said enthusiastically.

"Me too!" TJ piped in.

"Let me check the paper to see whether the Astros are playing in town today." I picked up the paper and scanned the sports section for the schedule.

"The ballgame starts at 7:05 tonight. If you want to go we should probably go see Joel this afternoon. Does that sound all right?"

"C'mon," TJ said. "Let's go."

"Whoa there. Go get washed up and I'll see if I can get some tickets to the game." I checked with Becky Sue and Hildy but neither one of then was too enthusiastic about going so it was going to be me and the four boys. I started to call the ticket office and reserve tickets for the five of us when I had a bright idea. I called the Levins and talked to Alan to see if he, JR and Bran would like to go to the game. I didn't think Benny would be ready to go yet but I made the offer to Alan just the same. He said Benny was still recovering but the rest of them would like to go. I told him to meet us at the 'Will Call' window at 6:45.

Then I made the call to the ticket office and reserved a box down the right side in back of first base. I was lucky to get such good seats. The box would actually handle ten people so I reserved all ten.

I had four boys waiting impatiently for me when I finished my call.

Joel was surprised when we showed up since I had told him I was spending the afternoon with his brothers. He understood when I explained it to him but was not happy he couldn't go to the game as well. It tore my heart up that he couldn't go, but I knew the rest of the family couldn't just stop living because Joel was sick. My mind knew that, but my heart didn't like it.

Our visit included, as it always did, a trip to the cafeteria for a frozen yogurt sundae. Tony was also included in the excursion. The six boys never seemed to stop talking.

"Tony always seems so much better after your boys visit. He is in so much better spirits after they leave. I know it does as much good for him as it does for Joel," Karen said, dabbing at the corner of her eyes with her handkerchief.

"I must say they are amazing boys," I said. "I am truly blessed that they came into my life."

It wasn't long before both Tony and Joel started showing signs of fatigue. Karen and I noticed it at about the same time and suggested we return to the room. Although the boys grumbled a little, I think they could see our patients were getting tired so they didn't put up too much of a fuss.

I told Hildy when we got back to the apartment that since I was taking the boys to the ballgame this evening we would eat junk food at the ballpark. She said she would put out the antacid.

A little after six, I loaded the boys into the van and headed to the Astrodome to meet up with Alan and his crew and to pick up the tickets from the 'Will Call' window. As it happened they were waiting for us at the window when we got there. As soon as my bunch saw JR and Bran they ran up to them and surrounded them with hugs. I hadn't told them we were going to have company at the game.

As Alan and I herded the boys toward the entrance, he recognized a young Hispanic man with his son who appeared to be about seven or eight years old. "Hey, Fernando, how are you doing?"

"Mr. Levin, it's good to see you," Fernando replied.

"Crane, this is Fernando Cruz. He repaired our roof when a limb fell on it in a storm earlier this year. He did a quality job.

"Fernando, this is Crane Johnson and four of these 'rug rats' are his sons," Alan said, sweeping his hand to indicate the boys. "The other two are my grandson and my foster son."

We exchanged small talk as we walked toward the gate. Fernando's son clung tightly to his father's hand with one of his hands and in the other clutched a baseball glove to his chest.

"Are you going to catch a ball tonight?" I asked him.

He just looked down at his shoes so his father answered for him, "It's not likely. We are way back up in the 'cheap seats'. It would have to be a powerful foul ball to reach us."

"Well look, I have two extra tickets for our box. Why don't you sit with us? It's right behind the dugout down the first base line," I said. When he started to decline, I interrupted, "If you don't use them they'll go to waste. Besides I'm sure these six 'rug rats', as Alan called them, would love to have your son join them. What's your son's name?"

"Mr. Johnson, thank you so much for your hospitality. My son's name is Antonio. He's a little shy around strangers."

"He won't be around strangers long if I know these guys," I said, as I handed the tickets to a young female ticket-taker at the gate.

By the time we found our seats after seemingly walking a mile inside the dome, Antonio was beginning to come out of his shell and was interacting with the rest of the boys. I found out he had just turned seven which made him only a couple of months older than TJ. He grabbed hold of Antonio's hand and introduced him to his brothers and friends as only a six year old could do.

"This is Chris and this is Larry and this is Lenny and this is JR and this is Bran and I'm TJ." All of the boys said, "Hi" as they were introduced. "What's your name?"

"Antonio," he said shyly.

"C'mon, you can sit by me," TJ said, taking one of the seats in the front row of our box.

The box's ten seats were arranged in two rows of five. After a little shuffling we ended up with Larry, Lenny, TJ, Antonio and Fernando in the front row and the rest of us in the second row. The adults were seated by the opening to the box so none of the kids could slip out without us knowing about it. JR sat between Bran and Chris.

Shortly after we were seated a handsome young man approached us to take our food order. I took a look at the menu before telling the boys what they had available. I should have known they would want hot dogs, chips and cokes, at least to start out with. Alan and I decided on the bratwursts with sauerkraut and hot mustard. When it was time for our guests to order Fernando politely refused saying he would go to the food court and get something for Antonio and him. I could tell he was uncomfortable with the prices of the items on the menu. They were high almost to the point of extortion but for the convenience of not having to fight through the crowds and waiting in line, to me they were worth it.

"Fernando, I do not wish to embarrass or insult you, but tonight you and your son are my guests. Please order whatever you and Antonio would like."

"Can I have a hot dog too, dad?" Antonio asked.

Seeing the pleading look in his son's eyes, he relented. "Yes, you can, son. Thank you, Mr. Johnson, sometimes it's hard to give my son all the things I would like to being a single parent."

The game started a few minutes after our order was taken but before it was served. The Cubs came up to bat and were put down in order. The Astros were more successful in their half of the inning when the first two batters got a hit and a walk. Jeff Bagwell batting third hit two foul balls in our general direction but not close enough for Antonio to get to use his glove. On the third pitch he hit a towering home run just inside the foul pole down the right field line. It was a good thing our food hadn't arrived by that time or it would probably have gotten spilled when the boys all jumped up and cheered Jeff as he trotted around the bases to be greeted at home plate by the two runners whom he had driven in.

The rest of the game was less memorable than the food that was consumed. At various times after our original order we ate nachos, peanuts, cotton candy and ice cream bars. The nachos were messy. By the time they finished eating them the boys' hands and faces were covered in the cheese sauce. I had asked for the jalapeños on the side because I didn't know whether any of the boys would like them. Chris and Bran were the only ones brave enough to try them with the nachos and they both liked them, much to my surprise.

Taking the boys to the restroom was an experience. The urinals, if you can call them that, were long porcelain troughs with a drain in the middle and a small amount of water trickling down from a horizontal pipe with holes in it. There was room for three or four of the boys to line up to urinate at one time. My crew had never seen anything like it before and could hardly do their business for laughing. TJ and Antonio were not tall enough to use it without Fernando and I holding them up which caused the boys to laugh even harder.

It was nearly ten o'clock when the game ended with the Astros winning 5-2 over the Cubs. Antonio never got to use his glove. There were a couple of foul balls hit into the stands near us, but not close enough to catch. By the end of the game Antonio had really come out of his shell. He was laughing and talking with the other boys like they were old friends. It was good to see the way he and TJ got along. Although the seating arrangement was in a constant state of change, the two of them always seemed to remain seated together.

As we were leaving the Astrodome I heard Fernando say to his son, "I hope the last bus hasn't left yet."

"Where do you live Fernando?" Alan asked.

"We live just off Richmond near Eldridge," he answered.

"That's not that far from our house. Why don't you ride with us? I have the minivan so there is plenty of room."

"Thank you, Mr. Levin, we would like that."

Before we parted, Fernando thanked me profusely for the hospitality he and his son had received. He was truly sincere in his thanks. I knew he could not treat his son to the type of evening they had experienced tonight. It made me even more grateful for the blessings I had.

Hugs and goodbyes were exchanged all around and then we headed off to our van and they went to find Alan's minivan.

It was nearly eleven o'clock by the time we got home after fighting the traffic to get out of the dome parking lot. TJ had fallen asleep and the twins were nearly there. I had to carry him into the apartment. He woke up enough to change into his pajamas but was not coherent enough to brush his teeth. I told the boys they could take their showers in the morning before I tucked them in bed.

My head barely hit the pillow before I was asleep. The next thing I knew there was a tapping on my bedroom door. I glanced at the clock as I struggled out of bed. It was 7:45. I slipped on my dressing gown before opening the door. Hildy was there looking concerned.

"I thought something might be wrong. You never sleep this late," she said.

"It was a late night. The game seemed to go on forever and the boys didn't want to leave. I imagine they will sleep in a bit this morning also. Let me get my shower taken and then I'll get them up."

It was eight-thirty before I was able to get the boys up. I think they could have slept more but Hildy had breakfast ready and waiting for all of us. I was finishing my bowl of cereal when the phone rang. It was Alan Levin.

"Good morning, Alan. Do you have a couple sleepy boys this morning?"

"Yes, I thought I was going to have to hire a derrick to haul them out of bed."

"Same here. What could I do for you?"

"Well, my problem is not with JR and Bran. It's Benny. He has been crying and asking for his brother. The kid is inconsolable since he found out he's in Houston. Do you think it would be all right with the Boises if we took Benny to see Tony?"

"I am absolutely positive it would be. Karen is very anxious for them to be reunited. What time do you want to be there? I'll go to the hospital early and prepare Karen for his visit."

"I thought we would try to get there around ten o'clock. Do you think would be okay?"

"Yes, I'm sure it would be." I gave Alan the instructions on how to get to Tony's room before we hung up.

I told Hildy what was going to happen before picking up another book for Joel since he had finished the last one I took.

"Can I go see Benny too?" TJ asked.

I'm afraid not, little one. There will be too many people there and he might get more frightened than he already is. Besides, you have to take your shower. Remember? And don't forget to brush your teeth," I told him, as I gave him a hug and a kiss on the top of his head. "I love you."

The other three lined up for their goodbyes as I started to leave for the hospital. I gladly obliged.

Karen was coming back from the cafeteria with a cup of coffee as I approached the boys' room. "Karen, I'm glad I caught you. I hate to spring this on you but the Levins want to bring Benny in to see Tony. I told them I didn't think you would have any objections ..."

"Oh no, no objections. There is never a day that Tony doesn't ask about his brother. It has been hard to keep from telling him about Benny. When are they going to bring him?"

Looking at my watch, I answered, "Alan said they would try to be here around ten. That's about twenty-five minutes from now. Do you want to tell Tony or do you want to surprise him?"

"I think surprise. I don't think he could stand the suspense of waiting even twenty-five minutes."

We went into the room and tried to act as natural as possible. I gave Joel the new book and placed the other one where I would remember to take it home. I was telling Joel about the ballgame we went to last night when Alan Levin poked his head in the door. I was about to introduce Karen to Alan when Ethel entered the room ushering Benny ahead of her, with JR and Bran behind her.

Tony looked over at Benny for a moment before recognition set in. "Benny, is that you, Benny?"

Benny turned to Ethel and asked, "Who's that?"

"Benny, it's me, Tony," he said, ripping off his surgical mask.

Benny looked hard at the unmasked Tony before he realized it really was him.

That was all it took. Benny launched himself at Tony and was in the bed with him before any of us could react. "Tony!"

"Benny … Benny … Benny, I missed you so much," Tony sobbed, as he wrapped his arms around his brother. "Where have you been? What did they do to you? You're so skinny."

There was not a dry eye in the room as Benny clung to Tony for dear life. They cried and laughed at the same time. Their emotions were raw. They didn't seem to be able to get close enough to each other.

Karen placed her arms around both of the boys and just held them, enjoying the love they radiated for each other. After a few moments she looked up and, I think, saw Ethel for the first time. "Thank you for caring for Benny. Tony's been so worried about him. It's so wonderful to have them together again. I can't tell you how much this means to both of us and Bill too, when he learns about it."

Several minutes later, Tony and Benny recovered enough from the initial shock of seeing each other to begin talking to each other. They had a million questions for each other and both were trying to ask them at the same time.

Karen interrupted, "Tony, you need to put your mask back on."

"Okay, mom."

"Is she your mom?" Benny asked.

"Yeah, she's my foster mom and I have a foster dad now too. His name is Bill. You'll like him. He's great. We have a house out in the country and a yard to play in. Dad and I like to play catch in the back yard. That is, we did before I got sick."

"What's the matter? How come you're sick? Why don't you have no hair? Why do you have to wear that mask?"

"I have leukemia and I lost my hair 'cause the stuff they put in my arm makes it fall out. I'm supposed to wear my mask so I don't get more germs to make me sicker. How come you're so skinny? You didn't use to be skinny."

"My foster mom and dad wouldn't let me eat hardly nothing. They hit me if I tried to eat very much and they cut my hair all off too. They said I hadda look sick. I'm glad I'm not with them no more. Gram is taking care of me now. She's nice."

"Who's Gram?"

"That's Gram over there. That lady," Benny said pointing at Ethel.

At that point, Ethel stepped over to the side of the bed and introduced herself to Tony. "Hi, Tony, my name is Ethel and that man over there is my husband. His name is Alan."

"How come Benny calls you Gram if your name is Ethel?"

Before she could answer, Benny spoke up, "She's like our old grandma before she died. Besides, she lets me sit on her lap and she's all soft and warm. I like sitting on her lap."

"I like having you sit on my lap, too. You can do it as much as you want, son," Ethel said.

Noticing that everyone was just standing around, I suggested, "Why don't the rest of us leave the boys and let them catch up on the time they have been separated. We can all go to the cafeteria for hot chocolate or something. Don't worry, you two, we'll bring some back for you."

As we started to leave Karen spoke up, "Mrs. Levin, would you mind staying here? I would like to talk to you and I want to stay here in case the boys have any questions."

"Of course, I would like to talk to you also," Ethel answered.

"All right guys, there's food to be had," I said, as I began pushing Joel's wheelchair out the door.

CHAPTER 16

We did bring Tony and Benny disposable cups of hot chocolate when we returned about an hour later from the cafeteria. JR raced ahead with Bran pushing Joel's wheelchair while Alan and I followed behind trying to keep them in sight.

Benny was resting with his head on Tony's chest exhausted from the outpouring of emotion. Tony's arms held his brother tightly as if not wanting to ever let go again. Karen and Ethel were sitting across the room from the boys as we entered. Both women were tightly clutching handkerchiefs as they talked quietly.

"Tony," Bran said, "we brung you some hot chocolate."

"Thanks, Bran," he said, sitting up in bed with Benny. "Did you bring Benny some too?"

"Yeah, and we put little marshmallows in them too," JR added, handing Benny a cup.

I helped Joel get back into his bed while the hot chocolate was being delivered. I stayed with him until his lunch arrived. After I made sure he could manage everything on his tray, I gave him a hug and a kiss and then left telling him his brothers would be coming this afternoon.

Benny was still there when I brought the rest of the boys to visit Joel. After they had greeted their brother they began looking over at Tony's bed.

"C'mon guys, I want you to meet Benny," I said, and led them to Tony's bedside. I introduced each one of the boys in turn.

When I introduced TJ, he said what I think all the boys were wondering, "Do you have leukemia too? Is that why you don't have no hair?"

"TJ, that's not nice to ask questions like that," I chided him.

Benny blushed as Tony answered for him, "No, he had some bad mom and dad. They cut all his hair off so he looks like me." Tony hugged his brother even tighter.

Alan, JR and Bran returned with containers of lemonade as the boys were talking to Benny and Tony. That brought the expected reaction from my troop. We had to go to the cafeteria to get them some. I helped Joel into his wheelchair and began pushing him out the door but not before TJ took his usual position on Joel's lap. Chris gently pushed me aside and grabbed the handles of the wheelchair as we started down the hall. The twins flanked the chair.

It seemed like a reversal of roles. Joel had always been the one to protect his brothers, and now they were the ones looking after him, if only in their own small way.

"Where's Hildy and Becky Sue?" Joel asked.

"They went grocery shopping. Your brothers have eaten everything in the apartment," I said, smiling at the other boys.

Before long, Tony arrived at the cafeteria in his wheelchair followed by his entourage. I wasn't too surprised. They joined our group pulling up another table so we could all sit together. They all began talking and laughing like boys will do. Despite being cautioned to keep the noise level down a couple of times, the chatter kept getting louder as everyone was trying to be heard over the other voices.

When I noticed several customers giving us nasty looks, I got the boys' attention, "Hey, guys, why don't we go outside in the garden where we won't disturb anyone?"

That met with agreement from all of them, so the nine boys and four adults made our way outside. For a June 2nd in Houston, it was a remarkably pleasant day. The temperature was only in the lower eighties which is unusual. Despite the comfortable temperatures, first Tony and then Joel began to show signs of fatigue. Both of them resisted weakly when we started to wheel them back to their room about a half an hour after we went outside. During this time, Benny had opened up and was interacting, although timidly, with the other boys. It was a little intimidating for him because all the others knew each other and he had just met them.

Once back at the room, my four said their goodbyes to Joel and to Tony before turning to JR and Bran and whispered something to them. I guessed it was about the birthday party for Joel tomorrow, but I didn't ask.

We got back to the apartment shortly after Hildy and Becky Sue returned from their food safari. They were still unloading the bags of groceries and putting them away in the pantry and refrigerator.

"Hi, guys," Becky Sue said. "If you go put on your swimwear, I think we have time for your lessons before supper."

It didn't take long for the boys to return dressed for the pool carrying towels. They waited impatiently while Becky Sue went to her apartment to change.

"I think a swim sounds like a good idea. Hildy, if you don't need me for anything I think I'll join the boys in the pool." It had been quite a while since I had played with the boys in the pool. I don't know who enjoyed it more. It did take my mind off Joel's problem, at least for a little while.

The rest of the evening, after we had eaten supper, was spent wrapping the boys' presents for Joel. Hildy spent the evening baking and decorating the cake for the party. The boys went off to take their showers and I sat down to read the rest of the morning paper when the phone rang. It seems like there was some sort of conspiracy to keep me from finishing the paper.

It was Jack.

"Jack, it's good to hear from you. What's SAPD's finest cop calling this late for?"

"I've got some news," he said. "I just heard from Billy Joe Slocum. You remember him. He was the investigator working on the boys' mother's murder. He told me Harry Andersen was found dead in the prison's food storage area. He had been brutally murdered and mutilated."

"Oh, my god! When did that happen?"

"They found him after breakfast this morning. I've seen this happen a couple of times to other sexual predators over the years. What's strange is that because of the plea deal, he was never charged or convicted of sexual assault of a child. That's the reason he wasn't segregated from the rest of the prison population as is the case with other predators."

"Have they found out who did it or why?"

"No, and they probably never will. The hierarchy among prisoners places sex offenders at the bottom and ones who molest their own children are considered almost fair game. Evidently someone found out about him raping Joel and put out the word. From what I have been told, it took more than one person to do this."

"I don't think I'll lay this on the boys right now. I don't want to put a damper on Joel's birthday party tomorrow. Besides, I don't think they would care anyway. I have never heard them even mention him in the eight months they have been with me. What will happen to his body?"

"If nobody claims it, they'll bury it in the prison cemetery in an unmarked grave."

"Thanks Jack, I appreciate you letting me know. By the way, have you heard anything new about Chris' parents?"

"The last I heard was they were trying to negotiate a plea to involuntary manslaughter which would put them in jail for maybe 15 years. I'll see if I can find out anything from my contacts over there. Oh, and tell Joel 'Happy birthday from the Hogans', at the party tomorrow. I wish we could be there, but Carolyn's folks are coming to visit tomorrow. Timmy misses the boys."

"I will, Jack. It'll be two to three weeks before we'll be back in town."

As I hung up the phone, TJ climbed into my lap. "My, you smell good," I said, kissing the top of his damp head. "Let's get you guys tucked in. We have a big day tomorrow."

On our way to the bedroom, we made a side trip to the kitchen where Hildy was finishing up the birthday cake.

"Wow, Hildy that's pretty," TJ said.

"Thank you, son, do you think Joel will like it?"

"Oh, yeah!"

"Hildy, that looks like it came from a professional bakery. How did you do it?" I asked.

"Well, I guess all those years working in the bakery taught me something," she said, smiling. "Do you think it will be big enough? As I figure it, there'll be around 18 people at the party. I baked another one-layer cake that I didn't decorate just in case."

"Hildy, there is enough sugar in there to keep the boys wired for a week. With the ice cream and cookies and soft drinks, there'll be more than enough for everyone. What would we do without you?" I said, as I gave her shoulder a hug.

"Good night, little one," she said, as I started to lead TJ toward the bedroom.

TJ turned and ran to her, throwing his arms around her waist, "G'night, Hildy. I love you."

Putting her hands on either side of his head she tilted his face up toward hers. "I love you too," she said, kissing his forehead.

I was surprised but very pleased when we reached TJ and Chris' bedroom. Chris was propped up in bed reading a book. He always liked it when I read to the boys, but I had never seen him pick up a book and read it just for fun.

"What're you reading there, son?"

"*Hunting for Hidden Gold*," he replied.

"Oh, one of the Hardy Boys books. I always liked those."

"I only got one page to go in the chapter. Can I finish it?"

"Sure, I'll go tuck the twins in and then be back for you guys."

Saturday morning I grabbed a clean pair of pajamas for Joel and took off for the hospital. I wanted to get there before the nurse came in to give him a sponge bath. He had been very good with everything that was done to him by the hospital staff, but on having someone give him a bath, he drew the line. I just made it in time.

"Good morning, son," I said, giving him a hug and a kiss on the forehead. "Happy birthday, you are now officially a rotten teenager."

"Yeah," he giggled. "I guess I better start practicing."

"You better not or I'll let the nurse give you a bath instead of me helping you into the tub. How are you feeling today? Can you make it by yourself or do you need me to steady you?"

"I feel good, but I think you better hold on to me, dad."

He didn't have any trouble getting to the bathroom after we got the plastic wrapped around his left arm. He was a little unsteady and probably could have made it on his own. He sat on the edge of the tub while I started drawing the water and adjusting the temperature. I got everything ready for him when he told me he needed to use the toilet but thought he could do it by himself. I stepped outside but told him to give a yell if he needed any help.

While Joel bathed, I chatted with Bill and Tony. Karen was busy doing the laundry and would be in later in the morning. Bill said Dr. Kerner indicated if everything went all right, Tony might get to go home next Friday or Saturday.

"Joel is going to miss him when he does go home, but I know Tony is anxious to get out of here. I don't blame him a bit," I said.

A few minutes later, Joel called out for me to come help him back to bed. "Look at my hair," he said, when I got there. "It's really falling out now."

It was. There were large patches where the hair had fallen out completely and other places where the hair was still in place.

"We knew this was going to happen," I said, giving him a hug. "No one's going to care. Everyone who sees you will still love you whether you have hair or not. Come on, let's get your hat to put on if you want."

When we came out of the bathroom, Dr. Kerner was waiting for him. "Let me see how you are doing this morning," he told Joel, as I helped him back into his bed. Dr. Kerner went through his regular examination routine before writing something on Joel's chart. "Now," he said clearing his throat, "you have an IV treatment scheduled for Monday morning and another on Thursday. You will also have to take another round of those big pills on Wednesday, the ones you called 'horse pills' last time."

"How do things look, doctor?" I asked.

"Everything is going just as we expected. He is well on his way to beating the cancer. We just have to keep after it to be sure it's completely beaten into submission. With the results we have so far it looks very positive."

"Thanks, doc, this boy means the world to me."

"Aw, dad," Joel blushed.

Dr. Kerner left a few minutes later. I read to Joel and Tony from the book I had brought to him several days ago. That lasted for about forty minutes until the boys' lunch trays were delivered. Food then became their major focus. After I made sure Joel could manage everything on his plate, I gave him a hug and told him I would bring his brothers this afternoon around two o'clock.

Since the conference room I had reserved was down the hall and around the corner from Joel's room, I went to check on it before I left to go back to the apartment. It looked like it was set up and ready for us. I just hoped the cafeteria would have the soft drinks and cartons of milk delivered by the time we were ready for them.

When I got back to the apartment the boys were bouncing off the wall with excitement. After I grabbed a quick bite to eat, I had the boys take their presents for Joel to the van. I told them they had to come back and help Hildy and Becky Sue carry all the party things too. TJ took the paper napkins, Larry took the bag of paper plates, Lenny took the plastic forks and spoons and Chris took the two half gallons of ice cream. The rest of us took the two cakes and the cookies.

It was only 1:30 when we left for the hospital. I told the boys they had to help Hildy set up for the party before they could go see Joel. As it was we had to make two trips from the van, one with the food and the second for the presents.

They made quick work of setting up for the party and then tugged on my hand for me to take them to Joel's room. He was napping when we arrived, but TJ soon took care of that as he climbed into bed with him.

"Hi, TJ," Joel said, giving him a hug. "Hi, guys."

After everyone had given and gotten their hugs, I suggested we go for a stroll and invited Tony and his mom and dad to go with us. I didn't know of any other way to get Joel to the party without giving it away. It only took a few minutes and we were set to go. TJ took his position on Joel's lap while Chris took over pushing the wheelchair and the twins flanked the chair.

We made our way down the hall away from our usual path to the cafeteria.

"Where're we going?" Joel asked.

"Oh, I thought we'd try going someplace different," I said.

When we reached the door to the conference room where the party was to take place, Lenny ran to the door and opened it. Chris quickly pushed the wheelchair into the room.

Hildy had strung a banner across one side of the room that said "HAPPY BIRTHDAY". The table was loaded down with the cake and cookies. Becky Sue was still arranging chairs around the tables so everyone could sit.

TJ turned on Joel's lap and threw his arms around Joel's neck, kissed him on the cheek and said, "Happy birthday, Joel. Open your presents. We wrapped them. I helped."

"Hold on a minute, son. Let's wait until everyone gets here. JR, Bran and Benny should be here in a few minutes. Why don't you take Joel to see his birthday cake that Hildy decorated?" I said to the boys.

"It's chocolate," Chris said.

"That's my favorite," Joel said.

"Mine too," chorused the others, including Tony.

As the boys were admiring the cake I saw a few cookies disappear off the table which brought a smile to Hildy's face and a shake of her head. The cake was decorated with chocolate frosting, little flowers made of red and white icing and swags of icing along the edges and sides. Hildy had written, "Happy 13th Birthday, Joel", and under it "June 3, 1995".

The door to the room opened and Ethel and Alan arrived with Bran and Benny. "Eric and JR will be here in a minute. They are parking the car," Alan said.

Benny headed to where Tony was standing and grabbed hold of his brother's waist before saying hello to the other boys. Bran made a beeline for the table where the cake was. When he saw Hildy standing there, he looked at her with pleading eyes. She pointed to the tray of cookies and raised one finger. He took one, content that he at least got something.

A couple of minutes later, Eric, JR and John came in the room. Chris, the twins and TJ all ran to the newest arrivals giving them each a hug.

"John," Joel choked out, propelling himself toward the group. "Why didn't you tell me you were going to come?"

"I didn't know until after we talked the other day. I wanted to surprise you, too," John replied, leaning down and giving Joel a hug.

"I'm so glad you came. I miss you," Joel said quietly.

"Okay, everybody, I think we're all here now. I know Joel is anxious to open his presents. TJ you come sit with me while Joel opens his presents. Maybe you could help by handing them to him."

"Yeah. Here, this one's from me," TJ said, as he handed a box to him.

Joel opened the box revealing a soccer ball. "Thanks, TJ, I hope we can play with this when we get back home."

The next box was from Chris. It was a new video game. "Thank you, Chris. John, this is the game Kevin was telling us about at school. He said it was really neat."

Next was a joint present from Larry and Lenny. It was a small box that contained a gold chain for Joel to wear around his neck. "Thanks, Larry, thanks Lenny, I've always wanted one of these."

"I got one of those for my birthday too," John said, displaying the chain around his neck.

"Can you fasten it for me, Lenny?"

"Sure," Lenny replied.

Then it was time for my present. I handed it to TJ who gave it to Joel. Joel carefully removed the ribbon and bow before ripping the paper off the box. He took the hinged box in his hands and slowly opened it. "Oh, dad, it's a wrist watch, a gold wrist watch. It's beautiful."

"Turn it over."

"TJ, I can't see, your head's in the way," Joel said, as he gently pushed his brother out of the way.

"What's it say?" Lenny asked as he brought his head alongside Joel's.

"It says, '*Joel, You bring joy to my life. Dad*'."

"Let me see it," Chris said.

As Joel handed his new watch to his brothers to look at, John leaned down and whispered something in his ear. Whatever he said made Joel smile broadly.

"Come, Joel, it's time to light the candles," Hildy said.

John pushed Joel's wheelchair up to the table where the birthday cake was sitting. Hildy struck a match and began lighting the thirteen candles.

After an absolutely horrendous rendition of *Happy Birthday*, Joel blew out the candles to everyone's applause.

"Thank you, everybody, I never had a real birthday party before. Mom would bake a little cake or a pie but I never had a party," he said, with his eyes beginning to glisten with tears of joy for the present and sadness for the past.

Hildy cut the decorated cake into large pieces, took out the corner piece and scooped an equally large portion of ice cream onto the plate. That first plate went to Joel. Ethel moved in beside Hildy and helped her dish up and hand out the heaping plates, first to the boys and then to the adults. My resolution to skip desserts melted at the thought of Hildy's chocolate cake. I did ask for a smaller piece. After all, I did have some will power.

We hadn't planned any organized games for the boys to play because both Joel and Tony would get worn out before the games could be played out. They didn't seem to mind. They were having too much fun talking and laughing. It was a little loud, but with ten teen and preteen boys, what could you expect?

I was enjoying myself talking to Eric. It had been a while since we had seen each other and as we talked I realized how much I missed seeing him. As we were talking, Karen came up to me and said they were going to take Tony and Benny back to the room. Tony was showing signs of fatigue. That brought me back to reality. I went to check on Joel to see if he, too, were tiring.

"How are you doing, son? Are you getting tired?"

"A little, but can't I talk to John some more?"

"Okay, a few more minutes and then you should get back into bed," I said, in my best fatherly tone.

"How's he doing?" Eric asked, as I returned to our table.

"He is starting to tire, but he doesn't want to go back to his room. By the way, when are you going back home?"

"Mom wants us to stay for lunch tomorrow after church. That means we'll probably start back around two. Why do you ask?"

"I thought maybe John could stay here at the hospital and I would take him back to your folks' place this evening. I have to take the other boys home after the party, but I'll be coming back later this evening so I could take him with me when I left."

"I don't see why that wouldn't work. It's quite a round trip from here to the house and then back to your apartment."

"I know, but those two seem to be developing a special relationship. I think it would do Joel's attitude good to have his friend with him a little longer. Dr. Kerner says a positive attitude is very important in his treatment. I know Joel is not looking forward to another round of chemo next week so this might keep his spirits up."

A few minutes later I could tell Joel was definitely beginning to tire. It had been about an hour and a half which was about as long as he had been out of bed since the chemo had started affecting his stamina.

"Joel, let's go back to the room. I don't want you to get too tired."

"All right, dad, I am feeling a little weak."

"Say goodbye to everyone. The boys and I will take you back to your room and then we'll come back and help Hildy clean up in here."

"Thanks, Hildy, the cake was wonderful," he said, stretching his arms up to give her a hug and a kiss on the cheek.

"Honey, it was my pleasure. I'm glad you liked it," Hildy said, returning his hug.

"Can John come with us?"

"Of course he may," I said. "Come along, now."

By the time we got back to the room, Joel was really showing how worn out he was. I think he was putting on a front so he would have more time to spend with John. I got Joel in bed and told him to get some rest before his brothers crowded around to hug him and again wish him a happy birthday.

"John, I asked Eric if you could stay and talk to Joel and I'll take you back to his parents' house tonight after I come to visit Joel. Just don't let him get too tired. He may need to take a nap."

"Thank you, Mr. Johnson," John said, wrapping his arms around my waist. "I promise I'll make him take a nap. I don't want him to get sicker."

"Okay, then, I'll be back around seven o'clock. You boys behave yourselves."

The boys and I helped Hildy and Becky Sue clean up the party room and carried all the garbage and what few leftovers there were to the car. TJ carried the soccer ball he had given Joel.

"Joel really liked my present, didn't he?" TJ stated, more than asked.

"Yes, son, he liked all the presents he got. But the best present he gets every day is his brothers' love."

"And yours, too," Larry and Lenny said together.

Surprisingly, or maybe not, the boys weren't too hungry when it came time for supper. Hildy fixed some tuna salad sandwiches and chips to satisfy what appetite they had.

On my way back to the hospital, I realized John probably did not get any supper. I didn't know whether he had any money to get something from the cafeteria. I should have given him some and showed him where the cafeteria was. To remedy my oversight, I stopped at the Wendy's on the way and picked up a couple of cheeseburgers and fries at the drive-through window.

Feeling guilty as I got to Joel's room, I saw the curtains had been drawn around his bed. I just assumed one of his doctors was there examining him. I didn't see John any place. I opened the curtains a crack to look in. What I saw surprised me. No, a better description was shocked.

Joel and John were in a serious lip lock.

CHAPTER 17

"Ahem!"

I could barely keep a straight face as John jumped away from Joel's bed, turned a deathly white and froze like a statue. Joel, on the other hand, turned a bright red.

"Ah ... Hi, dad, I didn't expect you so soon."

"I could tell that. Why don't we go someplace and talk?" I said to both of them.

"Yes, sir. I'm sorry Mr. Johnson," John almost whimpered.

"Bring Joel's wheelchair over here," I said, as I began getting Joel's slippers and robe.

John pushed the chair as we made our way to the waiting room which was empty, thankfully. I indicated we should sit at a small table with two chairs in the far corner of the room. All the while we were on our way I was trying to figure out exactly what I was going to say to them. We arranged ourselves around the table so we were all looking at each other.

"I'm sorry, Mr. Johnson, I won't do it again," John sobbed.

I reached out and took John's hand and gave it a squeeze. Then I turned to Joel and said, "Please tell me what was going on, son."

"Well ... ah ... John just gave me this thing to put on my chain," he said, showing me a small charm that had been attached to the chain Larry and Lenny had given him.

"That's very nice," I said, examining the charm. "It looks like it has some writing on it. I can't read it in this light. What does it say?"

"It's my name is all. But, see it's only half. John has the other half. Show him, John," Joel said.

"See," John said, "if you put them together, they fit."

"Oh," I said. "So you were just thanking John for his present?"

"Yeah ... well ... and ... well, I like John too. You said it wasn't bad, didn't you?"

"Yes, I did and I still mean that. John, do you think that you like Joel the same way?"

"Yes, sir," he answered without hesitation.

"I don't want to interfere with the feelings you guys have for each other. I want to caution you again about public displays of affection until you are old enough and secure enough to handle the reactions you'll experience from others. John, you know how your parents first reacted to your feelings for Joel. That was mild compared to how people who don't love you will respond."

"But, we pulled the curtain, dad"

"Yes, I know you did and that was fine. It still didn't give you much privacy. Did you think what might have happened if a nurse or orderly had walked in on you? They might have reacted much differently than what I did."

"Yeah, Mr. Johnson, I guess we didn't think about that," John said.

"There is another thing I want you to think about. Did you see Tony always wears that surgical mask except when he is eating?" I asked. "Do you know why?"

"Yes, dad, you said he wears it so he won't get sick."

"That's right. The doctor will probably ask you to begin wearing one very soon. John, the reason the mask is necessary is the medicines Joel is getting make him very susceptible to germs. Kissing, like you two were doing, is a very effective way of passing germs. Even if you had just a slight cold, those germs could easily be passed to Joel. Any infection could be very serious for him."

"Gee, I didn't know that. I sure don't want Joel to get sick 'cause of me," John said.

"I know you don't, John. I want you guys to be good friends. I also want you to be careful. While Joel is sick, your relationship will have to be restrained. After that if you still have feelings for each other, you will have to decide how you want to proceed. Now, if either one of you ever has any questions about anything, I want you to know you can always come to me. I don't know if I'll always have the right answer, but I'll always be honest with you."

"Thanks, Mr. Johnson, I wish my dad and mom could understand like you do."

"I know they're trying. Give them time to adjust. You know they love you and don't want to see you get hurt," I said.

"Yeah, I know. It's just sometimes … oh, I don't know. Sometimes I get the feeling they wonder what they did that makes me like Joel the way I do."

"It's not their fault. It's nobody's fault," I told him. All the while we were talking the boys were eating the burgers and fries I had brought for them. "Do you guys think you have room for some ice cream or frozen yogurt?"

Joel looked at me and giggled, "Yeah, dad."

"Me, too," came the expected response from John.

"God, I hope I handled that right," I thought, as we headed off to the snack bar.

John was very quiet as he pushed Joel's wheelchair down the hall. Joel chatted away about the party and the gifts he got and how good the chocolate cake was.

After the boys had their ice cream and Joel returned to his room, I suggested to John that we needed to get him back to the Levins' house before it got too late. I told him to say goodbye to Joel while I went to say goodbye to Tony and his family.

I got the impression Bill and Karen wanted to ask me something about John and Joel but didn't know how to bring up the subject. I didn't volunteer anything. If they had asked about the relationship, I don't know what I would have said. It really wasn't any of their business.

John was quiet as I started to take him back to the Levins' house. After about ten minutes, I asked, "What's on your mind, son?"

"I just feel so bad for Joel. I wish he wasn't sick. Sometimes I wish it was me instead of him."

"I know how you feel. I would give anything in the world for Joel not to be sick. We both love Joel in our own ways, and it's difficult for us to accept that he's sick."

"I guess I do love Joel. When I'm around him I don't stutter or stop in the middle of talking because the words won't come out. He makes me feel good. I don't know what I would do if he wasn't around. I miss him so much when he is not home."

"I understand, John. Joel is a remarkable boy."

The rest of the trip was made in silence. JR, Bran and Benny were playing kickball in the front yard with a couple of neighborhood kids when we arrived. Eric was sitting on the front step with his dad watching the boys play.

"C'mon John, we need someone on our side," JR panted as he ran up to the van.

"Okay," John yelled as he jumped out of the van and ran to join the game.

I joined Eric and Alan on the front step to watch the game for a while. It wasn't long before Ethel called for Alan to come help her with something or other. That left Eric and I alone to talk.

"Only four more weeks before you sell the business," Eric said. "Are you looking forward to it?"

"I guess. It's going to be strange not having a real job after working there for seven years. I am looking forward to getting the foundation started. I hope Darcie is as excited as I am. I know she'll do a fantastic job. She cares so deeply about kids in need. We can't solve all of the problems, but saving one child from the horrors of abuse or not knowing a caring family will make it all worthwhile. I'm sorry, I didn't mean to get preachy," I said.

"No, that's okay. I know you feel strongly about what you're doing. I just hope you don't let your heart overrule your head. You say you know you can't solve all of the problems. Just remind yourself of that every once in a while."

"Thanks, I'll try to keep that in mind."

"Is there going to be room in your new life for us?" Eric asked, looking into my eyes.

"I hope there is. Things are a little hectic right now. My first priority at the moment is making sure Joel gets well. Which reminds me, I had better be getting back to my boys before they wear out Hildy and Becky Sue. Thanks for bringing John with you. His visit really brightened Joel's day."

"It was my pleasure. He was so excited on the way here. He couldn't stop talking about Joel. That kid has it bad for Joel, as much as he tries to hide his real feelings from others. He's a good kid, though."

As we got up from the step I gave Eric a hug before calling to the boys telling them I was going. This brought the game to a halt as four of them came rushing to say goodbye. John was the first to receive a hug.

"Thanks, Mr. Johnson, for letting me come see Joel," he said.

"I'm glad you could be here for Joel's birthday. It meant a lot to him."

"Goodbye, Mr. Johnson," JR said, getting his hug.

"Did you enjoy your visit this week?" I asked.

"Yeah, I got to make two new friends," he said, smiling.

"Mister," Benny said, "Gram says you got me here. Is that right?"

"In a way, I guess I did, but there were a lot of other people involved."

"Thanks," he said, throwing his arms around my waist, muffling a sob.

"Do you like it here?" I asked.

His only response was the movement of his head against my stomach. I leaned down and kissed the top of his head and gave him a tight hug before he released his hold on me.

Bran was standing there with his hand extended for me to shake which I took and shook.

"Are you too big for a hug?" I asked.

"No, sir," he whispered, looking down at his feet.

"Come here, then," I said, as I pulled him into my arms. Then in a quiet voice, "Are you doing okay here?"

"Yes, sir, they are so good to me. Why are they? They know what I am. Why don't they hate me like my dad does?"

"There is no reason to hate you, son. The Levins love you for the person you are. Believe that. They don't judge you."

I gave him another squeeze before he let go. He looked up at me for a moment then nodded his head as if to say he understood.

Hildy had sent the boys off to get their showers taken before I got back to the apartment. This seemed like an awfully long day. I was exhausted as I collapsed into the lounge chair. It wasn't long before I had a lap full of a clean smelling, pajama-clad six year old. He was soon followed by the twins sitting on the chair arms and Chris nudging TJ over to one side of my lap so he could sit there also.

"I hope this chair doesn't break down," I said, trying to get my arms around all of them. "Did you have your snack before I came home?"

"Yeah," Chris answered, "Hildy had some cookies she didn't take to the party."

"Did you have a good time at the party?" I asked.

"Uh-huh," TJ said, "but everyone was bigger than me. I like Benny. He's not mad at me for asking 'bout his hair."

"That's good. I think it is about time you all were in bed. Hop down and I'll tuck you in."

Sunday morning Hildy fixed our breakfasts before taking off for church. Before she left she took me aside and told me she thought Becky Sue needed some time off. She hadn't seen her boyfriend or had a day off since we came to Houston. I guess I had been rather insensitive to Becky Sue's needs. My thoughts were on Joel. I decided to have a talk with her before I went to see him.

I could tell Becky Sue was getting a little homesick when I talked to her. She had planned on spending a lot more time with her boyfriend this summer. I got the impression they were on the verge of becoming engaged. When we finished I decided to send her home for a few days so she could see her boyfriend. I arranged for her to fly out this afternoon and to fly back on Wednesday afternoon. It would be a strain on Hildy and me to take care of the boys with my trips to the hospital, but I thought we could manage it for a few days.

We managed while she was gone, but it was a lot easier when she got back and all three of us could share the duties. Joel's chemotherapy went without a hitch. Tony did not get released from the hospital as he expected on Friday because he had developed a slight cold and Dr. Kerner wanted to make sure it didn't develop into something more serious. It was the following Monday when he finally got to go home.

Although Tony was happy he was going to get to go home, it was still an emotional goodbye when he checked out around ten o'clock. I'd brought the boys to visit Joel in the morning because I knew it would be the last time they got to see Tony, at least for a while. Everyone got their share of hugs before Tony was wheeled out of the room.

"I'm gonna miss you, Tony," Joel said, through his surgical mask. "It was nice having someone to talk to."

"I'll miss you too," Tony replied. "You've got my mom and dad's phone number. Call me anytime you can."

Tears came to Joel's eyes as his friend left the room.

"It'll be all right, son," I said, trying to soothe him. "You will probably have another roommate soon."

I was right. When I returned in the afternoon the other bed was occupied by a cute little blond boy who looked to be about ten years old. There was no one with him. When I asked Joel about the new boy he said all he knew was the boy's name was Mathew Rollins III.

"His momma was here when they brought him in but she left about five minutes later and hasn't been back," he whispered to me. "She didn't even hug him or kiss him or nothing. She just said goodbye and left. He hardly even wants to talk to me. He just lays there and cries a little."

"Well maybe his mom had to go to work and couldn't be here with him," I said trying to give her the benefit of the doubt.

"I don't think she hasta work," Joel said. "She was all dressed up in really nice clothes. I never saw anybody dressed up that fancy that had to work."

I stayed with Joel for a couple of hours talking and reading to him. I noticed when I was reading, Joel's roommate listened intently and didn't cry, as far as I could tell. As I got up to leave I gave Joel a hug and kissed his forehead. I made sure that Mathew heard I would bring the rest of the boys this evening. I was about to leave when I decided to introduce myself to him.

"Hello, my name is Crane Johnson. Joel is my son," I said, holding out my hand for him to shake.

He cautiously reached out his hand and took mine. In a voice that was barely above a whisper he said, "Hi, my name is Mathew."

"It is very nice to meet you Mathew. I hope we won't disturb you when I bring Joel's brothers to visit him tonight. They can get a little boisterous."

He gave just the hint of a smile before he released my hand and slid down in his bed.

Hildy was reading to the boys when I got back to the apartment. She put down the book as the boys rushed to greet me. Becky Sue had gone to the University of Houston Library to do some research for a class she would be taking this fall.

"Can we go swimming?" Chris asked.

"That sounds like fun. Go get your swimsuits on. It will be a while before supper."

They were in their bedrooms before I finished talking. I quickly followed after I found out from Hildy when supper would be ready. We had a good two hours to play in the pool. After playing with the boys for a while I realized how much I had missed these times with them. I also realized that despite my best intentions I had been somewhat neglectful of them while I concentrated on Joel's illness. In another week or week and a half he would be able to come home, and we could resume a somewhat normal life.

I could tell Becky Sue's swimming lessons were beginning to pay off for the boys. It was especially noticeable with TJ. He could hold his own in most of the water games that required swimming. Chris had improved his technique and the twins had reached a level where Chris was before Becky Sue's instructions. Hiring her was one of my better decisions as a father, other than hiring Hildy.

After supper was over and the dishes all rinsed and put in the dishwasher, we took off for the hospital. Becky Sue elected to stay at the apartment to catch up on some reading. On the way I explained to everyone that Joel had a new roommate named Mathew who was a little shy so they were not supposed to overwhelm him with attention. My admonition to the boys did nothing to dampen their enthusiasm when it came to greeting their brother. As usual, TJ assumed his position beside Joel on the bed and the twins and Chris climbed up on the side rails so they could hug Joel. It was a little while before Hildy and I could get close enough to greet Joel.

As I leaned down to hug Joel, he whispered in my ear, "He's scared."

"Did you talk to him? Did he say he's scared?" I whispered back.

"No, he hardly says anything. He just lays there and cries. He needs someone to hug him. His mom or dad haven't been here."

I just about lost it. Here was my wonderful son, sick with a serious disease and what was on his mind was the welfare of someone else. God, I hope he never loses his caring nature.

"Come with me, guys, I want you to meet Joel's new roommate," I said, lifting TJ out of the bed.

Hildy followed us as we approached the other bed.

"Mathew, I told you this afternoon that Joel's brothers were going to visit him this evening. Well, here they are. This one is TJ. He's six. The twins are Larry and Lenny, they're nine," I said pointing to first one and then the other. "Chris is right over there. He's ten. And this lady, who takes care of all of us, is Hildy."

"Hi," came his soft reply.

"How old are you?" Chris asked.

"Ten."

"Do you have any brothers or sisters?" Lenny asked.

"No," he said, in an almost whimper.

"Are your mom and dad gonna come and see you?" Larry asked.

"No, they're too busy."

That was too much for Hildy. She pushed past the boys and took Mathew in her arms, hugged him to her breast and started cooing to him. That's all it took. The dam burst and he began sobbing his heart out.

I ushered the boys back to Joel's bedside leaving Hildy to comfort Mathew.

"Can we go get some of that jogert?" TJ asked.

"You mean frozen yogurt, don't you?" I chuckled.

"Yeah, that."

"Get Joel's wheelchair and we'll go get some," I said.

On the way to the snack bar we stopped by the nurses' station to see if Mathew had any food restrictions. I wanted to bring him back yogurt also. He didn't have any restrictions which was good to know for future reference. With my troop, it seemed like after greeting Joel the next thing on their minds was something to eat.

"How come his mom and dad are too busy to come see him?" Larry asked after we got settled in the snack bar.

"I don't know, son," I said, trying to come up with any reason I could think of to explain their actions. I could not think of any.

After washing the chocolate off TJ's face, I asked the boys what flavor of frozen yogurt we should get to take back to Mathew. If the snack bar had more than three flavors they would have come up with more suggestions. As it was, since they couldn't agree on a single choice, I filled the paper dish with a sample of chocolate, vanilla and strawberry.

We started back in what was now becoming our standard way of traveling. TJ was sitting on Joel's lap, Chris was pushing the chair and the twins were flanking Joel on opposite sides. This never failed to get smiles from the nurses or visitors we passed in the halls.

Hildy was holding Mathew on her lap in the chair beside his bed when we got back to the room. When she saw us coming, she whispered something to him. He looked up and smiled the first real smile I had seen on him. TJ jumped off Joel's lap and took the dish of yogurt from me and walked it over to him.

"Here, we brought this for you. We didn't know what you liked so we got some of ever'thing," TJ rambled.

Mathew continued to sit on Hildy's lap as he ate his treat. I think TJ was a little jealous of him, but didn't say anything. I helped Joel get back in bed whereupon TJ resumed his customary position beside his brother.

It wasn't long before Dr.. Barrow came in on his nightly rounds. He gave Joel the usual examination before he removed Joel's cap. TJ watched carefully as Dr. Barrow closely looked at Joel's now totally bald head.

"He doesn't have any eye browns either," TJ volunteered.

"Eye browns? Oh ... I see," Dr. Barrow said stifling a chuckle.

"They are eyebrows," I said, correcting TJ.

Dr. Barrow then went over to check Mathew. "I see you've found a friend," he said to Mathew.

"Uh-huh," he responded.

"You get your first treatment tomorrow, Mathew. Is your mom or dad going to be here with you?"

"No, mom said she might come tomorrow night. Maybe"

"Okay, why don't you hop up into bed so I can check you out?"

I could see Hildy was barely able to hold her tongue as she hugged Mathew and kissed his cheek before she let him down to climb in bed. "What time does his treatment start?" she asked Dr. Barrow.

"It's scheduled for nine o'clock. Why?"

Hildy shook her head and came back over to Joel's bed. We stayed another half an hour before deciding Joel was beginning to tire. After he received his usual hugs from his brothers, the boys went to say goodbye to Mathew. I guess because they had seen Hildy give him a hug and a kiss earlier, that made him one of the family and they also gave a very surprised Mathew hugs all around. Hildy was the last to approach his bed. She leaned over and kissed his cheek and whispered something in his ear before turning and walking out of the room.

I didn't ask her what she had said to him but I was pretty sure I knew what was coming.

I was right. Tuesday morning Hildy announced she would be accompanying me to the hospital to be with Mathew when he started his chemotherapy. She had discussed it with Becky Sue and they had decided Becky Sue could manage the boys by herself and prepare the boys' lunch if she was not back by that time. I knew better than to argue with her and I was confident the boys would be well taken care of.

It was just after 8:30 when we arrived at the hospital. This was earlier than I usually arrived, but Hildy was determined to be there with Mathew when his treatment began. She greeted Joel and spoke briefly with him before going to Mathew's bedside and greeted him the same way she had greeted Joel.

CHAPTER 18

A few minutes past nine, Dr. Kerner and a nurse came in to begin Mathew's first chemotherapy. Hildy was still sitting with him, talking quietly when they approached the bed.

"Good morning, Mathew," Dr. Kerner said. "Are you ready to start?"

"I guess," Mathew replied timidly.

"It's going to be fine, honey," Hildy said softly. "I'll be right here with you."

"Thanks," he more mouthed than said.

Hildy got up and moved around to the other side of the bed so she could hold his hand while the nurse inserted the catheter. Mathew winced as the needle was inserted into the vein of his left arm that had been immobilized to keep him from twisting it.

Dr. Kerner picked up both IV bags from the cart the nurse had pushed up along side of Mathew's bed and examined them. He compared medicines against the chart he was carrying before he hung them on the IV stand and inserted the needles into a "Y" shaped tube the nurse had attached to the catheter. After starting the drip he adjusted the rate of each bag.

"Is it gonna hurt?" Mathew asked.

"You might feel a sting like a mosquito bite, but it shouldn't last too long," Dr. Kerner said.

"Don't you worry, son, I'll be right here beside you. If it hurts, you just let me know and we'll get it fixed," Hildy said, looking directly at Dr. Kerner.

"That's right. You just let Miss Hildy know and we'll get you something to make it stop. Now, I want you to take this pill," he said handing Mathew a small paper cup with a pink pill in it and a cup of water. "This will make you a little sleepy."

Mathew took the pill and then the cup of water. He looked to Hildy who nodded and then he swallowed the pill.

Hildy sat with him for about an hour holding his hand until he dozed off. She stood up, leaned over and kissed his cheek before coming over to Joel's bed. Her eyes were glistening with unshed tears. "I cannot understand a mother or, for that matter, a father, who would allow a son to face this alone. They don't deserve to be called parents. I'm going to stay here until they come," she said with steel in her voice.

Joel held out his arms indicating he wanted a hug from her. She obliged. "I love you, Hildy."

As I left a few minutes later, Hildy picked up the book Joel had by his bedside and began reading it to him. Mathew was still sleeping peacefully. I wondered what would happen if his parents showed up while Hildy was there.

The boys were in the swimming pool receiving their lessons from Becky Sue when I returned to the apartment. I was just about to change into my trunks when the phone rang. It was Foster from the office asking if I could be in the office tomorrow for a meeting and take care of some paperwork that needed my attention. I told him I would be there by ten in the morning. I then called the airport to see if I could get a flight to San Antonio before eight tomorrow morning.

By the time I had made all of the arrangements, I was surrounded by four boys in wet bathing suits wanting their hugs.

"Hey, guys, go jump in the shower and get the chlorine off and then we'll go get something for lunch." Then turning to Becky Sue, I said, "I'm going to take the boys out for lunch. You're welcome to come with us and then we'll go to the hospital."

"Thanks, but if it is all the same to you, I think I will stay here and work on the research for my class this fall."

"That's fine. I need to spend some time alone with the boys since I will be gone all day tomorrow."

I decided to take the boys to Pappadeaux Seafood Kitchen for lunch. It had been a while since I had any good Cajun food and their menu was probably as varied as you could get in Houston. Their gumbo, crawfish etouffee and jambalaya are really good. The place was beginning to fill up when we got there, but we were able to get a table without waiting. After looking over the menu, I decided to get three of the Pappadeaux Platters for the five of us. Even with the boys' appetites I thought three of them would be more than enough to satisfy them. The platters contained fried shrimp, fried oysters, fried catfish fillets, stuffed shrimp, stuffed crabs, crawfish and French fries.

I wasn't sure they would like the oysters or crawfish, but after they asked what they were, they disappeared along with most of the rest of the food on the platters. There were a few pieces of the seafood left after the boys had their fill. I had the waiter put the leftovers into a styrofoam carton so we could take them with us.

As we got up to leave, I noticed we needed to go to the restroom to wash their hands and faces because much of the food had been consumed without the aid of utensils. I'm sure Hildy would have enforced better table manners if she had been there, but fingers were efficient tools for eating most of the seafood.

TJ insisted we take the lunch leftovers into the hospital for Joel. I thought perhaps Hildy might be in more need of them if she hadn't gotten away to get her own lunch. Joel and Mathew were just finishing their meals when we arrived. Hildy had made sure they both could eat their lunches one-handed since each had one forearm immobilized.

Before TJ assumed his usual position beside Joel, I whispered to him that Hildy might be hungry.

"Here, Hildy, we brought you some fish," he said, handing her the carton he was carrying.

"Why, thank you, little one," she said, giving him a hug.

"Yeah, we went to the Poppa place," Chris said. "We even had oysters, but we ate them all."

"They were good, too," Larry added.

"And the crawfish and crabs were yummy," Lenny said.

"My, it sounds like you had a feast," she said, opening the carton TJ had handed her.

Hildy went to get something to drink and stretch her legs as TJ took his position beside Joel. After greeting their brother, Chris and the twins went to greet Mathew as well. He did not seem to be quite as shy as he was yesterday and greeted them enthusiastically. During the next twenty or so minutes while Hildy was out of the room there was a constant stream of boys traveling back and forth between the beds. Even TJ climbed down and went to visit with Mathew for a minute or two before returning to Joel.

Mathew appeared to be having fun talking to the boys when Hildy returned to the room. I was pleased to see the change in his demeanor. God, I love my boys and their unconditional acceptance of others in troubling situations. I got a lump in my throat and tears came to my eyes as I watched them with Mathew.

Hildy saw what I was feeling and gave me a hug and said, "I know. They are amazing."

After about an hour, I told the boys it was time to go and let Joel get some rest. That was met with a little resistance, but they, too, could see Joel was beginning to get tired. Turning to Hildy, I told her I would be back this evening and would take her home then. Getting a nod from her, I ushered the boys out of the room after they had given hugs to both Joel and Mathew.

Since it was one of those miserably hot and humid June afternoons in Houston, I decided it might be nice to take the boys to a movie. *Toy Story* had just been released and was showing at a theater not too far from the apartment.

The boys loved the movie as much as the popcorn and sodas. All of the kids in the audience cheered Buzz Lightyear and Woody. Some of the younger members of the audience were disturbed by Sid and his room full of "cannibal toys," but TJ just thought they were funny. All in all, it was an enjoyable afternoon at the movies.

When we got back to the apartment they all had to tell Becky Sue the whole story of Andy and his birthday party and Buzz and Woody. It was hard to tell if Becky Sue understood any of it with all four of them talking at the same time.

After I saw that the boys had their supper, I took off for the hospital to visit Joel and pick up Hildy. Mathew was sleeping when I got there and Hildy was reading softly to Joel. I approached the bed and gave Joel a hug and received one in return.

"How's he doing?" I asked, inclining my head toward Mathew.

"He's doing fine. He was so upbeat after the boys were here. I think it did him a world of good. I think he even forgot for the moment about his chemotherapy."

"Have either of his parents been here yet?"

"No," she said bitterly.

"Will you be able to come to the hospital tomorrow? I have to fly to San Antonio to take care of some business and won't be back until around six o'clock."

"Of course. I was planning on it anyway. I'm confident Becky Sue can handle the boys for a few hours by herself. I'll take a taxi so you will have the van to bring the boys to visit tomorrow night."

"Thanks, Hildy. I don't know what we would do without you."

"Me neither," Joel added.

"Oh, I was going to tell you. I was talking to Mathew and I asked him if he knew a Frank Rollins. You know, the pastor at my church. He said he did. Reverend Rollins is his uncle. I need to call him and let him know. As compassionate as he is, if he knew his nephew was in the hospital, I'm sure he would be here."

We talked for another half an hour when an overly dressed woman entered the room and looked over toward Mathew's bed.

"That's Mathew's mom," Joel whispered.

Hildy immediately got out of her chair and approached the woman. Putting out her hand to the woman she said, "Hello, I'm Hildy Ramirez, you must be Mathew's mother."

"Yes, I'm Eleanor Rollins."

"I've been anxious to meet you. In fact, I have been here all day, waiting for you," Hildy said, with the steel starting up in her voice again.

"Oh, really? Why?"

"Could we step into the hall? I'd like to talk to you and I don't want to disturb the boys."

Hildy didn't wait for an answer but took Mrs. Rollins by the arm and steered her out the door and closed it behind them. Curiosity got the better of me and I went to the door to see if I could overhear the conversation. It was faint but I was able to discern most of it.

"Why weren't you here when your son needed you? When I heard you were not going to be here I came and sat with your son as he went through the very frightening experience of his first chemotherapy."

I could almost see Hildy shaking her finger under Mrs. Rollins' nose.

"I had a very important social engagement I simply had to attend. Someone of my social standing in the community has to make an appearance at these functions," Mrs. Rollins said. You could almost visualize her nose being raised by the tone of her voice.

"Oh, was Celia Berger there?" Hildy asked.

"Why, yes, she was. We had a very nice conversation."

"We are talking about the Celia Berger who writes the "Celia's Society" column in the *Chronicle* aren't we?"

"Yes, I'm sure I will get a mention in her column tomorrow."

"Celia is my niece."

"Oh?" Mrs. Rollins said, with just a touch of panic creeping into her voice.

"Yes, she is. You know, I wonder what would happen to your precious social standing if Celia wrote a column telling Houston's social circle of the callous attitude you display toward your critically ill son?"

"Oh, my God, you wouldn't do that. I'd be ruined. Everything I have worked for to attain my position would be for naught."

"In a heart beat, I would," Hildy said. "Answer me one question. Do you love your son?"

"Well, of course, I'm his mother."

"That's not what I asked. I know that you are his mother. I asked if you love him? Really love him?"

There was silence for a moment or two before Mrs. Rollins answered. "Yes … Yes, I do love him. I guess I forgot about him and was only thinking about myself. Oh my God, I've been such a fool. I didn't want to admit Mathew was sick. It would interfere with my life. As long as I wasn't here with him, I could pretend everything was all right."

"I hope that means you will concentrate on him from now on. It's going to be a long struggle to get him well. I plan to follow his progress. I've become attached to him in the last couple of days. He is a frightened little boy who needs his mom and dad. By the way, where is his dad?"

"He's in Dallas trying to close a deal."

"He would risk losing a son rather than risk losing a deal?" Hildy asked, with as much anger in her voice as I had ever heard. "It sounds like he needs to rearrange his priorities also."

The voices faded as I assumed they had begun walking away from the door. I would have loved to have been a fly on the wall so I could have heard the rest of the conversation. It sounded like Hildy was giving, in no uncertain terms, her opinion as to what Mr. Rollins priorities should be. Unfortunately, all I could hear were faint words here and there but could not make out the conversation.

I was barely able to get away from the door as I heard footsteps approaching before Hildy strode into the room. Joel tried unsuccessfully to suppress a giggle behind his hand. Hildy gave me a knowing look as she approached Joel's bed.

We secretly watched as Mrs. Rollins approached Mathew's bed and stood there watching him sleep as if it were the first time she had seen her son. I saw her dab at her eyes before she leaned over the bed and lightly kissed her son's forehead.

Mathew stirred slightly before his eyelids started fluttering as he began waking up. It took him a few seconds before he was able to focus his eyes. "Hi, mom," he mumbled, his voice still filled with sleep.

"Hi, son," she said brushing the hair off his forehead. "How are you feeling?"

"I'm a little sleepy. Where's Hildy?"

"I'm right here, son," Hildy said as she approached his bed.

"Mom, Hildy held my hand all the time they stuck the needle in my arm. I was scared. She said I did good, didn't you?"

"Yes, you were a very brave boy," Hildy answered.

"I wish you'd been here, mom."

"I wish I had been too, son. I will be from now on," Mrs. Rollins said. Then looking directly at Hildy, "I now realize how much you mean to me. I'm glad Hildy was here for you when it should have been me."

"I'll see you tomorrow," Hildy said, leaning down and giving Mathew a hug before walking over to Joel and doing the same for him.

We left the hospital shortly thereafter.

I was on my way to the airport the following morning by 5:30. My day in San Antonio was filled with signing contracts, meeting with client management and handling personnel matters. The latter was the part I liked least. Foster had recommended one of our consultants be terminated for cause. He had been discovered to have been drunk on the job. That was a clear violation of his contract so it was my unpleasant job to give him his walking papers.

Still I was able to catch a flight back to Houston by four o'clock. Again the traffic was horrible between Houston Intercontinental and the apartment. I only wished there were better service between San Antonio and Houston Hobby airport. It would have made the trip much shorter.

Instead of being greeted by four boys when I entered the apartment there were five of them. I received hugs from my four, the other one just stood there watching. He looked to be seven or eight years old.

"Who's this young man?" I asked, after the hugging was over.

"That's Jimmy," TJ said. "He swims with us."

"Hello Jimmy, it's nice to meet you," I said.

"Hi," Jimmy said.

"His mother had to go pick up his dad downtown and he didn't want to get out of the pool and go with her so I told her he could stay with us until she got back," Becky Sue explained. "I hope that's all right."

"Of course it is. I'm glad they're making some friends while we're here. When are his parents supposed to be back?"

"Mrs. Samuels said it would take her about an hour to pick up her husband, so it should be another fifteen or twenty minutes. Supper should be ready about that time. If they're not back by that time there is enough for him also. We're just having meatloaf and macaroni and cheese so it is nothing fancy."

When it came time for supper, Jimmy's parents had not arrived so he joined us in our meal. We all had just begun eating when the doorbell rang. It was Jimmy's mom. I told her we had just begun to eat and he might as well finish and then we would bring him home. After checking that Jimmy was all right, she consented which was greeted with approval from all five of the boys.

We took Jimmy home after we had eaten and before we readied ourselves to go to the hospital. I was a little surprised when we got there that Mrs. Rollins and a man whom I assumed to be Mathew's father were by his bedside.

Hildy and Joel both got their share of hugs and kisses from the boys and me when we arrived. When the commotion had subsided, the boys looked over at Mathew's bed but didn't rush to greet him. I guess they were intimidated by his parents being there. I chatted briefly with Hildy and Joel, finding out how the day had gone and making sure there had been no problems.

I could tell the boys wanted to go say hi to Mathew so I walked over to his bed. "Hello, Mrs. Rollins, it's good to see you again." Turning to the man, I said, "You must be Mr. Rollins. I'm Crane Johnson, Joel's dad."

"I'm happy to meet you, Mr. Johnson. Please call me Matt," he said.

"These are my other sons, Chris, Larry, Lenny and the one in Joel's bed is TJ," I said pointing out each of my sons.

Each one shook Matt's hand before going quickly to Mathew's bedside and giving him a hug.

"Are they always so friendly with strangers?" Matt asked, as he watched the boys greet Mathew.

"They are not exactly strangers. They met him the day he was admitted and quickly became friends. My sons are very outgoing and make friends easily. Hugging a friend is the most natural thing in the world for them."

"May we talk … privately?" he said.

"Sure, let's go out into the hall. We can talk there."

I told the boys I'd be back in a little while and then followed Matt into the hall.

"That Hildy lady is something else," he said. "My wife called me last night after she got home and ordered me to get here as soon as possible. She said

Hildy had talked to her like no one had ever talked to her since she was a little girl and made her feel like a spoiled brat. I guess we both deserved that. Both of us have been so wrapped up in our own lives that Mathew sort of got pushed into the background and … and I'm ashamed of that."

"Yes, Hildy is something. She is the rudder that keeps the boys and me on track. I don't know what we would do if she weren't around. She's like a mother to me and a grandmother to my sons."

"You are truly fortunate to have her as part of your family. By the way, I have called my brother. I understand he is the pastor of Hildy's church. He also gave me a tongue lashing for not letting him know about Mathew's condition. He said he would be here first thing in the morning. He would have been here sooner, but he had a wedding and a funeral today."

"I have met your brother. He preached at the funeral for my sons' mother. I was impressed with him."

I saw that my comment about my sons' mother confused him. I was tempted to leave him hanging but then thought better of it.

"My sons are all adopted. It's a long story but four of them are biological brothers and the other one, Chris, is their brother by adoption."

"Oh," he said, nodding his head.

A few minutes later we returned to the room. The room was a little crowded with four adults and four boys alternating between beds. It was also a little noisy, but it was a happy noise.

Later, when we returned to the apartment, the boys gave Hildy her good night hug and ran into the apartment, I walked her to her apartment. "Hildy, you are amazing. What you did for Mathew and his parents was unbelievable. The changes in them are nothing less than remarkable. I don't know how you do it, but however you do it, don't stop," I said giving her a hug and a kiss on her cheek.

When I got back to our apartment, the boys had already started getting their evening snack ready. Becky Sue had left a note saying she had baked some oatmeal raisin cookies. The boys had set out the glasses for their milk and Chris was filling a plate with the cookies from the cookie jar.

After I got the boys settled into bed, I sat down with the video tape Collin had sent me with the confession of Benny's former foster parents. I needed to decide what I was going to do with it and the best way to proceed. I had been putting this off for a couple of weeks and needed to take care of it before we returned to Canyon Lake. More than anything I wanted to see Betty Venisti was dismissed from CPS and hopefully prosecuted on some charge. I would also like to see her scumbag husband disgraced, but that was of secondary concern.

As I was mulling over my options, the phone rang. It was Hildy. She apologized that she had forgotten to tell me that Dr. Kerner said he was going to give Joel what may be his last chemotherapy treatment at nine tomorrow. That sort of took care of what I would be doing tomorrow so I put the video tape aside and prepared myself for bed.

CHAPTER 19

I rushed off to the hospital the next morning so that I would be there when Joel received his last chemotherapy treatment. There were a lot of questions that I had for Dr. Kerner about the treatment Joel would need after he left the hospital.

It was just past 8:30 when I arrived at Joel's room. Joel and Mathew were just finishing their breakfasts. I was a bit surprised Mrs. Rollins was there already. She was wiping what looked like oatmeal from Mathew's face with a napkin. I greeted Joel with a morning hug and asked him how he was feeling and how he slept.

"My mouth is kinda sore, specially when I brush my teeth," Joel said.

"We'll ask Dr. Kerner if he can give you something for that. You remember he told you this could happen, don't you?"

"Yeah, but it keeps getting worse."

I talked to Joel for a few more minutes and then turned to the other bed and greeted Mathew and his mother.

"Good morning, Mrs. Rollins. It's good to see you here."

"Thank you, Mr. Johnson," she said sheepishly.

"And Mathew, how are you this morning?" I asked.

"Fine … Is Hildy gonna come?"

"I think she will be here this evening when I bring the boys," I said. Mrs. Rollins looked surprised at her son's question, but then recovered.

"Your Hildy has certainly made an impression on Mathew," she said.

"She makes quite an impression on everyone, most of all me and my sons."

"Good morning, Joel," Dr. Kerner said, as he walked into the room followed by his nurse.

"Hi, Dr. Kerner," Joel replied.

"Are you ready for your last treatment while you're in the hospital?"

"Yeah, I guess."

"Okay, then. You have had these medicines before so there shouldn't be any problems. You'll get an IV and have to swallow some of these big pills you call 'horse pills'," he chuckled.

"My mouth is really sore today," Joel said timidly.

"Oh, let me take a look," he said, removing Joel's surgical mask and then retrieved a pen light from his smock pocket. "Mmmm. Yes, your gums and the roof of your mouth are definitely irritated. How long has this been bothering you?"

"About a week, I guess. It wasn't bad at first."

"After we get your IV started and you take the pills, I'll get some mouthwash that will help with the pain."

Before starting Joel's medications, Dr. Kerner did his usual examination of him. "The lymph nodes are slightly swollen, but that's to be expected at this stage. Everything else seems to be fine."

Dr. Kerner gave Joel his 'horse pills' and started the IV. He then scribbled a prescription on a pad and gave it to the nurse and asked her to get it from the pharmacy. Mathew was next to receive his attention.

Before he was finished examining Mathew the nurse had returned with a bottle containing a red liquid. When Dr. Kerner was finished he returned to Joel and explained to him how to use the mouthwash.

"This is an antiseptic as well as a pain killer. We don't want your gums to become infected. You pour a small amount, about an inch, in one of these small cups and then swish it around in your mouth for about twenty or thirty seconds. Don't swallow it. It could upset your stomach. Then spit it back out into the cup. You can do this whenever your mouth starts to hurt, but try not to do it too often. One of the side effects of it is you won't be able to taste too much for a while after you use it. It might make your tongue feel numb also."

After he finished with Joel, I started asking all the questions I had about the follow-on treatment after we took him home and when that would be.

"I will give you a schedule for Joel's treatment. Dr. Greene should be able to administer it without any problem. If the blood tests and the spinal tap we'll do on Monday don't show anything unexpected, Joel should be able to leave the hospital on Wednesday."

On hearing that, Joel's eyes brightened, and I could tell he was smiling under his surgical mask.

I read to Joel most of the rest of the morning from a book I had gotten from the hospital lending library since we had read all of the books I had brought from home.

About an hour after I started reading, Reverend Rollins walked into the room. He glanced around the room before spotting Mathew and his sister-in-law and then went directly to Mathew's bed. I don't think he recognized either Joel or me.

"Uncle Frank!" Mathew said excitedly.

"How's my favorite nephew?" he asked, as he gave Mathew a bear hug.

"You say that every time. I'm your only nephew," Mathew giggled.

"Yeah, but you're still my favorite."

Mrs. Rollins was sitting there all the time while the two bantered back and forth. Finally Frank turned to her and greeted her coolly.

Turning back to Mathew, he said, "How about we get you out of that bed and go for a walk? You don't have to stay in that bed all of the time do you?"

"No," Mathew said, not waiting for an okay from his mother. "Do you know Hildy is here?"

"Yes, I talked to her on the phone. I'm glad she was here for you," he said, giving Mrs. Rollins a critical look.

After Mathew put on his robe and slippers, he took his uncle's hand and they walked out the door followed by his mother.

I went back to reading to Joel for about another hour before they returned to the room. I had never seen Mathew as animated and happy as he was when they returned. As Frank helped him back into bed I could tell he was getting tired. The chemo really sapped his strength.

When the lunch trays arrived, Frank said, "I have to meet a fellow pastor for lunch. I'll be back to see you in a couple of hours. You be good while I'm gone."

"I'm always good, Uncle Frank. You know that," he laughed, and gave his uncle a hug.

"Dr. Kerner was right. I can hardly taste anything," Joel said, as he ate his lunch.

"That's too bad. Does your mouth hurt?" I asked.

"No, it just feels funny."

I read a little more after lunch but the medicine tended to make Joel sleepy so he napped about half of the time. While he was asleep, I tried to go over my options on how to handle the video tape I had received from Collin. Since I was not familiar with the Houston establishment, I decided to call Collin and ask him if he had any suggestions on the best way to maximize the impact of the tape.

I stepped out of the room for a quick trip to the cafeteria to grab a sandwich. The place was nearly deserted when I got there so I chose a table in the corner and used my cell phone to make the call and to give me a little more privacy.

"Crane, how much do you want to be involved in all of this mess?" Collin asked, after we exchanged greetings and I told him what I wanted.

"Well, I really don't have any desire to have my name associated with it, but I don't know how I can avoid it," I answered.

"I think I can offer you the opportunity to accomplish your goal without you being associated with Betty Venisti's downfall. I'm not sure the tape will have any impact on her husband. It might embarrass him but he is so entrenched in the political machine he will probably be able to survive the embarrassment."

"That'd be great if you could keep me out of it. How are you going to do that though?"

"Over the years, I've cultivated relationships with several of the investigative reporters at the major TV stations in the area, as well as a couple of the columnists for the local papers. I'm sure if I provide them copies of the tape as a confidential source they could do the rest. I know one columnist who is very critical of the local CPS office here in Houston and would probably jump at the chance to dig up some more dirt on them."

"Would Benny's identity be protected?"

"Oh, absolutely, that would be one of the conditions I'd demand before I would release the tape to my contacts."

"Have you verified everything on the tape the Bensons said?"

"Yes, we have. We even have a photocopy of the check they gave to Venisti's campaign. We also have a copy of Benny's case file at CPS."

"How in the world did you get those?"

"Don't ask," Collin said, suppressing a chuckle. "I'd have to kill you if I told you."

"Okay, okay, I get it," I said.

"There won't be any charge for doing this. The only payment I want out of this is the satisfaction that one more corrupt caseworker is exposed. I hope it rubs off on her supervisor and he gets his. If he'd been doing his job instead of just drawing a salary this would never have happened. Our agency has investigated too many cases of CPS incompetence or corruption. Many times nothing resulted from it being exposed. They just swept it under the rug and went about their business as usual. This time I intend to make it my mission to keep up the heat until something is done."

"Bless you, Collin. If you ever need any help or support from me, don't hesitate to ask."

"Thanks, it's been good doing business with you. Let me know if you need any more detective work," he said.

Shortly after we finished our conversation and I had returned to the room, Joel woke up.

"I'm hungry," he said.

"What would you like, son?"

"Something cold."

"I'll go get you some frozen yogurt. What kind would you like?"

"Chocolate."

Turning toward the other bed, I said, "Mathew, would you like some frozen yogurt too?"

He looked at his mother for her okay before nodding his head.

"What flavor do you want?"

"Can I have the same as you brought me before?"

"Some of each coming up," I said, as I took off for the snack bar. I noticed his mother had a quizzical look on her face.

Frank Rollins had returned by the time I returned to the room. The frozen treats were well received by both of the boys. I resisted the temptation of having some myself. My sedentary life the past month had not done anything good for my waistline.

It wasn't long after Joel had finished his snack that Dr. Kerner returned and removed the IV which was almost empty. He then removed the catheter that had been in Joel's arm for nearly a month, telling Joel to apply pressure on a ball of cotton he placed over the puncture site. He also removed the splint that kept Joel's arm from twisting.

"Oh, I'm glad to get that off," Joel said. "Sometimes I would forget and bang myself in the head with it."

After a couple of minutes, Dr. Kerner checked to see if the puncture was bleeding. When he found it was not, he put a fresh cotton ball on it and covered it with an adhesive plaster.

"Now, try not to exert that arm too much for the next couple of hours. I don't want it to start bleeding. If it does, ring for a nurse and she'll take care of it."

I stayed with Joel until nearly five o'clock before giving him a goodbye hug and telling him I would be back with his brothers after supper. I also waved goodbye to Mathew.

"Hi, dad," TJ said, jumping up into my outstretched arms as I entered the front door. "I missed you."

"I always miss you, son," I said, giving him a kiss on the cheek and receiving one in return. "Have you been a good boy while I was gone?"

"Yeah," he giggled, as the other boys gathered around to receive their hugs.

"What have you guys been doing all day?"

"We went swimming this morning," Chris said. "I'm learning to hold my breath a real long time."

"Becky Sue took us to the park so we could play," Lenny volunteered.

"She's teaching us to play checkers, too," TJ added. "I got a king, didn't I?"

"That sounds like fun," I said, putting TJ down. "Do you want to go see Joel after supper?" I knew that was a dumb question, but I was nearly knocked over by the response.

Becky Sue elected to stay at home and work on her research while the rest of us took off for the hospital after eating another of Hildy's delicious suppers. I saw Hildy put something in her large purse before we left.

Joel's room was crowded when the six of us arrived. With Mathew's three visitors there were nine of us not counting the two patients. I hoped that nasty Nurse Grantham didn't come by. She would probably have a fit. Joel was sitting in a chair beside his bed.

"How come you're not in bed?" TJ asked, as he squeezed in beside his brother.

"My back got tired and the nurse said I could sit up a while," Joel said, giving TJ a hug.

With Joel in the chair it made it easier for the other boys to greet their brother. At least they didn't have to climb up on the bottom rung of the side rails to reach him.

"Hi, Hildy," Mathew almost shouted when he saw her.

"Hello there, Mathew, I'll come see you in a minute," she said, waving at him.

After we all had talked to Joel for a while, Hildy went to visit with the Rollins family. She first gave Mathew a hug and talked quietly to him for a moment before turning to her pastor and greeted him with a hug. "Reverend Rollins, it is so good to see you. I've missed your inspirational sermons. The pastor at the church where I've been going is well meaning, but he's an awfully dull speaker."

"Thank you," he said with a smile. "Unfortunately, the clergy is cursed, in a large part, with well meaning but dreary speakers. It is even more unfortunate that some only preach fear and hate for those who disagree with them. They seem to forget the 'Judge not' teaching of our Lord."

While Hildy was talking to the Rollinses, Larry whispered to me, "Can we go see Mathew?"

"Sure, just do it quietly. Don't interrupt the adults."

With that, TJ slid out of Joel's chair and followed in single file behind his brothers over to Mathew's bed.

"Although I didn't recognize Joel when I came in this morning, I do remember these twins and the youngest. He's TJ, isn't he?" Reverend Rollins asked Hildy. "I don't think I've met this other boy though."

"Yes, that's TJ and the twins are Larry and Lenny. Chris is the one you haven't met. He became part of the family some time after the funeral," Hildy said.

The boys didn't stay long at Mathew's bedside but they did get a little exuberant despite my admonition. They spent most of the time with Joel and enjoying each other's company. Joel began to tire after a while so I helped him back up into his bed. TJ didn't need any help to join his brother.

Reverend Rollins left first, saying that he had to get back to Canyon Lake because he had a wedding to perform tomorrow. We left after it was apparent that Joel was very tired and needed to sleep. The boys made their usual goodbyes to both Joel and to Mathew before we left.

I saw Hildy take a couple plastic bags out of her purse before we left and handed one to Mathew and one to Joel, along with a kiss to each of their foreheads.

"Is Joel gonna get to come home?" Chris asked as we were on our way to the parking lot.

"If everything goes right, Joel will get to come home on Wednesday. If that happens, we'll go home on Thursday. That's not too long from now," I said to all of them.

That was reason enough for a round of high fives among the four boys.

The days until Monday seemed to drag on forever, but it finally came. I got to the hospital early hoping Dr. Kerner would come and do his tests. All of the tests that had been run on Joel up to this point had been encouraging, and I had no reason to be apprehensive, but I was. I knew we wouldn't get the results back today so I don't know why I was worrying.

Joel seemed to be in good spirits when I arrived. His bright attitude soon had me feeling more upbeat as well. It wasn't long before Dr. Kerner and Nurse Sharon came in to take the samples. Although Joel had a blood sample taken every week, he only had a spinal fluid sample taken once since the initial one on being admitted to the hospital.

He knew what to do when Dr. Kerner told him what he wanted and curled up in a ball so the needle could be inserted into the base of the spine. I stood at the head of the bed and rubbed Joel's shoulder until it was over. There was just a hint of a tear in the corner of his eye when Dr. Kerner finished the procedure.

I leaned over and kissed Joel's forehead, "We'll be going home soon, son."

"I hope so, dad. I miss John and I miss Tony."

"Why don't you call John and then call Tony. I'll bet they would like to hear from you. I know John misses you."

"Thanks, dad."

"I'll go get a cup of coffee so you can call your friends in private."

I walked to the cafeteria for my cup of coffee. The cinnamon rolls were calling to me as I passed them in the line, but I successfully resisted their siren call. I took my cup of coffee to a table and was about to sit down when my cell phone rang.

"Hello."

"Crane, this is Collin Cupp. I just thought I would give you a heads up. You might be interested in watching the ten o'clock news tonight on Channel 2. You might also want to pick up a copy of the morning paper tomorrow."

"I hope this is what I think it is."

"You won't be disappointed, I can assure you. Take care, my friend. Goodbye."

I finished my coffee with a light heart but my sense of anticipation was that of a child the night before Christmas. When I got back to Joel's room he was wrapping up his call to Tony.

"Tony said he gets to see his brother a couple of times a week and talks to him on the phone every day. How come they can't live together, dad?"

"Joel, that's a little difficult to explain so that you can understand it. However, the simplest explanation I can give you is that Tony's dad doesn't make enough money."

"Oh ... that's too bad," Joel said.

I stayed with Joel until he had his lunch and then left, telling him I would be back this evening with his brothers. I was planning to spend some time with them. Although they realized Joel needed extra attention, they also felt neglected because I didn't spend very much time with them.

It was nice just spending some lazy time with the boys. We swam for a while and then I read to them. They had their snack. I had an apple. We simply enjoyed each other's company all afternoon. I cherished these times with them and thanked the day Joel came into my life that made it all possible.

Our visit to the hospital to see Joel went without incident. Mathew got his share of attention from the boys. I was glad to see both Mr. and Mrs. Rollins were there. Of course Hildy got an enthusiastic welcome from Mathew. I knew he would miss her when we all went back home and I felt sorry for him. I also knew Hildy would keep tabs on him to make sure his parents didn't revert to their previous behavior.

When we got back to the apartment, I told Hildy what Collin had said about watching the news and invited her to stay and watch it with me if she wanted. She accepted my invitation.

The boys had their snack then went to take their showers and prepare for bed. They had the added treat of having Hildy tuck them in as well as me. TJ gave her an extra big hug and kiss when it was his turn to be tucked in.

There was about half an hour before the news was scheduled to come on so I filled Hildy in on what Collin Cupp had told me. When I had finished she sat there for a minute thinking.

"Crane, I think I need to call my niece," Hildy said, getting up to go make the call. She used the one in the kitchen so I didn't hear the conversation.

The story was not the first one on the news program, it was the third. The news reader introduced the investigative reporter and headlined the story.

NEWS READER: "We now turn to another shocking story of Child Protective Services failing in their job to protect our most vulnerable citizens. Here is KXXX-TV investigative reporter David Campo with more on the story."

The screen shifts to the reporter superimposed on the video of the Bensons apparently detailing the scheme to someone off camera.

DAVID CAMPO: "This reporter has been given a taped confession of two individuals who allege they made a $5000 contribution to Richard Venisti's campaign so his wife, Betty Venisti, a case worker with CPS, would give them a foster child to use in a fraudulent attempt to scam money from sympathetic individuals. I have been provided with evidence that the contribution was made and accepted by the campaign. *(Screen changes to show an image of the cancelled check.)* I also have a copy of the case file of the child involved showing gross irregularities in not only record keeping but also showing clear violations of standard policies of CPS. When this reporter attempted to interview Mrs. Venisti, I was rebuffed at every turn. *(Screen changes to show the reporter following Mrs. Venisti down the street with a microphone and then back to a full face shot of Campo.)* Attempts to get a statement from her supervisor were unsuccessful. Over the next few days, I will have more reports on this new scandal in the already scandal-ridden CPS. I will also be reporting on the alleged involvement of the politically powerful Richard Venisti in this matter.

"This is David Campo reporting. Now back to you in the studio."

I switched off the TV and turned to Hildy, "Collin doesn't think anything will happen to Richard Venisti because of his political clout and social standing in the community. It's not a crime to accept a political contribution and as long as he or his political campaign were not directly involved in any *quid pro quo*, there is probably nothing that can harm him personally."

"There might be other ways," Hildy said as the phone rang. "That's probably for me. I asked Celia to call me after she saw the news."

Hildy went into the kitchen again to answer the phone so I was unable to hear the conversation. When she came back into the living room she had a broad smile on her face.

"You look like the cat that swallowed the canary," I said. "Tell me what's up."

"Well, Celia wants to help 'throw the scoundrels out' as she put it. It seems the Venistis are social climbers of the first order. They have been sucking up to the cream of Houston society for a long time in order to further his political career. These people have been a source of campaign contributions for him. Now, Celia believes, with a few calls to her contacts among the social leaders, the money may start to dry up. If there is one thing these people don't want, it's bad publicity. Being associated with public corruption is not in their best interest.

"Celia also said her Thursday column will be devoted to the story. If Houston society is anything like that in San Antonio, they will begin avoiding the Venistis like the plague. If that's the case, his campaign funds will dry up."

"We can only hope," I said. "I just wish they had said whether Betty Venisti had been fired. If not, she is still free to wreak more havoc on the system. I guess we'll just have to wait to see what the paper says in the morning."

Hildy left and I went and got ready for bed, not completely satisfied with the outcome.

The coffee was ready and Hildy was beginning to prepare breakfast when I exited the bedroom the next morning. I poured myself a cup of coffee and sat down at the table. The newspaper was laid out on the table open to the 'Bayou

City Beat' column. The guy writing under the name of Steve Larue was a real muckraker. He provided much more information than the guy on TV last night. He wrote that Betty Venisti had been suspended from her job and a termination hearing was scheduled the following week. He also interviewed several of her co-workers who said the only reason she kept her job was because of her husband's political influence. They said she was lazy and although she had a fair amount of cases to handle that she rarely made the required home visits for the children placed in foster care as specified by CPS regulations. It was well known in the office she routinely falsified her reports and the supervisor knew about it but was too afraid of her husband to do anything about it.

"This guy is good," I said to Hildy.

"I thought you would enjoy his column. I know I did. I just wonder what the status is of the kids she was supposed to be supervising."

"I should call Cindi Sessions to see if she has any more information. I would like to find out what she knows about Bran and his long term status and also Benny, of course." I said.

I left for the hospital after finishing my coffee. Joel was sitting up in bed when I got there, having just finished his breakfast. We talked until Dr. Kerner came in with the test results.

"All of the results so far are very good. We are still waiting for one more result before we can discharge Joel," he said, looking at me. "That result should be available either late today or first thing in the morning. Either way, if it turns out as I expect it to, Joel will be discharged at noon tomorrow."

"Yes!" Joel said.

CHAPTER 20

Joel's test was fine when we got the results on Tuesday, so Dr. Kerner said he would be released Wednesday morning. I was sure his brothers would be anxious for him to be back with them all the time. My next problem was to figure out the logistics of getting everything back to Canyon Lake. I didn't want to drive the van back because I thought Joel would be worn out from the three to three and a half hours it would take to drive. I also had the BMW at the airport in San Antonio. It wouldn't hold us all so I needed someone to drive it back to the house.

I called the private air service to reserve a jet to take us back to San Antonio on Thursday. After I had made all of the arrangements for the plane, I called the limousine service to have them pick us up and take us to Hobby at one o'clock.

Having made all the travel arrangements, I began making calls to let everyone know we would be leaving for home in a couple of days. The first call was to Eric's parents to see how they were getting along with Bran and Benny.

"It's so good to have kids around again," Alan beamed, after we had exchanged greetings. "Ethel is in heaven. She dotes on those boys. Benny is really coming around. He's so happy. The only time he's sad is when he and Tony get separated after a visit. But that doesn't last too long. He and Bran are becoming really great friends. I think Bran has adopted him as his little brother. And speaking of Bran, he has really cleaned up his language since he's been here. He still slips now and then, but Ethel just gives him a disappointed look and he apologizes."

"That's great," I said. "What's Bran's status? Is there any chance he'll be returned to his dad?"

"I don't know if I told you, but Cindi Sessions has taken over Bran's case as well as Benny's. It's unlikely Bran's dad will ever get custody of him. He's indicated he has no desire to have Bran come back to live with him. I know Bran doesn't want to return. He's told me that, in no uncertain terms. We're willing to keep him as long as he wants to stay with us."

"What about Bran's mother? I never did hear anything about her."

"She's dead. Bran said she had cancer and passed away about a year and a half ago. One of the few times he gets upset is when he talks about his mother," Alan said.

"I'm well aware of how it is to lose your mother. How is Ethel handling the boys and dealing with Darcie's up-coming wedding? I'd have thought it would be a mad house with the wedding less than two weeks away," I said. "I suppose you'll be going up there to help soon."

"In fact," Alan said, "we are heading up there this weekend. We're going to stay at Eric's place. I know it's going to be a tight squeeze with just his three bedrooms, but I plan to put in a couple of sleeping bags and the boys can make it a campout."

"I'm sure they'll enjoy that. The boys will have to come over and visit my sons while they're there. I have plenty of room and I know my boys would love to have them come and spend a night or two. Hey look, I have a proposition for you if you are interested. I have to get the van back home, but we're going to fly back because I don't want Joel to get worn out. If you would be willing to drive the van to Eric's house, I will loan you either the Land Rover or the BMW to use while you are there. I don't want you to feel obligated ..."

"That sounds like a great idea. My little Toyota Corolla would have been overloaded with all the stuff we're going to take. The minivan is in the shop with a broken axle. When are you leaving?"

"We're flying out around two o'clock on Thursday."

"We weren't planning on leaving until Friday ... but Ethel has been hinting she would like to go earlier. Hold on, let me ask her if Thursday would be better."

I could hear an animated conversation going on in the background, but couldn't hear what they were saying.

"Crane, Ethel is packing already. She would leave today if we had everything ready. She has the final fitting on her dress for the wedding this afternoon and it should be ready to pick up tomorrow around noon. That means Thursday would be a great day to leave. I was not looking forward to her driving one of the cars back here. We're bringing Darcie's car back so the newly weds will have a car when they return from their honeymoon. They're going to spend the July 4th holiday in Houston and then drive back later in the week. Ethel's eyesight is not what it should be. She is going to have cataract surgery on her right eye at the end of September so this will work out really well."

"We have a lot of stuff to pack in the back of the van, but with the roof rack and carrier I think we will have room for everything," I said. "If we can't get it all in I'll have the courier service take some of it. That's what we did when we moved to the apartment. We'll take as much as we can on the plane."

We talked for a few more minutes, working out the details of getting the van to them on Wednesday evening, before we hung up.

I then called Karen Boise. I wanted to talk to her about whether they still wanted to adopt Tony.

"Karen," I asked, after we had exchanged greetings, "are you and Bill still of a mind to adopt Tony?"

"We would give anything to," she said with a noticeable catch in her voice. "I talked to our new caseworker, Alan Carson, yesterday. Mrs. Venisti is no longer Tony's caseworker. He couldn't give us any hope it would be possible to adopt. Bill works hard but his income just isn't enough for us to qualify for the criteria they set. Even with the stipend the state provides, we still don't qualify."

"I just wanted to check to see if you were still interested. Since you are, I'll contact the foundation I told you about and they'll get in touch with you, probably the middle of July, to see if there is anything they can help you with to make adoption possible."

"That would be wonderful. I just wish there were some way we could reunite both Tony and Benny, but I suppose that's asking too much," she said.

"Well, when Darcie Glenn calls you to talk about Tony, you can mention it to her and she'll see if there is anything she can do."

"You seem to know a lot about this foundation. What's its name?"

"The ASEC Foundation, they specialize in helping people adopt kids who would normally not be good candidates for adoption. They also provide financial support if the adopting family needs assistance. It is fairly new. I've passed on to them a lot of information about you, Bill and, of course, Tony. I really think they can help you. Good luck, I'm sure Tony will be hearing from Joel. He, as well as the rest of the family, would love for you to come and visit us some time."

"By the way, how is Tony?"

"He's doing just fine. He is gaining strength every day. I told him this morning I thought I could see a little fuzz coming back on his head. We still have to be careful about any infection, but life is returning to normal ... almost. He has to go for another treatment tomorrow, but the doctor said it shouldn't have too big an effect on him. I hope he's right."

"Fantastic, I hope Joel does as well. Tell Tony the boys ask about him all the time."

After I finished talking to Karen, I decided to call Cindi Sessions to see what she could tell me. She was most informative, filling me in on all the gossip concerning Betty Venisti. It seems that her filing false reports on the children she was supposed to be supervising were actually violations of state law. She said it was something akin to perjury for filling out state forms falsely. She said the penalty for each infraction is 2 to 5 years in prison. So far they have uncovered at least a dozen instances of false reports being filed by her.

Cindi also said there were two more cases where Betty approved children to be placed in foster homes when the families had not gone through normal procedures or training. It seems these placements were made close in time to donations made to Richard Venisti's campaign by the foster parents involved. She said one of the assistant district attorneys had interviewed everyone in the office and had asked some very pointed questions about the office manager as well as Betty.

I thanked Cindi for the information and told her I would like to meet her at Darcie's wedding since we had only talked on the phone.

There was only one more call to make and that was to the limousine service in San Antonio to arrange for them to pick us up at the airport and drive us home.

As I finished my calls, the boys burst in the front door, fresh from their swimming lesson and looking for their afternoon snack. I knew Hildy had baked some brownies because I could smell them while I was on the phone.

"Hey, guys, why don't we take some of the brownies and go to the hospital? I'm sure Joel and Mathew would like some," I said.

They looked a little disappointed they would have to delay their snack for a while, but the idea of seeing their brother overcame their disappointment. Their feet nearly set the carpet afire as they ran to the showers so they could change and go see Joel.

To keep the drool off the carpets of the van, Hildy let the boys have a brownie before we got to the hospital. Needless to say, the brownies were a big hit with Joel and Mathew as well as the other boys. Since you can't eat brownies without milk we had to visit the snack bar to stock up. Hildy made sure there were enough for the two patients to have a couple of brownies after we left the hospital.

When we got back to the apartment I told everyone to sort out the things they would need between now and Thursday when we were to leave for home. The things we didn't need we'd begin to pack in the boxes we had saved from our move a month ago. Hildy and I helped them figure out what clothes to keep out. When we finished our inventory it seemed like we were leaving with an awful lot more than what we brought. Looking over the stuff we would have to put in the van, I decided by the time we got it loaded there would be no room for any passengers. I called the same courier service we had used to bring part of our things to Houston and arranged for them to come and pack what we couldn't get in the saved boxes and pick up everything Wednesday afternoon.

It was supper time before we got everything sorted out we needed to box up for the courier.

"Dad, is Joel really gonna get to come home tomorrow?" TJ asked, as he hugged my waist and looked up into my eyes.

"Yes, son, he really is going to come home. Do you want to go to the hospital to bring him home in the morning?"

"Yes!" was the immediate response from all four of the boys.

"Okay then," I said. "We need to set out some clothes for Joel to wear. I don't think he wants to ride home in his pajamas. Right after supper we'll pick something out for him. Now get washed up, I think Hildy has supper ready."

You would have thought we were picking out an outfit for a coronation when we went to set out Joel's clothes. Each one had their own idea as to what he would like to wear. We did finally decide, but it was definitely a compromise.

It had been a while since any of the boys had climbed in bed with me, but around 1:30 in the morning I was awakened by my bedroom door being opened. I then heard the patter of bare feet on the hardwood floor as they approached the bed. I could tell it was TJ as he slipped under the covers and snuggled up against my back.

"What's the matter, little one?" I asked, as I turned over and wrapped my arms around him.

"I don't know. I couldn't sleep."

"Are you worried about Joel?"

"Uh huh."

"I know you miss him, son."

"Is he gonna get well and ever'thing?"

"Yes, but he is going to be weak and won't be able to do a lot of the things he used to do, at least not for a while."

"Can I sleep with you tonight?" he asked timidly.

"Of course you may," I said, and kissed his forehead. "Now go to sleep."

It wasn't long before I could tell from his regular breathing that he was asleep. I wasn't quite as fortunate. I kept going over my lists of things to do before we took off for home. It's the curse of a list maker.

TJ was not in my bed when I woke up. That surprised me a little. I went to check on his and Chris' room and he wasn't there either. Now I was really starting to get worried. I slipped on a pair of shorts and started toward the kitchen to see if Hildy had seen him. I was relieved to see he was sitting on her lap talking very seriously to her. I couldn't hear what he was saying from my position just outside the kitchen, but I did see Hildy give him a big squeeze and a kiss on the cheek before he hopped down and started back towards me.

"Hi, dad," he said, and jumped up into my arms.

"Good morning, son. You got up awfully early."

"I wanted to go get Joel."

"It will be about three hours before Joel can come home. Dr. Kerner has to examine him one more time and he won't be there until after nine o'clock. Why don't you go wash up and get dressed, I'm sure Hildy will have breakfast ready by that time."

"Okay," he said, wiggling out of my arms and running into his bedroom.

I thought I was going to have to tie the boys down before we left for the hospital. They were so excited. I finally relented and we left to pick up Joel around 8:30. TJ insisted on carrying the clothes they had been picked out for Joel. Naturally Dr. Kerner had not been in to examine him yet when we arrived, but the boys didn't care. They were just glad to see their brother.

"I got your clothes," TJ hollered, as we entered Joel's room.

"Hi, TJ, thanks," Joel answered. "Hi, guys. You're early."

"They would have been here at seven if they could have talked your dad into it," Hildy chuckled. "Are you ready to go home?"

"Yes. Just being in this room all the time really gets boring. I want to see Samson again. I hope he remembers me," Joel said sadly.

"Oh, I'm sure he will. We should be home around four o'clock tomorrow," I said. "I'll call Eric and see if he will bring Samson over after he gets home."

Mrs. Rollins had not arrived yet so Hildy went to talk to Mathew. She gave him a big hug and received a kiss on the cheek. They talked quietly for several minutes before Mrs. Rollins came in shortly after nine.

The boys alternated between Joel and Mathew until Dr. Kerner came in to examine Joel about ten minutes after ten. That caused the boys to all crowd around the bed to see what Dr. Kerner did. He was very good about the boys watching as he explained to them everything he was doing and whether it was good or bad.

"Well, Joel, it looks like you're fit to go home," he said, when he finished.

"Yeah! Yeah!" the boys chorused.

"Now, I don't want you to overdo it. I want you to try walking around the house several times a day. Always have someone with you so you don't fall. Get out in the sun a little. Don't stay out too long. I don't want you to get sunburned. You'll have to go see Dr. Greene a couple times a month for treatments, but they won't be too bad," Dr. Kerner said, patting Joel on the shoulder. "I'll send a orderly to accompany you to the front door."

"If you guys will help Joel get dressed, dad will go sign all the papers so Joel can leave the hospital. I'll be back in a little while. Stay here until I get back," I told them.

It took me about twenty minutes to get all the paperwork signed, the bills paid and back to the room. Joel was dressed and sitting in the wheelchair ready to go. TJ was sitting with Joel, Larry and Lenny each had one of the handles on the wheelchair and Chris was carrying a bag with all of Joel's hospital clothes. The orderly walked behind.

As soon as they saw me, the entourage started for the elevator. It was an impatient group that waited for the elevator to arrive. Thankfully, it was empty so all of us could get in. When we got to the lobby near the front door of the hospital, I told everyone to wait and I would drive the van up to the front door. Chris decided to go with me and put Joel's clothes in the van.

It didn't take long before we were driving up to the hospital door. As I stepped out of the van, I saw Rodney talking to Joel who was all smiles.

"You take care of yourself, ya hear?" Rodney said to Joel. "I'm going to miss ya my little friend."

"I'll miss you too, Rodney," Joel replied, as he shook Rodney's hand. "Goodbye."

Larry and Lenny wheeled the chair out to the curb where the van was parked and to my surprise reached down and set the locks on the wheels so it wouldn't move. I opened the sliding door of the van and after Joel stood up I put my arm around him and half lifted him up the step into the van. TJ crowded in around us and sat himself in the seat next to Joel even before I had Joel's seatbelt fastened.

By the time we got back to the apartment, Joel was getting tired so I suggested to him that he lie down on the couch and rest until lunch time. I steadied him as he walked to the couch with a lot of help from TJ on the other side. Hildy came out of the kitchen with a tray with glasses of orange juice for all of the boys.

"Now don't spill any," she warned. It was not her custom to allow the boys to eat or drink anything in the living room, but today she made an exception.

"Thanks, Hildy, I missed having you look after me," Joel said as he got his glass.

"You're welcome, son. It's so good to have you home again," she said, turning and rushing back to the kitchen, dabbing at her eyes with her apron.

Joel finished his orange juice and then stretched out on the couch. TJ snuggled up beside him. "I'm so glad you're home. I missed you so much. I don't ever want you to leave me again," TJ sobbed.

Joel wrapped his arms around his little brother. "I promise. I won't ever, ever leave you again."

About an hour later Hildy called everyone to the lunch table. Again, TJ and I assisted Joel to the table. Everyone watched as Joel filled his plate and made sure he had everything he wanted. He seemed to be happy he was back with his family, among the people who loved him and whom he loved.

After lunch I left to go pick up Alan so he could bring me back to the apartment and then take the van back to his house. Joel went to take a nap and the rest of the boys were going to have their swimming lesson after their lunch settled.

Alan was ready when I got to their house and so were Bran and Benny. They had convinced Alan they needed to say goodbye to my boys before we left tomorrow. It didn't matter we would all be in Canyon Lake at about the same time tomorrow.

"Where is all the stuff you were going to pack in the van?" Alan asked.

"I decided if we packed everything in the van there wouldn't be any room for you guys to ride. And since I was going to have to have the courier service take some of it anyway, I decided to let them take it all. I don't know how we accumulated so much stuff in such a short time," I said.

I let Alan drive the van back to the apartment so he could get used to the way it handled while I was there to give him tips if he had any problems. I didn't have to worry. He drove it like it was his own van.

The courier service was there to pick up the boxes when we drove into the apartment parking lot. Hildy was showing them what needed to be taken. Since the boys were not there supervising, I assumed they were still having their swimming lesson. They must have seen the van drive in, because it wasn't more than a couple of minutes before they burst into the house.

When they saw Bran and Benny, there were hugs all around. By the time they got to Alan and me, most of the water from their swimming suits had been transferred so we didn't get too wet.

With all of the commotion going on with the couriers and six boys talking all at once it was no wonder Joel woke up. I was the first to notice him leaning up against the doorway of the bedroom. I quickly went to him and helped him to the living room couch so he could talk to the other boys. Six hugs later, he was talking and laughing with the others.

A few minutes after the couriers left, Hildy announced she had their afternoon snack ready. It was her version of strawberry shortcake. Hers started with a slice of pound cake in a bowl topped with a scoop of vanilla ice cream and sliced strawberries that had been macerated in sugar with whipped cream on top of all of it. I held to my resolve and declined a serving, as did Becky Sue. I still think I gained weight just by looking at it. All seven of the boys made quick work of theirs and washed it down with large glasses of milk. Alan made us promise we would not tell Ethel he indulged.

Our visitors left after they had finished their snack but not before my sons extracted a promise from Bran and Benny that they would come to visit us when we got home.

The rest of the day was spent enjoying Joel being home. Hildy prepared one of his favorite meals to celebrate his homecoming. The only time we got to see his smile was when he had to remove the surgical mask to eat. He would have to continue wearing it if there were a significant chance of him coming in contact with a source of germs at least for a couple more weeks.

When bedtime came I wondered whether the boys would revert to their old way or decide on some new sleeping arrangements. I guess old habits die hard. As they finished their showers and were ready to be tucked in, it once again was Joel and TJ in one bed and the other three in the other as if nothing had happened.

I woke up early the next morning. The aroma of fresh coffee tantalized me as I made quick work of my shower and morning ritual.

Hildy was humming to herself as I entered the kitchen.

"You're happy this morning," I said, pouring myself a cup of coffee.

"It's just so nice to have all of my boys back together again. This has been the longest month I think I've ever been through. I've been so worried about Joel. I know he still has a long way to go, but at least we have him home," she said.

"Yes, according to Dr. Kerner he has another year of treatments before he can be considered cured. And even then, he will still have to be watchful that there isn't any recurrence of the cancer. We also have to be aware of any unusual effects resulting from the chemotherapy such as delayed puberty or stunted growth."

"I'm just glad he's made it this far. I know he's going to be cured totally. He just has to," she said, almost in a whisper.

"Dad, Joel wants to come out for breakfast," TJ said, as he pushed under my arm to get his morning hug.

"Good morning, son. Sure, let's go help your brother," I said, picking TJ up and carrying him to the bedroom. "Did you guys wash your hands and face?"

When they said they had not, I helped Joel into the bathroom and steadied him while he and TJ washed up.

"Okay, you get on one side of Joel and I'll get on the other and we'll both help him. How's that?" I asked.

"Okay," TJ said, slipping under Joel's arm and grasping his hand.

TJ beamed with pride all the while we helped his brother to the kitchen table. He wasn't all that much help since I was doing most of the steadying but he thought he was and that was what was important. The other boys joined us at the table a minute or so after we sat down.

"How did you guys sleep?" I asked the trio.

"It was fun, just like before," Lenny said, getting nods from Larry and Chris.

"Oh boy! Waffles!" Joel said, as Hildy placed a plate stacked high with enough waffles to feed a small army.

I picked up the morning paper and went back to my neglected cup of coffee. I usually start with the business section before I read the front page. When I got to the front page I couldn't help but smile with satisfaction. It wasn't the headline story but it was a prominent story. The heading of the story read **"Venisti Arrested for Campaign Violations"**. The story went on to say the special grand jury had been investigating political corruption in the city for some time. A video tape received from a confidential source was the final piece of evidence that led to the issuance of the arrest warrants for Venisti and his campaign manager. The alleged violations of law centered on non-reporting of campaign contributions. A footnote to the story said that his wife had been arrested on unrelated charges of filing false documents with a state agency.

That made my day. My life was getting back to normal. Joel was back at home with his brothers and all those who love him. I had everything to look forward to. The business would be sold at the end of the month. My foundation would soon be in operation to help kids get the happiness they deserve with parents who loved them.

The morning went by quickly as we readied everything to vacate the apartment and head for home. The boys got in one last swim. Joel sat in a deck chair on the side of the pool under a beach umbrella enjoying his brothers frolicking in the water.

Hildy prepared a lunch of sandwiches for the boys at noon. By one we were ready for the limo to arrive. It was only a couple of minutes late, but I knew we had plenty of time to get to Hobby Airport before our scheduled two o'clock take-off time.

The limo drove us to the general aviation terminal and stopped at the private air service I had contracted with. I didn't see a plane similar to the one I was expecting. I left the boys in the limo and went into the office. The manager there told me the larger jet on the tarmac would be taking us to San Antonio. It seemed it had to be flown there anyway for a rental so instead of dead heading, they had decided to fly us there in it and save some money. That seemed entirely reasonable since it was a much more luxurious plane than I was expecting. I asked the manager if they had a wheelchair we could use to board my son. He said he would have one brought to the limo.

I went back to the limo and directed the driver to drive around to the side of the office. The ground crew met us and began removing our luggage and taking it to the plane's cargo compartment. The manager I had spoken to came out pushing the wheelchair for Joel. It only took a few minutes to get everything and everybody loaded. We were actually ready to depart shortly before two.

I was impressed with the plane's interior. It would seat fifteen in soft leather high back seats. It had a table where the busy executive could work. There was even a small kitchenette and wet bar. Everything was first class. I was glad I was not paying the actual rental cost on this plane.

We got the boys all strapped into their seats and we were ready for take off. It didn't take us long to get to cruising altitude. The steward came by and served all of us soft drinks and various snacks which the boys devoured.

I looked at my watch and noted to myself that we should be landing in San Antonio in less than fifteen minutes. I saw a light go on over the cockpit door and the steward quickly enter the cockpit. He was in there for several minutes before coming out. He looked a little shaken. He motioned for me to come forward with him.

"Mr. Johnson, we have a problem. It seems we have a hydraulic leak in the landing gear assembly and we can't lower it. The pilot is going to try to cycle it down, but he doesn't think it will go down or if it does it will only go part way down. He has declared an emergency so we will be given priority for landing but we will need to burn off some fuel before he will attempt a landing. That will take at least another half to three quarters of an hour before he thinks it will be safe to try a belly landing."

"What are our chances of a safe landing?" I asked, through a very dry mouth.

"Our pilot and co-pilot are very experienced, but you have to realize they don't practice these landing except in simulators. He thinks our chances are better than even of sustaining no physical injury to any of the passengers or crew."

"Okay," I said, taking a deep breath. "What do you want us to do?"

"I think it would be better if you were to tell your party as much as you think they should know. It would probably be less traumatic, if that's possible, coming from you. After that, I will run through the emergency procedures and make sure everyone is properly buckled in."

"You're right, of course," I said, and turned back toward everyone and prepared to deliver the news.

The boys were wide-eyed as I explained the situation. Becky Sue's face was as white as a sheet. Hildy was calm. After I finished outlining what was going to happen, the steward began going over the emergency procedures. He checked all of our seatbelts and made sure they were tightened properly. Then he gave each of us a pillow and told us to place it on our lap.

"When the captain announces over the intercom to prepare for landing, I want you to lean forward and wrap your arms around your knees and squeeze hard and stay that way until the plane stops. Do you have any questions?"

No one did. It was dead silent in the plane for the next thirty minutes. Finally, TJ broke the silence.

"Dad, are we gonna be okay?"

"Yes, we are," I said with more conviction than I felt. "We should be on our way home in a few minutes."

Just then, the pilot came over the intercom, "We will attempt our landing in approximately three minutes."

That was a long three minutes. I was reminding the boys what they were supposed to do when the intercom announced, "Prepare for landing."

I glanced around and all the boys were doing as they had been instructed.

The intercom came alive with a countdown, "Five … Four … Three … Two … One …"

"I love you, sons," I shouted as the intercom announced "ZERO" and all hell broke loose as the belly of the plane hit the ground to the accompaniment of a horrible screeching sound.

CHAPTER 21

The horrible screeching sound of the plane's aluminum skin scraping on the runway seemed to go on forever. The pilot had cut the engines just as the plane touched down but the absence of their roar went unnoticed as we spun around down the concrete.

"Is this the way I'm going to die? Am I going to go the way my parents did—in an airplane accident? God, please, don't let anything happen to my boys," I prayed.

The noise finally subsided to deafening quiet as the plane came to rest. The next thing I became aware of was the steward and the captain trying to open the door of the plane. It seemed to be stuck, probably from the distortion of the airframe slamming into the ground. After a short struggle they were able to force the door open and inflate the emergency escape slide.

"Quickly, get the kids out of their seatbelts and bring them to the door," the captain shouted to us, as the steward exited the aircraft.

Hildy and I immediately unfastened our seatbelts and began working on the boys' restraints. Joel was closest to me so he got my attention first and then TJ was second. I grabbed their hands and hustled them to where the captain was standing next to the open door. I saw the steward standing at the bottom of the slide waiting to assist the boys when they slid down.

"Joel, grab hold of TJ and then jump on to the slide. When you get down go as far away from the plane as you can," I said, and gave them both a hug.

As I turned back to the others, Hildy was trying to release Chris' seatbelt. Larry and Lenny were standing there waiting for their brother to be freed from his restraint. Looking over, I saw that Becky Sue was sitting in her seat, sobbing uncontrollably. She had not moved since the plane had come to a rest. I turned back to Chris just as Hildy got his seatbelt released.

"Come on, guys. Let's get you out of here. Hildy will you see to Becky Sue?"

I quickly led the three remaining boys to the door where I gave them the same instructions I had given their brothers. Then each jumped onto the slide one at a time to be caught at the bottom by the steward.

"Crane, can you help me?" Hildy shouted.

I looked to see what was going on only to see Hildy trying to lift a now clearly unconscious Becky Sue out of her seat. I rushed back to help and at the same time the copilot emerged from the cockpit and ran to help me. Although Becky Sue was not a big person, her dead weight was not easy to lift and carry in the confined spaces of the plane. We managed to get her to the exit. I wondered how we were going to get her down the slide when the copilot wrapped his arms around her and expertly jumped onto the slide making a perfect landing at the bottom and carried her away from the plane.

Hildy hesitated as she approached the exit door. "Ma'am, if you will sit down on the edge of the slide we will give you a push to get you started," the captain, said realizing her reluctance to jump.

She thanked him with her eyes as she complied and soon joined the rest of the family on the ground. The captain then indicated I was to go next. I did, and he followed quickly behind me.

In all of the commotion inside the plane I was unaware of all the activity going on outside. When I started away from the plane I realized we were far from being alone. The airport fire apparatus surrounded the airplane and there was an ambulance with paramedics who had the boys in tow. Their main concern seemed to be Becky Sue who was lying on a stretcher with an oxygen mask covering her mouth.

I ran to the boys and Hildy to make sure they were okay and to see how frightened they might be. To my surprise, the boys were laughing and giggling about their adventure. The fireman who was there with the boys looked at me, shook his head and smiled.

"That slide was fun, daddy," TJ said, as I gave him a hug.

"I'm glad you liked it but I don't want to try that again anytime soon," I said. Then turning to the rest of the boys, "Is everyone okay?"

"I skinned my elbow," Lenny said as he showed me his right arm.

"We'll have the paramedic take a look at it, but it doesn't look too bad," I told him.

When one of the paramedics seemed to be free, I led Lenny to him and asked if he could take a look at the boy's elbow.

"You know you guys sure as heck are lucky to get out of that plane with no more than a scratched elbow," the paramedic said as he applied an antiseptic salve and a bandage to Lenny's arm.

"I know," I answered, as it all began to sink in what we had gone through. "I think I need to sit down."

It was then I noticed the fire trucks spraying a foamy substance on the undercarriage of the plane. My only thought was I hope they don't get our luggage wet. It's funny what my priorities were at a time like this after I realized everyone was safe.

Becky Sue was sitting up being attended to by Hildy and the other paramedic. She still looked a little shaky, but at least she was conscious.

Joel came and sat down beside me. I wrapped my arms around him and he laid his head on my chest. "How are you feeling, son?"

"I'm awful tired," he said quietly. "My legs feel so weak. I haven't run in a long time. But I had to get TJ away from the plane like you said."

"You did a good job, son. I'm proud of you," I said, kissing the top of his head.

It wasn't long before all the boys were sitting with us on the ground. We sat there a few minutes watching the firemen finish spraying foam on the plane and then begin putting their equipment away. As we sat there another vehicle approached. When it got closer, I saw it was a small bus that had come to take us to the terminal. It had never crossed my mind how we were going to get there. I guess my thinking was not too straight yet.

Becky Sue decided she was well enough to ride with us and declined the paramedic's offer to take her to the medical clinic. She did appear a little sheepish when she climbed into the mini-bus.

It took us several minutes to get to the private air service's terminal where the mini-bus let us out. Thank goodness the limo was still waiting there for us. After I got everyone situated in the limo I went into the office to make arrangements for getting our luggage. They assured me that as soon as the authorities made the plane available, they would retrieve our luggage and have it delivered to the house. I thanked them and left to join the family in the limo for the welcome ride home.

I had completely lost track of time in all the commotion until we got on 281 and started for home. I wondered why the traffic was so heavy until I looked at my watch and noticed it was after five o'clock, peak rush hour. All I wanted to do was to get home as quickly as possible and make sure my boys were safe. When I turned to check on the boys, Joel had his head on Chris' shoulder and appeared to be asleep. I'm sure this ordeal had severely taxed his weakened condition. I just hoped it didn't have any lasting effects. Hildy was holding TJ close to her breast and stroking his hair. Larry and Lenny were sitting side by side doing their humming thing. It had been a long time since I had noticed them doing that. Becky Sue was still pale, but seemed to be recovering from the incident.

It seemed like it took a long time before the gate to our property came into view. I don't think I was ever happier than I was when I saw it. I stepped out of the limo and punched in the code to open the gate before we proceeded on to the house.

I was surprised to see Eric's car parked in front of the house as we drove up, but then I remembered I had asked him to bring Samson back when he got off work. Evidently they heard the limo coming up the drive and as we stopped, I saw three boys and a dog running at full steam around the corner of the house toward us. As I opened the door, Samson took one sniff at me before leaping into the limo and landing in Joel's lap as he was just waking up.

"Samson! Boy, have I missed you," Joel said, as he hugged and got his face tongue-washed by one happy dog.

The other boys quickly released their seatbelts and gathered around their dog receiving the same treatment that Joel had. Soon there were three additional boys crowded into the vehicle. It was a large limo, but eight boys along with Hildy and Becky Sue made for a tight squeeze.

It took a while before we got the boys out of the limo and started toward the house. Eric had joined us by that time and asked why we were so late in getting here.

"It's a long story, Eric. Let's get Joel and the boys in the house and I'll explain everything. I think Joel needs to lie down for a while."

I helped Joel into the house and got him settled on the couch. He didn't want to lie down. He wanted to play with Samson. I relented but made him promise to let me know if he was getting too tired.

"I'm hungry," TJ said to Hildy, looking up at her with those beautiful eyes.

"Well, little one, let's see what we have. I'll bet there is some ice cream in the freezer. Would that be all right?" she asked, leading him into the kitchen followed by seven other boys with Chris and Larry helping Joel.

"What do Bran and Benny think of the Hill Country?" I asked Eric. "I know what they think of ice cream."

"Except for Benny's very brief trip to Mexico, I don't think either of them has been out of the Houston area. Both are fascinated by all the deer. They were in the back yard chasing them when they heard the car drive up. Bran couldn't believe it when a roadrunner raced across the yard. I think he expected it to go 'beep beep' and be chased by the coyote," Eric chuckled. "Now what is this I heard your boys say about a plane crash?"

"Well, it really wasn't a crash, but we did make an emergency landing with the gear up ..." I started, as Mary Jane arrived to pick up her sister.

"Hi, Mary Jane," I said. "Your sister is in the kitchen with the boys. I think they're eating ice cream. Feel free to join them if you want."

"Thanks, Mr. Johnson, but I think I'll pass. I know my folks are anxious to see Becky Sue so we'll take off real soon."

Becky Sue must have heard her sister talking because she rushed into the living room and hugged her. "It's great to see you again. I didn't think I was ever going to see you again," she said.

"How come?" asked a puzzled Mary Jane.

"I'll explain on the way home. Good night, guys," she said. waving at the boys still enjoying their ice cream. "I'll see you tomorrow."

"Becky Sue," I said, "why don't you take tomorrow off? I think you need a little time to recover from our experience. We'll see you on Monday."

"Thanks, Crane, I think I could use a little time with my mom."

"Okay, are you ever going to tell me what happened?" Eric asked impatiently.

I went through the whole story with Eric, leaving nothing out. I could see he was horrified by the story.

"My God, Crane! I can't believe the boys are acting so nonchalant about your experience."

"I know. When I got to them after I got out of the plane they were laughing and having a good time. I expected they would be in shock. They may yet have a reaction to it. You know some type of post traumatic shock. I may see if Dr. Adams will see the boys as a group. Joel is scheduled for an appointment next Thursday for one of his follow up sessions."

"That'd probably be a good idea. They do draw strength from each other but I'm sure Dr. Adams will be able to tell if there is anything that might surface later."

"Dad, can we go swimming?" Chris asked, as the boys came back into the living room.

"I guess so. Does Bran have a swim suit? I think JR could wear one of the twins' suits. I don't know about Benny. I don't suppose it would be a crime if they swam in their underwear."

"Thanks for the offer, Crane, but we need to get back home. Mom and dad will be wondering what's happened to us. We've been here longer than we expected," Eric said, looking at JR. "Next time we come you guys can bring your swim suits. Now say goodbye and we'll be on our way."

"I'll follow you home in the Land Rover. I promised your dad he could borrow it while they were here. It will be big enough to carry all three of the boys. Also, if you would stop by and pick me up on your way to work, I need to pick up my car at the airport." I said. Then turning to Hildy, I said, "I think I'll stop by Canyon Pizza. Why don't you give them a call and order three large ones for me to pick up. I'm sure the boys won't mind eating pizza tonight."

"Good idea, I didn't know what I was going to fix for supper. Everything is frozen," Hildy replied. "Pick up a couple gallons of milk while you're at it. We don't have anything to drink except soft drinks and I don't think they need caffeine to rev them up."

I was right. The pizzas disappeared in a flash almost before I brought them into the house. At least our excitement today didn't affect their appetites.

After we finished eating and the table was cleared, Hildy said she was going to her Thursday evening church meeting, and I gathered the boys in the living room to talk to them about the airplane incident. Joel and Chris sat on either side of me on the couch while TJ climbed onto my lap. Larry and Lenny sat on the floor facing us.

"Tell me what you guys think about what happened on the airplane this afternoon," I said, trying to make my voice calm.

"The noise was awful loud and kinda scary," TJ volunteered.

"Yeah, and when we started spinning around, it felt funny. It was like being on that thing at the fair," Lenny said.

"How about you, Larry?" I asked.

"The scariest part was when it banged on the ground and bounced. I didn't like the noise either. I could feel it in my teeth," he said, with a grimace.

"Chris?"

"I guess the noise was the worst, but jumping down that yellow slide was kinda fun," Chris said, with a grin. That got agreement from TJ nodding rapidly.

I looked over at Joel and saw he was asleep. I guess I'll talk to him later. From the sounds of things, it didn't seem the boys were unusually traumatized by the airplane incident. For that I was very happy.

It wasn't long before it was time for the boys to get ready for bed. Since we had eaten supper so late they didn't have time for a snack. The day's events seemed to have started to take their toll and they didn't complain when I sent them off to shower and get into their pajamas.

I let the boys sleep the next morning although I had to get up early to meet Eric so I could recover my car from the airport parking lot. I would much rather have stayed in bed. It was a little bit surprising that I didn't have any of the boys in my bed when I woke up. It was a good sign that they were handling the airplane incident better than I had anticipated. Hildy was already in the kitchen humming to herself and trying to see what she could scrounge for the boys' breakfast.

"Crane, I need to go to the grocery store. I think I have enough frozen orange juice and some sausages that I can fix along with pancakes but there is not much else. Lunch could be rather slim if I don't get to the store," Hildy said.

"As soon as I pick up my car, I'll come back so you can go shopping. I should be back by 8:30 or 9," I replied. "You seem very happy this morning. Any special reason?"

"No … No, it was just good to get back to my church and be with my friends," she said, but I could detect a slight blush on her face.

I hadn't quite finished my second cup of coffee when I saw Eric's car on the security camera as he drove through the gate. I poured my half empty cup of coffee into a thermal mug and filled the mug from the pot before heading out the back door.

Usually after we got to 1604 and headed west toward the office the traffic was not too bad, but today we had to continue on 281 to the airport and the traffic was horrible. There was probably an accident somewhere ahead so we hopped off onto the access road and slowly made our way to the airport. I would like to have killed the idiotic civil engineer responsible for the interchange (or lack of interchange) where Loop 410 and 281 intersect. The Marquis de Sade could not have designed a more tortuous or devilish intersection.

We finally made it to the airport parking lot and I was able to get my car. The last logistical obstacle had been hurdled. Now to get back home so Hildy can go get the groceries.

Hildy was still in unusually high spirits when I entered the house. I knew something was going on but I didn't want to pry any more than I had earlier.

"Hi, dad," TJ said and jumped up into my arms, "I missed you."

"I missed you too," I said, giving him a hug and carrying him back into the family room where his brothers were.

"Dad, are we going to get to play baseball this summer?" Chris asked.

"I don't know why not. You signed up for it. You guys have missed about a week of practice, but that shouldn't be too hard to make up," I said, as I rummaged through my briefcase for the team assignments and schedules. "Chris, your team, the Redbirds, are scheduled to practice at two o'clock. Larry, Lenny your team, the Roadrunners, practices at four. This is going to be fun trying to keep up with your schedules. TJ, thank goodness your T-ball team doesn't practice today also. That would really confuse things."

I glanced over the equipment the players needed to have and noticed we were lacking a very important piece of equipment for my three baseball players. As soon as Hildy returned we would have to make a quick trip to the sports equipment store in New Braunfels. I was glad they were interested in getting involved in sports right away, thinking it would occupy them so they would have less time to think about yesterday's airplane incident.

Hildy returned around 10:30 with her car loaded down with sacks of groceries. It took the four boys and I almost ten minutes to carry them all in. TJ was more of a hindrance than a help and Joel didn't participate. Looking at all the food Hildy had purchased made the boys hungry, as if they needed a reason. Hildy washed some apples and gave them to the boys telling them it was too close to lunch for anything else.

I explained to Hildy that I had to take them to the sporting goods store to get some needed equipment telling her we would be back around noon. Joel decided he would stay home saying he was tired. Although TJ didn't need to go, there was no way we could go anywhere without him.

"What do we need to buy, dad?" Lenny asked. "We have our shoes and gloves and everything."

"Well, according to the rules of the league, you have to wear a cup."

"How do you wear a cup? That's stupid. I never saw anyone wear a cup," Larry chimed in, as Chris doubled over laughing.

"What's so funny?" Lenny asked.

"Son, the kind of cup we are talking about is one you wear to protect your testicles. It fits in a special jock strap," I said, trying to control a chuckle. "Chris knows what they are because he had to wear one last year when he played."

"Oh ... We never had a jock strap before," Larry said.

"Can I get one, too?" TJ asked.

"You don't need one to play T-ball," I started, but when I noticed his face drop, I continued, "Sure, I don't see why not."

The young salesman nearly cracked up when TJ walked up to him and announced in a loud voice, "I want a jock strap and a cup."

The other boys turned red in the face and quickly looked around to see if anyone heard him. Thankfully, there were very few customers in the store and they were middle age men looking at golfing equipment on the other side of the store.

I explained to the salesman what we needed and he led us to the section where there was a display of athletic supporters. He grabbed a measuring tape and took each of the boys' waist measurements. Looking over the display he selected the appropriate boxes containing the supporters and then selected the protective cups that would fit in them.

"Would there be anything else?" our salesman asked.

"I think we should get three baseball bats and some baseballs so you guys can practice at home. Oh, and a T-ball tee, a couple balls and bat. Can you guys think of anything else you might need? How about you?" I asked the salesman.

He didn't suggest anything so we paid for our purchases and left for home.

It was just past noon when we arrived back at home. TJ had to run in and show Hildy what he got and explain to her what it was for. It was all she could do to keep from laughing at his explanation.

"That's nice, son. Go put it in your room and get washed up. Lunch will be ready in a few minutes. That goes for all of you," she said to the rest of us. We quickly complied.

After lunch the boys went to get changed into their practice clothes even though it was about an hour before it was time for Chris' team to practice. Hildy packed a cooler with bottled water, soft drinks and most important a snack for later in the afternoon. I put it in the van while the boys were changing. TJ insisted on wearing his new equipment along with Chris and the twins. I added a pair of his underwear just in case he decided the supporter and cup were uncomfortable.

Joel decided he wanted to go with us so I put some folding lawn chairs in the van and added an old golf umbrella I had been given that would keep him from getting too much sun. I figured if he got too tired he could always sit in the van since the seat backs reclined and he would be fairly comfortable.

After we arrived at the ballpark and got everything unloaded I took Chris over to meet his coach and explain why Chris wasn't able to practice with the team before now. The coach introduced himself as Phil Leonard. He was very understanding and welcomed Chris to the team. I liked the coach immediately. He appeared to put the kids and their having fun ahead of winning at any cost. He took Chris aside and asked him what positions he liked to play and what he thought he did best. Then he asked him to throw a ball as far as he could to see if he would be better in the infield or the outfield. I was surprised when Chris was able to throw the ball much farther than what I remember he could last year, and straighter.

"You guys have been working with Chris, haven't you?" I asked, turning to Larry and Lenny.

"Yeah, he was really bad," Lenny said.

"We threw a ball with him every recess at school," Larry said. "He finally learned how to throw long."

"I'm proud of you," I said, giving them a hug. "You guys are something special."

The coach was really impressed when he pitched a few to Chris and saw how well he hit the ball. By that time, all the other boys had arrived and practice began. I could have sworn that either Jack and I copied his coaching style or he copied ours. Each kid on the team regardless of skill level received his attention and encouragement. The kids responded to him and not only had fun but listened to him when he asked them to do something. The only time he raised his voice was when he was telling the kids in the outfield to do something or change their position and only then so they could hear him. The more I saw of Coach Leonard, the more I liked him. He certainly had a way with young boys.

Chris' practice lasted for ninety minutes. That gave the team time to get all their equipment picked up before the next team came in to practice.

It was time for a snack when Chris came off the field so I dug into the cooler and handed out soft drinks for the boys and checked out what kind of snack Hildy had prepared for us. It turned out she had sent a couple dozen peanut butter cookies. I hoped that would be enough to feed the famished boys and me.

When the twins' coach arrived I took them and went to introduce us and explain why they hadn't been to practice before. Craig Latimer was the exact opposite of Phil Leonard. He indicated he didn't appreciate the fact the twins hadn't been to practice even after I explained to him the reason. I didn't take an immediate liking to him, but was willing to give him the benefit of the doubt.

His coaching style was one of yelling at the kids, berating them when they did something wrong. It was all I could do to hold my tongue. He had some of the boys crying when he humiliated them in front of the other boys.

The twins' practice was about half over when Joel asked if he could sit in the van. He was getting very tired. I helped him to the van and started the engine so the air conditioners would keep the van cool. Chris was playing catch with TJ. When I returned, I approached one of the other dads who was there watching his son practice.

After I introduced myself and finding out his name was Peter Hammond, I asked, "Is Coach Latimer always this way with the kids?"

"Yeah," he said disgustedly. "He knows a lot about baseball, but he sure doesn't know how to deal with kids."

"How come the league lets him coach then?" I asked.

"No one else wants to, so he gets to by default. I'd like to but I don't know enough about baseball to coach. I never played. I grew up in England and all we ever played was soccer or football as we call it," Peter said.

"I hate to see the kids being treated this way by the coach. If I could find someone to coach the team, how would I go about replacing him?"

"I'm sure if you could find someone the league president, Jason Calloway, would replace him in a minute."

"Listen, Peter, if I volunteered to coach the team would you be willing to help? I'm not going to bring my twins back to be berated by that man again. This game is supposed to be fun for them and from the looks on the kids' faces it sure doesn't look like they're having fun," I said.

"Have you ever coached a team before?"

"Yes, I coached a police summer league team in San Antonio for three years with a policeman friend. We never won a league championship, but at least the kids enjoyed themselves."

"You have yourself a deal. I'll call Jason tonight and have him contact you. I feel the same way you do about not bringing my boy again as long as Latimer is coaching."

I gave Peter my business card after I wrote my home number on the back. He gave me his card and we shook hands, sealing our deal.

"What have I gotten myself into now?" I mused to myself as I walked back over to where Chris and TJ were playing catch.

CHAPTER 22

After the twins finished their practice and we were on the way home, I asked them how they liked their practice. Chris had already let me know how much he enjoyed his.

"Okay, I guess," Lenny said quietly.

"That doesn't sound very enthusiastic. What's the matter?"

"Well ... Coach Latimer is always yelling at everybody and everything," Larry volunteered. "I just want to have fun, but it's not fun with him yelling at me."

"I think it will be better next practice on Tuesday," I said.

Joel was completely worn out by the time we got home. I helped him into the house and made him lie down on his bed so the other boys wouldn't bother him. He started to complain, but he realized he was much too tired to protest.

Shortly after we finished eating supper, I received a call from Jason Calloway about coaching the baseball team. He told me Peter had called and relayed my offer to help out. He almost begged me to follow through on it. When I said I would, he couldn't thank me enough. He said he would call Latimer and let him know that his coaching days were over.

We still had a little daylight left so I asked TJ if he wanted to try out his new T-ball equipment. Since he had never played it before, I had to go over some of the basics with him. I must confess I did not know that much about T-ball. If it hadn't been for the hand-out we parents had been given by the organizers I would have been lost.

I set up the tee and adjusted it to a height I thought TJ would be comfortable hitting and then positioned Chris at first base so TJ would know where to run when he hit the ball off the tee. After a couple of swings that missed the ball and a few hits that didn't go the required ten feet, I stepped in to give him some hitting advice. TJ's main trouble seemed to be not keeping his eyes focused on the ball as he swung the bat. With a little coaching, he managed much better. None of his hits would have been home runs, but they were respectable. He was thrilled he was able to get to first base without the twins being able to throw him out. It only took him about a half an hour to get tired from swinging the bat and running to first base.

When we went back inside the house, Joel was sitting on the couch reading a book. He looked up as TJ ran excitedly to him and began telling him all about hitting the ball and running to first base. Joel listened patiently to the telling before giving his little brother a hug and telling him how proud he was of him.

"Dad," Joel said, turning toward me, "may I ask John to come over for a while tomorrow?"

"I don't know why not," I answered. "I just don't want you to get too tired. You maybe over-did it a little today."

"Yeah, I'm kinda tired, but we'll just play with the video games so I won't get tired."

"Okay, go call him but I don't think he should stay all day, maybe just tomorrow morning or afternoon. You guys decide."

"Thanks, dad."

Later as I was tucking the boys in bed, Joel told me John was going to come over about 9:30 and his dad would be back to pick him up around one.

Saturday morning TJ was up almost before I had my first cup of coffee. He was anxious to go to his T-ball practice. I don't think I had ever seen him this excited since Christmas. His team was not scheduled to start practice until 10:30 but he was ready to go by 8:30. I tried to settle him down by playing catch with him, but I was only partially successful.

John arrived right at 9:30 much to Joel's delight. Although the boys had talked on the phone, they hadn't seen each other since Joel's birthday. They greeted each other with hugs and happy smiles before heading into the house to see if Hildy had a snack for them. At the mention of a snack the others followed closely behind them. Since it had not been that long since they had eaten breakfast, Hildy only let them have some fruit.

I invited Bruce in for coffee but he refused saying he had to take Pauline and the girls into San Antonio so they could do some shopping. His wife needed him to watch the girls while she scouted out the sales.

Finally it was time for us to go to TJ's practice. Larry and Lenny decided they wanted to go along so we piled into the van and took off for the practice field. Chris elected to stay home.

TJ was one of the first players to arrive. I looked around to try to pick out the coach of his team to explain why he hadn't been able to practice before now. I went up to a woman who had a couple of young boys hanging around her and asked where I could find the coach of the team. I was a little surprised when she said she was the coach. She introduced herself as Ellen England.

It took me a moment to recover before I explained to her about TJ's absences from practice. She was very understanding, even asking about how Joel was and wishing him well.

I told her I had been helping TJ with his hitting, but I didn't really understand the finer points of T-ball.

"Finer points," she laughed. "Sometimes the finer points of T-ball are trying to get the boys to run to the right base after they hit the ball, if, indeed, they run at all. You would be surprised at how many of them just stand there after they have hit the ball."

"Well, I hope we were able to get TJ to run after he hits the ball. Isn't that right, TJ?" I said, squeezing his shoulder.

"Yeah, dad."

The practice went fairly well with all fifteen of the boys getting a chance to bat several times and to play in the field. There were not a lot of fly balls caught, but that didn't seem to bother them. The most important thing was that they were having fun and learning a little bit about the fundamentals of baseball.

"Bye, Coach England," TJ said, when practice was over. "That was fun!"

During the hour TJ was practicing, Larry and Lenny were playing catch with a couple of other boys there with their younger brothers. They were a little reluctant to leave their new friends until I reminded them it would be nearly lunchtime when we got back to the house. I was nearly trampled as they ran to the van.

Lunch was almost ready when we returned home. Joel and John were in his bedroom playing one of the many video games the boys had accumulated. I could tell they were having fun from the giggles coming from the room as I went in my room to wash up. Chris was outside playing with Samson. He was tossing a baseball into the air and hitting it. Samson was acting as his outfielder by chasing down the balls and bringing them back to Chris. I watched this for a minute or so before calling him to come get washed for lunch. I was impressed how well he was hitting the ball. I think Samson needed the rest as well.

John joined us for lunch. He fit right in with the Johnson clan in the eating department. Everyone treated him as if he were one of the family. We had just finished eating and the boys had gotten all of the dishes put in the dishwasher when John's dad buzzed for us to open the gate.

We all went out to greet our guests as they drove up the drive. It looked like they had just returned from their shopping trip from all the packages that were visible in the back of the SUV. Pauline and the girls got out when Bruce stopped in front of the house. Larry and Lenny's eyes lit up as they saw Linda and Cassie.

"Pauline, it's good to see you again. Won't you come in for a cup of coffee?" I asked, shaking her hand.

"Thanks, that's very kind of you," she replied. "I must be getting old. I used to love going shopping, but anymore it really wears me out. I guess I didn't to have three like-minded shoppers to contend with."

"I know what you mean. When I take my five shopping, it usually turns into a real circus. Bruce, how did you survive?"

"Just barely," he said shaking his head. "I think the only reason I was invited along was so I could be the pack mule. I had to make two trips to the car to unload."

As we walked in the front door John ran up to his dad and gave him a hug before doing the same to his mom. "Dad, did you know Joel was in a plane crash?"

"What? No! Crane, is that true?" Bruce asked, wide-eyed.

"Well, not exactly. You see, on the way back from Houston the private plane had landing gear problems and we had to make a belly landing. It was scary, but no one was hurt. Lenny got a scraped elbow out of it is all."

"You know I saw on TV the other night where a plane had made an emergency landing at the airport, but I never in my wildest dreams thought about it being you folks. One of the stations showed pictures of it from their news helicopter," Bruce said.

"Yeah, it is not something I want to repeat," I said, as we took our seats in the family room.

Hildy appeared with the coffee and cups. As she finished pouring the coffee the twins came in the patio door and stood looking at us. I knew they wanted to ask something and were trying to work up the courage to do so.

"Dad ..." Larry started.

"Can we ... ah ... can we take Linda and Cassie and show them the lake?" Lenny blurted out.

"I'm sorry, son, not without an adult. Those steps down to the lake are too steep," I said, seeing their faces drop. "Why don't you go see if Hildy will let you have a cupcake? I know she baked some while we were gone this morning."

The consolation prize was enough for their faces to perk back up. I think the mention of cupcakes, although made in a voice I was sure could not be heard by the others, immediately got transmitted to them via kid telepathy and all nine of them converged on Hildy with such pleading looks on their faces that she couldn't refuse them.

We chatted over our coffee while the kids enjoyed the cupcakes. When they finished their snack, Bruce and Pauline rounded up their four and said their goodbyes. Although I could see Joel was beginning to tire, he insisted on walking John to the car to say goodbye to him. Joel gave John a quick hug and whispered something in his ear before saying goodbye to Bruce and Pauline.

Before they left, John asked, "Can Joel come watch me play soccer next Saturday?"

"Oh, I'm sorry, son. We have to go to a wedding in Fredericksburg next Saturday. Maybe the next week," I said.

As the Gordiniers drove down the driveway, I told Joel he needed to go in the house and rest. He didn't resist and leaned against me as we made our way back into the house.

"I like to have John come over," Joel said. "He makes me feel good."

"I'm glad you have such a good friend. By the looks of it he enjoys coming to visit you too."

Joel went to rest and the other boys went back outside to play a little baseball. I went to talk to Hildy. She had been acting a little strange and I was beginning to worry about her. I was afraid the stress of Joel's hospital stay topped off with our airplane incident had taken their toll on her. After all, she was not a young woman anymore.

I was just about to ask her if anything was wrong when she said, "Crane, I would like to have the evening off. Some friends and I would like to go out for the evening."

"Of course, the boys and I can manage by ourselves for the evening," I said. "You go and enjoy yourself. You certainly deserve some time off. You work much too hard and we don't let you know how much we appreciate everything you do for us."

"Thanks, Crane, taking care of those boys is a labor of love for me. They are the children and grandchildren my late husband Emilio and I could never have," she said, with just a hint of a tear in her eyes.

I decided not to ask what I had intended to ask when I came in. Instead, I decided to go for a swim. When the boys saw me dive in the pool they all headed back inside to change and join me. We had played in the pool for about 45 minutes when Joel came out with Samson and sat in one of the poolside chairs. Maybe next week I'll ask Dr. Greene if it would be all right for Joel to get into the pool if he feels strong enough.

From time to time one of the boys would climb out of the pool and go sit beside Joel and pet Samson for a while before rejoining the rest of us. It seemed like there was an unspoken rotation of the boys visiting Joel.

"Hey, guys, what would you like for supper?" I asked, after we all climbed out of the pool. "Hildy is going out with friends this evening so we are on our own. Do you want me to start the grill and fix some hamburgers and hotdogs?"

"Yeah! Hamburgers! Hotdogs!" was the unanimous cry. Even Samson gave his woof of approval.

I started the grill while the boys went in to shower the chlorine off and then I went in the house to fix the hamburgers. I figured if I made six large burgers and twelve hotdogs, that would be enough to stave off their starvation. After I got everything ready to go, I also went to take a shower.

The boys were waiting impatiently for me when I emerged from my bedroom.

We were just starting to take all of the fixings outside when the gate buzzer sounded. The security camera showed a late model Chevrolet waiting to enter. I activated the speaker and inquired what the visitor wanted and was informed by the gentleman sitting in the driver's seat that he was here to pick up Hildegard. I chuckled to myself and pushed the button to open the gate. No one ever called Hildy, Hildegard.

"Chris, go knock on Hildy's door and tell her someone is here for her," I told him, just as she entered the kitchen. "Never mind, son."

"Wow!" TJ said when he saw Hildy. "You look pretty."

"Thank you, TJ," Hildy said, leaning over to give him a squeeze.

"And smell good, too," he added.

The front doorbell rang and all of the boys took off to see who was there. "Guys, remember your manners," I said, following behind them.

When I opened the door, a tall, handsome man stood there. His once blond hair was peppered with white giving him a very distinguished appearance. The bright blue eyes under heavy eyebrows sparkled as he extended his hand.

"Hello, I'm Manfred Strasser. I'm here to pick up Hildegard."

"Crane Johnson, please come in," I said, shaking his hand. "Oh, and these young boys staring at you are my sons."

"I have heard all about you," he said, shaking each one of their hands as I introduced them.

"Who's Hildegard?" TJ whispered.

"That's Hildy, son," I said.

"But why does he call her Hildegard?" he asked.

"Because that is my full name, little one," Hildy said as she joined us and patted him on the head.

"Oh," TJ said, still a bit confused.

We watched as Manfred escorted Hildy to the car and opened the door for her before walking around and getting in. As they drove off, Hildy waved goodbye to the boys.

"Does Hildy have a date, dad?" Joel asked.

"I guess you might call it that, son. She is going out with some friends tonight and I guess Mr. Strasser is her date."

As we went back inside I told them I needed help in taking all of the dishes and condiments out to the patio table and assigned each of them tasks so everything would be ready when the burgers and hotdogs were cooked.

I put the meat on the grill which was absolutely perfect for grilling burgers. I went to get the rest of the food out of the refrigerator and the buns. It was going to be a rather simple meal with carrot and celery sticks and of course potato chips. I grabbed the vegetable sticks and a gallon of milk and asked TJ to carry the potato chips and Lenny to carry the buns.

The boys had done a great job of setting the table. They had set out the catsup, mustard, pickles, pickle relish and even brought the sliced cheese to make cheeseburgers.

It wasn't long before our impromptu picnic was ready. The first round consisted of the burgers, but it wasn't long before they were ready for the second round of hotdogs. We ate all but two of the hotdogs which pleased Samson. He got to eat the leftovers. Normally he didn't get to be fed from the table scraps, but tonight I made an exception.

About an hour after supper, the boys started asking what they were going to have for a snack. There were still some cupcakes left from this morning's ravaging by the boys and their guests and with some ice cream it seemed to satisfy them.

After the boys brushed their teeth and I tucked them in bed, I decided to sit up and read for a while and I guess, deep down to wait up for Hildy. It was about 12:30 when I saw the headlights of a car shine in the front windows as it drove up the driveway. I felt a little guilty.

It wasn't very long before the front door opened and Hildy and Manfred walked in.

"Oh, Crane, I didn't think anyone would be up. I was going to make some coffee. Would you like a cup?" a startled Hildy asked.

"If you have some decaf, I would like a cup. I guess I got wrapped up in my book and I lost track of time," I lied, not about the coffee but about the book.

"Come in the kitchen and I'll lay out some cookies the boys haven't discovered yet," she said with a smile.

Manfred and I sat at the table and talked while Hildy busied herself with the coffee. I found out he was a retired Air Force colonel. He had been retired about ten years and that his wife died about three years ago. He was now living in New Braunfels in a townhouse. He had moved back from California to his birthplace. He had one son, unmarried, who lived in Chicago and taught at a university.

"How did you meet Hildy?" I asked him.

"We went to school together in New Braunfels so many years ago. We even dated a couple of times. But, alas, she only had eyes for Emilio after he moved into school," he teased. "I must admit he cut a rather dashing figure and had many a girl swooning at his feet."

"Manfred, you make him sound like Rudolph Valentino. He was a handsome man though," Hildy said wistfully. "Do you use cream and sugar?"

"Sugar, please."

We drank our coffee and chatted for maybe fifteen minutes before I decided I had intruded on them long enough and excused myself, reminding Hildy to set the house alarm before she went to bed.

I slept later than usual Sunday morning. That is until TJ jumped into my bed and wrapped his arms around my neck.

"I'm hungry," he said, kissing my cheek.

"You're always hungry," I said, tickling his ribs. "Let dad take a quick shower and I'll fix you some breakfast after you've washed your hands and face. How does that sound?"

"Okay," he giggled, taking off for his bedroom.

Hildy came down from her apartment on her way to church as the boys were sitting down to the breakfast I fixed of hash brown potatoes, two dozen scrambled eggs, two pounds of sausage and about a dozen and a half slices of toast. This was washed down by large glasses of milk and orange juice. I settled for coffee and some eggs and toast. After saying goodbye to the boys, Hildy headed out the door.

"Is Hildy going to get married and leave us?" Joel asked seriously.

"I don't think so, son. Mr. Strasser and she are just old friends," I said, hoping I was right.

It started raining shortly after breakfast so outdoor activities were out of the question. We spent the day with me reading to them or them playing videogames. They went exploring the upstairs after lunch. They had never spent much time up there because it wasn't long after it was finished that we had to take Joel to Houston. The campout they had when JR stayed overnight was the last time they has spent any real time there.

"Can we invite JR over again?" Chris asked.

"You know Benny and Bran are staying with JR, don't you?" I asked.

"Yeah, can they come too?" Joel piped up.

"I'll call Eric," I said.

After Eric asked JR and the others if they wanted to come visit and stay overnight and got their enthusiastic reply, he said he would bring them over in about half an hour.

When Eric arrived with the three boys, he asked me if I were insane wanting to have eight active boys in the house all night. I assured him we would be able to manage. When I asked him where his mom and dad were he said they were with Darcie helping with the last minute arrangements for the wedding.

"Why don't you stick around then? Maybe the sun will come out and we can go swimming with the boys. I hope they brought their suits," I said.

"Oh, yeah, I think they would go swimming in the rain if I'd let them. It did look like it was clearing off in the west as we drove over here."

It did clear off and the ten of us went swimming. I let Joel get in the pool as long as he promised me he would let me know when he started to get tired. The pool was full of happy laughing boys and two adults. TJ stayed close to Joel, showing him his new swimming skills that Becky Sue had taught him. It only took Joel about twenty minutes before I saw him climb out of the water and head for a chaise lounge where Samson joined him.

When it came time for supper neither Eric nor I felt like cooking so we decided to order some pizzas which met with enthusiastic approval from the boys. We decided four large, sixteen-inch pizzas and breadsticks would probably be enough to feed the ten of us. Eric volunteered to go pick up the pizzas and asked Bran if he would go along and help.

Usually it took about forty-five minutes round trip to the pizza place, but they were gone nearly an hour before they returned and I could see Eric was visibly upset. The boys immediately attacked the pizza boxes. The thirty-two pieces and the breadsticks seemed to evaporate before our very eyes.

We were just cleaning up the mess from our meal when Hildy returned. Instead of getting hugs from five boys, she received hugs from all eight.

"My goodness, so many handsome boys," Hildy said.

"Are you gonna get married?" TJ asked innocently.

"What makes you think I'm going to get married?"

"Well, you had a date. Don't you get married after you have a date?"

Hildy could barely stifle her snicker, "It's a little more complicated than that, little one. I could never leave my little TJ."

With that, TJ wrapped his arms around her waist and said into her stomach, "I'm glad. I thought you were gonna go away. I love you, Hildy."

"I love you too, son. I love all of my boys," Hildy said quietly, patting TJ on the back.

When I explained to Hildy that all of the boys would be spending the night and part of tomorrow, she suggested that I call Becky Sue and have her bring her sister with her in the morning so there would be two of them to watch the boys. I made the call and Mary Jane agreed to come with her sister in the morning.

The boys went off to play and I took Eric aside. I wanted to know why he was upset when he and Bran returned from getting the pizza.

"Crane, it takes a lot for me to get riled up but a couple of idiots at the pizza place made a racist remark when Bran and I were waiting to pick everything up. There was a man about 25 or so and a teenager. They said something like 'we don't let niggers in here' and I nearly went ballistic. The man was a little guy. He was the one who made the comment, but the teenager agreed with him and laughed. I went over to them and asked them to apologize to Bran for their remark. They laughed at me.

"Now, I'm pretty strong from lifting weights and I grabbed the man by the front of his shirt and lifted him up out of the booth he was sitting in until his head was nearly touching the ceiling. I asked him again to apologize and again he refused. So I dropped him. His feet were probably three feet off the floor and when he dropped his feet went out from under him and he fell on his butt.

"That was bad enough to have to have Bran insulted by a pimple-brained bigot, but then the manager came out and told us to take our pizzas and get out."

"I'll be damned," I said. "He didn't say anything about the racial slur the guy made?"

"No! In fact he was very solicitous of the bigot. That is the last time I ever get pizza there," he said angrily. "I don't know many people around here but everyone I know will hear about our treatment."

"I know a lot more and they too will hear of it. Hildy knows everyone and I'm sure she will be happy to spread the word. I won't do business with people who condone racism or people who do business with them," I said emphatically.

"I won't either."

"Come on, let's go see what kind of trouble the boys are getting into," I said, draping my arm across his shoulders.

CHAPTER 23

❀

I thought handling five boys was a chore, but eight of them was something else. They were all upstairs when Eric and I returned to the house. You could hear their laughing and chattering all over. Hildy just smiled and shook her head as we went up the stairs to join the boys.

Joel and TJ were sitting on the couch cheering Chris and Bran as they battled each other in a table tennis match. I was surprised Chris was able to hold his own against his much older opponent.

"Hey, you're supposed to let me win," Bran said. "I'm older than you."

"Right!" Chris said, as he started giggling so hard he was unable to return Bran's serve.

Larry and JR were matched up against Lenny and Benny in a boisterous game of foosball. They were laughing and shouting encouragement to each other and rooting against their opponents.

It was a noisy bunch of boys, but the important thing was they were enjoying each other and having the time of their lives. I was beginning to wonder if we would be able to calm them down enough for them to get to sleep sometime this evening. The fun continued until around eight o'clock when Hildy came upstairs to see how the boys were doing.

As soon as she arrived, the boys took it as a sign that a snack was not far off. They were right.

"Is anyone ready for a snack?" she asked, with a broad grin on her face.

This was followed by a thunderous chorus of, "YEAH!"

"Crane, Eric, I need your help to get things ready," Hildy said, as she turned and led the troops down the stairs. "Everybody wash your hands and then find a place at the kitchen table."

It was a good thing the house had multiple bathrooms or there would have been some crushed boys. Fortunately, they paired up and headed off to get washed up. Eric and I followed Hildy into the kitchen where she made us wash our hands in the kitchen sink. After we were suitably clean Hildy gave us our instructions on what she wanted us to do to prepare the snack quickly. She had filled eight bowls with vanilla ice cream and placed them in the freezer before she had come upstairs. Our job was to top each bowl with hot fudge sauce, chopped pecans and whipped cream. She had set up an assembly line so everything could be done quickly.

By the time the boys had returned displaying their freshly scrubbed hands to Hildy, we had set out the bowls and were beginning the assembly line process. It took us less than a minute to complete our job with Hildy doing the honors of placing the bowls in front of the boys and escaping with all of her fingers intact. I think the hot fudge sundaes were gone before the fudge had a chance to cool.

When the dishes were rinsed and placed in the dishwasher, Hildy stopped Bran. "Bran, you have really changed since I first saw you a month ago. I haven't heard you use a single swear word all the time you've been here. I'm proud of you," she said, giving him a hug.

"My foster mom doesn't like me to talk that way," he said shyly, before running off with the other boys.

"Mom says he is a changed young man. His whole attitude has turned around. He's happy and very protective of Benny. They are almost inseparable. He helps Benny deal with his separation from Tony," Eric said.

"It looks like Benny is doing well also. His hair is growing back nicely. I hope Joel's comes back soon. At least I hope he has some before school starts," I said.

Hildy went to her apartment and Eric and I went to check on the boys.

"Where are they all going to sleep?" Eric asked.

"Well, I hadn't given it too much thought. We have six beds I'm sure can hold them all. I suppose we ought to ask them what they want to do," I said.

When we did ask they were a little surprised. They hadn't given it any thought either until JR piped up, "Can we camp out like we did last time?"

"Oh, you mean sleep in the three beds up here? But it might be a little crowded for the eight of you. The last time there were only six of you," I said.

"Yeah, but if we shoved them all together they would be big enough," Chris answered.

"Okay, Eric and I will shove the beds together while some of you start getting your showers taken. I think you will have to shower in shifts. I don't think there is enough hot water for all of you to shower at the same time."

As the boys hurried off to start getting ready for bed Eric hollered to JR, "Don't forget to brush your teeth."

"That goes for the rest of you, too." I added.

We finished getting the bedroom rearranged about the time the first group of boys emerged smelling clean and dressed for bed. Chris asked if they could watch a video before they went to bed and I agreed. Joel was tired so he climbed into the triple queen size bed. He could still see the TV if he wanted to watch. Soon the rest of the freshly scrubbed boys made their appearance.

Chris selected *Abbott & Costello Meet the Keystone Cops* and popped it into the VCR. I have always been a fan of the duo and have a fairly large collection of their films. This was one of my favorites. Absolutely no redeeming social value but hysterically funny slapstick comedy.

Eric and I watched for a while with the boys before he said it was time for him to get back to his house. He figured his folks would be wondering where he was. He said goodbye to all of the boys.

I walked him out to his car. Saying I would see him at work tomorrow, we embraced for a moment before he got in his car and drove away. I watched his car all the way to the gate leaving the property.

When I went back in to check on the boys I could tell they were beginning to get sleepy. Benny's eyes were closed and only popped open when the others laughed at some of the antics on the screen and then quickly closed. I went over to him, picked him up and laid him down on the bed.

"I'll take care of him," Bran said, and laid down beside him.

The tape only lasted a few more minutes so it wasn't long before all of the boys had crawled in bed. They arranged themselves in informal pairs, Joel and TJ, Bran and Benny, Larry and Lenny and the final pairing of Chris and JR. The bed was full of sleepy but happy boys.

It had been a while since I had to get up to an alarm and it startled me when it went off. Grudgingly, I got up and started getting ready to go to work. Hildy was already up preparing breakfast when I entered the kitchen for my morning cup of coffee.

"Do you think we have enough food in the house to feed them all?" I asked, pouring myself a cup of coffee.

"It's going to be touch and go," she said laughing. "I'm scrambling two dozen eggs and fixing a couple pounds of hash brown potatoes and bacon. If it takes more than one loaf of bread for toast I'm in trouble. Maybe I should fix a couple tubes of biscuits and put out some jam."

"Do you gotta go to work today, daddy?" TJ asked, as he squeezed under my arm and onto my lap.

"Yes, little one," I said, giving him a hug and a kiss on the cheek. "Daddy has a business to run for a couple more weeks then I'll be home almost all the time. How come you are up so early? Breakfast is not even ready yet."

"I didn't want you to leave before I got to see you," he said, snuggling into my chest.

"How would you like a glass of orange juice while daddy finishes his coffee?"

"Okay."

The warmth of his little body against my chest filled my soul with an overwhelming sense of joy that brought tears to my eyes. I don't know what I would do if these boys were not in my life. They make me whole.

When I finished my coffee I suggested we go wake his brothers and guests as Hildy almost had breakfast ready. He threw his arms around my neck and I carried him up the stairs to the mass bed. Samson met us at the top of the steps. I didn't realize he had spent the night up here with the boys. He had made himself scarce with all the noise the boys were making earlier last evening. He must have joined them after they all went to bed.

Samson helped rouse the boys by jumping up on the bed and barking. He also licked Joel's ear causing him to giggle before he rolled out of bed, soon followed by the others.

"Go wash your hands. Hildy will have breakfast ready by the time you get to the table," I said. That started them off in a hurry.

I went to talk with Hildy while the boys were washing up. I wanted to know if she was going to be okay with all the boys here since they were staying until this afternoon.

"Well, I'm going to have to go grocery shopping before lunch. Five boys eat a lot but eight eat an awful lot more. I'm sure with both Mary Jane and Becky Sue here today we won't have any problems. They will probably be outside most of the day swimming or playing ball or something," Hildy said.

As the boys arrived in the kitchen, I gave them each a hug before I left for the office. I hadn't gone far down the road from the house when I passed Mary Jane and Becky Sue heading for the house.

It was almost strange being in the office again. Carol was not at her desk when I opened the door to my office. What was waiting for me was a mountain of paperwork. I decided that before I could face it, I needed to get a cup of coffee. On the way to the break room where the coffee pot was located I met Carol coming out.

"Good morning, Crane. Welcome back. How's Joel?" she asked.

"He's doing fine, but still a little weak. I see you have my day planned out with all that paper on my desk. Thanks a lot," I said. "When Foster comes in, I think we need to meet to bring me up to speed on the projects."

"Okay, I'll tell him. Most of that paper is for your information only. The small pile on the right side of your desk is the one that needs your signature or approval."

I grabbed my coffee and started wading through the papers that required my attention. When Foster arrived we spent the rest of the morning and part of the afternoon going over the status of each project. He had several recommendations on moving people between projects to better utilize talents and to move projects along that were lagging behind their schedules. We didn't even take time out for a lunch break. Instead we had sandwiches delivered from the deli down the street.

I did finish all the important paperwork Carol had laid out for me and still had time to call Dr. Adams to see if he would talk to all five of the boys about our airplane incident. He agreed saying it would be helpful in Joel's treatment as well. After the call, I said to heck with it and left the office for home.

I saw the Land Rover in front of the house as I drove up the lane. Alan and Ethel were probably here to pick up their boys.

"Hi daddy," TJ said, around a mouthful of chocolate cake.

All eight of the boys were sitting around the kitchen table enjoying their afternoon snack of chocolate cake and a glass of milk. Alan and Ethel were sitting on the stools pulled up to the breakfast bar drinking cups of coffee. Alan was looking with envy at the cake the boys were eating but he knew his wife would object if he asked for some.

I greeted the Levins and sat down beside them. "How are the wedding plans coming along?"

"Fine, I guess," Ethel said. "I'm glad we only have one daughter. I don't think I could stand going through this more than once. I'm glad it's only a small wedding."

"Yeah, small in size, but not in cost," Alan added.

"Oh hush, you know you'd do anything for your daughter," she said, emphasizing your.

"It doesn't look like I'll have that problem. I know I'm a glutton for punishment taking on these five boys but adding a girl to the mix is definitely not in the cards," I laughed.

By this time the boys had finished their snack and Mary Jane and Becky Sue joined us from the family room. After my boys put their plates in the dishwasher they came and gave me a hug and kiss before running outside to play.

"Don't go too far," Ethel said to her boys. "We'll be leaving in a few minutes."

"Okay, gram," Benny said, as he disappeared out the patio door.

It wasn't long before our guests left, much to the regret of all the boys. Joel appeared to have overtaxed himself. It was even more apparent after supper. I was sitting on the couch reading the newspaper when he sat down beside me and leaned up against my shoulder. I wrapped my arm around him and kissed the top of his head.

"Am I ever going to get well, dad? I get so tired. I can't do anything," he sobbed quietly.

"Yes, son, you're going to get well. It's just going to take time. You've only been out of the hospital a few days. I know it's hard for you to understand. Every day you are going to get stronger. Soon you will be able to play with your brothers just like you used to."

"I don't want to be sick. Why did I have to get sick?"

"Joel …" I said, my voice cracking. "If there were any way that I could have been the one who got sick instead of you, I would have without giving it a second thought. You've been through more in your short life than anyone should endure in a lifetime. I wish I had some magic that would make your leukemia go away as if it had never happened. Unfortunately, I don't. All I can do is love you with all my heart and do my best to protect you."

"I know, dad. Sometimes I get so sad."

"That's understandable, son. Whenever you feel that way I want you to promise me you will come talk to me or, if I'm not here, talk to Hildy."

"I promise," he mumbled.

We sat there cuddling for maybe twenty more minutes before the other boys joined us. It was a squeeze but all six of us ended up on the couch. My newspaper was long forgotten.

On Tuesday I only spent a half a day at the office. The twins and Chris had baseball practice in the afternoon. I had not told the twins I would be coaching their team. They didn't even tumble to it when I put on my coaching clothes.

Joel decided to stay at home and read. I thought it was a good idea. I didn't want him to overexert again today. TJ was torn between staying home with Joel or going to practice with the other boys. Going to practice with us won out. On the way to the practice field we stopped and filled the cooler with sodas and ice. We also picked up enough cookies to satisfy the Cookie Monster on *Sesame Street*.

Chris' team practiced first as they did last time. I chatted with Coach Leonard for a little while before practice started. When TJ and the twins weren't playing catch or cheering Chris, they were shagging foul balls. TJ especially like running after the balls fouled off to the right side of the field where we were watching.

Practice only lasted an hour today for Chris since his team had a game scheduled for Friday as did the twins' team. Thank goodness they weren't scheduled to play each other's team. When his practice was over, I told him to invite his teammates to have some of the sodas and cookies we had brought. That was certainly a big hit.

Peter Hammond showed up with his son about fifteen minutes before our team was to begin practice. The rest of the team straggled in until most of them had arrived. None of them looked too enthusiastic about being here. I told the twins to go round up their team and bring them to the dugout. They looked at me funny, but did what I asked.

When everyone had gathered around I said, "Hi, guys, let me introduce myself. My name is Crane Johnson and I'm going to be your new coach. Peter Hammond here is going to be helping me."

"Really, dad?" the twins said in unison. "Cool!"

"But ... but where's Mr. Latimer?" one of the boys asked.

"He isn't able to coach anymore. Now I know we have a game to play on Friday, so we have a lot of work to do. The first thing I need to do is find out what all of your names are," I said, and began going up to each one of the boys and shaking his hand as he told me his name. Peter did the same.

We had a much happier practice. No one was brought to tears, but there was a lot of laughing and we practiced the fundamentals over and over until everyone was tired. The hour seemed to fly by. We could have used more time. Every coach wants more time to practice. It would not have done much good because the boys were showing their fatigue. They were ready for the sodas and cookies when we ended practice.

As everyone was finishing up their snack, Ronnie, one of the older boys, came up to Peter and me and said, "I'm sure glad y'all are coaching now. I was going to tell Coach Latimer I was going to quit playing. I didn't like the way he treated us. He always made Harry cry before practice was over. He wanted to quit, but his dad wouldn't let him. Now he doesn't want to quit. Neither do I."

"Thank you, Ronnie. This is a game we are playing, and games are supposed to be fun. Too many adults forget that," I said, patting him on the back.

It was supper time when we got back home. We just had time to change our clothes and get washed up before Hildy had the food on the table. Everyone had to tell Joel all about practice and the twins had to tell him I was their new coach.

After I got the boys in bed, I took a look at my schedule for the rest of the week and found it to be rather full. TJ was scheduled for his T-ball practice on Wednesday; the appointment with Dr. Adams was on Thursday; Chris and the twins had ball games on Friday; Darcie and Mel's wedding was on Saturday and finally TJ had a T-ball game on Sunday afternoon.

I guess I had better get used to having a full schedule with five active boys and Joel was not even able to be involved this summer. It looks like I'm turning into a stereotypical 'soccer dad'. I wouldn't have it any other way.

Wednesday I finally got through all the paperwork that was piled on my desk. I even had time to take Foster and Carol to lunch to thank them for all the hard work they had done in my nearly-month long absence. I left the office around 2:30 so I could be home in time to take TJ to his practice. When I got home I found Chris, Larry and Lenny in the back yard with TJ working on his hitting the ball off the tee. I watched for a few minutes from the patio door before I went out to interrupt them. Actually, TJ was hitting the ball quite well and he even ran to the right base after he hit it. I chuckled at remembering his coach say that was a problem with some of the kids.

Chris decided to stay home with Joel and play video games, but Larry and Lenny wanted to go to TJ's practice. I think one of the reasons was the sodas and cookies we were going to take.

"Let's go, dad," TJ said, grabbing his helmet. "I got my cup on."

"That's good," I said, chuckling.

Practice went very well. TJ even caught two fly balls when he was in the outfield. He missed a few too, but that didn't matter to him. All he could talk about were the ones he caught. He even had to tell Hildy all about them when we got home. She gave him a big hug and told him how proud she was of him.

I hadn't told the boys about their appointment with Dr. Adams tomorrow so after supper I called them together to tell them what was going to happen.

"You guys know Joel goes to see Dr. Adams about every month. Well, tomorrow he wants to talk to all of you when Joel goes. Joel can tell you what happens when he sees Dr. Adams, but all he wants to do is to talk to you. No needles or medicines," I said. "He's not that kind of a doctor."

They took the news without batting an eye. I guess after being around doctors all the time while Joel was in the hospital it just seemed natural they would go see another one. It never ceased to amaze me how resilient and adaptable these wonderful boys were.

Regardless, I was a little nervous when we got to Dr. Adams' office on Thursday. Dr. Adams greeted Joel and then turned to the others and asked them their names. He made them feel very much at ease. I was anything but, as he escorted them into his therapy room.

It was a very long forty-five minutes I spent in the waiting room looking through magazines and at my watch. A couple of times I thought I heard laughter coming from the room, but I wasn't sure if it was just my imagination.

Finally, the door opened and the boys came streaming out followed by Dr. Adams. TJ ran to me and started telling me all about what they had talked about in the session. "Whoa, little one, you can tell me all about it on the way home. Right now, Dr. Adams wants to talk to me. You guys behave yourselves."

Dr. Adams closed the door behind us before he said, "Mr. Johnson, those are five very remarkable young men."

"I know. I am very proud of them."

"Although each of them expressed fear at what happened on the airplane, no one seemed to have any lasting trauma from it. In fact they seem to find some humor in the situation. I don't believe they will have any problems as a result. However, if any of them should show signs of unnatural fear or have recurring nightmares, I would like to know about it so we could deal with it quickly. I doubt that will be the case. They seem to draw on a collective strength. One thing they know for certain is they are loved and are secure with you," he said.

"They are loved, that's for sure," I replied.

"Keep doing what you are doing with them and I don't think they will have any problems."

"Thanks doctor," I said, as I left his office.

"I'm hungry, dad," TJ said, wrapping his arms around my waist.

"You're always hungry," I said.

"Yeah, I know," he giggled.

"Well then, I suppose we ought to stop at the Dairy Queen."

"Yeah," he said, dragging me toward the door.

Everyone decided to have a Blizzard: two had Oreo cookie, two had toffee and one had chocolate chip cookie dough. I had a small cone.

When we got home, there was still time to play before Hildy would have supper ready, so after we all changed our clothes, I took the boys outside to practice. Three of them had games tomorrow afternoon so I took a bat and hit them some fly balls. TJ wanted to play too so I hit him some soft ones. After a while I gave them some batting practice. They seemed to be doing pretty good.

After supper I called Eric's house to see if the boys would like to go to the games tomorrow. I thought I might give Eric's parents a break. He thought it would be a good idea and offered to have Mary Jane bring them to the ballpark. I gave him the time and directions for her to follow to get there if she didn't know where it was. I also told him I would bring them back to our house for supper. I would grill some hamburgers and we could eat out on the patio. I invited him to come by also. He accepted.

Hildy left to go to her church meeting and I suspect to see Manfred. I was happy for her finding someone her own age to be with. I just hoped, like the boys, that she didn't leave us. She was such an important part of the family.

When I got home from work on Friday, Chris and the twins were dressed in their uniforms and ready to go to the ballpark. I quickly changed and we headed out. Joel decided to come with us today so I loaded a folding lounge chair so he would have something comfortable to sit in to watch the games. Samson started to put up a fuss about being left behind. I saw the look in the boys' eyes, which meant we couldn't leave him, so I got his leash, he jumped into the van and we were on our way. I told Becky Sue to take the rest of the afternoon off before we left.

We had a thoroughly enjoyable afternoon. Chris' team won their game by one run, 10 to 9. My team was not as lucky. We lost, 8 to 4, but everyone tried their best and I was satisfied the team had the potential to win some games before the season was over. Each of the twins had two RBI's so their day was not a complete loss.

Mary Jane had arrived with her boys just before Chris' game started. They were enthusiastically greeted by everyone. I hadn't told the boys they were going to come to the game or that they would be going home with us.

Joel tolerated our outing much better than I expected. He did spend most of his time in the lounge chair but did walk around some when Samson got restless. Samson was not the happiest camper being on the leash. He rarely had to wear it. He had free run of the house and yard since our property was completely fenced. He did enjoy the attention he got from all of the boys who came over to pet him.

It's a good thing the van would seat nine. It was loaded down with eight boys, Samson and me. When we got home I told the boys about our trip to Fredericksburg tomorrow to attend Darcie's wedding. I told them they would have to wear their best clothes.

"Where's Freddyberg?" TJ asked.

"Fredericksburg is a town about seventy miles away. That means we'll have to leave just before noon so we can be there in time for the wedding at two o'clock," I said. "Okay now, run change your clothes."

I was getting the fire going in the grill when Eric arrived. JR was playing soccer with the other boys in the side yard. When he saw his dad he ran to him and gave him a hug which was followed by seven more from the other boys and one more from me.

Hildy came out and started setting up everything for our picnic. "Crane, I hope you don't mind, but I invited Manfred to come tonight."

"No, of course not, he's welcome anytime. You're part of this family too," I said.

The fire in the grill was just about right to begin the burgers when Manfred arrived. I hadn't noticed his arrival until he came out of the house with Hildy carrying a tray with twenty-four burgers ready for the grill. Hildy was carrying three packages of buns that she added to the table that was already loaded down with all kinds of condiments. She had fixed potato salad, baked beans, carrot and celery sticks, radishes, chips and salsa.

As soon as the first batch of burgers hit the grill there were eight boys crowding around looking as if they were starving. Hildy quickly shooed them away to get cleaned up for supper. The burgers were not quite done when the boys returned.

I went to the table to grab a soda when I heard TJ ask Manfred, "Are you gonna marry Hildy?"

"Why do you ask that?" Manfred asked, a little stunned.

"Because I don't want Hildy to leave me," he said. "I don't want you to marry Hildy."

"There is one thing I know, TJ, and that is Hildy would never leave you no matter what. She loves you way too much," he said.

I didn't hear any more of the conversation because I had to get back to the burgers. I didn't want them to burn with eight hungry boys waiting on them. It wasn't long before the meal was ready and the boys made short work of filling their plates to overflowing. I was so full by the time I had finished eating the main part of the meal, I couldn't eat any of the cherry cobbler Hildy had fixed. That didn't stop the boys, however.

Despite their pleas that their friends spend the night again, Eric insisted his charges go home with him to sleep. A round of hugs for all as they left for home and then I sent my sons to get their showers taken and get ready for bed. We had a long day ahead of us tomorrow.

CHAPTER 24

I don't know what I would do without Hildy. I had totally forgotten about wedding presents for Darcie and Mel with everything that was going on in my life. Hildy saved me. She knew Darcie had registered with Foley's and she had purchased, with her household credit card, china place settings, crystal and silverware for me and the boys to give to the happy couple. We didn't physically have the presents in hand. Instead Hildy gave us cards we signed which would be exchanged for the actual gifts by the bride and groom. This made it so much easier on everyone concerned, especially the mother of the bride whose job it was to take care of all the wedding presents.

Over breakfast I tried to explain to the boys what was going to happen today. None of them had ever been to a wedding and I wanted them to know how to behave. I also wanted Joel to know he was to wear his surgical mask since we would be around so many new people. I didn't want him to pick up some bug with his weakened immune system.

June 24th was turning out to be a gorgeous day for a wedding. It was going to be a little warm this afternoon. The weatherman forecast the temperature to reach 92 degrees by late afternoon. I hoped the church was air conditioned. If it wasn't there would be a lot of sweaty people in the church.

I let the boys play as long as possible and still have time for lunch and to get dressed. It had been a while since any of them had worn their sports jackets. I had them try them on to make sure they still fit. They did but just barely. All of the boys had grown and put on weight since they became my sons. It looked like we would be going clothes shopping before school started. They did look handsome in their dress clothes even though they were none too happy to have to wear them. I didn't make them wear the jackets and ties on the trip to Fredericksburg. Hildy put them all on hangers and hung them in the back of the van.

After making sure everyone had gone to the bathroom, we took off for the wedding shortly after 12:30. It was going to be over an hour's drive to Fredericksburg so I had checked out a book on tape from the library. It was *The Secret of Pirate's Hill*, one of the Hardy Boy mysteries. I thought it would hold their attention most of the way up and back. It worked. They were enthralled by the story. It didn't hurt that Hildy hauled out some peanut butter cookies about half way there. We didn't pack any milk so they had to make do with bottled water. At least it would dry if they spilled any.

We found the church without any trouble due to the excellent directions Darcie had provided along with the wedding invitation. It was a small church on the outskirts of Fredericksburg in a beautiful hill country setting. Between Hildy and me we got the boys into their coats and ties. Joel donned his surgical mask and we headed toward the church doors. Once inside I was pleased to note the place was well air conditioned.

The inside of the church was very nice. It was plain but at the same time elegant. The pews were wooden but were comfortable even though they had no cushions. There was probably room for a hundred or so worshipers to fit comfortably in the pews. The pulpit was a simple raised platform with a lectern. Behind it was the area for the choir and behind them was a small pipe organ. All in all, it was a very pleasant, unostentatious place of worship, unlike some of the more ornate churches in San Antonio.

We were escorted to a pew by one of the ushers, a handsome young man, who I learned later one of Mel's cousins. Since we were a little early we were seated in the third pew from the front behind where Darcie's family members would sit. Hildy sat on one end and I sat on the other with the five boys in between us. Joel was seated beside me. He objected slightly when I told him he would have to remove his ever present hat when we entered the church. He leaned into me trying to bury his hairless scalp in my shoulder. I tried to soothe him by placing my arm around him and telling him nobody cared that he didn't have any hair.

A few minutes after we sat down, Eric arrived, leading JR, Benny and Bran to the pew right in front of us. This seemed to enliven everyone as the boys began whispering to each other. Even Joel seemed to forget about his baldness for the time being. The whispering began to get louder after a while. It took Eric, Hildy and me to quiet the boys down as the organist took her seat and began playing. For being a small pipe organ it certainly sounded like a much larger one. It filled the little church with its music.

Mel and his two groomsmen took their places as the preacher took his. The bride's maids, flower girl and ring bearer also made their way to the front of the church. Ethel was escorted to the front pew before the organist began the "Bridal Chorus" from Lohengrin. Everyone stood and turned to watch the bride approach from the rear of the church. As I turned I felt a little body squeeze by me. When I looked down there was TJ sticking his head out into the aisle to see what everyone was looking at. I grabbed hold of his shoulder fearing he would completely step out of the pew.

Darcie was dressed in a long ivory gown that looked like it had pearls sewn on the bodice. She walked slowly up the aisle on the arm of her father. TJ looked up and me and mouthed something I couldn't hear over the organ music. When I leaned down, he repeated, "Who's that lady wearing the mask?"

"That's Darcie," I said in his ear chuckling, at his reference to Darcie's veil being a mask.

As Darcie came next to our pew, TJ said, "Hi, Darcie."

She turned her head toward him and smiled while I blushed and steered him back to his seat. Eric barely controlled his snicker when he saw my embarrassment but patted TJ on the head as he returned to his seat next to his brothers. The rest of the wedding went off without a hitch. Darcie Marie Levin became Mrs. Melvin Eugene Glenn.

Except for TJ's minor lapse of proper etiquette, I was very proud of the way the boys acted throughout the nearly forty-five minutes they had to sit quietly in the pews.

After the wedding ceremony, everyone was invited to the reception at a local VFW hall. When we got there the band was just setting up and the caterer was readying the food which immediately caught the eyes of the boys. I restrained them saying we had to wait for Darcie and Mel to arrive. That didn't go over that well, but they grudgingly agreed.

Soon the newlyweds arrived and the reception line formed. We got in line about in the middle of the seventy or so people who were at the wedding. As we were approaching the happy couple I told the boys it would be proper if they gave Darcie a kiss on the cheek and they should shake hands with everyone else.

"Daddy said we could kiss you on the cheek," TJ said, when it was his turn to greet Darcie.

"Only if I can give you one, too," Darcie replied, as she leaned down and gave TJ a kiss.

The other boys followed suit. We shook hands with Mel, the Levins and Mel's parents. Mel's mother was a very heavy woman whose face still showed the beauty that she was in her younger and slimmer days.

"Oh, you're the Johnson my son has told me about," she said, as I introduced myself to her. "I think it is very courageous of you to take on raising five boys."

"Thank you, they are the light of my life," I said.

As I introduced each of the boys to her she hugged them to her ample bosom which almost made them disappear, especially TJ.

Going through the reception line I was able to meet Cindi Sessions. She was so helpful in getting Benny settled in the Levins' home. I was looking forward to meeting her and to thank her for everything she had done. She stuck out her neck for a complete stranger so a child could have a good home to live in. She wasn't afraid to cut through the bureaucracy and do the right thing. I have been very critical of Child Protective Services, but she was one of the good guys in a thoroughly broken system.

We found an empty table and sat down to wait for the cake-cutting ceremony to begin. Eric and his three charges came and sat down at the table next to us. We chatted for a moment before TJ whispered in my ear that he had to go to the bathroom. I looked around for the restrooms. At first I didn't see them but at last I spotted them just inside the front doors. When I told the rest of the boys I was going to take TJ to the restroom they all decided they needed to go as well. It must have been catching because Eric's three decided they had to go also. The ten of us trooped off to the restroom. Thankfully there was no one using it when we arrived.

There were two urinals and two stalls to be shared among the eight boys ranging in age from 6 to 15 years. Bran and Joel were tall enough to use the urinals, but the other boys had to use the toilets. TJ made a beeline for one of the stalls and made it just in time from the sounds of it.

After the boys washed their hands we returned to the tables. Hildy had been kind enough to save them for us. We had no more than sat down when the bride and groom approached the four tiered wedding cake for the cutting ceremony. It seemed like half of the guests rushed forward with cameras to take pictures. The boys watched in fascination as Darcie and Mel cut the cake and then fed each other a piece. Then came the part I know all of them were waiting for. We got in line to receive the cake, bridal mints and punch. They couldn't decide between the bride's cake which was white with white frosting and the groom's cake which was chocolate with chocolate frosting so they had a piece of each.

The band started playing while the refreshment line continued. A few couples started dancing while they waited to go through the line. As people finished their refreshments more and more of them started dancing. Then it was time for the bride and groom to dance and the floor cleared. After that it seemed like everyone danced with everyone else. Pretty soon, after they had consumed the cake, the boys started getting bored so I suggested to Hildy that we make our goodbyes to the happy couple and head back to Canyon Lake.

By the time we reached home the boys were becoming very restless and irritable. I could tell Joel was completely worn out. Although he objected, he didn't put up too much of a fight when I asked him to lie down for a while. We compromised by him agreeing to use one of the lounge chairs by the pool while the rest of us, except Hildy, changed into our swimsuits and took a dip in the pool. I made sure the large umbrella shaded him so his pale skin wouldn't get sunburned.

Sunday was very relaxed. The only thing on the schedule was TJ's T-ball game at two o'clock. I had never seen a T-ball game before. My only experience with it was the practice session last week. It was really something else to watch. I laughed until my sides were sore. A couple of the boys ran to third base after they hit the ball. One boy ran toward second base chasing the ball he had just hit. Some of them would hit the ball and then just stand there not running to first base. One boy just stood there with his bat on his shoulder and refused to swing at the ball on the tee.

I don't know what the score was or who was winning the game. All I knew was that TJ enjoyed himself and that was what mattered to me or to him.

My last week at the office was hectic. I spent most of my time in meetings with Gerald and Carlos making sure everything was ready and in order for the turn over of the business at the end of the week. There were all of those last minute details to take care of before I gave up ownership. The hardest part was making sure I received all of the profits generated by the company up through Friday when my ownership ended.

The week was also complicated by Joel's first chemotherapy treatment since he left the hospital. I was glad Dr. Greene could do it in his office. It took a little over two hours for the IV to complete and another half an hour before Sam allowed him to leave.

Thankfully, Joel's treatment didn't occur the same day that one of the boys had baseball practice. By the end of the week I didn't know if I were coming or going. With three different practices and then two games on Friday, I was worn out. The new management team had arrived mid-week and when I wasn't meeting with Carlos and Gerald I was meeting with them, going over everything I could think of they might need to know about the business.

On Saturday morning, John had a soccer game Joel wanted to attend so we packed up the van and all of the boys and I took off for the game. The soccer game was a time for me to relax. I could sit in the bleachers, as hard as they were, and watch the game and four of my sons as they ran along the sidelines cheering John. Joel sat with me. The chemotherapy had sapped his strength but that didn't take away from the enjoyment of watching his friend on the field. John was really pretty good. He wasn't the biggest kid on the field but he was quick and could control the ball with his feet as good as or better than anyone else out there.

John's dad saw Joel and me sitting in the bleachers after a while and came up and sat beside us. He inquired as to Joel's health and we chatted for the rest of the match. You could tell he was proud of the way his son was playing from the way he cheered John on. Bruce seemed to have mellowed since I had talked with him last. He didn't make a single comment about the relationship between Joel and John. I gathered it may have partly resulted from the new preacher his church had hired. From the way he talked the new guy preached a much more tolerant attitude toward others who didn't believe as they did.

By the time the match was over Joel was completely exhausted. That did not stop him from wanting to talk to his friend. After Bruce had congratulated his son on his team's win, John ran to Joel. We gave them some space for a few minutes before I insisted that Joel and the rest of us head for home so he could get some rest.

TJ's T-ball game on Sunday afternoon was again a source of amusement. I know it is not nice to laugh at the youngsters but some of their antics were classic. However, some of the parents were obnoxious. They yelled and screamed at their sons when they didn't do everything right. I was ashamed of them. One father who was sitting near me was particularly obnoxious. My first instinct was to move away from his boorish behavior. Instead I moved closer to him. When he started yelling at the boy in the batter's box trying with little success to hit the ball off the tee, I pointedly asked him if that was his son.

"Yeah, the little shit never listens to me when I show him what to do," he said.

"How old is your son?" I asked.

"He just turned six."

"He must be one of the youngest kids on the team then."

"Yeah, but …" he started, I think seeing where I was going.

"Well, maybe he just needs a little time to develop. Maybe he needs a little encouragement instead of criticism. I've found that to be the case with my five sons," I said.

He looked a little ashamed. "I guess you're right. He's my only son and I want him to be good so badly."

When the game was over, TJ ran to me and jumped into my arms, all excited. "Did you have fun?" I asked.

"Oh, yeah! We won!" he said, his smile nearly splitting his face in two.

I noticed the son of the man with whom I had been talking approached his dad with his head down and a hint of a tear in his eyes. The boy was totally taken aback when his father picked him up, hugged him and told him he thought he did a good job. The boy's face lit up like it was Christmas, and he started telling his dad all about the game even though his dad had watched the whole thing.

Tuesday was the Fourth of July holiday. I remember my parents always made a big deal of it no matter where we were in the world. After consulting with Hildy, I invited a number of families to an afternoon barbeque and swim. It turned out to be a fairly large number of people: Eric and JR, Bruce and Pauline Gordinier with John and his three sisters, Harold Nicholas and Joey, Max and Janet Sutton with their son Billy, Jack and his family and finally Manfred Strasser. That was twenty-six people if everyone showed up. Mary Jane and Becky Sue were also invited but they had plans to be with their family.

Hildy started preparing food on Monday morning and I don't think she stopped until well after all our guests arrived. Most everybody insisted on bringing something for the barbeque. I let Hildy coordinate that. I was going to handle the meat to be put on the grill. She was going to do the side dishes and desserts. I cheated a little. I bought a couple of briskets at a smoke house in New Braunfels. I didn't have the time to tend to them for twenty-four hours while they slow cooked. All I would have to do was to put them on the warming rack in the grill and then slice them when they were ready. The other meats would be cooked from scratch on the grill.

On Monday, I went to the party supply store in New Braunfels to pick up folding tables and chairs. I also went to the grocery store for paper plates and plastic cutlery. We didn't have enough plates and utensils in the house to serve everyone.

Manfred arrived early on Tuesday morning, shortly after the boys and I had finished breakfast. He insisted on helping Hildy with the preparations of the day. She tried to dissuade him but he was adamant. It turned out he was a big help. He loved to cook and considered himself to be a gourmet cook. It wasn't long before the kitchen was humming with activity. The boys went to get dressed for the day, and I went to start setting up the tables and chairs.

Chris helped me set up the long tables while the twins and TJ helped arrange the folding chairs. Larry and Lenny did a good job of setting up the chairs. They were very precise in aligning the chairs around the tables. TJ was not so neat which caused the twins to straighten the chairs that TJ shoved up to the table. He only did a couple of chairs so it wasn't a burden on the twins.

I suggested to Joel that he remain inside and rest because it was going to be a long day and he would need all of his strength. I also asked him to let me know during the day if he was getting tired. I didn't want him to miss any of the fun, but I didn't want him to overexert himself and set back his recovery. He said he would. I gave him a hug and kissed his naked head.

After we got the tables and chairs set up, I started the grill and put the briskets on the warming rack before I went into the house to get the cut up chicken that had been marinating overnight. They would take the longest to grill compared to the bratwurst, hot dogs and hamburgers.

Our guests started arriving shortly before noon. John and his family were the first to arrive. Joel had been watching the picture from the gate security camera for some time before they arrived. As soon as he saw their car he was out to the front step waiting to greet them. His face lit up as he saw John peering out of the side window as they drove up. The twins were there also to greet Linda and Cassie. After we had greeted everyone, I directed Bruce where to park his car at the side of the house while Pauline took her covered dish into the kitchen to join the rest of the food. Rachel, the tomboy of the family, went to join Chris and TJ who were playing catch.

John and Joel walked into the house and sat down on the couch in the living room to talk. I was glad to see Joel was trying to conserve his energy so he could last most of the day.

Over the next half hour, the rest of the guests arrived. While I was greeting our guests, Manfred was tending the grill. He probably did a better job of it than I would have. Everything looked delicious when I went to check on it. The chicken was done to perfection and the brats were beginning to sizzle along with the hot dogs and hamburgers. Manfred took the briskets and began slicing them, placing the slices in a pan, covered them with sauce and placed it back on the warming rack.

By this time we had the majority of the kids hanging around just waiting to start eating. Hildy and the rest of the women started bringing all the food out and placed it on the tables. It fell to the men to corral the kids and see they washed their hands before they were allowed to eat. It looked like an awful lot of food when it was all spread out. The adults paired off with the kids seeing they got their plates filled before we filled our own.

The kids' table rang out with laughter as they pointed to each others' faces covered with barbeque sauce. It was all good-natured teasing and no one got their feelings hurt. The four girls didn't seem to be intimidated by the eleven boys. They gave as good as they got.

Everybody enjoyed the meal and, if anyone came away hungry, it was their own fault. As we were cleaning up the dishes, throwing away the trash and putting the leftovers away, Chris came up to me and asked if they could go swimming.

"I think you had better wait a while until your food settles. In about an hour we can all go swimming. Go play with your friends for now," I said, giving him a hug.

"Okay, dad," he said, and ran off to play with his friends.

With everyone's help we cleared the tables in no time. Hildy emerged from the house with large glasses of iced tea and bowls of lemon slices for those who liked lemon in their tea. To me, putting lemon in tea was a crime. If I wanted lemonade, that's what I would drink. But from the looks of it, I was a minority of one. Also the Southern tradition of sweet tea was an abomination to my way of thinking. It was so sweet it could give you diabetes just by looking at it. Hildy knew my preferences so the tea she brought was unsweetened but there was ample sugar for our guests to indulge themselves.

Manfred followed with glasses of lemonade for the kids that they quickly took off his hands. As TJ took his glass I saw him talking earnestly to Manfred. I wasn't close enough to hear what was being said, but when they finished talking Manfred gave TJ a hug and received a big smile in return.

Before long the women went inside leaving the men to watch the kids. It wasn't a difficult job because they were having so much fun playing tag. Their laughter echoed through the hills and out onto the lake almost forcing us to watch their antics. Joel and John sat watching the others with envy for a while before Joel asked if they could go in and play with his video games. I could see he was getting tired so I readily agreed.

I think it was almost exactly an hour when Chris came running up to me. I knew what he was going to ask so I just shook my head and said to all the kids, "Go get your swimsuits on but wait until there is an adult here before you get into the pool. Chris, you go show our guests where they can change. Show the girls upstairs."

"Come on, let's go. I'll show you," he said, and took off for the house.

Max and Bruce said they didn't swim but the rest of the men including Manfred all went in to change. Pauline, Carolyn and Janet were supervising the girls changing as well as getting changed themselves. Some of the boys were already changed and hurried past us as we made our way inside. I'm sure there were piles of boys' clothes all over the floors of the downstairs bedrooms.

I always thought our pool was pretty good sized until we got twenty people in it. Some of us were content to sit on the sides of the pool and let the kids enjoy themselves. A couple of the men usually were in with the kids giving them boosts into the air so they could cannonball back into the water. Manfred was in excellent shape for a man in his mid-fifties. You could tell he worked out and took care of himself.

After about an hour I decided to go into the house and check on John and Joel. The door was open to the bedroom when I approached. When I looked in I saw that Joel was asleep on the bed. John was sitting beside him with his hand resting on Joel's. As I walked in, John looked up at me. I could see a worried look on his face. I carefully sat down beside him and put my arm around him.

"Is Joel ever going to get better?" he asked quietly.

"Yes, son, but it's going to take some time," I said.

"I like him so much. I don't want him to be sick," he said, burying his face in my chest.

"I know. We would all give anything if he could be back to normal. He will. We just have to be patient. Joel needs our support to help him get well. I know he really appreciates that you didn't abandon him when he got sick."

"Oh, I could never do that. He's my best friend. It makes my stomach hurt that he's sick and I can't help him," he said, as I felt his tears beginning to drip on my bare chest. "I love him."

"Yes, I know you do."

I sat there for several minutes holding John before Joel started to stir.

"Hi, dad. Is something wrong?" he asked, looking at John in my arms.

"Nothing's wrong, son. How are you feeling?"

"Okay, I guess. Just tired."

"You guys want to come outside? I think Hildy should be about ready to serve dessert," I said

"Yeah, in a minute, dad, we'll be there."

I went to check with Hildy to see if she was indeed about ready to serve the desserts. She and two helpers were busy cutting the cakes, pies and brownies that covered the breakfast bar. As I entered the kitchen, she told me to grab a couple half-gallon containers of vanilla ice cream out of the freezer so they would start to soften. I was also told to take a stack of paper plates, plastic utensils and napkins out to the patio. Hildy and her helpers followed me with their hands loaded with the desserts.

It was amazing how fast thirteen kids could evacuate the pool as they saw the treats being brought out. The adults were only a little bit more dignified in their exit. I sent Chris into the house to bring the ice cream out while we got everything organized.

The rest of the afternoon went by quickly. I spent so much time talking to all of our guests that I really didn't have much time to talk to Eric. It seemed we were always surrounded by others. I did have a short conversation alone with Jack. He said he had submitted his papers to the police department to retire at the end of July. He had worked out an agreement with Collin Cupp and Independent Investigators to open a branch office in San Antonio. He just wondered if my offer of a retainer to do work for the foundation was still good. I assured him it was and I already had an assignment for him as soon as he got started.

Supper was a simpler affair consisting mainly of leftovers. The remaining brisket made excellent sandwiches and with more hamburgers and hotdogs everyone had plenty to eat. After everyone had their fill, we began sending the kids into the house to shower and get dressed before the fireworks began.

The hill our house was built on was one of the highest around the lake and commanded a view of almost every place that had fireworks planned. Shortly after nine the fireworks started. One of the subdivisions to our west in Spring Branch was the first to start their show. It had hardly gotten underway when the Canyon Lake Forest subdivision on the south side of the lake started their display. It was difficult for the kids as well as the adults to make up their minds which one to watch. To make it even more difficult, the marina started setting off their fireworks. We were literally surrounded by brilliant flashes of light, starbursts of all colors and fiery rain all followed by loud bangs strangely out of sync with the display.

TJ was beside himself. I don't think he had ever seen a fireworks display before. He was running around, grabbing hold of whichever person was nearest. When he got to me he grabbed my hand and yelled, "Look, look daddy, look! Oh wow! That's so pretty!"

I gave him a quick hug before he was off to share his excitement with someone else. This made the whole day worth all the effort we put in to it. I was surprised when he gave Sara a hug even though she had been tagging after him all afternoon.

All the fireworks displays had ended by 9:30 and our guests started to leave. You could still hear firecrackers going off and could see an occasional sky rocket go off from houses around the lake, but the organized displays were over. Unfortunately, we would probably hear firecrackers going off most of the night.

As our guests were leaving, Chris came up to me and asked if JR could spend the night. He was backed up by TJ and the twins.

"I don't care, but you will have to ask his dad," I said.

He took off with his three brothers close behind to confront Eric. It looked like JR was hitting his dad up as the boys approached him. I couldn't hear what was being said by Chris but Eric looked at me as if asking for my assent. When I nodded my head he must have said it was okay with him from the reaction of the five boys. They raced into the house as Eric walked over to me.

"Are you sure you really want another kid here tonight after having fifteen here all day?" he asked.

"What's one more boy? Five or six you can hardly tell the difference," I said, as we followed the boys into the house.

All of our guests had departed except for Manfred who was helping Hildy clean up things in the kitchen. When I saw him, I went into the kitchen to thank him for all the work he had done today.

"Crane, no thanks are necessary. I haven't had so much fun since my son was a little boy twenty or so years ago. I should be thanking you for allowing me to be part of your celebration," he said.

"You're welcome here anytime," I said. Then turning to Hildy, "You are amazing. I don't tell you often enough how much the boys and I appreciate your looking after us and how much we love you." I hugged her and gave her a kiss on the cheek.

"Are you going to tuck us in?" TJ asked, interrupting our conversation as he padded into the kitchen in his pajamas.

"Of course I am. Is everybody ready? Did JR get some pajamas?" I asked, as I picked him up and carried him to his bedroom.

"Yeah, Larry gave him some of his."

Eric followed us into the bedroom as I tucked TJ and Joel in bed and gave them their goodnight hugs and kisses. Eric followed suit. Going into the next room the twins were in bed by themselves. Chris was missing.

"Where's Chris?" I asked.

"He's with JR," Lenny answered.

The twins got tucked in by both Eric and I following our usual routine. Then we went to the fourth bedroom that was rarely used. I guessed that was where Chris and JR were. I was right. I didn't think they would sleep upstairs by themselves.

"Hi, dad. It's all right if we sleep in here isn't it?" Chris asked.

"Of course it is," I said, as I sat on the side of the bed and brushed the hair off his forehead. "Just make sure you go right to sleep. It's been a long day."

"We will," he said, giving me a hug which I returned with a kiss.

Eric was doing the same to his son before we switched.

As we left the room, Eric said he had taken tomorrow off from work. That brought up an infinite number of possibilities.

"Let's talk," I said, as I led him into the living room.

CHAPTER 25

I sat down on the couch in the living room. Eric sat beside me. I didn't quite know how to begin to say what I wanted to say. Placing my hand on Eric's forearm, I began, "Eric, it's obvious that I am attracted to you and I believe that it is reciprocated."

"Yes, you know it is," he replied.

"The problem is, I really don't know you. In the few months we have known each other we have never really had the time to explore each other's hopes and dreams. It seems every time we are together the boys are always here keeping us from having a serious discussion. The only time we have been alone together was when we went to the concert and that was only while we drove to and from the event. If our relationship is going to go anywhere, I need to know who you really are.

"I have been hurt in the past and I don't want that to happen again. I am not interested in just a sexual relationship. I am interested in a relationship based on trust, respect and a mutual understanding of each other's needs, one that is based on a friendship that transcends the physical. I want one that will last beyond the sheer act of sex. I guess what I really want is one based on love.

"Am I making any sense?" I asked.

"I think I understand," Eric said. "I don't want a one-night stand either. I'm not into bed-hopping. I want a stable relationship, one I won't be ashamed of no matter what the rest of the world thinks."

"How do we begin to decide if what we have is for real or just physical attraction?" I asked.

"I don't know. I guess we just need to open ourselves to each other, really get to know one another," Eric answered.

That is exactly what we did for the next three and a half hours. It wasn't always easy, and there were times of awkward silences, but we did learn a lot about each other. I shared with him all the important events in my life from my parents' death to the painful memories of my failed love affair in graduate school with Cassie. I let him know what I wanted to do with the foundation and the dreams I had for it in the future. Eric shared the good and the bad of his life including his marriage. We both were honest with each other about what we were looking for in a partner.

Around two o'clock we were worn out both emotionally and physically. The revelation of our life stories had begun to wind down. When Eric said he should be getting home, I suggested he spend the night in one of the upstairs beds. I wasn't yet ready to make the commitment to take him into my bed, as tempting as that was. He accepted and we both went to our separate beds after a quick hug and a friendly kiss.

It seemed like I had only gotten to bed when I felt a little body slip in beside me and put his arms around my neck. When I opened my eyes, I was looking into the beautiful azure eyes of my little TJ.

"I'm hungry, dad," he said, kissing my cheek.

"You're always hungry," I said, reaching around to tickle his ribs, getting a high-pitched giggle from him. "Go wash your hands and face. I'll bet Hildy has breakfast waiting for us."

I looked at the clock as I rolled out of the bed and saw it was almost eight o'clock. I don't know how long it had been since I had slept that late, certainly not since the boys had come to live with me. I washed up and threw on a pair of shorts and a tee-shirt and headed to the kitchen.

To my surprise, Eric was sitting at the table drinking, a cup of coffee and looked to be having a serious conversation with Hildy.

"How long have you been up?" I asked Eric, as I poured myself a cup of coffee.

"Oh, not too long," he said. "Just long enough to drink a half a cup."

"How did you sleep?" I asked, sitting down at the table with him.

"The bed was great. I didn't have any trouble falling asleep. It just didn't last very long," he said.

"Dad, what are you doing here?" JR asked, as he jumped on his dad's lap. "Do I have to go home right now?"

"In a little while, son," Eric said giving his son a squeeze and a kiss on the top of his head. "Dad stayed the night also."

Joel, who had entered the kitchen at the same time as JR, glanced first at me and then at Eric, looking like he wanted to ask a question.

"Yeah, your dad slept in one of the beds upstairs. We talked so long. It was too late for him to drive home," I said, more to Joel than to JR.

A smile flickered on Joel's lips as he took his place at the table that Hildy quickly loaded down with breakfast. The other boys joined the group at the table after getting hugs from Hildy and me. Samson went to his bowl and had his breakfast also.

Eric decided it was time to leave about an hour later, much to the chagrin of JR and the rest of the boys. Eric told JR they had some work to do at the house and he needed him to help. JR rushed to Hildy to say goodbye before all six of them went out to the car. Since Mary Jane and Becky Sue had the day off, Eric and I had to watch the boys.

I walked Eric out to his car and gave him and JR a hug before they took off for home.

As the boys and I walked back into the house after Eric's car exited the property, Joel came up to me and took hold of my hand.

"Dad, can I talk to you?" he said.

"Of course, you may," I said. "I'll always make time to talk to you. Let's go into my study."

I sat on the couch and motioned for Joel to take a seat beside me. "Now, what is on your mind?"

"I heard you talking to Mr. Hogan about a foundation. What's a foundation?" he asked.

"Well, son, this foundation is going to help deserving young people who don't have parents to get adopted by their foster families if those foster families want to adopt and don't have enough money to qualify. People like Mr. and Mrs. Boise who would like to adopt Tony and maybe even Benny."

"But if they don't have enough money, how are you gonna help them?" Joel asked.

"See, that's what the foundation is going to do. It will give deserving parents, who need it money to help them qualify to adopt. They will get the money until the adopted child leaves home or graduates from college. The amount of money the parents receive will be determined by how much they need to maintain an acceptable life style for the adoptee. Do you understand?"

"Yeah, but won't that cost a lot of money? How is the foundation gonna get all that money?"

"Well, dad is going to give the foundation a lot of money to get it started," I said, not wanting to reveal exactly how much I was giving away. "After that, we hope to get donations from others to help to keep the foundation going and to expand the number of kids that we can help."

"Oh," Joel said after a moment.

"Joel, you look like you have a question you want to ask. What is it?"

"I was just thinking about Tony and Benny and how happy they would be to be back together all the time. That's all Tony talks about when I phone him. I hope you can do it. But ..."

"But what?" I asked.

"Can I help?" he asked, barely above a whisper, looking up at me with those beautiful eyes.

I knew I could never refuse him. In fact, it made a lot of sense to have a child help us. I had Jack who would be investigating the proposed parents but there was no one who could get the story from the child. What could be more natural than one adopted kid finding out the feelings of a kid going through the adoption process?

"Joel, that's an excellent idea. I'm so proud of you for wanting to help. You can help in any way you feel comfortable. I have a meeting with Carlos and Gerald this afternoon to finalize some details about the foundation. If you want to, you can attend. You will learn more about the foundation and maybe help figure out how much you want to be involved," I said, putting my arms around him and pulling him into my chest. "You make me so proud."

"Dad, can we go swimming?" Chris asked, sticking his head in the study door.

"Now that's a good idea," I said. "Go get your suits on and I'll be there in a couple minutes."

"Son, we'll talk some more after the meeting this afternoon and I'll try to answer any more questions you have at that time. Why don't you get your swim suit on and let's join your brothers in the pool," I said, getting up from the couch.

Samson was waiting for us at the patio door when we started toward the pool. He followed us to the pool, but one thing Samson never did was go in the water. He never minded water when he was bathed, but showed no interest in going into the pool. He would sit and watch the boys or run up and down the side of the pool if the boys were involved in a game of dodge ball.

Joel played with us for maybe fifteen minutes before he became tired and got out of the pool. He sat in a lounge chair under the beach umbrella watching his brothers and me. Samson, as usual, went and sat beside Joel to get his ears scratched.

A half an hour or so later, Hildy emerged onto the patio carrying a tray with a large pitcher of juice and a half dozen glasses. It was like a giant vacuum cleaner had sucked the boys out of the pool. They were beside her before she could reach the table to set her tray down.

"Thanks, Hildy," TJ said, as he gave her a wet hug.

The other boys echoed his thanks as well.

"You're welcome, boys," Hildy said, looking at me, smiling and shaking her head.

After lunch Joel and I took off for San Antonio to meet with Carlos and Gerald about the foundation. The meeting went off very well. Everything was set to begin operations as soon as Darcie returned from her honeymoon. All the necessary paperwork had been completed to meet the government's requirement to operate as a charitable entity. Gerald informed us that $10 million from the sale of the business had been transferred to ASEC bank account to start the foundation.

"That idea of yours to donate 68.97% of the business to the foundation as of June 30th before the sale went through saved you a lot of taxes," Gerald said. "Your tax liability on the $4.5 million is going to be hefty enough. Of course the donation will favorably impact your overall taxes for several years to come."

I could see that Joel was just itching to ask a question but he refrained until we were on our way back to the house.

"Dad, did you really donate $10 million to the foundation?"

"Yes, son, I did. Why?"

"Are you rich?"

"I guess we are rich by most people's standards," I said, emphasizing the 'we'. "But the main reason that I'm rich is because I have you and your brothers. I could be the poorest man in the world and still be rich if I had you guys."

"Thanks, dad," he said. "I guess I'm rich too because you found me."

I didn't tell him that he and his brothers were actually rich in their own right. Each of their trust funds was worth over $4 million as of the first of the month.

"Dad …?"

"Yes?"

"Ah … do you like Mr. Levin?"

"Of course I do. Why?"

"I mean, like I like John?"

I paused for a moment debating how to answer. "That's hard to say. I am very fond of Eric and I think he likes me too. If you are asking if I love him, I can't honestly say. Would it bother you if I did?"

"No … I was just wondering."

The rest of the drive home was in silence.

I received a call from Darcie on the 14th telling me she was back from the honeymoon and was ready to go to work on the foundation. It surprised me a little bit. I didn't think she would have their households straightened out for another week or so, but I was pleased she was ready. I invited her and Mel to come over to the house on Saturday for a barbeque and we could discuss how to get organized so everything would be in place by the first of August.

The rest of the week was spent between baseball practice and games. Chris and the twins each had games on Saturday morning so we barely made it back to the house in time to grab a quick lunch before Darcie and Mel arrived. I had invited Eric and JR to come for the barbeque also.

The boys were getting ready for a swim when Eric and JR arrived. They quickly joined the boys in the pool. Mel and Darcie were not far behind. Mel also changed and made his way to the pool where Chris was giving JR pointers on breathing between his swimming strokes.

Darcie and I went into my study and started discussing our ideas on how to start up the foundation and the way we both thought it should operate. She had some definite ideas I found quite surprising. She was going to be a driving force in the foundation, and I was so impressed with her command of what I was trying to do. I could tell from what she presented that she had given the foundation a lot of thought. I knew right then I had made the right choice of her to head up ASEC.

When we finished our discussions, Darcie went into the spare bedroom to change into her bathing suit so she could join the rest of the crew in the pool. I went to check with Hildy to see how the preparations for the barbeque were coming before I, too, changed into my swim trunks. I stopped by the barbeque pit and started the fire going before I joined everyone in the pool.

Mel was sitting on the side of the pool as I finished starting the fire. "Man, how do you keep up with these boys?" he asked, panting.

"First of all, I don't try. They have much more energy than I do. I think they could go non-stop all day long and usually do," I said, laughing.

"Crane, you know I'm jealous of you."

"Why are you jealous of me?"

"Because, Darcie spent the majority of our honeymoon talking about you and your foundation. She is so excited about it she can barely wait to get started," he said.

"Well, I'm glad to know she is excited about it. I know she'll do a good job. She has a passion for helping kids and that's what's necessary for us to succeed," I replied.

I enjoyed playing with the boys and our guests for another hour before it was time to start getting the meat put on the grill. I had chosen some great looking ribeyes. Before I began grilling, I asked everyone how they liked their steaks and then suggested they go grab a quick shower and change clothes.

As I was going into the house to follow my own advice Hildy stopped me. "I hope you don't mind, I invited Manfred to join us this evening. He's going to take me to the movies afterward. He should be here any minute."

"That's fine. I should have thought to ask him myself. You take off anytime you want. The rest of us can clean up," I told her.

By the time I emerged from the shower, Manfred had arrived and was playing with the boys. I guess they had decided if he liked Hildy and she was their 'grandmother', then he could be their 'grandfather'.

I put the steaks on the grill while Hildy brought the rest of the food from the kitchen. Most everyone wanted their steaks cooked medium except for Manfred and Mel who wanted theirs cooked rare. To be on the safe side I made sure the boys' steaks were done so there was no pink in the middle. It took some planning but I was able to get all the steaks grilled and ready to be plated at the same time.

Hildy, Eric and I cut the boys' steaks for them. Joel and Chris decided they could cut their own. It didn't take long before we were able to join the rest of the adults to enjoy our own meals. Both tables were not only filled with good food but with good conversation and above all, laughter. Sitting there surrounded by people I loved or deeply respected, I realized again how blessed I was.

After we finished eating, Hildy began to clean up but I stopped her. "You and Manfred run along. We can handle the clean-up. Enjoy the movie," I said, as I shooed her away from the tables.

She looked at me as if she was going to argue until she saw I was determined. Shrugging her shoulders, she went to the boys and gave each of them a hug. Manfred followed behind her doing the same.

"Okay, guys, each of you grab your plate, your silverware and your glass and take it into the kitchen. Then go wash your hands," I told the boys.

With everyone helping it didn't take long to get everything cleaned up and the few leftovers put in the refrigerator. Darcie insisted on loading the dishwasher and making sure the kitchen was cleaned up so there was no mess left for Hildy.

The six boys went into the bedrooms to play with the video games while the four of us adults retired to the living room for coffee. Mel and Darcie sat in the loveseat while Eric and I sat on the couch. We chatted about nothing in particular for a half an hour or so until TJ walked timidly into the room and climbed onto my lap.

I hugged him and gave him a kiss on the back of his head. I knew he had something on his mind. He turned his head and put is lips to my ear and in his best stage whisper said, "Can JR stay all night?"

"I don't care, but you have to ask his dad," I said, imitating his stage whisper.

It was all Darcie, Mel and Eric could do to keep from laughing, but they did a pretty good job of keeping a straight face.

TJ turned in my lap to face Eric and with that innocent expression on his face that only a six year old could attain, asked, "Can JR stay here all night?"

"Did JR put you up to this?" Eric asked.

His answer was a wide-eyed shaking of his head no.

"I guess it would be all right," Eric said, looking at me, shaking his head and releasing his pent up smile.

As TJ took off for the bedrooms, I said, "I think we were set up. They knew it would be hard for us to refuse a request from the youngest."

Mel and Darcie just laughed at us. "You guys are just pushovers," she said.

Changing the subject I said, "Which of your two houses did you decide on living in?"

"Were going to live in Mel's house in Bulverde," Darcie said. "It's much bigger than mine and besides it has a much better view. It's also much closer to the ASEC office you've rented in Thousand Oaks."

"Oh, that will be convenient. The office should be ready the early part of next week. The only thing holding us up is the installation of the phone lines. Southwestern Bell promised they would be in this last week but so far they haven't delivered. Hint, hint, Mel."

"Hey, don't look at me. I'm just some dumb computer geek there. I don't have anything to do with the installations," Mel said, laughing.

Around nine o'clock, Mel and Darcie decided to take off for home and went in to say goodbye to all the boys. After getting and giving each of the boys a hug, they took off for Mel's house. Eric and I followed them out to their car to say our goodbyes.

"When are you two going to get together? Or have you?" Darcie said, as we stood beside Mel's car.

"What? What do you mean?" I stuttered.

"Darcie!" Eric chided.

"Well, for heaven's sake. It's obvious that you like each other. Don't tell me you don't. Remember, Eric, I have known you for a long time and you're so easy to read. Crane, you're pretty transparent as well. Even the boys know you two have the hots for each other," she said, getting into the car.

Eric and I were speechless as they drove off down the lane.

Entering the house we were met by Larry. "Dad, we haven't had our snack yet."

"Okay, you go get the others while Eric and I see what there is for your snack."

Luckily, Hildy had a plate of chocolate frosted brownies in the refrigerator. The brownies and some large glasses of milk staved off starvation in the six of them. Eric and I each grabbed a brownie before they were all gone even though we did get a few dirty looks.

After they finished their snacks, Chris rinsed the glasses and plates and stacked them in the sink. The dishwasher was full of freshly washed dishes from the barbeque.

"Time to get your teeth brushed and ready for bed," I told them as they started back to the bedrooms. I was surprised when I didn't get any complaints. I guess the day's activities had worn them out. "I'll come tuck you in bed in a few minutes."

I went back into the family room and turned on the TV since it was coming up on ten o'clock. I wanted to see what the weather forecast was for tomorrow. If it were going to be decent, I thought I might take the boys out on the boat fishing, since TJ didn't have a T-ball game tomorrow and we hadn't been out for a few weeks. The local weather on the Weather Channel was just beginning as I tuned to the channel. The two minute synopsis of the local weather indicated it was going to be partly cloudy with temperatures near 95 and winds 5-10 mph. It looked like it would be a good day to take the boat out.

I gave the boys a few more minutes to get ready for bed before I went in to say goodnight followed by Eric. The bedtime ritual had become quite standard. The first room I went into was Joel and TJ's. I gave each of them a hug and a kiss on the forehead. Tonight they got the same from Eric. As we left the room I switched the lights off and then pulled the door almost closed. This was repeated in the twins' room and finally in the spare room where Chris and JR were.

As we were leaving after tucking them in, JR said to his dad, "I wish I had a brother to sleep with all the time."

"Maybe someday," his dad said.

Eric and I went back into the family room and talked for another hour or so before we were both beginning to yawn.

"Do you want to spend the night?" I asked.

"Yes, I think I would like to," he said standing up.

As he started toward the stairway to the spare beds upstairs, I took his hand and pulled him toward my room.

CHAPTER 26

I made sure I was up and dressed before any of the boys woke up. The coffee pot had not started perking when I got to the kitchen so I started it. Hildy had not made an appearance either. When I went to get the Sunday paper from down the lane, I noticed Manfred's car parked in the driveway. "Good for her," I said aloud, as I walked to get the paper.

Hildy, looking a little flustered, entered the kitchen just as I was pouring myself a cup of coffee. I sat my cup down, walked over to her and gave her a hug.

"What's that for?" she asked.

"Oh, I don't know. I guess I'm just happy for the both of us," I responded.

She cocked her head to one side with a questioning look on her face until Eric walked out of the hallway and entered the kitchen. "I see," she said, blushing and then her face took on a knowing look.

"It's Sunday, you don't have to fix our breakfasts today. I usually take care of it while you go to church," I said.

"I know, but ..." she said, trailing off.

"Let me help you. You tell me what to do. I don't want you to miss your services."

"We ... I mean, I think I'll go to the late service this morning," she said as she started stirring up a large batch of pancakes with more concentration than was necessary.

Eric poured himself a cup of coffee, gave me a one-armed hug and sat down at the table. I smiled at him and then turned to the refrigerator to retrieve a three pound package of link sausages and began to brown them in a large skillet. When Hildy was about half finished with the stacks of pancakes, I asked

Eric to watch the sausages so I could wake the boys and get them ready for breakfast.

While I was gone he set the table and poured each of the boys a glass of milk and one of orange juice. I put the maple syrup in the microwave to warm up when I returned. Manfred poked his head in the back door to the kitchen.

"Manfred, welcome to the morning madness of the Johnson household," I said. "Come on in and join us. There's plenty of food for everyone."

He looked at Hildy and when she gave him a nod he joined us in the kitchen. To my surprise, he walked up to Hildy and gave her a kiss on the cheek before going to pour himself a cup of coffee. She turned a bright red and playfully pushed him away.

Hildy was taking the last of the pancakes off the grill when the boys started rushing into the kitchen. Everyone, including Manfred, received a hug from each of the boys. Manfred was a little surprised when JR gave him a hug also.

"Dad, did you stay here last night?" JR asked, as he hugged his dad.

"Yes, I did," Eric answered, without any further elaboration.

"How come you're here?" TJ asked Manfred.

"TJ, don't be rude to our guest," I scolded.

"That's all right, Crane. Ah … I … I'm going to take Hildy to church," he said.

TJ shrugged his shoulders and went back to eating his stack of pancakes that quickly disappeared along with the rest of his breakfast.

After breakfast Eric and JR left for their house saying they would meet us at the marina around ten o'clock so we all could go fishing. Hildy and Manfred took off for church and I began putting together some sandwiches to eat on the boat. The boys finished getting dressed and ready to go.

When Samson saw the fishing tackle being loaded into the van, he got all excited and started running around and barking. He knew we were going fishing and he would get to go. Although he didn't like the boat that much, he did like to go with us. I think he just liked to go in the van with the boys. Before we left, I made sure the boys had a liberal coating of sun-block. The sun can be murderous in July in South Texas.

Everyone put on their life jackets before we got on the boat. Even Samson had his on. Darrell had serviced the boat after I called him earlier so it was all gassed up and ready to go when we got there. He even had the bait on board for our fishing expedition. We had everything loaded and ready to go when Eric and JR arrived, apologizing for being late. Eric's parents had called, saying they planned to bring Bran and Benny up next weekend for a couple of days to get away from the heat and humidity of Houston. I was sure that a sleepover was on tap for all the boys next weekend as soon as the rest of the boys heard the news.

I backed the boat out of our slip and slowly eased it out of the marina area before I gave it more speed. While I steered the boat, Eric worked with the boys to get their tackle ready to fish. When I got to a spot where we had some luck fishing the last time, I cut the engine and let the boat drift. Since there wasn't much current in the lake, we barely moved from the spot. I did keep watch to make sure we weren't in the way of the speedier boats and jet-skis. The lake was quite crowded and I didn't expect we would catch many fish. It turned out I was wrong. The fish seemed to be hungry and shortly after the boys resumed fishing after lunch they had nearly caught their limit. We had more fish than I really wanted to clean but I didn't think any of the boys would take kindly to throwing them back. I hadn't told them about 'catch and release' fishing.

I was surprised and pleased that Joel held up as well as he did. Every once in a while he would reel in his line and come sit beside Eric and me to rest for awhile before going back to join his brothers.

When I suggested that we head back to the marina, I received some dark stares until I said we could stop and get some ice cream at the marina snack bar. That was received with enthusiasm since I had not packed anything for an afternoon snack.

Samson made a beeline for the nearest tree as soon as we walked off the dock with Chris running after him. I didn't think Samson would run away but Chris wanted to make sure. When they returned, I told Chris to put his leash on. Comal County has a leash law and I didn't want to get fined for Samson running free.

We said goodbye to Eric and JR after everyone had feasted on ice cream and we had divided up the fish so they would have enough for their supper. Also, I didn't relish the idea of cleaning all of them. We were left with more than enough for our supper after they were cleaned and filleted.

As we drove up the driveway to the house, Manfred was leaving in his car after dropping off Hildy. I stopped the van and spoke briefly to him through the rolled down window before driving on to the house. Samson jumped out of the van as soon as the door was opened and raced around the yard, happy to have a chance to stretch his legs after being cooped up most of the day.

I told the boys to go in and take a shower while I took care of the fish. I was still working when they started trickling out to watch me. I was nearly finished and thankful that I was. I never really liked the messy job of cleaning fish.

However, I liked the final results. I had to keep reminding myself how good fresh fish tasted all the time I labored over them.

I had planned on grilling the fillets on the outdoor grill, but as I was getting ready to start the fire, the weather decided otherwise for me. One of South Texas' famous afternoon thunderstorms blew up and ruined my plans.

Hildy came to my rescue and although it was her day off, she took the fillets from me and said she would bread them and fix supper for us. I thanked her profusely and went to take a much-needed shower. I stunk to high heavens from fish offal.

As I entered the kitchen feeling much fresher, the boys were rushing around setting the table. Hildy was putting a large pan of deep fried fish in the oven to stay warm. A large bag of frozen French fries was waiting its turn in the deep fryer. When the fries were finished, they joined the fish in the oven and Hildy began dropping spoon-sized dollops of hushpuppy batter into the hot oil. When the first batch of about twenty hushpuppies was ready, she told Joel to get the milk out of the refrigerator and fill the glasses. Chris was instructed to retrieve the tartar sauce and the catsup and put them on the table.

Since everything was hot I decided it would be prudent for me to serve the food. I loaded each plate with fish, hushpuppies and French fries and passed them to the boys. Hildy set a basket of bread on the table followed shortly by another heaping plate of hushpuppies which quickly made their way onto plates around the table. It was not the healthiest of meals but it sure tasted good. I'll bet Hildy will ensure our diets are healthier in the coming week.

Since it was still raining when we finished supper, I asked the boys if they would like for me to read to them. That met with unanimous approval so I went to my study to pick out a book I thought they all might like. I selected one of Mark Twain's lesser-read books called *A Horse's Tale*. I had always thought it was one of Twain's better stories, but I also understood why it didn't have as wide appeal as some of his other works. I believed the boys would enjoy it. I think more than anything, we all just liked sitting around together, sharing a quiet time.

TJ took his usual spot on my lap, Joel sat on my left and Chris on my right. Larry and Lenny took their positions on the floor on their stomachs with their heads propped up on their hands. I read to them for about an hour and a half before they began to get restless. My leg was also going to sleep from having TJ sitting on it.

We watched a little TV until it was time for a snack. That was quickly followed by preparations for bed. As I tucked the boys into bed I told them I had to work all week, but I would be home for their baseball and T-ball practices.

It seemed strange to walk into the office after almost a month. The first thing I did was to check with Carol to see where my office space was. I assumed someone from the new owners had my old one.

"Carol, how are you?" I said, as I came up behind her.

"Crane," she said, turning to greet me, "it's good to see you. How have you been?"

"Oh, I'm doing fine. It's just a little strange to be back in the office again. Which office am I supposed to use?"

"The one next to your old office is set up and ready for you. You're looking good. Retirement must suit you."

"Well, I'm not really retired. I'll be in here a week every month and then there is the foundation we are just getting started which will take a lot of my time. Then there are five young boys that keep me on my toes," I said, laughing.

"If the foundation every needs a good secretary, let me know," she said, in a hushed tone.

"That I will," I said, as I gave her a quizzical look. "Is there something wrong?"

"No, not really, it's just not the same around here anymore," she sighed. "Go check out your office and I'll bring you a cup of coffee. Brandon Hines, the new manager, is not in yet. I'm sure he'll want to meet with you when he arrives."

I did meet with Brandon Hines when he arrived about a half an hour later. He looked to be around forty, graying around the temples and the start of a paunch. He impressed me as being highly intelligent but also a bit abrupt with those around him. We spent over an hour talking about what the new owners expected of me in my one week each month at the office. That turned out mostly to be working with young project managers helping them in developing project plans and staffing schedules. I was also to advise projects that appeared to be veering off schedule and helping to get them back on track.

After I met with Brandon, I worked with a couple of project managers who had come with the new owners. It seemed they were both managing their first project and they needed help. Both appeared to be competent but a little overwhelmed at everything they had to juggle to keep a project on track.

I hadn't made plans for lunch so I decided to call Jack to see if he were available. Unfortunately, he was in court testifying and I was unable to reach him. As I was leaving the office to get some lunch, Carol was on her way out also. I asked her if she had plans and when she said she didn't, I suggested we eat together. I would have invited Foster, but he was out of town.

By the time lunch was over, I could tell that Carol was not happy with the new management. She didn't say so in so many words, but I got the distinct impression she was not happy. I made a mental note to discuss with Darcie whether we needed a secretary for the foundation.

I had no more than sat down at my desk when Ronnie, one of the new project managers, stuck his head in the door to see if I was ready for our afternoon session.

"Give me a few minutes," I said. "I need to make a phone call before we start up."

"Okay," he said, leaving me to make my call.

I took out my address book and looked up the number I wanted to call. I used my cell phone since this was a personal call.

"Hello, Karen," I said, when she answered. "This is Crane Johnson. How are you?"

"Oh, Crane, it's nice to hear from you. We are doing fine. Tony asks about Joel all the time."

"Joel talks about Tony, too. They developed quite a friendship in the hospital. That's one of the reasons I'm calling. The Levins are going to be visiting their son this weekend and are bringing Benny and Bran. I was wondering if you and Bill would like to come up this weekend and visit us. It would give the boys a chance to see each other again. We have plenty of room for you. I'm sure all of the boys will be staying at the house Saturday night. They like to have a sleepover."

"Thanks for asking. I'll talk with Bill when he gets home this evening. I know what Tony's answer will be. I'll call you after I've talked to Bill," Karen said.

We talked for a few more minutes before we hung up and I got back to business. The rest of the afternoon went by quickly as I worked with Ronnie on his project. I was ready when it was time to go home. It seems my three weeks off had gotten me out of the habit of putting in a full days work.

I drove home as fast as the traffic would let me, which wasn't that fast. Not being the boss anymore, I had to wait until four o'clock before I could leave the office. Becky Sue was still at the house when I drove in and parked the car. As I entered the back door I was attacked by TJ jumping into my arms.

"Hi, daddy, I missed you," he said, giving me a kiss on the cheek.

"I missed you too," I said, giving him a squeeze and returning the kiss. "What have you been doing all day?"

As I carried him into the family room, he told me in detail everything he had done all day including what he had for lunch. We were greeted on our way by Joel and his brothers who surrounded us in a group hug. God, how I loved these boys. We sat on the couch and they told me all about their day until Becky Sue came in to tell them goodbye.

Tonight's supper was much healthier than last nights, but the boys seemed to enjoy it as much as they did yesterday's. Hildy had fixed us roast chicken, wild rice and steamed broccoli along with a mixed greens salad.

We had just finished with supper and had all the dishes loaded into the dishwasher when the phone rang. It was Karen phoning to say they would be happy to come for a visit. I gave her the directions to get to our house and told her to call if they got lost. The directions were not that complicated until the last couple of miles before you got to our house. I told her if they left by nine in the morning they should be here by noon and if the weather held we would have a cookout. I also mentioned that if they wanted to swim to bring their suits.

After we hung up I called the boys and told them Tony was going to come for a visit this weekend. That was met with enthusiasm by all of them. It had been quite a while since they had seen him. Even Samson seemed to be excited.

"Dad?" Joel asked quietly.

"Yes, son."

"John called today and wants me to come over to his house tomorrow. Can I?"

"I guess that would be all right. What time are you supposed to be there?"

"He thought maybe ten."

"Well, you know that dad will be at work. Have you figured out how you are going to get there?"

"I thought, if you said it was okay, maybe Hildy would take me, and then you could bring me home when you got off work."

"Okay, let's go ask Hildy if she will take you," I said, getting up off the couch and heading for the kitchen where Hildy was still cleaning up from supper.

"Hildy, Joel has something he wants to ask you."

"Um … Could you … ah … Could you take me to John's house tomorrow? Please?"

"Of course, sweetheart. What time do you want to go?" Hildy replied.

"Thanks, Hildy, you're the best," Joel said, giving her a big hug. "Could we go a little before ten?"

"Sure, I'll get the directions from your dad," she said, returning the hug.

When I gave her the directions she said, "I know where that is. One of my friends from church lives on that same street. In fact, from the address it should only be a couple of houses away."

"Something else I wanted to talk to you about. I've invited Tony and his foster parents to come visit this weekend and was thinking of inviting several others also for Saturday afternoon. If everyone comes there will be about twenty-six people including twelve kids. You do enough around here and I don't want to put you to the trouble of all those people. I thought we could have it catered. There's that barbeque place in Bulverde that caters. It's pretty good, I hear. What do you think of that?"

"That would be easy enough. Why don't we have them cater the main meal and I'll take care of the desserts?"

"That's fine if you want to do that. Would you work up a menu and give them a call to see if they can do it? Although there will only be twenty-six at the most we should plan to have extra food since there'll be a dozen kids," I said, smiling as I thought about the amount of food my tribe could put away.

The rest of the week went fairly smoothly. I picked Joel up at John's house on Tuesday. Wednesday I had to take Joel for his chemo treatment at Dr. Greene's office. I had to make arrangements with the office to come in next Wednesday to make up for missing one of my scheduled days. I made all of the boys' practices including coaching the twins' team. TJ was making surprising progress. I suspected either Becky Sue or the other boys were helping him during the day while I was at work. I was proud of him, as I was of all of the boys.

Saturday morning was going to be rough. Chris' team was playing the twins' team I coached. Before the game started I took the twins and Chris aside and talked to them. "It's not important which team wins or which team loses. What is important is you all play the game the best you know how. If you do that nobody is a loser. I love you no matter what the outcome is. Now let's go out there and have fun." I gave them all a hug and sent Chris over to his team.

Both teams played their hearts out, but in the end Chris' team came out on top by a score of 5 to 4. My team may have been able to win if I had left the starters in the whole game, but I had a strict policy that everyone on the team got to play at least three of the six innings. The rules of our league only require every team member had to play at least one inning.

We made it back to the house in time for the boys to get cleaned up from the game before our guest started to arrive. The caterers had arrived and were setting up the tables when we got there. I went to check on them and to see what was on the menu. Hildy had taken care of that and I hadn't even thought to ask what it was. Jeremy, the caterer in charge, told me we were having brisket, ribs, and chicken for the entrée and cole slaw, ranch beans and potato salad for the side dishes. There would also be pickles, sliced onions, jalapeños and all kinds of condiments. He indicated they would be ready to start serving around one o'clock.

Since it wasn't quite noon, I went back in to check with Hildy to see if she needed any help. Before I was able to ask her the phone rang. It was Bill Boise. He wanted to check the last part of the directions with me before he started down some winding road. I laughed but assured him he, indeed, was on the right road. I told him he was only about a mile and a half from the house.

When I told the boys Tony and his mom and dad would be here in about five minutes they all went out on the front porch to wait. Samson went too. I monitored the gate security camera and when I saw them approaching, I activated it so they could get in. The car had barely stopped when it was surrounded by excited boys. Tony was the first to emerge and was swallowed up in the hugs from the boys. Karen and Bill received the same treatment as they stepped out of the car.

I noticed Tony had some hair growing again although it was a little spotty. Joel noticed it too and ran his hand over his friend's head. He said something to Tony I couldn't hear that brought peals of laughter from the six of them. Then they ran off to show him the lake with Samson circling them as they went.

I embraced Karen and shook hands with Bill. "Let me help you with your luggage. I'll show you where your room is."

"I must say you have a beautiful home and the view is fantastic," Karen said. "This is the first time I've been to the Hill Country and I've lived in Texas all my life."

"That goes for me too," Bill said. "I've been to San Antonio several times but never ventured far from the downtown area. It's difficult for us 'flatlanders' from Houston to drive up and down all these hills."

"Dad! Dad! Come quick! They've got deer in the back yard and you can get real close to them. Come on!" an excited Tony said, grabbing his foster dad's hand and dragging him around the side of the house.

I chuckled, grabbed their two suitcases and started for the front door. Karen and I had started up the steps to the house when Hildy appeared at the front door. She stepped outside, gave Karen a big hug and started chatting away like long lost friends. I took the suitcases to the spare bedroom and then went outside to join Bill and the boys. Joel was giving Tony the grand tour of the yard and pool, showing him the lake. He had his arm around him pointing out the dam when I arrived.

"This is spectacular," Bill said. "This is so much different than where we live. It's so flat in Fort Bend County. How much land do you have here?"

"We have thirty-five acres. It is mostly covered with trees, Live Oak and Mountain Cedar. Not much good for farming or raising cattle. The deer manage quite well; in fact, too well most of the time," I said.

As we were standing there admiring the view, Eric and JR arrived in their car followed by his folks with Benny and Bran. When Tony saw his brother he ran to him and lifted him up in the air in a bear hug. They were quickly surrounded by the rest of the kids, everyone talking at the same time.

Before they were done greeting each other, Jack and his wife and three kids showed up. They weren't out of the car yet when Darcie and Mel drove up. By this time the boys had noticed the food being set up by the caterers and were beginning to circle them like a flock of vultures.

"Hey, guys, the food won't be ready for about another half hour. Besides not all of our guests are here yet," I told them.

I was kept busy making sure everyone got introduced to everyone else. The boys pretty much took care of their own introductions. Sara, Jack's little daughter, ran up to TJ and gave him a hug. TJ looked at me like a trapped animal. I just shook my head and smiled at him.

Dr. Sam and his wife Carol arrived and were closely followed by Manfred driving up. When Manfred got out of the car he carried what looked to be a large cake into the house before joining the rest of us on the patio.

Jack Jr. and Bran seemed to be hitting it off. They were about the same age so it seemed natural that they pair up. Since Benny had his brother to look after him, Bran didn't need to act in the protector role he usually maintained.

It was nearly a quarter to one but I could see the boys were getting restless and kept gravitating toward where the food was being set out. I went to talk to Jeremy to see how soon they would be ready. When he indicated it would only be a few minutes, I yelled at the boys to go wash their hands. They didn't need to be told twice and all ran off to get cleaned up. I would be willing to bet all five bathrooms were used to produce clean hands.

I noticed as the boys were returning from their clean-up that Darcie and Karen were having a serious conversation. "Good," I thought. Since they were going to be the foundation's first potential recipients, it was good they get better acquainted. I wanted Darcie to be as sure as I was that the Boises were good candidates for our assistance.

The food was set up buffet style. We let the youngsters go through the line first with the help of the adults to make sure they didn't spill their overloaded plates. The rest of us followed with Manfred and me bringing up the rear. The caterers had set up some extra tables so all twenty-six of us could sit down to eat. Hildy was fussing over everyone making sure they had everything they needed until I insisted she sit down. Manfred had saved a seat beside him for her.

I had barely sat down and started eating when Lenny came up to me and whispered in my ear, "Can we have some more?"

"Of course you may. Help yourself. Try not to spill your plate though," I told him.

He ran off almost before I finished talking waving to the other boys it was all right to get seconds. They quickly joined him in trying to deplete what was left of the food. A number of the adults also went back for seconds. It was a good thing we had ordered extra because there was very little food left when everyone was finished eating.

When Hildy announced there was dessert, I think all of the adults just groaned. The reaction of the boys was the exact opposite. As much as they had eaten, I don't know how they had any room left. She instructed them to bring their paper plates and plastic utensils, dump them in the garbage bag she was holding, then go inside and wait for her.

I went to check on them and to see what kinds of desserts she had prepared. I was amazed at the selection. There was a chocolate cake, a white cake, apple pie, peach pie, apple cobbler and a big bowl of chocolate pudding. In addition, she had set out a gallon of vanilla ice cream to top things off.

Manfred came in unnoticed and began helping Hildy speed up the process of handing out the desserts. He manned the ice cream scoop while she dished up whatever each boy wanted. I grabbed another gallon of milk and took it out to the boys' table to fill their glasses in case they needed more.

Ethel, Carol and Karen were busy cleaning up the dishes from the adults' table. The caterers were busy wrapping up in foil what few leftovers there were. Jeremy motioned me aside and handed me the bill for the food. I led him back into the house to my study where I wrote him a check and thanked him for the excellent job he and his crew had done.

Hildy came out onto the patio, coffee pot in hand with Manfred right behind carrying a tray with coffee mugs and cream and sugar. Several of the adults refused the coffee but most accepted. We sipped our coffee and watched in disbelief as the boys ate their desserts.

The afternoon went by rapidly. We let the boys go swimming about an hour after they finished eating. Many of the adults joined them at times in the pool. Eric and Mel were having a ball playing with the kids. So was Bill. Tony and Joel took frequent breaks from the goings on in the pool to rest but they were never far from each other. Their bonding in the hospital still seemed to be strong.

Dr. Sam had Karen engaged in an animated discussion of which I'm sure Tony was the subject. I saw him motioning toward Tony as he talked.

Hildy and Manfred had disappeared shortly after she had brought the coffee out, but I hadn't really noticed with so much going on. It wasn't until they returned that I realized they had been gone. I thought that was a little strange. Usually Hildy hovered around all of us like a mother hen tending her chicks. I guess they just needed some time away from the crowd.

Around five o'clock I decided to start the grill. It would take a while for it to get hot enough to cook on. I planned to fix hamburgers, hot dogs and bratwursts for everyone who wanted to hang around. We could also bring out the leftovers from lunch if anyone wanted them.

Dr. Sam and Carol thanked me and Hildy for the hospitality, but they had to leave to get ready for their bridge party this evening. Darcie and Mel also said they had to leave. They were going to the movies with another couple.

Jack and Carolyn decided to leave also saying Sara was getting a little crabby and needed to get home and go to bed. They didn't leave until they admonished Jack Jr. and Timmy to behave themselves and reminded them they would be picked up around ten in the morning.

That left eight adults and eleven boys to feed. While I started getting everything ready for the grill, I told the boys to go jump in the shower and wash the chlorine off. I told them they would probably have to shower in shifts since I didn't think there was enough water pressure for all the showers to be used at once. I later learned they all climbed into two showers, the big one in my bedroom and the big one I had built upstairs. I thought I heard a lot of giggling from inside as I worked at the grill.

Eric walked up to me at the grill and put his arm around my shoulder, "Thanks for a great day. JR is in heaven. He wants a brother so badly. He loves being here with your boys. It's the next best thing since I'm pretty sure he won't have a natural brother."

"I'm pretty sure that Chris would adopt him," I said, as he withdrew his arm from my shoulder. "Chris really takes him under his wing when he visits. It reminds me of Joel and TJ's relationship."

Ethel and Alan had been talking to Bill and Karen while Eric was talking to me. When I turned to them, Bill and Karen were looking at us strangely. I let it pass. I didn't think they needed any explanation.

After supper, all the boys went upstairs to watch some videotapes we had rented. The adults retired to the family room except for Hildy and Manfred. They went up to her apartment after she had served us coffee.

When it came time for bed, I sent everyone to get their teeth brushed and get into their pajamas while Eric and I pushed the three queen size beds together. He had brought two sleeping bags and I had two if we needed them.

Jack Jr. and Bran decided to use a couple of sleeping bags on the floor. Tony and Benny wanted to put two of the sleeping bags together so they could sleep together. That left only seven for the beds. It was after ten when they were all hugged and tucked into bed.

Eric and his parents left shortly after all the boys were bedded down. I wished he could stay, but from the questioning look we got from the Boises I didn't think that would be a good idea. It would just complicate things too much.

Karen and Bill soon decided it was time for them to get to bed so I showed them where everything was and made certain they had clean towels and washcloths. I went back out and started to button the house for the night.

I was just getting ready to turn out the lights and head to my bedroom when Hildy came into the kitchen.

"Crane, I need to talk to you," she said cautiously.

"Okay," I said.

"I don't know how to say this ... Manfred asked me to marry him," she blurted out.

"Oh," I said, groping for a chair to sit down.

CHAPTER 27

To say I was stunned by her announcement was an understatement. The ramifications of her revelation were exploding in my brain. I found the chair and sat down or more accurately fell into it. I was unable to speak for a moment. I could see our happy family crumbling at the loss of an important member.

When I regained the power of speech I mumbled, "When ... When are you going to marry?"

"We haven't set a date," she said. "That's what I want to talk to you about. The last thing I want to do is to leave my boys. They've become a most important part of my life. Ah ... That is ... When Manny and I do get married ... Well, do you think he could live here with me?"

"Oh my God, yes!" I almost shouted. "I don't think we could manage without you. When Manfred first started coming around here, I know TJ was upset you might leave us. I was too. When you said he had asked you to marry him, I could just see our family collapsing. But as much as I want you to stay, your apartment above the garage is rather small. You only have a bedroom, living room and a kitchen/breakfast room and of course a bath."

"I know, but we can make do. I couldn't leave my boys."

"Let me think about what we can do. Thanks for letting me know. I'm relieved you don't plan to leave us," I said. "You know you're an important part of this family and the boys and I love you."

"Thanks, Crane," she said, leaning over and giving me a hug. "See you in the morning."

I finished closing up the house for the night and went to check on the boys one last time before I went to bed. As I started up the stairs where the boys were bedded down I heard some muffled giggling. I couldn't tell which of the boys it was coming from at first until I approached them. The closer I got, the more it seemed to be coming from the sleeping bag containing Tony and Benny. The other boys seemed to be asleep.

They didn't see me as I walked up to them. Tony was whispering to Benny who would then giggle softly. I knelt down beside their sleeping bag. They were startled when I said, "You boys need to get to sleep. I know you enjoy seeing each other. Maybe someday you can be together all the time. Now try to go to sleep." I patted each one on the head and started back toward the stairs.

"Thanks for inviting us here, Mr. Johnson," Tony whispered.

"You're welcome. Goodnight."

It had been a long day and it didn't long after I crawled into bed before I was fast asleep. About two-thirty I was awakened by someone crawling in bed with me. When I turned over, I could see in the dim moonlight that it was Chris.

"What's the matter son?"

"I think I ate too much. My stomach hurts," he said, as he squirmed against my side.

I rolled over and placed my hand on his forehead. He didn't appear to have any fever. "Let me get you something to make your stomach feel better," I said, as I slid my feet over to the edge of the bed. I remembered the last time this happened with TJ. At that time we didn't have anything except a home remedy to take care of it. At least this time, we had a supply of antacid tablets.

I went into my bathroom and retrieved the bottle from the medicine cabinet. I shook a couple tablets out of the bottle and put it back in the cabinet. I filled a paper cup with water from the cold water tap and took it back to the bed.

"Here, chew a couple of these and then take a drink of water. This'll make your stomach feel better in no time," I said, sitting on the bed beside him.

"These taste pretty good but they stick to my teeth," he said, as he handed the cup of water back to me.

"Now try to get some sleep. If your stomach still hurts, you let dad know. Okay?"

He turned over on his right side and was asleep before I got back in bed. So much for the stomach ache.

When I awoke the next time, the sun was streaming in the window and my alarm clock showed it was just past six-thirty. I couldn't hear anyone else stirring but I decided I had best get up and prepare for the day. I showered, shaved and dressed. As I left the bedroom I heard Hildy in the kitchen. Since it was

Sunday, I didn't know if she would be fixing our breakfast or whether I would have the honors.

"Good morning," I said, as I poured myself a cup of coffee. "Is there anything I can do to help you?"

"Oh, you startled me," she said, as she continued cracking eggs into a large bowl. "Do you think three dozen eggs will be enough?"

"What else are you going to fix?"

"Well, besides the scrambled eggs, I thought I'd fix a couple pounds of bacon and sausage. Then I have the waffle iron heating up and was going to make waffles. Oh, and toast and preserves."

"I think that will be more than enough. I'll fix the meat and the toast. There is not too much chance I can screw that up," I chuckled.

For the next half hour we cooked away. We even were able to stay out of each other's way most of the time.

"Everything should be ready in about ten minutes. Why don't you go wake the boys and get them ready for breakfast?" she told, more than asked, me.

"I'm surprised they haven't been down here before now. Usually they can smell food a mile away."

I was about to mount the stairs when Bill and Karen emerged from their bedroom. "Good morning, I was just on my way to wake the boys. Breakfast is about ready. Grab a cup of coffee and I'll be right down."

It didn't take long to wake the boys. At the first mention of food they were up and headed to the bathrooms to get washed up. JR knew the drill about washing up before Hildy would let them sit down at the table, but the other guests had to be told by the other boys. I went back downstairs and woke Chris who was still sleeping in my bed.

By the time I returned to the kitchen the boys were beginning to arrive, still dressed in their pajamas. Hildy received hugs from the nine younger boys. Jack Jr. and Bran evidently decided they were too old for a hug. Hildy was having none of that. She walked up to Jack Jr. and wrapped her arms around him.

"Jack Jr., you are becoming such a handsome young man. I'll bet the girls' hearts are all aflutter over you," she said to a blushing teen.

Turning to Bran she said, "Come here young man. I just wanted to tell you how proud I am of you. I haven't even heard you come close to swearing." She gave him a hug and then turned to the rest of the boys, "Go sit at the table in the dining room. It's big enough for the eleven of you. We'll bring the food in there."

It took Hildy, Karen and me to carry all the food into the dining room. We all helped the boys fill their plates the first time. I just hoped there would be something left for the adults to eat when they were finished. Although the boys tried their best there was still food for us when they finished and took their plates to the kitchen. Joel rinsed the dishes and Chris loaded them into the dishwasher before everyone took off to shower and dress for the day.

The Boises, Hildy and I settled in to eat our breakfast amazed at the amount of food the tribe had eaten. Karen marveled at how easily Hildy had managed to prepare enough food in such a short period of time saying it took her longer to fix breakfast for Bill and Tony.

"How's Tony doing?" I asked. "Have you ever approached him about the possibility of you adopting him?"

"He is really doing well," Karen said. "Dr. Kerner says all his test results are excellent. He thinks a complete recovery is almost certain, thank God. It is a godsend that Dr. Kerner got that grant to pay for Tony's treatments."

Bill continued, "Yes, and we've talked to Tony about us adopting him. He seems to be enthusiastic about it but at the same time there seems to be something not quite on the surface that's bothering him. We think it has something to do with Benny, but he won't say. I think he's afraid his brother will get adopted and he'll lose track of him. He loves his little brother unconditionally. He is never happier than when Alan and Ethel bring him to visit us."

"I asked you once before if you ever considered adopting both of them," I said. "At that time you indicated you would but your main concern then was you didn't qualify because of income. I know you talked to Darcie yesterday when she was here. Did you bring up the subject to her?"

"No, I didn't," Karen said. "We talked about adopting Tony with the aid of the foundation is all. She asked a lot of questions about us, our house and about Bill's job and things like that. She said you were involved in the foundation also. I didn't know that. You never said."

"I'm on the board and help manage its operations," I said. "If you are serious about adopting Tony and want the foundation's help and support you'll need to undergo a background investigation by the foundation. Jack Hogan will be conducting it for ASEC. He will do a criminal background check. He will check your references and also look into your finances. It will be to your advantage to cooperate with his investigation. If everything checks out, we'll assist you in retaining legal representation for the adoption process. Over the next few weeks, Darcie will be explaining to you the specific details of what the foundation will provide."

"That sounds great," Bill said. "How long is all of this going to take?"

"There is no precise answer to that. The initial petition for adoption could go before the court in as little as two months. If the court agrees, you could be given permanent custody. Then, for the adoption to become final, it could take anywhere from ninety days to a year. There are a lot of variables, but the legal counsel we have has been known to be able to expedite things."

We chatted for a while over our coffee. Hildy cleared away our breakfast dishes and got ready to go to church. The boys began drifting in from taking their showers. TJ climbed onto my lap.

"What's going on, little one?" I asked, kissing the back of his head.

"Nothing, just wanted to sit on your lap," he murmured.

"Your hair smells so clean. Did Joel wash it for you?"

"Uh huh," he said. Then turning, he whispered in my ear, "Can we go down to the lake? Tony and Benny wanna see it."

"Sure, as soon as everyone finishes their showers we'll all go down to the lake," I said, for the benefit of the Boises.

I don't know what it is with boys, rocks and water, but when we got down to the lake level they all picked up rocks and started skipping them across the surface of the lake. With all eleven of them skipping rocks I thought it wouldn't be all that long before they would have the shoreline picked clean. The lake level was about five feet below its normal level so we had a little more shore for the boys to play on.

It didn't take long before both Tony and Joel started getting fatigued and came and sat down with Karen, Bill and me. "Are you doing okay?" I asked Joel.

"Yeah," he said, leaning into me. "I just get tired so easy."

"I know," I said, wrapping my arm around him. Bill was doing the same with Tony.

After a while the boys got tired of skipping stones and decided they wanted to go back up to the house.

"Don't forget, dad, I got a game this afternoon," TJ turned and said, before he started up the stone steps.

"I won't. Your game's not until three o'clock," I said, giving him a playful swat on the seat of his pants. He ran off giggling and grabbed Benny's hand as they started climbing the steps.

It wasn't long before Jack came to pick up his two boys. They didn't want to leave and break up their ragged game of kickball everyone except Joel and Tony were involved in. They were in the process of loading their stuff into the car when Eric came to pick up JR, Bran and Benny.

Tony hugged his little brother before Benny started toward the car with tears in his eyes. Tony turned to Karen and buried his face on her shoulder trying to hide the tears in his eyes.

"Eric, could you possibly let Benny stay a little longer?" I asked. "I know your parents aren't leaving for home until tomorrow. We could drop Benny by your house on our way to TJ's T-Ball game this afternoon."

"I think it would be all right," Eric said. Then turning to Benny, "Would you like to stay a little bit longer?"

"Yes sir!" Benny almost shouted. With the remains of tears in his eyes he ran to Tony and jumped into his outstretched arms.

"Come on, Bran, I'll let you drive back to the house now that you have your learners permit. That is if you want to," Eric said, as he held out his keys that were quickly snatched from his hand. "Well, I guess that answers that question."

"I'm glad I have a few years before I have to face a teenage driver," I laughed and clapped Eric on the back.

"Well, it's only for a couple of days. There is hardly any traffic on the road between here and our house so I feel relatively safe. He really is a safe driver. But just between you and me I still almost push my foot through the floorboard while he drives. I guess this is good practice for when JR gets old enough to drive," Eric said, before turning to Benny. "We'll see you later, son. Be good."

It wasn't long after Eric left that Chris came up to me and asked, "Dad, can we go swimming? It's getting hot."

"Sure," I said. "Go get your suits on."

We sat under the beach umbrellas while the boys frolicked in the water for the next couple of hours. Tony and Joel spent a lot of the time sitting on the edge of the pool just talking. Every so often they would join the fun in the water until they got tired and had to sit out for a while. It was good to see their relationship that started as the result of their shared affliction was now based on solid friendship. They never seem to be at a loss for something to talk about as they sat on the side of the pool.

Around noon I decided I had better figure out what we were going to eat for lunch. I excused myself to go inside. Karen insisted she help while she admonished Bill to keep an eye on the boys.

I was surprised when I opened the refrigerator. Hildy had prepared a platter of cold cuts consisting of sliced beef, ham, turkey and salami along with Swiss, cheddar and American cheeses. All the makings for sandwiches including lettuce, tomatoes and pickles were ready to be placed on the table. It looked like there was enough food to feed an army. I was mistaken. By the time the boys and the adults had finished eating there was very little of anything left to put away.

After lunch I told the boys to go take a quick shower to rinse the chlorine off and get ready to go to TJ's game. Although the game didn't start until three o'clock we had to leave around two so we could get Benny back to Eric's house and get TJ to the ballpark in time to warm-up for the game.

Bill and Karen took Tony and Benny in their car and followed us to Eric's house. They were going to leave Benny and then begin their three hour drive back to their home southwest of Houston. It was not a happy scene when the brothers were separated. After a tearful goodbye, Benny buried his head in Ethel's ample bosom and cried. He was still sobbing when we left for TJ's game.

We were among the first to arrive at the ballpark. There were a few stragglers left from the previous game that was played earlier, but the field was empty. I didn't pay any attention to them since they were sitting in the bleachers on the other side of the ball diamond. The twins and Chris immediately took TJ and had him start practicing hitting the ball off the tee while they fielded the balls he hit. We carried all the equipment in our van for just such contingencies. It wasn't long before the rest of the team members and coach arrived to start the warm-up and we packed away our equipment.

I was a little surprised when Eric arrived with JR and Bran to watch the game. Benny was still being comforted by Ethel according to Eric. Larry, Lenny and JR sat with Eric and me while Joel, Chris and Bran played catch behind our bleachers. I would check on Joel every so often. Most of the time, I could hear their giggles as they tossed the ball back and forth to each other.

The game was about half over when I heard a ruckus behind the bleachers where the boys were playing. Suddenly Joel was yelling, "Dad! Dad, come quick!"

I turned around and saw some young man in his mid twenties and a teenager attacking Bran and screaming racial slurs. Eric and I acted as one, vaulted over the back of the bleachers and ran to aid Bran.

"That's the same asshole that was at the pizza place," Eric said, between clenched teeth.

Eric grabbed the man from behind in a bear hug while I corralled the teenager by taking him firmly by both arms. "What's going on here?" I said, in my most authoritative voice.

"We don't want no niggers around here," the obviously intoxicated man in Eric's grasp spat out.

I could see Eric was livid. He had maneuvered the man's arms so they were twisted up behind his back. Hearing the racial epithet, Eric twisted the man's arms even farther up behind his back causing him to squeal, "Ow! You son-of-a-bitch, let go my arms."

"I think you had better leave here now before I get really angry. I don't ever want to see your ugly face again. Take that punk kid with you also," Eric growled.

"Hey, Crane, what's up?" I heard a voice behind me ask.

Turning, I saw the voice was that of Deputy Sheriff Jesse Cantu. "Hi, Jesse," I said, still holding onto the teenager. "These two were harassing this young man," I pointed to Bran.

"Dammit, LeRoy! When are you ever going to learn? Are you drunk again?" Jesse asked, as he approached the man being restrained by Eric. "You sure as hell smell like it. I'm going to take you in for being drunk and disorderly and let you sleep it off. I'll call your poor wife and tell her she can pick you up tomorrow morning as usual. Damn! I'm getting sick and tired of taking you in all the time. I hope one of these days the judge will sentence you to a rehab center." Then turning to the boy I was holding, he said, "You need to find someone else to hang around with; otherwise you are going to end up just like LeRoy, a drunk."

"Thanks, Jesse, this is the second time they have harassed Bran. This time they actually struck him. I intend to file a complaint for assault and battery on LeRoy, whatever his name is. I didn't see this one throw any punches." I told Jesse.

"LeRoy Mason is his name. LeRoy, it looks like you might not get out of jail in the morning after all. You'll have to see the JP (Justice of the Peace) for him to set your bail," Jesse told him as he removed his handcuffs from his belt and started putting them on LeRoy's wrists. "Crane, let me get him in the back of my patrol car and I'll get a form for you to fill out with all the particulars. That'll allow us to hold him until the JP sees him."

TJ's game was over before we had filled out all the forms and witness statements. I gathered up all the forms and handed them to Jesse, "Jesse, why were you here?"

"My son was playing for the other team."

"Oh, I guess I didn't realize you had a boy old enough to play."

"Yes, Ronnie will be six in October. I'm afraid he is not much of an athlete yet, but he has fun playing with the rest of the boys and that's what's important to me."

"Thanks, Jesse. Let me know if and when I have to testify against that jerk," I said, shaking his hand.

Bran was being comforted by Eric and the other boys as I turned away from Jesse. We all talked briefly before I suggested we should all go back home. Eric asked Bran if he felt up to driving the car back to the house. That seemed to take some of the sting out of the situation, but you could tell Bran was still upset.

As we were unloading the van when we got home, TJ came up and stood beside me with a confused look on his face.

"What's the matter, TJ?" I asked.

"Well … Joel said a man called Bran a nigger. What's a nigger?" he asked innocently.

"Let's go into the house. There is something I want to tell all of you," I said, making sure everyone heard me.

As we went through the kitchen, I grabbed soft drinks for everyone before we settled on the couch in the family room.

"Okay, everyone but TJ saw what happened at the ballpark to Bran. That man called Bran a nigger. That is a very hurtful word and I never want to hear any of you use it. It's used by stupid people to insult black people. People who do that are bigots. Bigots believe that just because someone's skin is dark that makes them inferior or not as good. Sometimes this unreasonable hatred or prejudice leads to violence as it did against Bran this afternoon."

"Did that man hit Bran?" TJ asked, his eyes open wide.

"Yes, son, he did. Bran never did or said anything to the man. That's what a prejudice can do. It can make you do unreasonable things for no apparent reason."

"Bu t … But Bran is nice," TJ sputtered. "He's my friend. I like him."

"I know, son. We all like Bran."

I answered a few more questions about the incident before I heard a stomach growl which changed the subject altogether. Since I didn't have a clue as to what to fix for supper I suggested we go get Mexican food. That seemed to please everyone so as soon as we all washed up we hopped into the van and headed off to New Braunfels to a good Tex-Mex restaurant.

Full to overflowing, we returned to the house, not wanting to do anything but turn on the TV, relax and watch some mind-numbing program. So that's what we did until it was bed time. I hadn't told the boys about Hildy's revelation that she was going to get married. I didn't want to upset them until we had everything worked out.

Tucking the boys into bed was still one of my favorite activities. It let me share the love I felt for them in a very tangible way. Even though Joel was now a teenager he still didn't object when I tucked him in and gave him a kiss on the forehead.

When I went into the twins' room I saw Chris and them were whispering quite seriously to each other. As I approached the bed the whispering stopped.

"Dad," Chris began. "We've been talking. Can we start sleeping upstairs in those beds?"

"Why sure you may. If you want too, you can start tomorrow night," I said. "Is that all right?"

"That'll be neat," Larry said.

"But remember, there'll be no horsing around when you're up there. When you go to bed you're to go to sleep."

"Sure, dad," Lenny said, sounding hurt that I would question them.

"Good night," I said, after giving each a hug and a kiss. "I love you."

My alarm went off at six-thirty. Darcie and I were going to go to the foundation's new office and try to get it organized this morning. I also wanted to talk to her about whether or not we needed to hire a secretary. Although the foundation was not officially in business for another four days on August 1, we wanted to make sure everything was in place so we could start helping deserving people and kids.

I was a little surprised to find Manfred sitting at the kitchen table when I arrived to pour myself a cup of coffee. "Good morning. I'm glad you're here. I need to find out what your intentions are for this young lady here," I said, smiling.

"Crane, behave yourself," Hildy chided.

"No, seriously; congratulations, Manfred. I'm just glad Hildy says you're not going to steal her away from us."

"I think if I made her choose between me and your sons, I would come out on the short end of the stick," he said. "I can see why, too. I'm quite fond of them myself. I may have to adopt them as my grandsons since my own son does not seem inclined to give me any."

"Are you sure you want to be an immediate grandfather to five boys?" I asked. "Oh, by the way, I haven't told the boys you're planning to marry. I thought I would wait until you had set the date and then maybe we could all sit down and tell them together. I know their main fear is going to be that Hildy would leave them."

"That's probably a good idea," Manfred said.

Becky Sue arrived as the boys were sitting down to their breakfast. "Crane, I need to talk to you," she said, "alone if we could."

"Sure, come into my office."

"The fall term starts August 19th. There are only three weeks between today and then. I need a little time to get ready for school so I thought if I could work this week and next then I would have a week off to get ready. I know that leaves you with two weeks without help before the boys start their own school," she said, almost apologetically.

"Of course, that will work out fine. I'm sure your summer job has provided you with more excitement than you ever expected. The boys will miss you. Next summer, if you are interested the job is yours again. And if you ever need a letter of recommendation I will be more than happy to provide one for you."

"Thank you, I do appreciate it."

Manfred had left when I once again entered the kitchen. The boys were all busy eating their breakfast when I gave them a quick hug before leaving for the new office.

Darcie had beaten me to the office and it hit me I had forgotten to give her a key to get into the office when I saw her standing outside the door. Thankfully, she had only just arrived. I quickly remedied the situation by giving her a key and apologizing for my oversight.

The first thing I did once we entered the office was to check the status of the phones. I was glad to see they were working. The Internet connections were also working, I discovered when I booted the computers.

Our office space consisted of a small reception area, two offices (one for Darcie and one for me), a larger conference room, a small area for a coffee pot and refrigerator and a toilet area.

Darcie and I discussed whether we needed to hire a secretary right away and ended up deciding that for the next month or so there would not be enough work to make it worthwhile to hire someone. The next thing we did was to try to establish the criteria we would use to evaluate potential parents and foster children we would help. This proved to be a difficult task. We decided the amount of financial aid each adopting family would receive would be determined by a number of criteria including family income, where they lived, housing required for the adopted child and the personal needs of the child. The latter was to include any counseling the child might require to adjust especially if they had come from an abusive or traumatic background.

I did take time out to call Harold Nicholas to see if he could drop by this evening to talk about some more renovations I had in mind. I looked forward to meeting with him and also invited him to bring Joey. I knew TJ would like to see him again.

CHAPTER 28

Harold showed up shortly after seven with his son Joey. TJ was waiting at the front door and ran to meet his school friend. They ran off around the side of the house to play while Harold and I went inside to talk about what I had in mind.

"Joel, would you keep an eye on TJ, Joey and your brothers while Mr. Nicholas and I talk a little business?" I asked.

"Sure dad," he said, marking his place in the book he was reading and went outside to mind the other boys.

"How's he coming along?" Harold asked.

"He's doing very well, thanks."

"That's good. Now, what was it you wanted to renovate? I thought we took care of everything the last time."

"Well you see Hildy, my housekeeper/cook/nanny is going to get married and they plan to make their home here in her apartment. The thing is, it is kind of small. It's fine for a single person, but will be a little cramped for two. What I want to do is to enlarge it to include another bedroom and bath and expand the living room. As part of this, I want to add garage space for two more vehicles and some storage space. My van sits out most of the time because it doesn't fit in any of the spaces so I want to make sure the new garage bays will accommodate it. Right now our six bicycles take up one of the three existing garage bays."

"Okay, let's go take a look at what we've got to work with. Let's start outside so I can see the footprint," Harold said starting back outside.

As we walked around, Harold jotted down some notes in a small book he carried. He muttered to himself and paced off what I assumed would be the new garage extension. After about fifteen minutes he seemed to be satisfied and suggested we go inside and take a look at the existing apartment.

Hildy had retired to her apartment when we got back inside. I knocked on her door and when she answered I explained to her what we wanted to do. Although she protested that it was not necessary, I could tell she was pleased.

Harold spent another twenty minutes surveying the inside of the apartment and again making notes in his book while Hildy and I watched. "I'll need to have my designer come and take a look, but I have a good idea of what is possible with what you have told me. He may have some ideas as to how to accomplish what you want. Do you think it would be possible for him to come tomorrow?" Harold asked.

"Yes, what time would he be here?" I asked.

"I'll send him around nine if that's all right?"

"That'll be great. Let's go see what the boys are up to."

I poured Harold a glass of iced tea and we settled ourselves into lounge chairs on the patio to watch the boys play. All of the boys except Joel were playing a game of kick ball. That brought to the surface of my mind something else I had been thinking about.

"Harold, I have been thinking of creating a bigger play area for the boys over there where that semi flat area is. What would it take to make that area big enough to play baseball or soccer?"

"Well, a lot of it would depend on how much rock would have to be broken up to get an area flat enough. The soil around here is only a few inches deep so we would have to bring in a lot of topsoil to make the surface safe enough to play on. We're going to have to do some excavating for the other project so we'll have all the equipment to do it. When Konrad gets here tomorrow, I'll have him look at it and see what he thinks about what it'll take," he said.

We sat and talked for an hour or so until the sun was casting its last light over the tops of the hills to the west. It finally got too dark for the boys to play and they rushed up to the patio wanting something to drink. It was time for their evening snack so I invited Joey to join my sons.

After the apple pie and ice cream was ravaged, Joey and his dad left for home and my boys went to shower and get ready for bed. Tonight was the night the twins and Chris were planning on sleeping upstairs in the bedroom I had built up there. I wondered to myself if they would make it through the whole night. They hadn't moved their clothes to the new bedroom so I wasn't convinced they had really made up their minds this was going to be a permanent arrangement.

When everyone was clean and dressed for bed, I asked if they wanted me to read some more of the book we had started, *A Horse's Tale*. I read for a little over a half an hour until TJ fell asleep in my lap. I picked him up and carried him to his bed and everybody else headed for their beds. I kissed my youngest and tucked him in before doing the same to Joel.

"Are they really going to sleep upstairs all night?" Joel asked.

"They said they wanted to. We'll have to see if they make it all night," I said, smiling.

I climbed the stairs to where my other sons were. I could hear them talking and giggling as I approached their beds. I was a little surprised they each were in a separate bed. I had just assumed they would keep the same arrangement of all sleeping in one bed. I didn't care because that's why I'd put three beds in the room. Chris was on the left. Larry was in the middle and Lenny was in the right-hand bed.

I started on the right and worked my way across all the beds tucking them in and giving each a kiss on the forehead. Before I left for downstairs I cautioned them to go right to sleep and no talking.

"Good night, guys, I love you," I said. "I'll leave a night light on in case you get up in the night and forget where you are."

"Good night, dad," they all three said in unison.

I went back downstairs and picked up a book I had been reading but hadn't had a chance to read recently. It was a book by Piers Anthony, one of my favorite prolific Sci-Fi Fantasy authors with a really warped sense of humor. I read for about ninety minutes before sleep started to overtake me. I quietly slipped upstairs to check on the boys and was pleased they were all asleep and each in his own bed.

Hildy was in the kitchen beginning her breakfast preparations when I entered to pour myself a cup of coffee. I took my coffee and went upstairs to check on the boys again. I don't know what I was worried about. They were totally safe up there. I chuckled when I saw they had all migrated to Larry's bed and were once again a tangle of arms and legs. Old habits die hard. I let them sleep and went back down to the kitchen to visit with Hildy.

We chatted a while before I asked, "Does Manfred have a job? I know he is a retired Air Force Colonel, but he is awfully young to just sit around his townhouse all day."

"Yes," she laughed, "he has a lawn and landscape maintenance business. He has, I think, ten crews. They work mainly in the New Braunfels area, but do some work in Canyon Lake. Why do you ask?"

"Well, as many times as he has been here, he has never mentioned what he did now. I guess I just wanted to see if he was a fortune hunter," I laughed, as I got up to pour myself another cup of coffee.

"Good morning, dad," Joel said sleepily, as he padded into the kitchen still wearing his pajamas.

"Good morning, son," I said, giving him a hug. "You're up early."

"I wanted to talk to you. Can you take me shopping for TJ's birthday present? It's on the seventh. Larry's and Lenny's are on the sixteenth. Are we going to have a party?" he asked.

"Of course we're going to have a party. We'll have one for TJ and another one for the twins. Why don't you come with me to work today and we can go shopping later. I'm only going to work at the foundation for a little while this morning. We can go shopping after that. Besides, I want to talk to you about Tony. Finish your breakfast and then go get dressed."

Becky Sue arrived right after the rest of the boys had settled down to eat breakfast. Konrad came shortly after she arrived. I talked to him for several minutes and told him to show himself around and to call me if he needed anything. I knew from the last time that all I needed to do was to give him a general idea of what I wanted and he would come up with something much better than I could have imagined. I gave all the boys a hug and then Joel and I left for the foundation office.

Darcie was already in the office when we arrived. I could tell by the sparkle in her eyes that she was excited at the prospects of what we were going to do with the foundation. She greeted us when we entered and gave Joel a hug.

"Are you going to help your dad this morning," she asked.

"Yes, ma'am," he answered, "then we're going shopping for TJ's birthday present."

"Oh, when's his birthday?"

"Next week."

"Darcie, I asked Joel to come to the office today so we could talk to him about the first prospective beneficiaries of ASEC. He spent a lot of time with Tony this last weekend so I think he has some insight into what Tony feels about the possibility of the Boises adopting him.

"Joel, why don't you go get something to drink out of the refrigerator while I take care of a few things and then we will sit down and talk to you. Okay?"

"Can I boot up that computer?" he asked pointing to the PC in the reception area. "I get to take a computer class this year in school and kinda want to get a head start."

I just nodded to him as I kicked myself mentally. For being a computer nerd for so many years, it never dawned on me the boys just might be interested in them too. It looks like I had better talk to Eric about setting up a home network so I could train the next generation of nerds.

It only took me about thirty minutes to take care of the business that needed my immediate attention. When I finished I asked Joel and Darcie to join me in our new conference room to discuss what Joel learned from talking to Tony.

"Son, is Tony happy living with Mr. and Mrs. Boise?" I asked.

"Yeah, he likes living with them, but he's afraid."

"Afraid? Afraid of what?"

"He said he was afraid those people might take him away from them."

"You mean CPS might take him away from the Boises?"

"Yeah, he said every time he started to really like the people he was living with, they took him away. They did it two times before."

"What did he say about Benny?" I asked.

"Every time I asked him about Benny, he got really sad. He wants him to live with him, but he says that's never going to happen. His old case worker told him his mom and dad can't have any more foster kids. How come, dad? His mom and dad are really nice."

"Did he say anything about his mom and dad wanting to adopt him?" Darcie asked.

"Yeah, he said his dad kinda talked to him about it. He just said his dad said they would like to adopt him."

"What did he think about being adopted?" I asked.

"He really wants to be but he wants Benny to be adopted too. He … ah … I don't know if I should tell you …"

"If you think it's important, son, maybe you should tell us. We need to know as much as we can if we are going to be able to help Tony and his brother," I said.

"Well … He really wants Benny to be with him. He said they might run away so they could be together. I told him not to do that 'cause he didn't have any place to live if he did. He said Benny needs him. I guess it's like TJ needs me. Benny feels safe when he is with him. He didn't want me to tell anyone. He said they would put him back in one of those awful places where you get locked up all the time. Don't tell anyone. Please dad?"

"I don't think we'll need to tell anyone. We need to see that he has no reason to run away. Did he say anything else? What do Mr. or Mrs. Boise do when he does something wrong?"

"They make him go to his room and he can't listen to his music. They never hit or spank him. He said his mom always hugs and kisses him after his time out and tells him she loves him. He said he usually cries when she does that."

"Would he be happy living where he is if Benny and he can both be adopted?" I asked.

"Oh, yes! He's so worried about Benny. Sometimes he cries himself to sleep after Benny gets to visit him."

"Thank you Joel, you've done a great job. I think you have helped your friend more than you know," I said. "Darcie, do you have any more questions to ask Joel?"

"No, I think he has done an admirable job for the foundation. Thanks, Joel," she said, squeezing his hand and giving him a smile.

"Can we go buy TJ's present now?"

"Sure, go turn your computer off and dad will be ready in just a couple of minutes."

Our shopping trip did not take very long. Joel knew exactly what he wanted to buy and where he could buy it. We parked at North Star Mall and were in and out in less than twenty minutes. He is definitely my kind of shopper. I really hate the crowds in malls.

I glanced at my watch as we were getting into the car and noticed it was only a little after eleven. "Do you want to stop and eat lunch or do you want to wait until we get home?"

"Let's stop. I'm hungry," he giggled.

"You're always hungry, just like your brothers," I said. "How about if we stop at Applebee's?"

"Okay."

I knew wherever we stopped would be fine with him. I hadn't found too many foods he didn't like. When we walked in the front door of the restaurant I was so proud of him. Despite being bald he removed his cap like a gentleman and didn't let the stares of the other customers bother him. I could have hugged him right there, but I waited until the waitress showed us to our booth.

"You know, you are one special boy. I don't know what I did to deserve finding you, but I'm sure glad that I did," I said, with a lump in my throat.

He just blushed and looked at the menu until the waitress returned with glasses of water and took our order. Joel ordered a bacon cheeseburger, fries and chocolate milk while I ordered what they called a Santa Fe Chicken Salad. Because we beat the lunch crowd our meal came rather quickly. Joel ate his burger and fries and then looked from the dessert menu to me and back.

"Go ahead, you can order something for dessert. I think I'll just have a cup of coffee," I said.

He ordered a dessert called Blue Ribbon Brownie. When I looked at the menu it was described as "Hunks of dark chocolate and nuts are baked into this massive mountain (brownie) that is draped in hot fudge and sweetly hugged by two scoops of vanilla ice cream." I think I gained weight just reading the description. He ate it all and looked like he could have eaten another one.

On our way to the car after paying our bill Joel asked, "Dad, can we go do something? Just you and me?"

"Sure, what do you want to do?"

"I don't know. I love my brothers, but … Ah … Well, sometimes I just need not to be around them all the time. Does that make me bad or something?"

"No, of course not. We all need to get away sometimes. How about if we go find a movie?"

"Yeah," he said, running the rest of the way to the car.

We ended up in one of those mega-movie complexes with a dozen or so different movie screens each showing a different film. After eliminating the "R" rated ones we settled on a "PG" rated one call *Jumanji* with Robin Williams. It was a dreadful movie. It was so bad we both laughed all the way through it. Thankfully, there were very few other patrons in the theater. The best part of it, besides the sinfully buttered popcorn, was Joel and I were sharing some time together, just the two of us.

"Thanks, dad," Joel said on the way back to the car. "That was fun."

"You're welcome, son. Remind me to do this again if I forget," I said, reaching my arm around him and giving him a sideways hug as we walked to the car.

Becky Sue was giving the boys their swimming lessons when we arrived home. Joel quickly changed and joined them. I went into my study and called Eric. I hadn't seen him in a few days and was anxious to talk to him. I also wanted to discuss what the best option was for a home computer network. He wasn't in the office so I left a voicemail message for him to call me if he had time and went to join the boys in the pool.

After I was in the pool for about twenty minutes I realized how negligent I had been about swimming my laps in the morning. It seemed ever since Joel was hospitalized I had not swum on a regular basis and I could definitely feel it. I vowed right then to start to remedy that the first thing in the morning.

When I hadn't gotten a call from Eric by eight o'clock I called his house. There was no answer. He didn't have an answering machine so I couldn't leave a message. He hated those abominable machines as much as I did. I was a little concerned but not overly so. After I put the boys to bed I called again and still there was no answer. Now, my concern level went up.

I made good on my promise to get up and swim laps the next morning. I pushed myself a little harder than I should have after having been away from my routine for a couple months and I was sure I would pay for it tomorrow.

I was getting ready to leave the house for my old office to make up the day I missed last week to meet my contractual commitments when Becky Sue came in. "Have you heard how Eric's mom is?" she asked.

"Why? What's the matter with Eric's mom?" I asked, stunned.

"I don't know," she answered. "He called Mary Jane last night and told her he was on his way to Houston with JR because his mother was sick. He told her not to come to work today. I just wondered if he had called you."

"What time did he call Mary Jane?"

"Oh, it was about eight, eight-thirty, something like that."

"Thanks, Becky Sue, I'll call his folks house to find out how she is. It must be fairly serious if he left for Houston last night," I said.

I hugged the boys and left for the office. Then it dawned on me. If Eric left for Houston last night, what about Darcie? I broke a few speed limits on my way to the office. I wanted to have time to call Houston before everyone else arrived for work.

I shouldn't have been surprised when I walked into the office and Carol was at her desk. She was almost always the first person to arrive. "Have you heard from Eric?" I asked.

"Yes, I had a voicemail waiting for me when I got in. He said he was taking a personal day, that his mother was very ill and he would call later if he wouldn't be back in tomorrow. Have you heard anything more?" she asked.

"No," I said, and rushed into my office.

I did a quick review of my voice mail messages to make sure I didn't have one from either Eric or Darcie before I dialed their parents' number on my cell phone.

"Hello," a voice said. I thought I recognized it as Alan's.

"Alan? This is Crane Johnson. I heard Ethel was sick and I called to see how she was."

"Oh, Crane, here's Eric, I'll let him talk to you."

"Crane," Eric said in a throaty voice. "I'm glad you called."

"Is something wrong? Is your mother all right?" I asked.

"Mom died," he said with a tremble in his voice.

"Oh my God," I gasped. "What happened?"

"She had complained of a headache yesterday morning before they took off for home. She took a couple of aspirins and it seemed to get better, dad said. When they got home she said she was going to lie down for a while and rest from the trip. She never woke up. The doctor said she had a massive stroke. I can't believe she is gone," Eric said, his voice clearly showing he was on the verge of tears.

"I am so sorry, Eric. Is there anything I can do? Do you need anything?"

"No, I don't think so. JR is really shook up about this. Benny is inconsolable. Dad says he hasn't stopped crying. Bran is a real trouper. He's doing everything he can to soothe Benny. I'm going to call Karen and Bill to see if they will take care of him at least until the funeral."

"Eric, I think that's a wonderful idea. Now remember, if there is anything you or anyone there needs, you let me know. You and your family are very special to me. And let me know where and when the funeral is going to be. Tell Darcie to take all the time she needs. I'm sure Alan needs her more than the foundation right now. Do call if you want to talk. I'm a good listener."

"Thanks, Crane, you're very special to me also. I'll call you when all the arrangements have been made."

We said our goodbyes and I went to tell Carol what Eric had told me. I spent the rest of the day coaching the two new project managers who I had worked with last week. The guys were sharp but the whole idea of looking at a project from all sides to help anticipate problems or bottlenecks had not quite been incorporated in their thinking. They were still locked into looking at their projects in a linear manner. They would learn, it would just take time.

I dreaded breaking the news to the boys when I got home, but they needed to know. They were very fond of "Grandma Ethel" as they called her. That's what JR called her so they just assumed it was her name. I think all of the boys with, I think, the exception of Joel had sat on her lap and been cuddled into her ample bosom. She had been a very warm and loving woman and it showed in her children.

I barely had time to change my clothes and rush off with the boys to baseball practice when I got home. The news about Ethel would have to wait until later. Chris went off to his ball diamond for his practice and I went off with the twins to coach their team. Joel and TJ played catch and watched their brothers practice.

When we got back home, I sent the boys off to shower before they sat down to supper. While they were out of the room I told Hildy of Ethel's death. She was visibly shaken but recovered before the boys returned.

"We're going to have a family meeting right after you get everything cleaned up after supper," I told them, as we were eating dessert. They barely looked up from the banana pudding.

A few minutes later we were all assembled in the family room. TJ took his usual position on my lap with the rest of the boys sitting beside me on the couch. I still had not figured out a good way of telling them. I guess the best way was to just tell them as gently as possible.

"Do you guys remember JR's grandmother?" I asked.

"Yeah, Grandma Ethel's nice," TJ said, getting nods from the others.

"Something happened to her yesterday. She went to sleep and didn't wake up."

"How come she didn't wake up?" asked TJ.

"Well, son, she went to be with your momma in heaven."

"Does that mean she's dead too?" TJ asked, looking into my eyes. I could see the tears beginning to form in his.

"Yes, son, I'm afraid she is," I said, giving him a hug.

As I looked around I saw Larry and Lenny holding each other. The same was true of Joel and Chris. There was no great sobbing, just quiet tears for a lady we didn't see that often but felt close to because she was such a fine person. The rest of the evening was rather subdued. Even their snack time was not as boisterous as usual.

I tucked the boys into bed, the twins and Chris upstairs and Joel and TJ in their usual room. Not being tired, I picked up my book and went to bed to read until I got sleepy. I read for an hour or so before I turned the lights out and settled under the covers.

It must have been around three o'clock when I was awakened by someone crawling into bed with me. My first guess was that it was TJ. When I turned over I discovered in fact it was him.

"What's the matter, little one?"

"Is Grandma Ethel really gonna see my momma in heaven?"

"Yes, I'm sure she is."

"But how will she find her?"

I had to think a moment before I could answer that. "Well, she will be watching her children just like your momma watches hers. Her children are Eric and Darcie and they live around here so I'm sure she will find a spot in heaven to watch them and your momma will be in the same place watching you."

"Oh."

I kissed his forehead and pulled the cover up over him. "Go to sleep son. Grandma Ethel is probably talking to your momma right now."

CHAPTER 29

The next few days were rather chaotic. Ethel's funeral was scheduled for Saturday morning, which meant I would have to get Peter to take over coaching the team's game. Although he hadn't had much experience with baseball he had learned a lot over the course of the summer and he did know how to work with kids. I also called Chris' coach to let him know Chris wouldn't be able to play on Saturday.

We planned to leave for Houston on Friday afternoon in the van. I didn't think Hildy or the boys were up to flying again, at least not for a while. I'm not sure I was either.

One thing I did get accomplished before we left for Houston was to contact Cindi Sessions and convince her to make Bill and Karen Boise the temporary foster parents for Benny. She wasn't hard to convince but she did have to stretch a few CPS rules to make it happen. When she heard what the foundation had in mind it made it easier for her to justify the placement.

Samson would have liked to come with us but that was not going to happen. The boys said their goodbyes to him and then I put him in the fenced area of the yard. It had shelter for him to get out of the sun and I made sure he had plenty of food to last until we got back on Saturday. There was also plenty of fresh water available that was refreshed automatically every two hours.

I made reservations at one of the hotels that offered multiple bedroom suites not too far from the Levin's home. I was thankful when we arrived that they offered bellhop service. It looked like we had packed for a month instead of a couple of days. I was grateful for assistance carrying the luggage into our rooms. The bellboy was equally happy with the large tip I gave him for his help.

We had arrived shortly after six in the evening and naturally the boys were hungry. I made them wait until I had called the Levin house. I spoke briefly with Darcie and found out the viewing for Ethel was scheduled for this evening from 7:30 to 9:30. I got directions for the funeral home before we left to go eat.

After loading everyone into the van we took off for an all-you-can-eat buffet I knew about that was just down the street a mile or so. Thankfully, it was not crowded when we got there. Hildy and I had a hard time convincing them they didn't have to take everything on their plate the first time through the line. They finally understood they could go back as many times as they wanted so they would have an opportunity to sample everything if they wanted to.

I helped TJ fill his plate and I do mean fill. I was sure his eyes were bigger than his stomach but once again I was proven wrong when it all disappeared and he went back for dessert. I tried to be restrained but did allow myself to have a small slice of cherry pie. At least I didn't cover my dessert with soft-serve ice cream as the boys did.

When we got back to the van I inspected the boys' clothes for food stains and was pleasantly surprised that all of their supper had made it into their mouths and not onto their shirt fronts. I explained to them that we were going to the funeral home to see Grandma Ethel before we went back to the hotel. I didn't know how the boys were going to react to seeing Ethel in her casket.

I shouldn't have worried. The boys were perfect gentlemen as we approached the casket. I did have to lift TJ so he could see in the casket and when he reached out to touch her I whispered to him not to do it. Darcie and Mel were there along with Eric. Alan was not there. Each of the boys gave a hug to Darcie as we went through the family line.

As TJ approached Darcie he said, "Daddy said Grandma Ethel is in heaven with my momma."

"Yes, she is," Darcie said, choking back the lump in her throat but with a tear running down her cheek. Giving TJ a squeeze and a kiss on the forehead she added, "I love you, my little one."

I put my arms around Eric when I reached him. All I could think of to say to him was that I was sorry. It seemed to be enough. His eyes were reddened from crying but there were no tears in his eyes now. I think there is always something special between an only son and his mother. We embraced for a while before I followed the boys to the side of the room where JR and Bran were sitting. They seemed to brighten as we approached them. I'm sure it was not a pleasant thing for them to sit quietly in a room full of mourners.

Alan walked in with two older women as we were talking to JR and Bran. He made his way to the casket with them and then went to Eric and Darcie. I went up to him after a minute or so to pay my respects. He introduced the two women to me as Ethel's sisters, Edith and Edna. Although he didn't say, they looked to be older sisters.

Turning to Eric, I said, "Look, why don't I take JR and Bran with me back to the hotel. It's going to be a long evening for them sitting around here."

He looked at Alan and nodded. I told him which hotel we were staying at and he said he would pick them up around ten. All the boys were enthusiastic about that.

As we walked to the van, Joel whispered to me, "Can we stop and get a snack? Bran's hungry."

"And I suppose you're not," I said, giving his shoulder a squeeze. "You know it's only been about an hour since we ate."

"Yeah, I know," he giggled.

We stopped at the Dairy Queen and everyone decided they wanted banana splits except for Hildy and me. We settled for a small cone. They put two of the staff in an assembly line putting together the seven high calorie concoctions. Joel saw to it that TJ got his banana split first. Away from the funeral home all the boys were more their animated selves as they waited for their treats.

Hildy and I just shook our heads as the boys laughed and talked and ate their treats. Even though Bran was a couple of years older than Joel he still seemed to fit in like he was a member of the family. He seemed to be very solicitous of JR. I had seen him act like that towards Benny, but since Benny wasn't around he seemed to know JR needed someone to lean on. It's amazing the change that has occurred in him since we first found him sitting against the wall of that apartment about three months ago. That sullen, withdrawn and scared little boy has blossomed into a confident, outgoing teenager.

I wondered what was going to happen to him now that Ethel was gone. Alan may not want to foster him without Ethel. I knew Alan had deep feelings for Bran, I just didn't know whether he would be able to manage a young teen and deal with his grief at the same time. One thing was for sure; I didn't want or need another boy to take care of no matter what my feelings for him were.

When we got back to the hotel the boys sprawled out on the floor in front of the TV and watched some mind-numbing program. I don't know how much they really saw of the program because of all the chatter that was going on among them.

Within a half an hour TJ had climbed up on the couch and snuggled under my arm. I guess the day had finally caught up with him. I brushed the hair off his forehead and gave him a quick peck. "Are you tired, son? Do you want to go to bed?" I asked.

"No," he said with a yawn.

"Well, you just sit here with dad. Eric will be here to pick up JR and Bran in a few minutes and then all of you need to hit the sack."

He didn't make it until Eric arrived. In fact he only lasted a few more minutes before I could tell by his regular breathing he had fallen asleep. I was tempted to pick him up and put him in bed but decided to wait until after our guests had left. I didn't want him to possibly wake up alone in a strange bed and panic.

It wasn't very long before Eric knocked on the door. I asked Bran to let him in. I didn't want to disturb TJ by jumping up to answer it. Slowly I laid TJ out on the couch and went to Eric. I could tell he was on the verge of breaking down so I steered him into the kitchenette and sat him down at the table. We talked and I consoled him for maybe ten minutes before he was more in control of himself.

He took Bran and JR and left but not before everyone got their hugs. I walked them out and down to the lobby of the hotel where I again embraced Eric. I'm sure the few people in the lobby thought it strange, but I didn't care. I was comforting a friend in need.

When I returned to the suite the boys were trying to decide which bed they would take. The suite had two bedrooms. One had two queen size beds and the other a single queen size. Hildy had her own room across the hall. Once the big decision was made I picked up TJ and carried him to the bed Joel had selected. I decided it was too late for them to take a shower tonight so they put on their pajamas while I started undressing TJ. Joel helped after he was ready for bed. I was surprised but TJ never woke up with all the wrestling of him we did trying to get his pajamas on.

Since the funeral was at ten I had to get the boys up fairly early in order for them to shower, dress and have breakfast. The latter being the most important to them, I'm sure. When we entered the restaurant in the hotel, the greeter did not seem too happy with the thought that five active boys might disrupt the tranquility of the upscale establishment. She took us to the far corner of the dining area in an attempt to isolate us from the rest of the patrons. I knew what she was doing and was a little bit ticked off but didn't want to create a fuss.

After our waiter took our drink order, we decided on the buffet breakfast, which would be faster than ordering from the menu.

Hildy and I escorted the boys to the serving line and they began loading their plates. We supervised to make sure they took a variety of foods rather than a plate filled with just scrambled eggs. I had to help TJ since he was hardly able to see over the edge of the buffet. Their plates were filled to overflowing with nearly everything on the serving line.

The boys' behavior at breakfast was excellent. They were quiet and as well-mannered as I could have asked for. Hildy never allowed obnoxious behavior at home so it didn't surprise me they were well behaved in the restaurant. Our waiter was a young man who appeared to be maybe twenty. He was very attentive to us and particularly the boys. He made sure they had all the milk and juice they wanted and even brought a plate of sweet rolls to our table for them.

"Hal," that was the name on his nametag, "I appreciate the service you've given us. Do all of your customers get this level of service?"

"Well, no," he blushed. "I have five younger brothers and three sisters at home and these boys remind me of them. I miss them. They're back in Tyler."

"Are you going to school in Houston?" I asked.

"Yes, I go to Rice during the day and work three nights and weekends here," Hal said. "My scholarship doesn't quite cover all my expenses."

"You must be a pretty good student to get a scholarship to Rice," I said, with renewed respect for this young man. Rice University is considered by many as 'Harvard on the bayou'.

"I do okay," he said, again blushing.

Hal finished clearing our table and then brought our check which I signed having it added to our hotel bill. As we stood to leave I shook hands with Hal and slipped him a large tip for his excellent service and wished him good luck with his studies. When he looked at the bill I had slipped him he shook his head in disbelief and when he recovered, thanked me profusely. Hildy and I took the boys back to the room to get ready for the funeral and get our luggage loaded in the van.

The church where the funeral was to be held was only a few blocks from the Levin house. We arrived about a quarter to ten and took our places in the pews. The organist was playing some solemn music on a large pipe organ. Ethel's casket was placed at the front of the church. Many of the people approached the casket as they entered church and before they took their seats. I didn't see the need to do that since we had been to the funeral home the night before and I really didn't want to put the boys through it again.

The service lasted longer than I had anticipated. It was far longer than most protestant services I had attended over the years. The minister could have put an insomniac to sleep. His voice was a droning monotone. It didn't take long for TJ to become restless. He climbed up on my lap and laid his head on my chest. The twins were fidgeting quietly in the pew. Even Hildy was beginning to get restless. Thankfully the service ended and the ushers led everyone past the casket as we left the church.

I hadn't noticed that Bill and Karen were there with Tony and Benny until we were on our way out of the church. We waited for them in the parking lot because Joel wanted to talk to Tony. Benny was upset and clinging to Karen as they approached us.

"How's he doing?" I asked Karen, after everyone had been greeted.

"He's happy to be with his brother," she said, "but he misses his Gram. He doesn't understand what's happened."

"I'm sure it's hard for him. He has been jerked around so many times in the last few months. Hopefully he will have some stability very soon," I said.

We chatted a couple more minutes before we loaded into the van and joined the procession going to the cemetery. I just hoped the minister would be a bit more dynamic and most of all shorter winded at the grave site. He wasn't. I learned later he was the associate pastor of the church and was filling in for the head pastor who was on a retreat in Northern Minnesota for a week.

We were invited back to the house after the burial as is the custom. Besides the family, the Boises were the only others there. Hildy immediately went to help Ethel's sisters and Darcie in the kitchen preparing the food. The nine boys went out in the back yard to play and work off some of their pent up energy.

There was so much food. Most of it had been brought by friends and neighbors. There were casseroles of all kinds plus cakes and pies. The women in the kitchen had made what seemed to be a mountain of ham sandwiches and plates of cold cuts. The food hadn't been laid out a minute before there were nine hungry boys rushing into the house. Hildy gave them a stern look and JR quickly led them to the bathrooms to wash their hands.

When Bill laughed, I said, "Has she gotten them well trained or what?"

"She certainly has. I think I had better go wash up myself. I wouldn't want her to look at me that way."

The mountain of sandwiches was reduced to a molehill by the time the adults got to it. I sat with Eric as we ate. He was still feeling down but the realization of his mother's death was beginning to sink in. That didn't make the pain any better but it was becoming manageable. When I asked him what was going to happen to Bran, he said he was going to take him back to Canyon Lake until his aunts left. He thought they would be staying with Alan all next week to help get Ethel's affairs taken care of and for Alan to have someone of his own age to grieve with.

Joel came and squeezed in beside Eric and me on the couch. I could tell he was getting tired. "Why don't you go lie down on Benny's bed for a while? We'll be leaving in about an hour. Okay?"

"Okay, dad," he said, as I gave him a hug.

Turning to Eric, I said, "I'll be so glad when his chemotherapy is over. It really saps his strength."

I noticed Tony had snuggled up to Bill and was resting as well. I know the weakness is part of the price the boys pay for the treatment to get well, but I still get angry they have to endure it.

Wondering what the rest of the boys were up to I went out to the back yard to check. Mel was there playing with them. It looked like he was having the time of his life. They were throwing a Nerf football around. He made sure everyone of the boys received their share of the throws. TJ was just getting his turn when I walked out the back door. He made a great catch for a six, almost seven, year-old. He tossed it back to Mel and then he saw me standing there and ran to me.

"Did you see? I caught it! I really did!" he almost yelled, as he jumped up into my arms.

"Yes, I saw you. That was a great catch. You're getting good. I'm proud of you," I said, giving him a squeeze before I put him down. He ran off with a big smile on his face to play with the other boys.

I watched for a while and then gave Mel a rest. Playing with seven boys can be very wearing. They have a much higher energy level than adults have. I had been throwing the ball to them for maybe ten minutes when Lenny came up to me and asked if they could get a drink.

"Okay, guys, let's take a break and get something to drink. It won't be too long before we have to leave to go back home," I told them. "You need to rest and cool down. It's getting hot out here."

Hildy drew up enough chairs around the kitchen table for the seven boys to sit down while she poured them all a large glass of milk and Darcie set out a heaping plate of assorted cookies. Tony was still sitting beside Bill and leaning his head against Bill's chest looking like he was asleep. Otherwise, I'm sure he would have been at the table too.

I went to check on Joel in the bedroom. He was lying on the bed but was not asleep when I walked in. "How do you feel now?" I asked, sitting on the bed beside him.

"Okay, I guess," he said. "I wish I didn't get tired so easy."

"I know," I said. "Why don't you go into the kitchen? Darcie set out some cookies and if you don't get there soon your brothers will have them all eaten."

That got him up off the bed in no time and he joined the others. Since there was no room for him at the table he hopped up on a stool at the breakfast bar next to Tony, who had been roused from his slumber by the sound of the other boys eating. Hildy placed a smaller platter of cookies in front of them along with their glasses of milk.

It was almost three o'clock by the time we got our goodbyes said and everyone loaded into the van. I made sure everyone visited the restroom before we started out. I didn't want to have to make a pit stop on the way. I wasn't looking forward to the three-hour drive back to our home but I was anxious to get there. "When are you going to come back to Canyon Lake?" I asked Eric, as the boys were getting buckled into their seatbelts.

"I think sometime tomorrow after church. I plan to go back to work on Monday. The project I'm working on will take my mind off things and it's also at a critical stage which needs my attention."

"Well, you know I'm here for you if you need anything. Why don't you send JR and Bran over to the house Monday? Tell Mary Jane she can help her sister out taking care of all of the boys. I think JR needs to be with the other boys to help him work through his grieving. Also, plan on staying for supper," I told him, before giving him one last hug and getting into the van.

"Thanks, Crane, I appreciate your support," Eric said, with just a hint of a tear in his eyes.

The boys waved to their friends until we were out of sight. The traffic on the freeway was heavy until we got past Katy on our way home. I never really liked driving from Houston toward San Antonio. The scenery was not interesting, there were few towns to break up the monotony and worst of all today the sun was shining in through the windshield all the way home. I was always happy when I reached Seguin. It seemed like I was almost home even though it was still close to fifty more miles to go. We made relatively good time and drove up to the gate just under three hours from the time we left.

"Hildy, we're hungry," Larry whined.

"Me too," TJ piped in.

"I don't know what we have in the house to eat that I can fix in a hurry. How about if I call Manfred and see if he'll pick up some pizzas for us? How does that sound?" Hildy asked.

"Yea!" was the response from five hungry boys.

While the boys helped me unload the van, Hildy went to phone Manfred. After we were finished with the unloading, Hildy gave each of the boys a banana to stave off starvation until the pizzas arrived. With their bananas in hand, they went to see Samson. He was all over them as they released him from the fenced in area. You would have thought he hadn't seen his boys for weeks instead of a single day. He stayed within reach of at least one boy the rest of the evening.

It was only about forty-five minutes before Manfred arrived with four large pizzas. I just hoped that would be enough. It turned out there was not a single slice left when we finished. A gallon of milk was also consumed.

Everyone seemed to be lethargic after supper. Hildy and Manfred went to her apartment and the boys and I settled into the family room. I turned on the TV to see if there was anything worth watching. I found a program about the tigers of India I thought would be both interesting and educational so that's what we watched.

A few minutes after we started watching the program, Joel whispered to me, "May I call John? I want to see if they won his soccer game today."

"Sure, tell him to say hi to his mom and dad for me."

"Okay."

It wasn't long before TJ climbed up on the couch beside me and tucked himself under my arm. "I know one little boy who is tired," I said, kissing the top of his head. "When Joel gets off the phone why don't you guys take your showers and then I'll read some more of the story?"

"Okay," he whispered, snuggling closer to me.

The tiger program ended on the TV and Joel hadn't returned to the family room and TJ was nearly asleep. I got up to see if he were still on the phone. He was going to use the phone in my study so the sound from the TV wouldn't bother them. When I entered the study he looked up at me with wide eyes as if to say "Am I in trouble?"

"I think you have been on the phone long enough. Say goodbye to John. I want you to make sure TJ gets his shower taken."

"Okay, dad. Can John come over tomorrow afternoon?"

"If his folks say it is all right, he may. Tell him to plan on staying for supper and we'll take him home afterwards."

"Thanks, dad!" he said, and then turning back to the phone, "He said it was okay. Tell your mom and dad we'll bring you home after supper."

I left the study door open as I went back into the other room but I heard Joel say, "I gotta go. I don't want dad to get pissed." Then, in a quiet voice I could barely hear, "I love you, too."

"Oh boy!" I thought. "How do I keep this relationship from getting out of hand?" I didn't want to stifle it. I just wanted to make sure that no one got hurt. "I'm too young to have to deal with teenage love. I don't even know how to deal with my own."

After they had taken their showers and put on pajamas, they wanted their snack. All we had was ice cream but that didn't seem to matter to them. With the dishes put in the dishwasher we settled into the family room again where I finished reading *A Horse's Tale* to them.

Sunday morning I was up early to fix everyone's breakfast. I didn't know what Hildy's plans were but today was supposed to be her day off. I did notice when I went out to get the newspaper that Manfred's car was still parked in the driveway. I was just putting the finishing touches on breakfast when Joel stumbled into the kitchen.

"The bacon woke me up," he said, rubbing the sleep out of his eyes.

"Good morning, son," I said, giving him a one-armed hug. "Why don't you go upstairs and wake your brothers and then see that TJ gets washed up for breakfast?"

It was a lazy morning. After breakfast the boys entertained themselves reading the Sunday comics and just relaxing. About ten o'clock, Chris came up to me and asked if they could go swimming. That's what we did for the next couple of hours until lunch time. Lunch was a quick one. I fixed sandwiches, chips and milk followed by some cookies that Hildy had taken out of the freezer last night.

I was getting the kitchen cleaned up after our lunch when the gate buzzer sounded. When I checked the security camera I saw it was John and his dad. I activated the gate opener and told Joel his friend was here. We all went out to greet our guests.

"Bruce, it's good to see you again. Can you come in? I was about to make a pot of coffee," I said as I shook his hand.

"Thanks, but I can't stay. We promised the girls we would take them shopping for school supplies this afternoon, but Pauline is not feeling well so I get the honors," he said with a snicker. "If I know my girls, they will also end up doing some clothes shopping."

"That sounds like a lot of fun. I'm going to have to take the boys to do the same one of these days. It won't be long before school starts."

"John, you behave yourself and do what Mr. Johnson tells you. I'll see you tonight," Bruce said. Then he turned to me, "What time do you think you will be bringing him home?"

"Oh, I imagine it will be around seven. I'm going to grill some hamburgers for supper and it'll be after that."

After Bruce left, the boys went into the house to check out the new video game John had brought. I followed them in to see if the game met with my approval. It turned out to be a NASCAR game where you raced cars. The most violent things in it were the car crashes when you couldn't keep your car on the track.

About an hour later it was time to get ready for TJ's T-ball game. His game was scheduled to start around three o'clock. He was all excited about going. He had already dressed in his uniform and informed me he was wearing his cup.

We were preparing to leave when Joel came up to me. I knew he wanted to say something but was having a hard time deciding how to start.

"What is it, son?"

"Well … Could I … That is could we …" he trailed off.

"Come on, son, what do you want to ask?"

"Can John and I stay here while you go to TJ's game?"

"Hmm," this took me a little by surprise. "I guess that would be all right. But, there are some rules you need to follow. Okay?"

"Yeah," he said hesitantly.

"One, no swimming while we are gone. Two, stay away from the lake. And three, don't eat too many cookies," I said, giving him a hug. "I trust you, Joel. Please don't disappoint me."

"I won't, dad," he said. "Thanks."

I knew we would only be gone a couple of hours, but this was the first time I had ever left him alone in the house. I tried to convince myself that after all he was now a teenager and needed to start becoming more independent. That didn't mean I wouldn't worry about him all the time we were gone. I also hoped those teenage hormones didn't overrule his good sense.

CHAPTER 30

"How come Joel gets to stay home?" Lenny asked, as we were getting into the van.

I knew that was coming and I hoped my answer would satisfy them. "Joel has company so he and John are going to stay here while we are gone. He's older than you guys. Besides, TJ needs you to cheer for him."

"Oh," Lenny replied, not entirely convinced.

I was surprised I got off that easily about Joel staying home. We drove to the ballpark with no further questions. TJ's team won their game but I don't think it made any difference to them. They were having too much fun playing the game to worry about silly things like winning or losing. That would change in a few years with all the emphasis and pressures that are placed on kids to win at sports in Texas. I hoped they would keep sports in a reasonable perspective as they grew older.

"We're thirsty," Chris said, as we climbed into the van.

"There're some bottles of juice in the cooler. Why don't you get some out for everyone? Don't spill it, please," I said.

"We're hungry, too," TJ added.

"We'll be home in about twenty minutes. Hildy laid out some cookies for us that you can have when we get there. I think they're oatmeal-raisin," I told him.

"Oh boy," TJ enthused. "They're my favorite."

"I thought chocolate chip cookies were your favorite."

"Yeah, them too," he giggled.

We made it home without any juice spills. As soon as we were parked, the boys flew out of the van and headed for the kitchen. "Don't forget to wash your hands," I called after them. Samson greeted them like they had been gone for a week.

I poured glasses of milk for the boys and set out a plate of cookies while they were washing up. I hadn't seen either Joel or John since I came into the house, but then I hadn't really looked for them.

It wasn't long before the cookie massacre began. I was surprised Joel and John hadn't joined in on the snack so I went looking for them. I found them in the family room. John was sitting on the couch and Joel was sleeping with his head in John's lap.

"He got tired," John whispered.

"How long has he been asleep?" I asked.

"I guess about fifteen or twenty minutes," John said, as he brushed the stubble of hair on Joel's head.

Joel must have heard us talking because he blinked his eyes and yawned. When he saw me he said, "Hi, dad. I must have gone to sleep."

"Are you feeling okay, son?"

"Yeah, John and I were riding the bikes and I got tired. Can we go swimming now? John really wants to, don't you?"

"Sure son, it'll be a couple of hours before supper. Did you guys have your snack?"

"Ah ..." Joel started looking at John and smiling. "Yeah, we did, but ..."

"Well, if you hurry there might be a few cookies left that your brothers don't eat." I had barely gotten the words out of my mouth when both he and John were heading to the kitchen.

Everyone thought swimming was a great idea so as soon as the cookies disappeared we quickly changed into our swim suits and headed to the pool. For the next hour we romped and played and generally had a good time. Joel did take time out to rest every so often when he started tiring. His stamina was getting better but he was still a long way from being back to his old self. Whenever he took time out to rest, John would sit with him on the side of the pool until he was rested.

The boys continued playing in the pool while I started the fire in the barbeque pit to cook our supper. I put the hamburgers on the grill as I sliced the tomatoes and prepared the lettuce. Our fare was going to be simple, just hamburgers, chips, carrot and celery sticks. For dessert there was vanilla ice cream with chocolate syrup.

When the burgers were done I called the boys. They hopped out of the pool and ran to the picnic table without even drying off. I didn't make them put on their shirts like Hildy would have done. I figured this was really a picnic and didn't see any reason for shirts.

I had to laugh at the burgers the boys built. By the time they had put the hamburger, tomato, lettuce, pickles and sliced onion on the bun it was so thick they had a hard time opening their mouths wide enough to take a bite. They did manage however.

After they had eaten their fill and we had everything cleaned up, it was time to take John home. Everyone jumped into the van and we took off. Joel and John were fairly quiet on the way. Their conversation was so low I could barely tell they were talking. Maybe it was just that the others were talking so loud.

Bruce and Pauline were in their front yard along with their three daughters when we arrived. The boys piled out of the van as I went to say hello to the Gordiniers. Larry and Lenny made their way over to Linda and Cassie. TJ noticed Rachel was holding a black puppy so he and Chris went straight to her. Joel and John went off by themselves.

"I see you have a new member of the family," I said to Bruce, as I shook his hand.

"Yeah, the kids have been wanting a pet so we went to the Canyon Lake Animal Society Shelter and picked him up. He looks like he's at least part Lab but mostly just dog," Bruce laughed.

"You know what this is going to lead to. The boys have been hinting at getting another dog for a while now, but I've been putting them off. I'd better talk to Hildy. She is the one who'd have to care for them while the boys are in school."

We chatted for a few more minutes before I called to the boys and told them to say goodbye to their friends and to get in the van. TJ was holding the puppy and was reluctant to give him up, but finally gave the puppy a hug and a kiss before relinquishing it to Rachel. I saw Joel give John a quick hug before walking back to the van.

I kept waiting for it and was not disappointed. About half way home, TJ whined, "I wish I had a puppy like Bubba."

"What about Samson? Do you think he would be jealous?" I asked.

"No, he needs a little brother," TJ said.

"Well, we'll see," I added hoping to put off any further discussion of the matter.

The rest of the evening went fairly well with only a few mentions of another dog. I knew it would not be the end of the discussion though. Joel had been quiet all evening after we had returned from John's house. He never said much even when I tucked him into bed. As I was tucking Chris and the twins into bed Larry asked if they could go shopping for TJ's birthday present since his party was on Wednesday. I told them I would take them shopping tomorrow and asked them to think of what they wanted to get for him because I didn't want to spend the whole day at the mall.

I think they spent an hour or so discussing what they wanted to get after I tucked them in and went back downstairs. I could hear a giggle every so often from them as I sat reading my book in the family room. I figured sleep would overtake them soon enough so I didn't try to settle them down.

I was just about to put my book aside and close up the house for the night when I heard footsteps coming down the hall. When I looked it was Joel. "What's going on, son? Can't you sleep?"

He crawled up beside me in the recliner and laid his head on my chest without saying anything.

I felt his forehead to see if he had a fever. His head was not hot so I didn't think he was sick. I put my arms around him and gave him a hug. "Can you tell dad what's wrong?"

He let out a big sigh before he said, "I'm confused, dad. How come I feel so funny when John's here?"

"What do you mean you feel funny?"

"It's like something is squeezing my insides and my face feels hot."

"It sounds like you really like John, maybe even love him. Do you think that might be it?"

"I don't know. Maybe."

"Does John feel the same way as you do?"

"Uh huh."

"Did he tell you he did?"

"No, but he likes to kiss me. Oh … I didn't mean to say that."

"That's all right, son. Do you like it when you kiss?"

"Oh, yeah!"

"I hope that before you do anything besides kissing that you'll talk to me first. I've explained to you the 'birds and the bees' but I want you to know that even if you know what and how to do it, that doesn't mean you are psychologically ready. Don't rush into something you're not ready for. I trust you to use your best judgment as to how your relationship with John will progress. Just remember that I'm always available to listen to you when you need someone. I won't tell you not to do something but if I don't think you're ready for it I'll try to explain why I think you shouldn't. Always know that I love you and I always will."

"I know you do. I love you, too. You're the best dad anyone could have," he said, stretching up and kissing my cheek.

"You're a pretty neat kid and I'm lucky you're my son. Now, I think it is time to get you back to bed," I said choking back my tears but with pride clearly in my voice.

TJ was the first one of the boys out of bed in the morning. He padded into the kitchen rubbing the sleep out of his eyes. "Good morning, little one," Hildy said, holding out her arms for her morning hug.

"Umph," he said sleepily, as he was enclosed in Hildy's arms.

"Did you have a good sleep?" I asked, as he crawled onto my lap.

"Yeah, I guess so. Joel is still sleeping. He must be tired," he said, giving me a hug before tucking his head under my chin.

TJ sat on my lap enjoying our cuddle as I read the morning paper. He was so quiet I had to look every so often to see whether he had gone back to sleep. We sat that way for maybe fifteen minutes before his stomach let out a growl. "I think we better feed that before it bites somebody," I laughed, and tickled his stomach. "You go wake Joel and get washed up. I'll go wake the rest."

"Okay," he giggled, as he jumped down off my lap and ran toward his bedroom.

After breakfast, I told Larry, Lenny and Chris to get dressed and we would go into San Antonio to shop for TJ's birthday present. When Becky Sue arrived I told her what was going on and that we would be back around noon. I also told her JR and Bran would be coming over with her sister shortly, that I had invited them to spend the day. They arrived about a half an hour later.

"Where are you going?" TJ asked Larry, as he was getting in the van behind his two brothers.

"We're gonna go get your birthday present," Larry responded.

"Oh, okay," TJ said, his eyes lighting up. "What are you gonna get me?"

"You have to wait 'til your birthday," Larry said, closing the van door.

We got to the mall just after it opened at ten o'clock. The boys had decided what they thought they wanted to get for TJ so it didn't take all that long for us to do our shopping. We did have to go to several stores before we found exactly what each wanted to buy. Since it was time for their morning snack they convinced me we needed to stop at the Cin-A-Bun shop for one of their sinful cinnamon rolls and a carton of milk each. I had a cup of coffee and drooled as they ate the sticky confection.

When they were finished, I cleaned up their sticky hands and faces as much as I could before leading them to the restroom for a more complete wash up.

"Come on guys, I want to stop by the foundation office and check my voice-mail before we go on home."

It was not that far to the office. When we got there I was surprised to see Darcie's car parked in front. "What are you doing here? I didn't expect to see you this week."

"I needed to work to keep my mind busy. Besides, dad has Aunt Edith and Edna to be with him. Mel had to go back to work today so I thought I would too. I may have to take off Friday. Mom's will is to be read in the afternoon."

"Take whatever time you need. The foundation is not going to be too busy until we start getting referrals. So far we only have the Boises to concentrate on," I said. "I'm only going to be here long enough to check my voice-mail before I have to get these boys back home."

"What have you guys been doing this morning?" Darcie asked.

"We bought TJ's birthday presents," Chris said.

"Oh, that's right. His birthday is Wednesday, isn't it? Are you going to have a party for him?"

"Yeah," Lenny answered. "He invited seven boys in his class to come."

"With JR and Bran, that will be fourteen boys. Do you want to come and enjoy the fun?" I chuckled.

"Thanks for the invite, but I think I'm busy that day," Darcie laughed.

I only had one voice-mail of interest. It was from Jack. He said the preliminary investigation of the Boises had been completed and he wanted to meet with me to go over the results. All that was left to do was a credit check and verify their financial statement. I called him back and left a message that I would be available all day Tuesday for a meeting. I confirmed that Darcie would also be available.

When we got home, the boys couldn't resist taunting TJ with the wrapped presents until I made them take the presents upstairs to their bedroom. I went outside to check on the other boys and saw Joel and Bran were paired off against Becky Sue and JR playing a game of badminton but without a net. It was more like seeing how long they could keep the shuttlecock in the air before someone missed it and it hit the ground. I hated to break up their fun but Hildy had told me lunch would be ready in about twenty minutes. They all seemed to be out of breath when I stopped them and were ready for a break.

I followed them back into the house when the phone rang. It was Jack returning my call and wanted to set up the meeting on the Boises for tomorrow morning at nine. I told him that would be fine with me but I would have to check with Darcie. He said he had already talked to her and she would be there at nine.

After lunch we sat down to plan out how to occupy fourteen boys at TJ's party. Hildy had the food and cake all planned. Becky Sue would act as life guard in the pool and Mary Jane would organize games and other activities for the group. I was in charge of decorating the game room upstairs and setting up the tables and chairs. I was going to have to go to the party store to rent a couple of folding table and chairs so all fourteen of the boys could sit down when the cake was served.

I took off for the party store when we finished to pick up everything so I could start the decorating process. Thank goodness they had all the things I needed, including the Happy Birthday banners, napkins, paper plates and balloons. I also picked up favors to give to the guests.

Eric came to pick up JR and Bran when he got off work. I bribed him into helping me decorate tomorrow night by inviting him to stay for supper. It didn't take much to twist his arm. I thought it might take his mind off his mother for a while. I could tell he was still a little depressed. I hated seeing him that way. He had always been such a happy and outgoing person.

TJ was so excited about his birthday coming up that he was hardly able to settle down to go to bed. I wondered how he would be tomorrow night. I don't think he ever had a birthday party before. Wednesday could not come quickly enough for him. I hoped Becky Sue would be up to his hyperactivity.

Tuesday morning I left early to meet with Jack and Darcie on the Boises. I got to the office a little early so I made a pot of coffee. I knew Jack would want a cup and I only had time at home for about a half a cup. Darcie arrived shortly after the coffee pot quit perking followed a few minutes later by Jack.

"Come on in, Jack. Grab a cup of coffee and join us in the conference room," I said shaking his hand.

"Thanks, Carolyn didn't fix any coffee this morning. She wasn't feeling well. I think it's her allergies," Jack replied.

"It's good to see you again, Jack," Darcie said, as he sat down at the table.

"Thanks, it's good to see you, too. Sorry to hear about your mother. I know how hard it is to lose a parent. I lost both of mine six years ago in an auto accident," Jack said.

"Well, Jack, what do you have for us?" I asked.

"They check out pretty clean. There is only one blemish we were able to find on Bill's record and that was a long time ago. It seems he was picked up for shoplifting merchandise worth less than twenty dollars when he was thirteen. He was given three months probation and twenty hours of community service."

"How did you find that out? I thought juvenile records were sealed," I said.

"You don't really want to know how we got the info. Just let it be said that it's nice to have contacts. The incident occurred in Gonzales County where I grew up. Other than that one incident he hasn't had so much as a traffic ticket since. Karen is also clean. There are no police records for her at all. It's all here in the report. Everything is detailed from their birth through school up to the present time."

"That looks promising," I said.

"The preliminary look at their financial status is also in the report," Jack said. "Bill doesn't make a lot of money and with Tony being sick Karen has had to give up her part time job to take care of him. They are making it but there's not much left over for luxuries. It would be even more difficult for them if they didn't have someone paying all of Tony's medical bills the state doesn't pay." The last he said, giving me a knowing look.

"Darcie, from your experience in the system, how much more would their income have to be to meet the guidelines to adopt Tony?" I asked, passing the financial report to her.

She spent several minutes looking over the report before she answered. "There are a lot of variables and there is some state assistance for expenses associated with the adoption process itself. If my memory serves me correctly the state will pay up to $1500 for non-recurring adoption expenses. They may even be eligible to receive monthly payments from the state because Tony can be classified as a 'special needs child' since he is over age six. If Benny were to be adopted along with Tony then both would be considered 'special needs'. Such payments could continue until each reached the age of 18. It's possible that each could be eligible for a waiver of tuition to one of the state universities.

"Now that's all a bunch of ifs and the paper work necessary could drag out the process for heaven knows how long. I know that hasn't answered your question but it's something to consider before we make a grant to them."

"I think we need to consider all possibilities before we make a decision but for the sake of this discussion give me your best guess at what additional income they would need to have the adoption of Tony approved," I said.

Doing some quick calculations on a small calculator before she answered, "I would say around $800 a month to meet the requirements most caseworkers look for."

"That would allow them to just maintain an even keel. They could not improve their standing or provide more for Tony. Hmm ..." I mused. "I think it would be a mistake to only provide the absolute minimum. What do you think if we were to provide a stipend of $1000 a month? Would that provide them with a little breathing room?"

"It won't make them rich, but it would allow them to have a few luxuries they otherwise wouldn't be able to afford," she replied.

"Now, let's put Benny in the mix. What additional financial burden would that add? How much more would we have to provide to maintain the same standard of living?"

"I think a good rule of thumb would be three-fourths of the amount given for the first child. Let's say around $750 a month and a little less for each additional child if we ever encounter that situation. Now if the state does provide a monthly payment then the foundations contribution should be reduced by that amount."

"So that means the foundation would be providing up to $20,400 a year to the Boises. That certainly won't break us. Our investments are providing about four times that amount each month. Are the three of us agreed that based on the information we have that we are in favor of supporting this action to the board for final approval?" I asked.

"I am," Jack said.

"I am, too," Darcie echoed. "If Bill and Karen are willing to adopt both of the boys, I definitely think the board should approve our suggestion."

"Great! Darcie, would you set up a board meeting for later this week? I think everyone is in town. Try to set it up for Thursday, if you can. That way you could go to Houston on Friday.

"Now if both of you will excuse me I have to go pick up TJ's birthday present and find someplace to hide it so he won't find it before tomorrow."

"Have fun," Darcie laughed, as Jack and I left the office.

As it turned out TJ's present wasn't ready when I got there and wouldn't be until tomorrow morning so I went on home to get started on the decorating for the party. When I drove through the gate I saw a parade of six bicycles riding on the long drive up to the house. Becky Sue was riding my bicycle. I got in line and drove behind them all the way to the house.

"Hi, Crane, I hope you don't mind my borrowing your bike. I was giving the boys some safety tips on riding in traffic," Becky Sue.

"No, that's fine. The bikes are there to ride," I told her, as the boys gathered. "Hey guys, isn't it about time to get washed up for lunch?"

That was all it took and they were off like a shot. Becky Sue and I followed at a more sedate pace. I made a mental note to tell them to put their bikes away in the garage if they weren't going to ride them anymore today.

Later in the afternoon I decided to swim. I again had been remiss in doing my laps in the pool for a while. Naturally the boys wanted to join me. When I started swimming my laps, Chris started swimming with me as he had done many times in the past. I was pleasantly surprised at how long he could stay with me. I'm glad that I was able to outlast him. It would have been embarrassing to be out done by a ten year old.

Eric arrived about 5:30 with JR and Bran to help me decorate for the party. We decided we would wait to start until after supper. I took Eric aside and asked him how he was doing.

"Okay, I guess," he said. "It's still hard to believe mom's gone. At least the last time I saw her I hugged her and kissed her and told her I loved her. That makes me feel better, but …"

"I know," I said, putting my arms around him as he started crying.

"I feel like such a baby," he said, after his crying had subsided. "Thanks, Crane, thanks for being here."

"You're welcome. You're very special to me," I said. "I want you to know that."

"I feel the same," he said. Then brightening, "I suppose we ought to see what the boys are up to. There's no telling what kind of mischief the seven of them can get into."

We found the boys outside playing with the badminton set I had put up earlier. Larry and Lenny were faced off against Bran and Chris. At first I thought it would be a mismatch since both Bran and Chris were older than the twins but it actually was the other way around. The twins seemed to have better communication between them as to which one of them should hit the shuttlecock when it was close. Bran and Chris on the other hand were continually running into each other or banging rackets. When they did, it invariably caused the twins to double up laughing, especially if one of their opponents fell down. Neither team was very good but they sure were having fun. Even the non-players were having fun watching and cheering.

It took Eric and me almost two hours to put up the decorations and set up the tables to Hildy's satisfaction. When we were finished, I must admit it did look good. It even passed muster of the boys. They even tried to help, but to be honest they tended to get in the way rather than aid in the process.

When Eric and the boys were ready to go home they went by the kitchen to say goodbye to Hildy. She was in the process of frosting TJ's birthday cake. There were seven set of young boys' eyes glued to the large cake. I'm sure there was drool trying to escape all of their mouths.

"There now boys, you'll have to wait 'til tomorrow before you can have any of this cake, but if you look in that cookie jar you might just find something that will satisfy you," she said, nodding her head toward the large cookie jar.

They didn't wait for a second invitation as seven hands tried to grab a cookie at the same time. Eric and I laughed at their struggles but in the end each had grabbed at least two cookies. We waited until the jar was clear of other hands before we reached in and got our treats.

Before Eric climbed into his car I gave him a hug and said, "I'm always here for you whenever you need someone to talk to or just to be with. You're always welcome here."

"Thanks, my friend, I do appreciate that."

TJ was even more excited when I tucked him in bed tonight. I tried to settle him down but it took Joel to finally get him settled down enough to lie still in bed. I just hoped he would sleep at least part of the night. He had a big day ahead of him tomorrow.

I was a little surprised TJ was not up when I walked into the kitchen on Wednesday morning. Hildy was busy making waffles and browning sausage when I poured my cup of coffee. I retrieved the morning paper and sat down to drink my coffee and wait for the seven year old tornado to appear. Joel appeared shortly with Samson and led him out to do his morning duty.

It wasn't long before the smell of the waffles brought all of the boys to the table suitably washed. I was surprised no one mentioned TJ's birthday. I guess they were to busy eating to remember. That didn't last long. After the first round of waffles Joel was the first to wish TJ a happy birthday. That jogged the others' memory and they too wished him a happy birthday.

After breakfast I sat the boys down and told them we would give TJ his gifts from us this morning. I didn't want the guests to feel badly because our gifts to TJ would probably be more expensive than the gifts they would bring. Of course that was just fine with TJ. He was a perfect gentleman as he opened each of the gifts as the boys gave them to him. After opening each he would thank the brother and give him a hug. Hildy gave him her present once the boys were through.

When he had opened all the presents TJ looked at me as if to say "Where's my present from you?"

"What? Are you looking for another present?" I asked.

He just giggled as an answer and looked at the floor.

"Of course dad has a present for you, but Joel and I have to go pick it up. Now all of you go get dressed and then we'll go pick up your present," I said.

It took us less than an hour to pick up the present and return to the house. TJ must have been watching the security camera aimed at the gate because he was waiting for us beside the driveway when we drove up. I got out of the BMW, went around to the passenger side and opened the door for Joel. He stepped out holding a white puppy with four black feet, a black tipped tail and black markings around his eyes that looked like he was wearing a mask.

TJ was ecstatic when he saw the puppy and grabbed it out of Joel's hands. "Oh, he's so cute," TJ said cuddling the puppy to his chest. "I love him! I love him! I'm gonna call him Bandit. Yeah, Bandit."

With that, Bandit peed on TJ's shirt.

CHAPTER 31

"Bandit, you bad dog," TJ scolded, as he laughed and held his new friend out away from him so the rest of Bandit's present harmlessly watered the yard.

Larry, Lenny and Chris were laughing so hard they were holding each other up to keep from falling down. Joel and I were trying our best not to laugh and were having a hard time doing it.

When Bandit finished, TJ hugged the puppy to him and received an enthusiastic tongue-washing. "I love you anyway. You're the bestest present I ever got."

"Okay, son, let's go get you cleaned up and show Hildy the new member of the family," I said, still stifling a snicker.

We hadn't taken a couple of steps when Samson greeted us. More to the point he headed straight for Bandit. I hadn't seriously considered that he might be jealous of a new dog in his territory and I was a little worried. When he got to Bandit he sniffed him thoroughly before stepping back and giving one bark. He then turned and led the procession back to the house. I drew a sigh of relief that Bandit was accepted so quickly.

Turning to the now only occasionally giggling twins and Chris, I said, "Will you guys get Bandit's bed and food bowl out of the car and bring them into the house?"

The twins grabbed the doggie bed and Chris the weighted bowl and followed us back into the house. I grabbed the bag of puppy food.

"Hildy, see my new puppy," TJ said, holding out Bandit. "His name is Bandit 'cause he's got a mask. See?"

"Oh, he's adorable," she said, taking the squirming puppy. As she held him up to her, he gave her neck a thorough licking. "And what is that on your shirt?"

"Ah ... He sorta had a accident," TJ said bashfully.

Hildy tried her best to suppress her laugh but her voice gave her away, "Well, I think you had best go change your shirt and wash up."

"Yes, ma'am," he said, holding out his hands for his dog. "Let's go, Bandit."

Off he went to his bedroom with his four brothers and Samson following close behind.

"You know what this is going to lead to, don't you?" Hildy asked.

"Oh yeah, it looks like we'll have a whole kennel full very shortly. I'd better have Harold build us some dog houses along with the remodeling," I said, shaking my head.

It wasn't long before Samson came into the kitchen and headed for his food bowl followed closely by Bandit stumbling over his own feet. When Bandit tried to eat out of Samson's bowl he was nudged over to his own bowl I had filled with his puppy food. After a couple of nudges he got the idea Samson wanted him to eat out of his own bowl. Hildy and I just stood there watching them and smiling.

"Smart little devil, isn't he?" I commented.

"Let's just see how quickly he gets trained to go outside to do his business," she replied.

"Yeah, I suppose it would be a good idea to line up a carpet cleaning service. This may take a while. Maybe Samson can help train him," I said hopefully.

Hildy had decided since TJ's guests would be arriving around one o'clock she would serve lunch earlier than usual. That didn't cause the boys any problem. Samson knew better than to beg at the table so he lay down on his rug while the boys ate. Bandit seemed to think that was a good idea and snuggled up against him and promptly went to sleep.

Becky Sue wasn't scheduled to come to work until noon. She arrived just as we were finishing our lunch. She said her sister would be bringing JR and Bran over in a few minutes. Mary Jane wanted to get the games and activities set up before all the rest of the guests arrived.

JR and Bran were greeted by TJ and Bandit as Mary Jane drove her car up the drive. JR was thrilled that TJ had gotten a puppy. He thought it gave him more leverage with his father to get him one too. He and Bran took turns holding and getting licked by a squirming Bandit. When TJ took him back, Bandit placed his head on TJ's shoulder as he was being held and appeared to go to sleep.

"I think we had better put the dogs in the fenced area before your guests arrive. It might be a little too much excitement for Bandit. Samson will take care of him. You can show your friends your puppy but I think it is best they don't hold him," I said, leading the boys back into the house. TJ wasn't too happy about letting his new little friend go but agreed when the gate buzzer announced the first of his school friend's arrival.

As each of the parents arrived I invited them in to check out the preparations for the party. Since I didn't know any of them except by name I wanted them to be reassured the party and the kids would be properly supervised. All the invited boys had been told to bring their swimsuits if they wanted to swim. I made sure the parents knew there was a Red Cross certified lifeguard on duty to see their sons were safe in the water.

By a quarter past one all the invited guests had arrived and the parents had gone. The party plan was for Mary Jane to organize the games for the first hour and a half. Then the cake, ice cream and other treats would be served. After that the last couple of hours would be for the boys to go swimming or games if they didn't want to swim.

Mary Jane did an excellent job of keeping the boys occupied for the first part of the party. She was going to make an excellent elementary teacher. She had a definite way with the six and seven year olds.

While all this was going on Hildy and I were getting the table ready. Eric and I, the night before, had arranged the two tables side by side so they looked like one large square table. There were four chairs along three sides of the table and two on the other side.

At about two-thirty I announced the cake and ice cream were being served, but that everyone had to wash their hands before we could start the party. I told my sons to show our guests where the bathrooms were so they could wash up. It didn't take long for fourteen boys to find their way upstairs to the table. The nametags put TJ's seven guest and JR on opposite side of the table with Bran, the twins and Chris at the end of the table. TJ and Joel sat on the other end where the cake was.

Hildy lit the candles on the cake and everyone sang an off-key rendition of *Happy Birthday*.

"Make a wish and then blow out the candles," I said, giving TJ's shoulder a squeeze.

"I don't know what to wish for," he said. "I got everything. I got my Bandit and everything."

"That's okay. Just blow out the candles."

"I know! I know! I wish that Larry and Lenny and Chris had a puppy, too," he said, and with a big breath he blew out the seven burning candles.

I could see three pair of eyes at the other end of the table all staring at me with 'puppy dog eyes'. I knew this was coming but I didn't know if the household could stand five boys and five dogs. When I turned to look at Hildy she had this funny-looking smile on her face and just shook her head trying very hard to suppress a snicker.

The cake was cut with TJ getting the first piece with a big dip of vanilla ice cream on top of the chocolate cake with chocolate icing. Hildy cut the cake, I added the ice cream and passed the dishes to the anxiously waiting and starving boys. There were bowls of nuts and mints on the table which were quickly added to the plates.

After everyone had their fill of cake, TJ opened his presents. They were mostly games or Disney videos. JR and Bran gave him a video game which I had made sure was not violent. TJ was very polite. He thanked each boy as he opened a gift. I was so very proud of him my heart felt like it was going to burst.

"Anyone want to swim?" I asked, after all the party festivities were finished.

"Yea!" came an almost unanimous reply.

"Okay, go get your suits on," I said. I noticed one of the boys didn't seem to be too enthusiastic about swimming. His name was Brad and he was the smallest of all the friends TJ had invited. He was lagging behind the rest of the boys going to get changed. "Brad? Don't you like to swim?"

He looked at me and appeared to be on the verge of tears before he said barely above a whisper, "I never been swimming before. I'm kinda scared."

"Well, I tell you what. You stay right by me. I'll make sure you're safe. How about that?" I asked, giving him a squeeze.

"Okay, you won't let me drown, will you?"

"No, son, now go get changed and wait for me beside the pool. I'll be right there."

Off he ran to change and I started to my own room to get ready. Hildy said she would start the cleanup. I thanked her and returned and gave her a hug. "What would I have ever done without her?" I thought to myself as I changed into my swimming trunks. Sure enough Brad was waiting for me beside the pool.

I jumped into the shallow end of the pool and then sat back up on the side of the pool motioning Brad to join me. I took his hand and helped him to sit beside me with his feet dangling in the water. After I thought he was comfortable, I slipped off the side and stood in the three foot depth of the shallow end. I turned to him and held out my arms to him. He nervously put his arms around my neck and allowed me to lift him in my arms.

"We'll stay right here where the water isn't so deep. Do you think you would like to stand in the water? It'll only come up to here," I said, drawing a line across his chest with my finger and then tickling his ribs.

"Okay," he giggled. "Don't let go."

"I won't, I promise," I said, as I gently removed his arms from around my neck and eased him down into the water. "See, that's not bad, is it?"

"Huh-uh," he said, while he clung tightly to my waist.

I walked him back and forth across the shallow end until I thought he was becoming more comfortable. "Now we're going to have some fun. Can you make the sound of a motor boat?"

"Like this," he said, and then made a fair imitation of a motorboat by puckering his lips and blowing air through them.

"Great, that's the way I do it, too. Now what we're going to do is do it like a real motorboat ... underwater. Here, I'll show you," I said. Taking a deep breath, I placed my face underwater and did my imitation of a motor boat. Brad was giggling when I lifted my face out of the water and cleared my eyes. "You want to try?"

"Yeah, you made lotsa bubbles."

"Just remember to take a big breath before you put your face in the water and lift your face up before you run out of breath. Are you ready?"

With the shake of his head he took a big breath and leaned over so his face was barely under the water. He started making the motor boat sound but before he was out of breath he started to giggle.

"The bubbles tickle," he said. "I want to do it again."

Each time he did his motor boat his face made it further down into the water until his ears were under.

"Do you want to try something else?" I asked, as he came up the last time.

He looked at me and shook his head yes, his eyes as bright as two new pennies.

"Okay, let's see if you can learn to float on your back. Put one hand on the side of the pool and then lean back. I'll put my hand under you so you won't sink." For the next fifteen minutes or so I worked with him until he was able to float for a fifteen or twenty seconds by himself before he would start to sink and panic. I was always there to catch him. After the first few tries the worried look on his face was replaced by a smile I thought might crack his face.

TJ came over to check on Brad. "Having fun?" he asked his small friend.

"Oh, yeah!" he said. "Your dad's been showing me lots of stuff. He's really neat."

"I know, he's the best," TJ replied.

"But, I'm getting kinda tired. I think I'll get out a while. Maybe I'll go sit with Joel. He looks tired too," Brad said, and then clambered out of the pool and went to sit on the lounge chair next to Joel.

"Thanks, dad, he never talks much. I'm glad he's having fun."

I joined the other boys and played in the water with them. We were all having so much fun that we lost track of time until the first parent arrived to take their son home. As it happened it was Mrs. Rasmussen, Brad's mom.

"Mom! Mom! Look what Mr. Johnson showed me," he said, running from his mom to the side of the pool. I knew he was waiting for me so I went and helped him into the pool. There he showed his mom the motor boat and then with just a little help from me his back float.

"That's great, son," Mrs. Rasmussen said, smiling at him. "Go get your clothes changed. We have to go pick up your dad."

"TJ, go show Brad where the towels are so he can rinse the chlorine off before he gets dressed," I said. "The rest of you had better go shower also before your folks come to get you."

"Okay, dad," TJ answered, and followed Brad into the house.

"How did you get Brad into the water? He has always been afraid to get in a pool," Mrs. Rasmussen said.

"We took it real slowly and he saw how much fun the other boys were having and that helped. I didn't push him to do anything until he was comfortable. I think he would really like the water if he had a chance."

"His dad probably tries to push him too fast. He so wants Brad to be an athlete. I don't know if he ever will be. He is so small and will probably never be a big person. His dad and I are both fairly short. But thank you for working with him. I can tell he had a good time," she said.

Brad came out carrying his wet bathing suit that Hildy had wrapped up in plastic wrap and the Star Wars action figure that each of the guests received as a party favor. "Thanks, Mr. Johnson, I had a great time," he said, as he ran to his mom's car.

One by one the other boys were picked up by their parents until only JR and Bran remained. It would be a while before Eric arrived to take them home. Becky Sue and her sister left shortly thereafter. Before Becky Sue left I asked her if she would be available to life guard on Friday of next week for the twins' birthday party. This was to be her last week of work for us so she could take some time off before her classes started. She said she would let me know and if she couldn't she would suggest someone who would be able to help.

By the time all the party guests were gone, I was exhausted. The energy level of six and seven year olds is amazing. The only time they were not going ninety miles an hour was when they were eating cake and then they were fidgeting. My admiration goes out to their teachers for being able to corral their energy and actually get them to learn.

TJ immediately went and rescued his puppy as soon as the last guest left. Bandit was excited to get released from the fenced in area and when he wasn't squirming in TJ's arms he was racing around the house investigating everything in site. He seemed to want to chew on almost anything he could get in his mouth. I could see having a puppy in the house was going to be a whole new experience. I put chew toys at the top of my shopping list.

When Eric arrived to pick up JR and Bran he was greeted by an excited JR who tried to tell him about the entire party in one breath until his dad got him to slow down. Eric made his way to the house and was introduced to Bandit. He gave me a resigned look knowing JR was not going to let up until he got his own puppy.

"You know I'll get even with you for this, don't you?" he said, in a mock threatening voice.

"Yeah, well, misery loves company," I retorted. "Why don't you join us for dinner? Hildy is fixing ham, corn on the cob and sliced tomatoes. I picked up the corn and tomatoes from that roadside stand down the road there on 306. They're home-grown."

"That sounds too good to turn down. And besides I haven't had a piece of birthday cake. Is there any left?" he laughed.

I went into the kitchen and told Hildy to set three more plates for supper. She told me Manfred was going to stop by also. I guess it was a good thing I bought two dozen ears of corn yesterday. She said that as soon as Manfred got here supper would be served.

Supper was delicious. From the amount of butter on the boys' faces from eating the corn I could tell they enjoyed it as much as the adults. We only had slightly less butter on our faces. Hildy solved the problem by bringing out wet paper towels to clean up with.

There was still enough of TJ's birthday cake for everyone to have a piece before Eric decided it was time for them to take off for home.

"Come on guys, we have to get home and get things packed so we'll be ready to take off for Houston when I get off work tomorrow. Say goodbye to your friends," Eric said. Turning to me, he said, "JR is really going to miss Bran. They have become very close this past week. I think Bran likes the idea of having a little brother. First it was Benny and this week it has been JR. He was a lot of company for JR."

"Well, you could always take over fostering him or even adopt him," I said, with a grin.

"Bite your tongue!" he said. "Sometimes JR is more than I can handle. What would I do with a fifteen year-old?"

"I asked myself something like that a million times before I decided to take on my five. Sometimes it's been a challenge, most of the time it's been a labor of love having them with me. I'm blessed to have Hildy. She has made it possible for us to maintain a semblance of a normal life."

"I don't know what's going to happen to Bran. I haven't discussed it with dad. I know he cares deeply for Bran, but whether he wants to try to handle a teenager alone at his age is not something I think he has even considered. When mom was alive it was a different matter. She needed to have someone to mother and dad was fine with that. He enjoyed the kids they fostered. Now I feel things may be different. I don't know."

"Whatever happens, Eric, I want to make sure Bran is taken care of and not returned to his dad. He's a sensitive boy and needs the love that a family can provide. Keep me informed," I said, as Eric headed toward his car.

I watched as their car drove down the lane. I wondered if our busy lives would ever give us time to explore a relationship I thought each of us wanted. When I returned inside TJ was sitting on Manfred's lap while holding Bandit. "Did you tell Mr. Strasser what Bandit did to you?" I asked TJ.

"No," he giggled. "When daddy gave him to me he pee-peed on me. He didn't mean it. He got all excited and couldn't help it, could you, Bandit?"

Bandit licked TJ's nose as an answer.

"Well, it wouldn't be the first time it happened to me," Manfred said, smiling. "When my son was little and we were stationed in Sacramento, we had three daschunds. Why we had three I'll never know. One day I came home from the Air Force base and there they were. My wife kept them all the time I was stationed there and when I was in Korea. When we moved to Minot, unfortunately, they didn't thrive in the cold of North Dakota and the three of them failed to survive the first winter. I guess they were warm weather dogs. My son was crushed but he never wanted a dog after that."

"Son, why don't you take Bandit outside? Take Samson and maybe he'll show Bandit that he is supposed to do his business outside and not on your shirt," I said.

"Okay," he said, jumping down from Manfred's lap. "Here, Samson, let's go outside. You can show Bandit what to do."

When the boys were finished with their showers and had gotten ready for bed, I went upstairs to tuck Chris and the twins in bed. I had a good idea of what I was going to face. I was immediately surrounded by the three of them and guided to sit on a bed. A twin sat on either side of me. Chris sat on the bed opposite me.

"Dad," Lenny began, "Can we get a puppy for our birthday next week? Please?"

"Yeah, dad, please?" Larry pleaded.

"How about you, Chris?" I asked.

"Yeah, but my birthday is not 'til November," he said, hanging his head.

"Well, I'll tell you what. If you promise to take care of them …"

"We will! We will, dad!" they almost shouted in unison.

"All right then, we'll go to the shelter on Friday and see what they have available. Now then, it's time you guys were in bed," I said. I received extra special hugs and kisses from them as I tucked them in.

I went downstairs to finish my nightly routine. When I entered Joel and TJ's room, I was not all that surprised to see Bandit in bed with TJ. "Now, TJ, you know Bandit can't sleep in bed with you. He needs to sleep in his own bed."

"But, he'll be lonesome," TJ said, sticking out his bottom lip in a pout.

"Give him a hug and let me put him in his bed. I'll put his bed right here beside yours," I said, shoving the doggie bed closer to the boys' bed.

"Okay," he reluctantly said, kissing his puppy on the top of his head. "I love you, Bandit."

I put Bandit down in his bed hoping he would stay there. That was not to be. He tried to climb back up into TJ's bed. Several times I put him back in his bed but he was having none of it. Finally I decided to try a different tack and took him around to the other side of the bed where Samson's bed was and put him down beside Samson. That seemed to work a little better. He turned around several times before he settled down and lay down next to Samson and appeared to be inclined to go to sleep. I hoped this would last at least through the night. With Bandit settled, I tucked Joel and TJ in for the night and went to my room to prepare for bed. It had been a long day.

Thursday morning was the first meeting of the board of directors of the foundation. I got to the office at about 8:45 to get things ready for the meeting. Darcie was already there when I got there and had almost everything prepared to present our first proposed recipients of the foundation to the board. All that was left for me to do was to make a pot of coffee. Gerald, Carlos and Jack all arrived shortly before nine.

Before we were able to take care of any business the board had to vote on the rules that would govern the operations of the board. Carlos had drawn up a set of rules that we all read through before we voted to approve them. The next order of business was to authorize me as President, CEO and Chairman of the Board to hire employees and to set salaries and compensation for all employees and to contract for services as I found necessary with oversight by the board.

With all the housekeeping items taken care of we took up the proposal to pay the Boises a stipend if they were willing to adopt Tony and an additional stipend if they also agreed to adopt Benny. Gerald suggested what we were proposing was a bit too generous and suggested we might want to trim back the $1000 per month to at least $900 and the second amount for Benny be reduced to $700 maximum.

After much discussion it was decided the amounts Gerald proposed were appropriate. It was also agreed that if the state provide any ongoing support to the Boises that our contribution would be reduced by 80% of the state aid. The aid would be available until each one reached the age of 18 or graduated from high school. At that time a determination would be made whether to continue the aid if either one attended a recognized institution of higher learning.

The meeting adjourned just before eleven. When everyone was gone, Darcie made a call to Karen Boise, which she put on the speaker phone, to explain to her what the foundation was proposing and to ascertain if they were still interested in adopting Tony or Benny or both.

"We want both of them. They are so happy these past couple of weeks to be back together again. To separate them again would be something I cannot bear to think of. Yes, we want to adopt and as soon as we can," Karen said.

"What you need to do to get things started," Darcie said, "is to contact Cindi and tell her what you want to do and find out from her what the state will contribute to the adoption process. Once you have done that, give me a call and I will coordinate with CPS to let them know what the foundation is willing to do."

"God bless you. If we hadn't met Joel and Mr. Johnson, none of this would ever have happened. God must have had a plan ..." Karen broke down. We could hear her sobbing over the phone. "I'm sorry. It's just nothing like this has ever happened to us. It's almost unbelievable."

"That's the purpose of the foundation: to find good people who want to adopt and provide them with the resources to make it happen," Darcie said. "You and your husband are to be the first recipients of the foundation's aid."

"Thanks, Darcie, I'll call Cindi as soon as I hang up and get everything started. I hope this all works out. It just has to," she said. "Goodbye."

"I'm going to like this job," Darcie said, after she disconnected. "It really makes you feel good to be able to help people like Karen and Bill."

"I'm glad we can do this. It does make you feel like you are doing something worthwhile," I said. "Well, I'm going to head on home. Let me know if you hear back from Karen. I won't be back in the office until tomorrow afternoon and I know you will be gone all day. I'm going to go by the animal shelter to see what they have to offer in the way of puppies. It looks like I'm going to be the proud owner of five dogs after tomorrow."

"You are a glutton for punishment, aren't you?"

"Yeah, five boys and five dogs, my carpets will never be the same," I said, getting up and heading for the door. "I'll see you on Monday."

I was surprised when I got to the shelter that they had a fairly large selection of dogs of all ages to select from. I saw three I thought would be good matches for the boys, but would have to wait to see what they thought tomorrow.

CHAPTER 32

I looked at my watch as I was leaving the Animal Shelter and noted it was almost half past noon. Not only was I hungry but Chris had baseball practice and I had to coach the twins' practice this afternoon. I had enough time since Chris' practice was not until two o'clock and the twins' wasn't until three.

As I drove up the drive to the house, I was met by TJ chasing Bandit toward the car. I stopped before I reached the house, afraid I might run over Bandit. TJ scooped up his puppy and opened the car door and climbed in.

"Hi, dad," TJ said, hugging Bandit.

"Hi, son," I said, reaching over to give them both a hug. "Are you and Bandit having fun?"

"Oh, yeah," he enthused. "I fed him and we went all around the house and he even went swimming with us. He's a good swimmer. He paddles all around and climbs up on my back in the water. He's funny and he only had one accident, but Hildy said it was all right."

"I'm glad you guys are having so much fun," I said, as I drove the car the rest of the way to the house and parked in the garage. "Have you had your lunch yet?"

"Yeah, we had tomato soup and grilled cheese sandwiches," he said. "I dunk 'em in the soup. Do you?"

"Yes, I do," I said. "I wonder if Hildy has some left for me. I hope you didn't eat it all."

He didn't answer as he took off around the corner of the house with Bandit at his heels. When I entered the house Hildy told me the tomato soup was gone but she could fix me a sandwich and some potato salad she had prepared for our supper. I thanked her and went to wash and change.

•

While I was eating my lunch, Becky Sue joined me at the table to tell me she would be unable to be the lifeguard for Larry and Lenny's birthday party next Friday. She did, however, have someone who was willing to do it. The person's name was David Wilson. He was a sophomore at UTSA (University of Texas San Antonio), nineteen years old and Red Cross certified. When I asked if I could meet with him before I made the final decision she informed me he could meet with us tomorrow afternoon after he got off work.

"If he has a job how is he going to be able to work next Friday?" I asked.

"This is his last week on his summer job. He helps his uncle build houses in the summer," she said. "I think he'll get along very well with the boys. He has four younger brothers and one sister at home. Besides he's cute."

"I thought you had a fiancé," I told a blushing Becky Sue.

"I do, but he says he can look, so I can too."

"Have him give me a call and we can set up a time to meet. Thanks," I said.

When I told TJ that he couldn't take Bandit to the ballpark, he decided to stay at home with Joel and Becky Sue. He said he and Bandit were going to take a nap. I gathered up Larry, Lenny and Chris and took off for the ballpark.

Chris ran to say hi to his coach after I had parked the Land Rover. He was one of the first kids to arrive so I went to talk to Coach Leonard. We chatted about our teams and how much the boys had improved since the start of the season. Before long, the rest of the team arrived. I told Chris the twins and I would be practicing on field number three when he finished with his practice and for him to come there and wait for us to finish. I pointed to our practice field to make sure he knew which one it was.

As Chris and his team began their practice, I got a ball out of the Land Rover and began playing catch with the twins. For almost ten year olds they weren't too bad at catching the ball and delivering it to the other one as if they were throwing it to a base for an out. We did this for maybe fifteen minutes before I told them to rest and watch Chris' practice. I didn't want their arms to be too tired to practice when it was our turn.

Peter Hammond, our assistant coach, arrived with his son about a half an hour later. When I saw him drive up, I ushered Larry and Lenny over to our practice field. The team that was practicing on it was just wrapping up their session as we approached. Peter and I got busy putting out the equipment so everything would be ready when the rest of the team arrived.

Practice went as usual. It always amazed me at the wide variations in abilities and athleticism in our little group of boys. Some of them couldn't walk and chew gum at the same time and others could make spectacular diving catches and come up throwing the ball. Peter and I made it a point that each and every boy on our team knew he was appreciated and most of all had fun.

After the practice was over, I had the twins help me get the sodas and snacks out of the car. Chris joined us in enjoying the refreshments. I think this was the boys' favorite part of practice.

I waited until all the boys had been picked up by their parents before we started home.

"Dad …" Lenny started.

"Yes, Lenny?"

"Are we really gonna go … you know … get our puppies tomorrow?" he asked.

"Yes, son, we're going to go see what they have at the shelter. If you see one you like we'll take it home. If you don't see a puppy you like we can check some other places until you do find one. Remember, this is your birthday present so don't expect another present next week. Okay?"

"Yeah," all three chimed in.

Becky Sue was getting ready to leave when we got home. She said she had spoken to David and he would call around eight tonight to set up some time to meet. I thanked her before she gave each of the boys a hug, said goodbye to Hildy and left for home.

Hildy met me at the kitchen door and told me Harold had called and would be by tomorrow at three to discuss the plans for the renovation of her apartment unless he heard from me to the contrary. I didn't know of anything that would conflict with that, but I asked her to be available to go over the plans also. If Manfred were available he was welcome to be there as well.

"Daddy," TJ said, jerking on my shirt tail, "Bandit is so smart. He knows he's 'posed to go outside to go to the bathroom."

"That's great, son," I said giving him a hug.

"But sometimes he doesn't know until it's too late and when he gets to the door he has a accident. But he really wants to go outside. He just doesn't know too soon," he said.

I tried not to laugh but a snicker slipped out. "He'll learn," I said, looking at Hildy and shaking my head.

"Samson's trying to teach him, dad," Joel said, as he came into the room. "He goes to the door and barks and Bandit follows him outside. I don't think Samson has to go as often as Bandit. You're not mad at him are you? He really does try."

"No, I'm not mad at him. In fact, I'm very proud of how quickly he's learning," I said, leaning down and scratching Bandits ears. "You're a cute little devil, aren't you?"

Bandit rolled over and waited for someone to scratch his belly. He got several volunteers.

I received a call from David Wilson right at eight o'clock. I told him what I wanted him for and he sounded excited about doing it. He even agreed to come early and help with the games. That made me happy since neither Becky Sue nor Mary Jane was going to be available. He told me he was working on his degree in Child Psychology and thought it would be fun to work with kids other than his brothers and sister. I asked him to come around ten and he could meet the family and help me set things up for the party. I decided after talking to him on the phone that I didn't need to meet him in person. I trusted my instincts and Becky Sue's recommendation.

Later when I was tucking the boys into bed, Chris and the twins were so wound up about going to get a puppy tomorrow that it took a long time before I was able to quiet them down. Even after I had gone back downstairs every once in a while I would hear one of their high pitched giggles. I knew it would only get them started again if I went up there so I just waited until sleep overtook them. It was probably only a half an hour after they were usually asleep, but I suspected they would be difficult to get up in the morning.

I was wrong. I heard their footsteps on the stairs before I had finished my first cup of coffee. They rushed into the kitchen and surrounded a surprised Hildy with a hug and received a kiss on the top of each head before they descended on me. All three tried to climb on my lap at the same time.

"Whoa, guys, I don't think my lap will hold all of you," I said. I gave each a hug and a kiss and directed them to a chair at the table. "You are up awfully early aren't you? Do you have anything special you plan on doing today?"

"Dad!" came the indignant response from all of them.

"Can we go to the animal place now?" Larry asked.

"They don't open until ten o'clock. That's over two hours from now," I told three disappointed boys. "Eat your breakfast. I'll go get your brothers out of bed."

When I went into the bedroom I panicked. TJ was not in the bed and he wasn't in the bathroom. I was about to shake Joel when I noticed TJ curled up on the floor with Bandit tucked in his arms. "That little stinker," I muttered, much relieved. Reaching down I picked him up and sat down on the bed cradling him in my arms. Bandit tried his best to climb up my leg but wasn't able to make it.

"Morning, dad," a sleepy TJ murmured.

"Good morning," I said, kissing his forehead. "How come you were sleeping on the floor?"

"Bandit was lonely," he said, burying his face in my chest.

"Okay, Bandit was lonely. I see. Go get your hands and face washed and then take Bandit outside. Hildy will have breakfast ready when you come back in."

Off he ran with Bandit in hot pursuit. I woke Joel and then went back to the kitchen to finish my coffee.

I had never seen the twins and Chris as fidgety as they were this morning. They kept checking the clock until finally at a quarter to ten I relented and we got in the van to go see if we could find them a puppy. TJ and Joel were going to stay at the house with Becky Sue. The shelter was about twenty-five minutes away, but you would have thought it was hours away, as antsy as the boys were.

The shelter was just opening when we arrived. It is a volunteer organization, so strict business hours are not rigidly adhered to. A lady wearing a nametag with Mary on it showed us back to the kennels where she told us they only had ten dogs up for adoption. There were others but they had not been spayed or neutered so they were unavailable. Two of the kennels held full grown dogs. Both were large breeds that I thought inappropriate for the boys. There were also two schnauzers but all they did was bark constantly. I was glad the boys didn't show any interest in them. The next kennel held a litter of five beagle mix puppies.

Mary informed me these five had just become available for adoption. There were three males and two females. I hadn't seen them when I was here yesterday and a couple of the ones I had seen were no longer around. She opened the kennel and the boys went in to inspect the puppies when they showed interest. They were immediately surrounded by all five of the beagles.

I could tell it was love at first sight as the boys hugged and played with the pups.

"Dad, can we have these?" Chris asked.

"If you want, you can each pick out *one*," I said, emphasizing one.

"But ..." Lenny started.

"No, you can only have one. We don't need any more."

That didn't meet with any great enthusiasm but they accepted that it was final. They set to the task of trying to decide which one each of them wanted.

After changing their minds a dozen times, at least, they made their final decisions. As it turned out the three they picked out were the males. They were nearly identical, but with just enough variation in their markings to be able to tell the difference. It took a little while to sign all the paper work, get the shot records of each pup and pay the neutering fee and other charges.

"Okay, guys, let's go get your new puppies their beds and collars. We had better stop and get some more dog food, too. I may have to start buying it by the truck load," I laughed, as we got into the van.

We stopped at the local pet supply store and picked up the items including a supply of flea collars. Fleas and ticks are big problems with all the trees around the area. None of the dogs we were now the proud owners of would be satisfied being exclusively house dogs. We had always let Samson have free run of the thirty-five acres but now with five dogs I didn't think that would be a good idea at least not until they were older. There were a lot of critters they might come in contact with that could be dangerous to them including skunks and rattle snakes.

As we were driving home, I asked, "Have you decided what you are going to name your new friends?"

Larry was the first to respond, "I'm gonna call mine Buddy."

I could see in the rearview mirror Lenny looking hard at his new pet before he said, "Buster, that's what his name is."

"I think I'll name mine Rusty," Chris finally answered.

"Well, that's settled. Let's get these guys home and introduce them to the rest of the family. I think Samson will be the most important introduction."

I was right. As soon as I parked the van in the driveway Samson was there to greet us. When each of the boys stepped out of the van with their new charge Samson sniffed each one in turn. Apparently satisfied that there was no threat to his position as number one dog he turned and led the group back into the house.

Hildy stopped work on lunch and gave each of the dogs a hug as they were introduced to her. "You're going to have to tell me how I can tell them apart. They all look so similar," she said, after they were all greeted.

This started a long dialog from the boys on the merits and special markings each of their dogs had. I must admit I had to look very closely to discern the subtle coloration differences among the puppies. Chris' was probably the easiest to tell apart. His dog had more brown coloring than the other two. I'm sure I would mix them up for quite a while.

Bandit took to the three new puppies as if he was one of their litter. Before we had any accidents I told the four boys to put their pups on leashes and take them outside. I was left with the task of bringing in all of the dog paraphernalia we bought at the pet store.

By mid-afternoon I had to make the boys put their dogs in the new doggie beds to give them a rest. They had been wrestled with ever since we brought them home and I could tell they were getting tired. Becky Sue said she would read the boys a story while their pets rested. They ended up with each dog in their basket with their master lying on the floor next to it while Becky Sue read a story to them. Since Bandit's basket was downstairs he slept in TJ's lap on the couch next to Becky Sue.

Harold arrived with the renovation plans shortly after three. Manfred had arrived earlier and had been introduced to all of the new arrivals. The plans had turned out better than I had anticipated. Konrad, Harold's designer, did an excellent job taking what I thought I wanted and making plans that were not only functional but were estheticly pleasing in relation to the rest of the house. With the new addition the total living area of the house would be just over 7000 square feet.

One feature he had proposed was an elevator to Hildy's garage apartment. Although she was not in any way handicapped, if she stayed around as long as we hoped, the day might come when climbing stairs would not be something she looked forward to doing. Both Hildy and Manfred were pleased with the plans and believed their apartment would be more than sufficient for their needs after their marriage.

After a few very minor changes to the plan I gave Harold the go ahead to begin the renovation with the proviso it would not begin until after next Friday. I didn't want any construction going on during the twins' birthday party. He laughed and said he probably couldn't start construction until the end of the month because all of his crews were tied up on other jobs.

Saturday was a madhouse. Chris had a ballgame at one o'clock and the twins' game wasn't until four. Joel wanted to go watch John play soccer at two. I was beginning to feel like a stereotypical 'soccer mom'. I finally asked Manfred if he would mind taking Joel to the soccer match. Thankfully he agreed.

It was difficult for the boys to leave their puppies at home, but we put them in the fenced area and made sure there was plenty of food and fresh water for them while we were gone.

By six o'clock, when we arrived home, no one was in the best of moods. That soon changed when the boys retrieved their puppies. It's a wonder what caring for another creature can do to lift your spirits. How can you stay in a bad mood when a puppy is giving you such unconditional love?

Sunday we took the boat out on the lake and had a picnic lunch while idling around the water. Again we left the dogs at home. I couldn't see us taking five dogs and five boys on a boat with a twelve person capacity. The boys loved the water even if we didn't fish. It was too hot for good fishing so we just cruised around for about four hours taking in the sights. I let each of the boys sit in the captain's chair and steer the boat when there was no boat traffic near us.

That evening Eric called and hinted he wanted to come over. It didn't take me long to invite him to come. I think he had a lot on his mind and needed someone to talk to. I was happy to oblige.

The boys were happy to see JR and I was surprised to see Bran was still with them. I was surprised but happy. JR, of course, was beside himself when he saw all of the new puppies. He gave his dad such a pitiful look that would have melted the coldest heart.

"Okay, JR," Eric said. "Next week we'll go look."

"Thanks, dad," JR said, jumping into his dad's arms and giving him a kiss on the cheek.

The boys went off to play with the dogs while Eric and I went into the kitchen for a glass of iced tea. After we fixed our tea we went back to watch the boys play. Eric didn't say anything for a long time, he just watched the boys with a far away look in his eyes.

Finally, I said, "Eric, something seems to be on your mind. Do you want to tell me about it?"

"Yes, I really need to bounce something off you. I'm trying to get permission to foster Bran. Dad is not capable of handling him at the moment. His grief over mom's death is overwhelming him. I've talked to Bran's caseworker and I've gotten temporary custody of him. I guess I need to know if I'm crazy for wanting this."

"You are probably asking the wrong person," I said. "Sometimes I think I was crazy to take on raising five boys. I will say one thing. I have never, even for an instant, regretted doing it. I love them more than my own life. But, I think you need to answer a couple questions for yourself. Are you doing this because you truly want him as part of your family? Or, are you doing this to help your dad out?"

"I've been asking myself the same questions. JR and he have become inseparable. He's like the big brother JR never had. I do love him. At least I think I do. I'm confused. What am I going to do? How am I going to raise both of them? I have the financial resources, especially after my inheritance from mom," he said, covering his eyes with both hands.

"The logistics of raising them both is the easy part. I think the hardest part of raising Bran would be the prejudice he would face in our overwhelmingly white area. For that matter you would also be on the receiving end of that prejudice because you would be raising him. Are you prepared for that? And another thing, he says he's gay. My God, gay and black in a redneck county, that's a lot of baggage for one youngster to carry. If he ever got exposed … Are you willing to face that?" I asked, putting an arm around Eric's shoulders.

"You know, you're not making this any easier for me. I came here for answers and all you've given me are more questions," Eric teased.

"What are friends for?" I retorted. "Come on, let's round up the boys. It's about time for their snack. Hildy made a strawberry-rhubarb cobbler I'm dying to try. You go see to it that they wash up. I'll set out the vanilla ice cream to top the cobbler."

With seven eating machines, it didn't take long for the cobbler and ice cream to disappear.

"Say goodbye to your friends," Eric said, after we had cleaned up from the boys' snack. "It's time to go home. I've got to figure out who is going to take care of you guys while I'm at work."

"Look, Eric," I said. "I don't think this is a long term solution, but why don't you bring them by here tomorrow. Maybe Hildy will have an idea of who might be available to stay with them and fix their meals at least temporarily."

"Yeah, can we dad?" JR pleaded. "Then I can get to play with the dogs."

"Okay, but just for tomorrow. Now scoot yourself out to the car. Thanks, Crane, I didn't mean to dump them on you," he said, and gave me a hug.

The week of the twins' birthday was filled with trips by the other boys to buy presents for them and with shopping for new school uniforms. School was due to start on Wednesday the twenty-first. I discreetly made a call to Corinthian Academy on Monday to see if the new freshman class was full. I was please to find out there were still a few vacancies that hadn't been filled.

"What have you done about Bran's schooling?" I asked Eric when he arrived to pick JR and Bran up Monday evening.

"Oh Lord," he said. "I hadn't even thought of that. I guess there have been too many things on my mind to even consider it. I wonder if JR's school has any room and if I can get Bran enrolled at this late date?"

"I checked. They do have room in the new freshman class. I took the liberty of scheduling him for testing on Wednesday morning. If you can't take off work, I'll take him to the school and pick him up after the test."

"Crane ... Thanks, I really appreciate you looking after Bran's interests. I guess I'd better get my act together if I'm going to be the father to two boys," he said.

"So, you've decided?" I asked.

"Yes, I'm going to fill out all of the paperwork to qualify to be a foster parent and then try to get Bran assigned to me on a permanent basis. Oh, by the way, I have a Mrs. Carson coming tomorrow to stay with the boys. I haven't met her, but I did talk to her on the phone and she seems quite nice. I'll let you know if I can't take Bran in for the testing."

Tuesday morning I made a few phone calls to Carlos, Gerald, to my stock broker and a few others. When I was satisfied I had all my finances and legal affairs in order I took Joel, TJ and Chris to buy the twins' birthday present. Larry and Lenny stayed at home with Hildy and the dogs.

Eric called in the evening to let me know he wouldn't be able to take Bran in for testing. He had to go to Dallas for his project there. He would be back on Thursday evening. Mel and Darcie were going to spend Wednesday night with the boys and Mrs. Carson would be there during the day.

Wednesday morning all the boys piled into the van as I got ready to go pick up Bran for his testing. Bran appeared to be very nervous as he climbed into the van and waved goodbye to JR. He soon calmed down in the company of my sons. By the time we got to Corinthian he was laughing and having a good time with the other boys. He held back a little as we trooped into the school.

Harry Lyle met us in the headmaster's office. I introduced Bran to him and said he was living with Eric Levin and his son JR. Something struck me as odd as I talked to Harry but couldn't quite put my finger on it. He said the testing and interviews would take about four hours and we should plan to be back around one o'clock. We all gave Bran a hug and I told him to try his best saying we would pick him up and take him to lunch when he was finished. He was the only prospective student taking the test today.

I called Mrs. Carson when I got home and told her I would come by to pick up JR and take him to lunch when I went for Bran. Naturally everyone wanted to go so the van was going to be full.

We arrived back at the school shortly after twelve-thirty. I thought possibly since there was only one student being tested that Bran might finish early. It turned out I was right. The boys went to play on the playground equipment while I went in to check on Bran. He was just finishing with his interview when I approached the secretary's desk. Bran looked like he was about ready to cry as he walked toward me. He didn't say anything, just wrapped his arms around me and buried his face in my shirt front.

"What's the matter, son?" I asked.

No response; he just looked at me and shook his head.

"Why don't you go outside and play with the other boys. Take a right after you go out the door and you will find them. Let me talk to Mr. Lyle."

He nodded and walked toward the door.

I walked to the secretary's desk and asked to see Mr. Lyle. She told me she would see if he was available and asked me to take a seat. I had to wait about five minutes before Lyle arrived.

"Mr. Lyle, it's good of you to see me. I was curious about the results of Bran's test and interview. His foster dad is out of town and asked me to get the results."

"Well … Ah … This is a little delicate. You see, he didn't pass the interview portion of the exam," Harry said.

"What do you mean? What part of the interview didn't he pass?" I asked.

"The interviewer didn't think he would fit in with Corinthian's … traditions."

"And just what does that mean?" I asked, becoming more distressed.

CHAPTER 33

"Well you see ... we don't have anyone like him enrolled here. We think he would feel uncomfortable without others like him," Lyle said, not looking me in the eyes.

"What you are really saying is that because he is black you don't think he would fit in. Is that right?" I said, in a measured tone becoming very calm.

"I didn't say that exactly ..."

"Well, what exactly did you say?"

"I just think it would be better if he found another school. Now, if that is all, I have things to do," Lyle said, getting up to leave.

"One more thing, is Mr. Pierce in his office?"

"Yes, he is, but he's very busy getting ready for the new school term."

"I think he'll see me. I have something very important to discuss with him," I said with as steely a tone in my voice as I could muster.

Mr. Lyle must have gotten the message because he motioned for me to follow him to Mr. Pierce's office door where he knocked. He opened the door and I followed him into the room.

"Mr. Pierce, Mr. Johnson would like to speak to you."

"Thank you, Harry. Come in, Mr. Johnson. What may I do for you?"

"I have just been informed that a prospective student has been rejected for what I believe to be racial reasons. Does this school discriminate on the basis of race?" I asked, after Mr. Lyle left us.

"Of course not, we have filed a statement of nondiscrimination with the US Department of Education and with the Texas Education Agency."

"How many minority students are currently enrolled?" I asked.

"I can't recall right offhand."

"I would be willing to wager that there is exactly zero. Do you think I might win that wager? Well, I'm sure you would welcome your first minority student, wouldn't you?"

"Of course, if he is qualified, but I understand he failed the interview portion of the pre-acceptance procedure."

"Not to change the subject, but how are you financing the construction of the new classrooms for your first freshman class?"

"Well, it's public record that we issued notes for the initial construction."

"I believe the amount issued was $10 million, correct?"

"Why, yes, that was the amount."

"I also understand they were Demand Notes, correct?"

"Yes," he said, getting noticeably paler.

"Yesterday, I had my broker purchase half of those notes. Now what do you suppose I might feel compelled to do if I thought for one moment the school I'm sending my sons to is racist?"

"Oh no, that would bankrupt the school," he said, collapsing into his chair. After a couple minutes of silence he asked, "What do you want?"

"Two things, first, I want Bran LeBeau admitted to the freshman class. He's qualified in every way that matters, including academics. Second, I would find it most agreeable if the school actively sought out qualified minorities for the student body," I said.

"Very well, he'll be admitted," he said. "Is there anything else?"

"Perhaps there is one more thing, I don't want to hear he is being discriminated against by the faculty or other staff or that they allow or encourage any discrimination against him. That young man is as dear to me as are my own sons and I would be compelled to respond as if he were, should anything happen. Now if you will excuse me, I'm taking my sons to lunch."

I left the office with the coppery taste of bile in my mouth. When I got to the front door all seven of the boys were there waiting for me.

"Is Bran going to get to go to school here, dad?" Joel asked. "He said he wasn't. Why can't he dad?"

Putting my arm around Bran's shoulder and looking him in the eyes I said, "Yes, Bran is going to go to school here, too."

That brought a round of cheers and a round of hugs from all of them. Then everybody headed for the van. We stopped for lunch at a local mom and pop cafe that served great made-to-order burgers and milkshakes.

Most of Thursday morning was spent shopping for new school uniforms and other clothes to replace all of the ones the boys had outgrown. I never knew boys' feet could grow so fast. Thank goodness Hildy went with us to do the shopping. She had much better sense about her when it came to choosing the boys' clothes.

By Thursday evening Larry and Lenny were so excited about their birthday party tomorrow I didn't think I would ever get them settled down so they could go to sleep. It was funny watching them. They told me they had never had a birthday party before. The most they had ever had to celebrate their birthdays was a cake their mother used to make for them. They never had any presents or friends to help them celebrate. It was nearly 10:30 before they finally got to sleep.

"Good morning, liebchen," Hildy said, giving first Larry and then Lenny their morning hugs. The puppies in their arms got hugs at the same time.

"Take your puppies outside. We don't want them to have an accident," I told them.

Chris had already made his way downstairs and had Rusty outside. I think he went to sleep long before the twins did last night. Joel and TJ had their dogs outside also. With all the playing the ten of them did, I would probably have to go drag them inside to eat their breakfasts. In reality all I had to do was go to the door and announce that Hildy's pancakes were ready and I was nearly run over by the rush of five boys heading for the bathrooms to wash up. I steered the dogs to their food dishes in the laundry room.

David Wilson arrived around 9:30. Becky Sue understated when she said he was cute. He was movie star handsome. Maybe handsome is not the right word. Beautiful is more descriptive even though that is an odd descriptor for a man. All the boys took to him immediately and dragged him off to see their puppies. He was as personable as he was good looking. Even Hildy was taken by him.

We soon got down to the business of setting up everything for the party. Even the boys got involved in helping. David and I could probably have done it faster without their help but it was important for them to feel like they were helping.

After an early lunch we prepared for the onslaught of ten friends of the twins plus JR and Bran. Janet Sutton was the first to arrive bringing her son Billy. Larry and Lenny had really developed a friendship with him after their incident of sitting on him at school. He had changed dramatically after he had their friendship. He was no longer the class bully.

David kept the boys entertained while I greeted each new parent bringing a son. It turned out he did card tricks as a hobby. All the boys were spellbound as they crowded around him trying to see how he did them. I think they would have spent the entire afternoon just watching him do the tricks.

I thought TJ's party was a madhouse, but with ten pre-pubescent boys added to my sons and Eric's two it was really bedlam. David appeared to love working with the boys and they were captivated by him. The first part of the party went off without a hitch. I think everyone was ready for some cake when we announced it was time to go inside.

The same tables we had for TJ's party were now set up with five boys on three sides and the twins on the fourth. Hildy had baked and decorated two birthday cakes. One was chocolate with white frosting and the other was white with chocolate frosting. They were both large enough to feed the entire group if they all wanted the same kind.

We again sang an absolutely horrible rendition of *Happy Birthday* before the twins blew out the candles. I asked them if they had each made a wish. They said they had but wanted to keep it a secret.

Five of the boys had been invited by Larry and the other five had been invited by Lenny. That way the guests would not feel obligated to buy presents for both of the twins. The presents would end up commingled anyway so it really didn't matter which twin got which present.

After everyone had eaten ice cream and cake, David entertained them with his card tricks for enough time for their treats to settle. Then it was off to the pool for everyone who wanted to go for a swim. All but two of the boys wanted to go swimming so Bran and I played volleyball with them until they tired. At a few minutes to five, I told everybody to go jump in the showers and get dressed, their parents would be here shortly to pick them up. I think they were all genuinely sad to see the party come to an end. I'm sure David had a lot to do with that.

Before he left I asked David if he would be interested in continuing the boys swimming lessons that Becky Sue had started. He readily agreed and we decided that since summer baseball would end this Saturday for Chris and the twins, and Sunday for TJ, he would come every Saturday afternoon after that. We agreed on compensation for the lessons and then I paid him for today and he left after getting a round of hugs from seven boys.

The dogs were released from the dog run and raced around, stumbling over their own feet being happy to be free. Samson just stood and watched as if he couldn't understand what was going on. When he decided it was time to go water one of the bushes, he had four puppies following him to help.

Bran slowly approached me and said, "What did you do to make the school let me in?"

"I just convinced them you would make an excellent addition to their new freshman class. You are a very bright young man. I just want you to show JR and Eric how great a young man you really are. Can you do that?" I asked.

Nodding his head, he wrapped his arms around my waist, "Thanks, Uncle Crane."

The last time someone called me "Uncle Crane" I ended up with five sons. "You are very welcome," I said, and returned his hug.

"Are Eric and his boys going to stay for supper?" Hildy asked, as I went back in the house.

"I haven't invited them yet. If you have enough for all of us, I will," I said.

"We're having fried chicken, mashed potatoes and corn on the cob. I can always fix enough for three extra mouths, even if two of them are young boys," she laughed, turning back toward the kitchen.

"I'll invite them, then," I said after her.

I went upstairs to see if there was any more cleanup necessary before the rental store came tomorrow to pick up the tables and chairs. Hildy had cleaned everything off the tables. She filled a couple of garbage bags with the trash which she left for me to carry out. I grabbed them and took them downstairs and out the back door. I decided to carry them down to the gate since they weren't that heavy. It was garbage pickup tomorrow and I wanted to get rid of as much trash as possible.

As I started down the drive with my two garbage bags in hand, Joel came up along side of me.

"Dad, what did you say to Mr. Lyle to made him change his mind about Bran?" he asked.

"It was really Mr. Pierce whom I convinced that Bran would be an excellent student," I answered.

"They weren't going to let him attend because he is black, right?" he said, looking straight into my eyes.

I didn't want to lie to him but I didn't want him to know exactly how I 'convinced' them to change their mind. "They just needed an incentive to do the right thing," I said, as we approached the gate.

"You're not going to tell me, are you?" he asked, with a big smile on his face.

I placed the trash bags outside the gate before I turned to him. "You know, for a thirteen year-old with fuzzy hair, you're pretty smart. I love you, Joel Jay Johnson."

"You're pretty smart for a thirty year-old. I love you, too," he giggled.

I put my arm around him and we started back up the drive. We were almost to the house when Eric drove up.

"Hi, guys," Eric said, as he stepped out of his car. "Crane, I see you're still here. I figured you'd have been carted away to the funny farm. How many boys did you have here today? Fifteen? Sixteen?"

"Actually there were seventeen. We had a great time, but I'm glad we don't have any more birthdays for a few months. I need some time to regroup. How's everything at the office? How's your project coming?"

"Oh, everything is going great. The project in Dallas is actually going to be wrapped up quicker than planned, at least my part of it. Everyone misses you at the office."

"I still owe them my week this month. I'll be coming into the office the last week of the month after I get the boys back in school," I said.

"Well, I'd better gather up my two and head off for home and figure out what to fix for supper. Mrs. Carson wasn't there this afternoon to fix anything for us," Eric said.

"Stay for supper with us. I already checked with Hildy and she is fixing extra. It's nothing fancy, just fried chicken," I told him.

"Thanks, that's the best offer I've had all day. I need to check on my two. I'll bet I know what they are doing. You know, since you got all of those dogs, I haven't had a minute's peace from JR. We're going to the shelter tomorrow morning to see if they have anything. I think we will be the proud owners of at least one dog. I only hope I can get away that easy."

The twins had to show Eric all the presents they had gotten at the party before we sat down to supper. When he asked them if they had received their birthday spanking, their eyes got really wide and they backed up against the wall. I had to explain to them that in some places it was customary to give the birthday boy a light spanking, one swat for each year old they were. They still didn't think too much of the idea. My guess was they remembered the abuse they had received at the hands of their abusive biological father. I didn't realize he was still having an effect on them. I realized I needed to let them know their old father was dead and would no longer be able to hurt them.

Our meal was excellent as always. Hildy's southern fried chicken is some of the best I have ever eaten. I don't know how many chickens she fried but I know there were at least a dozen drumsticks. She told me later that she bought packages of legs, thighs and breasts rather than whole chickens so she didn't have to spend the time cutting them up.

After the dishes were all loaded into the dishwasher, and the little food left over was put in the refrigerator, the boys went to play with their dogs while Eric and I retired to the family room. "May I speak to you privately?" Eric asked.

"Sure, let's go into my study," I said leading the way.

Eric closed the door behind us and then stepped up to me, wrapped his arms around me and planted a passionate kiss on my totally shocked lips.

"Wow! What was that for?" I asked, when he released me and I recovered.

"That was for helping Bran … and for me. I talked to Paul Coulter today and he said the word going around the school was that you applied a little pressure to the school's pocketbook to get Bran admitted. He said there are several versions of what happened, depending on who you talk to. He'd called Darcie about some foundation business and told her about it and then she called me. What was it exactly that you did do?" he asked.

"If you must know, I hold some notes the school is using to finance the construction of the new classrooms," I said, hoping this would satisfy him.

"So what? How does that give you any leverage with them? They pay you interest and then redeem the bonds at maturity in what ten or twenty years?"

"You see, they are not really bonds. What they issued were demand notes," I said.

"I don't understand. I'm not an accountant. What's a demand note?" he asked.

"It just means the lender or the borrower may at any time demand their redemption. I thought it was a good investment. They pay 8% interest which makes for a good annual income from them. I never threatened to redeem them, I just wondered out loud what I should do if I discovered the school my sons were attending was racist," I said, blushing.

"You are one sneaky bastard, a rich sneaky bastard, but one with a heart of gold. By the way, how much of the debt do you own?"

"I had my broker secure half of it."

"Oh my God! No wonder Pierce had to change his underwear after you left," he laughed. "Or at least that's how the story goes."

"I doubt that," I chuckled.

"They're really taking your implied threat seriously. They're holding meetings with everyone on the school's payroll as well as all the volunteers to let them know that discrimination will not be tolerated by anyone. Paul said they were told they would be terminated immediately if there were even a hint of discrimination. Not only will this benefit Bran, but it will help the new female students who will be attending this year also. "You're a good man, Charlie Brown," he said, hugging me.

This time I initiated the kiss. This time it was not a surprise to either of us. When we came up for air, I said, "I'd like to keep this up but I think we had better check on the boys. I'll take a rain check."

"You can redeem it any time," he said, giving me a final hug.

The boys were playing with the dogs as we went out to check on them. JR was holding Bandit and getting his face licked as if he were a lollipop. He was giggling so hard he could hardly hold the squirming puppy.

"I see there will be no getting out of looking for that puppy tomorrow," Eric said.

"No," I said. "There's no way you'll come home without at least one dog. Maybe two?"

"I think we had better try just one for a while. It'll be fine until the boys go back to school, but what will we do with it while we're all gone?" he asked, shaking his head.

"You'll just have to fix up a place where it can run, have plenty of shade and lots of fresh water and food. It'll do all right while you are gone. Don't worry," I said, patting him on the back.

As was the nightly ritual since getting the dogs, the last thing the boys did before getting tucked into bed was to take their friends outside one last time. I think Bandit was really getting the idea of being house trained. I wasn't too sure of the three Beagles, although to be fair we had only had them less than a week. All of them had been pretty good about sleeping in their doggie beds. Even Bandit was sleeping in his own bed and not with Samson anymore.

After all the boys were tucked in for the night, I received a phone call from Darcie. She said she had received two referrals for the foundation from two case workers she knew. I was a little surprised because we really hadn't advertised the foundation to CPS. I guess the grapevine was working overtime. Darcie said she would like to talk to me about the two cases. I told her I would be in the office on Monday morning and we could discuss them at that time. I told her to go enjoy her weekend and I would see her Monday.

Saturday was the last game of the summer season for Chris and the twins. Unfortunately, they were scheduled to play their games at the same time. That meant I wouldn't be able to watch Chris' game since I would be coaching the twins. I was glad Hildy agreed to come along with us so she would be able to keep track of Chris and also keep TJ reined in.

The day was sultry hot when we got to the ball fields but there were dark clouds in the west threatening rain. As the games got started all the coaches kept one eye on the approaching storm. At the first sight of lightning we called the games and everyone headed to the cars. I made sure all of my team were safe in their parent's cars before I felt comfortable to start home. It was starting to rain hard as we drove toward the exit of the complex.

"Crane, stop! There's a young boy over there by that metal shed," Hildy cried. "We can't leave him there. What if the lightning would strike?"

I looked to where she was pointing. I could hardly see him for the pouring rain. I headed the van toward the shed to get a better look.

"That's Chad. He's in our class at the other school," Larry said, opening the side door of the van. "Chad! Come on in the van!"

Chad looked a little surprised but didn't hesitate to jump into the van. Hildy immediately got a blanket wrapped around the soaked boy trying to dry him off.

"Chad, where are your folks?" I asked him.

"My brother's supposed to pick me up. He went to see his girlfriend and left me here," Chad replied.

"What's your phone number? I'll call them and let them know you are all right."

"But … Dickie will get in trouble," he said.

"I think Dickie is already in trouble," I said, and then dialed the number he gave me.

When I reached his parents on my cell phone I explained to them the situation. They were relieved to know he was all right. I told them I would bring him home. They gave me the directions and we headed out again. Chad lived not all that far from the ball fields, but it was in the opposite direction from our house. It only took us a few minutes to get to his house. His mom was waiting for us on their front porch with a large umbrella unfurled ready to make a dash to the van.

Chad's mom thanked us profusely for bringing her 'baby', as she called him, home safely. As she headed back to the house with Chad under the umbrella we heard her begin the questioning of Chad about where his brother was.

The center of the storm seemed to be right over our heads as we turned back on to 306 and headed for home. The lightning would flash and almost immediately it would be followed by a very loud clap of thunder. Each one elicited a nervous giggle from the boys.

"Are we gonna get home soon, daddy?" TJ asked.

"It'll only be a few minutes, son," I answered.

"Bandit's gonna be scared," he said.

"Samson will take care of him. I'll bet they're in the doghouse with him all cuddled up," I said, trying to be convincing.

I drove the van as far into the garage as it would go so we wouldn't have to get wet when we got out. I could hear the puppies yipping and crying as we started for the back door. The boys made a beeline for the dog run to check on their scared little friends. Hildy and I grabbed towels from the laundry room to dry off the dogs and boys as they rushed back into the house.

"Samson was taking care of them like you said," Chris announced, as he grabbed a towel and wrapped it around Rusty. It didn't bother him that he was wetter than his puppy.

"But Buster was still scared. See, he's still shaking," Lenny said, as he hugged his little pet.

It didn't take long for the dogs to settle down with all the love the boys were giving them. I just wondered if they would put them down long enough to eat. It would be a tough choice but I thought I knew what it would be. One thing for sure was there would be no dogs allowed at the table.

The rain stopped by the time we had eaten supper and we were treated to a magnificent sunset a couple of hours later. The boys were much more interested in finishing off the last of the birthday cakes than in watching the sunset.

Sunday morning meant I was in charge of breakfast. I usually fixed scrambled eggs, sausage and frozen hash browns. The toaster only made four slices at a time so I had to make three batches. I kept the toast warm in the oven while the others were being toasted.

The boys didn't seem to mind my lack of culinary skills. There was nothing left when they were finished eating.

Today was going to be fairly relaxed. The only thing we had going on was TJ's last T-ball game at two. We spent the morning swimming and playing with the dogs. Bandit loved the water and he and TJ had a ball in the water. Buddy, Buster and Rusty played in the water with their masters but were not as enthusiastic about it as Bandit. They spent most of the time in the boys' arms rather than swimming around. I was pleased at the progress the boys had made in their swimming ability. They all had dramatically improved over the summer. Becky Sue's instructions were apparent in their improvement.

TJ's team won their game. Afterwards he gave Ellen England, his coach, a hug and thanked her for being so nice. I also thanked her for making his first experience with organized sports so enjoyable. We took the long way home and stopped by the Dairy Queen for hot fudge sundaes. Nobody seemed to mind the extra time it took to get home.

Hildy and Manfred were sitting out by the pool when we got home. They were surrounded by the puppies trying to jump up on their laps and being petted. That was until the boys ran to their puppies and sidetracked them.

After a while I started a fire in the grill. I planned to fix some hamburgers and hot dogs. I invited Hildy and Manfred to join us if they didn't already have plans. They agreed and Hildy offered to fix some beans and cole slaw. Manfred said he would help me make out the burgers.

I fixed a couple extra burgers for the dogs. Although I didn't allow the boys to feed their pets from the table, I intended for them to give the burgers to the dogs in their regular food dishes. This was a special treat. Ordinarily they would be fed dog food. That way I knew they were getting the right nutrition to keep them healthy.

The more I was around Manfred the more I liked him. The boys adored him and he appeared to return their love. I hoped that once he and Hildy were married it wouldn't change things. I think I was a little jealous of the thoughts of having to share Hildy with him.

Supper was great, both the dogs and the boys enjoyed their meals. The boys had ice cream for dessert, the dogs had none.

I tucked the boys in at bedtime. The boys got hugs and kisses, the dogs got pats on the head. When I tucked Joel and TJ in bed I thought Joel had something on his mind. He seemed to be a little distracted.

"Son, is something bothering you?" I asked him.

"No, it's nothing," he said.

"Well, if you decide you need to talk to someone, I'll be in the family room reading for a while," I said, kissed him on the forehead and left the room.

I probably had read ten pages of my book when I heard footsteps coming down the hall. I could tell it was Joel from the sound. He approached and then squeezed in beside me in the recliner.

"What's the matter, son?" I asked, and put my arm around him.

"It's ... well ... school starts on Wednesday and ..." he started and buried his face in my chest.

"Yes, you'll be in eighth grade. You'll get to see all your friends again you haven't seen all summer," I said trying to be as reassuring as I could be.

"But ... But, what if they make fun of me 'cause of my hair?" he asked, choking back a sob.

"I suppose that is a possibility. Do you think they would make fun of you if they knew why your hair is like it is?"

"I don't know, maybe not."

"How could they find out what happened to make your hair look like it does?"

"Maybe you could tell them?" he asked, looking me directly in the eyes.

"Is that what you want? Do you want me to come to school and sit in each of your classes and tell your classmates you had leukemia?"

"No," he said, almost indignantly.

"Okay, is there any other way they could be told?"

"I guess I'll have to tell them," he said, after thinking for a moment.

"I think that's the best solution, then they can ask you questions about it," I said, giving him another hug. "You know there may be some of your classmates who still may make comments about your hair. There are always a few who make fun of people who may look a little different.

"Let me tell you a story of a boy I went to school with. It was a boarding school so we lived at the school as well as going to classes there. Cary was about my age. We shared a room in the freshmen dorm. He had a severe limp which caused him to take a step and then drag his other leg and then take another step and so on. Anyway some of the older students took to imitating how Cary walked. I know it hurt his feelings because sometimes at night I could hear him crying.

"One day he came upon a boy who was imitating him to a group of his friends. They were laughing at the imitation when Cary limped up to them. He looked the boy straight in the eye and said, 'I'm sorry you find it necessary to make fun of me to make you feel important. What you are doing is hurtful to me.' With that, Cary turned and limped away. I was a few feet away and heard the whole confrontation.

"The boy stood there stunned, not only that he got caught doing his imitation but that Cary had confronted him is such a direct way. I never saw him imitate that limp again."

"What happened to Cary?" Joel asked.

"The last I heard he owned a company in San Jose, California and was a multi-millionaire. I haven't heard from him in a couple of years."

"Thanks, dad," he said.

"You're welcome, son. Now I think it's time for you to go back to bed or you'll be a sleepy boy in the morning. I love you," I said, kissing his forehead.

"I love you, too," he said, slipping out of the recliner and heading for his bedroom.

I hope he will be able to handle the inevitable teasing he will encounter. I just hope he can defuse it before it gets to him. I must remember to talk to him about it after he gets started in school. God, I wish there were some way I could shelter him from it.

Sleep didn't come easy.

I awoke to the smell of bacon being fried. After showering and getting dressed I joined Hildy in the kitchen for my cup of coffee. I told her I would be going to the foundation office this morning, but I would be back this afternoon. She reminded me we still needed to get the school supplies for the boys before school started. I hadn't even thought of that. She handed me the list the school sent out for each grade. It looked like we would be making a trip to Office Depot this afternoon.

Darcie was in the office before I got there. I grabbed a cup of coffee and then went to talk to her about the two referrals she had received. I read through the material Darcie's friends had sent her. On the surface both files seemed to fit the criteria we had established for foundation help. The information was skimpy, however. We would need a lot more information before either one of the prospects could be approved.

I had Darcie call her friend Lucinda. She was a caseworker who had submitted one of the files. I had Darcie ask her if we could get more information about her referral. All we really knew was the referral was a divorced woman, thirty-five years old, who was fostering a ten year-old girl and wanted to adopt the girl. The woman worked as a cashier in a supermarket and her disposable income did not qualify her for adoption.

The other file was on Bruce, a single man, twenty-six years old, who taught mathematics in a local high school. He had been involved in the Big Brothers program with an eight year-old boy. It seemed the boy's mother was single and didn't know who his father was. The mother disappeared several months ago and the boy made his way to his Big Brother's house. He had been fostered with Bruce ever since. The mother had recently been found murdered in South San Antonio. It seemed Bruce was more likely in need of legal counsel rather than ongoing support from the foundation.

I called Jack and told him we had two more prospects we wanted investigated. He said he would come to the office and pick up the information we had and would begin his background checks. I suggested he wait to start the full background checks until after Darcie and I had interviewed them. If all went right, that would happen before the end of the week.

After getting off the phone with Jack I told Darcie I wouldn't be back in the office until Wednesday when the boys were back in school. I asked her to see if she could set up a time to talk to our two new prospects sometime later in the week if at all possible.

I got back home in time for lunch. Hildy said she had to go grocery shopping after we had eaten. I found the school supplies list and herded the boys into the van and we took off to get what they needed. We filled a shopping cart nearly to the top with the supplies for all five boys. I picked up a few things for the foundation office as well.

When we got home I had the boys put their school supplies in their backpacks so they would be ready to go to school on Wednesday. After they had finished, I gave them each a brush and told them they had to learn how to brush their dogs. Joel already knew how because he had been brushing Samson for some time. I told them they had to brush their dogs at least once a week. They were anxious to learn how. Joel demonstrated how he brushed Samson with long slow strokes. You could tell Samson liked being brushed. When the other boys tried it on their own dogs, both dog and owner seemed to enjoy the process.

Later that evening after the supper dishes were placed in the dishwasher I called the boys into the family room. They all came in with their puppies in their arms except for Joel and Samson. Samson walked beside Joel until he sat down and then climbed into Joel's lap. TJ took his usual place on my lap and the others sat on either sides of me.

"Chris, this does not directly affect you. There is something I have been putting off telling the rest of you. I put this off because at the time I became aware of it Joel was in the hospital and I didn't want to put any more stress on him than he had already. Since then I have just put it off because I didn't want to deal with it.

"You know your old dad was sent to prison for killing your mom, don't you?" I asked and received nods from everyone. I continued, "Prison is a very dangerous place. When it became known what he had done to Joel, it became even more dangerous for him. The danger finally caught up with him and someone killed him. Your old dad is dead."

Nobody said anything for a moment or two. Then Joel spoke, "He stopped being my dad when he killed my mom." There was bitterness in his voice. "I'm sorry he's dead, but I'm not sad. You're our dad now. He's just someone I once knew."

Larry and Lenny were nodding their heads in agreement. TJ didn't say anything for a while. He just stroked Bandit. Finally he said, "He hurt my mommy and Joel. I didn't like him. He can't hurt them no more."

"I love you guys," I said. "If you ever feel like you need to talk to me about your old dad, I'll always be here for you."

The revelation of their dad's death didn't put a damper on the evening. They were playing with their dogs and having a great time within minutes. It had gone better than I had expected, but I was still a little bit surprised at their casual attitude.

When I asked the boys what they wanted to do on their last day before they had to start back to school they said they wanted to go fishing. So right after breakfast I called the marina and had them service my boat. Hildy packed a lunch and a snack. I got the fishing gear ready, loaded it in the van along with a cooler containing our lunch and another with soft drinks and bottled water.

I almost relented when TJ looked at me with those beautiful pleading eyes while he held Bandit. I just could not see taking all five dogs on the boat. The dogs stayed at home. Hildy said she would take care of them. That helped a little bit.

Once we were on the boat, the dogs were forgotten. We cruised around until we came to our favorite fishing spot. I cut the engine and let the boat drift slowly. There was not much current or wind so we didn't drift very far. I broke out the fishing gear and saw to it that each one had a good lure before I gave the rod to each boy. I'm not much for using live bait when I have to put it on the hook.

As the sun rose in the sky, I liberally applied sunscreen to the boys and myself. I didn't want them to start school with sunburns. The fish weren't biting all that well. We did catch some fish. In fact everyone caught at least one fish. I think Larry did the best with three. After the boys enjoyed their morning snack I decided we had enough fishing for a while. I started the motor and we cruised the lake taking in its beauty and watching the other boats. There were quite a few speed boats and jet skis buzzing around. The boys really liked watching the jet skis and the plume of water shooting up behind them as they roared around. Maybe next summer I would rent one and take each of the boys a ride on it. Maybe.

After we ate our lunch, we continued our cruise slowly around the lake. I maneuvered the boat back to the marina. I could tell the boys were getting tired. I decided it was best to head home. We loaded all of the fishing equipment into the van as well as the empty coolers and the one containing our fish.

As usual, I got the job of cleaning the fish. There weren't that many so it didn't take me long, besides the boys had more important things to do, like playing with the puppies. Hildy said we had enough fish for supper when I finished cleaning them.

We went swimming when I finished with the fish. It did get the fish smell off all of us. The puppies were really beginning to take to the water. Samson still preferred to stand on the side and bark every so often. It was funny to see the four puppies when they got out of the water. They would try shaking the water off, but sometimes they got to shaking so hard they would fall over. That would cause the boys to go into fits of laughter.

The fish was excellent. Hildy served it with her wonderful hush puppies and a cabbage and carrot salad. It was a simple supper but nobody complained.

Nobody complained later when snack time rolled around. Hildy had fixed cream puffs. She had even frosted the tops of them with chocolate and then dusted them with powdered sugar. They were very messy to eat but they were heavenly. We had them all over our faces before we were through.

"Hildy, these are yummy," TJ said. He even had chocolate frosting on his nose.

It was barely dark outside when I told the boys to go get their showers taken and get ready for bed. They started to complain but I reminded them that school started tomorrow and they had to get up early to catch the school van. Reluctantly, they went off to their showers.

Even though they didn't want to go to bed, I could tell they were tired. I tucked them all in, giving them a hug, a kiss and telling them that I loved them.

Despite the fact they went to bed early, I had a hard time getting them to wake up in the morning. Finally they came dragging down the stairs and the hall to the breakfast table. By the time breakfast was over they were fully awake and chatting about going to school. I was glad to see they were excited to go back to school.

Everyone was ready in plenty of time to meet their van. They looked so handsome in their new school uniforms I had to take a picture of all of them together. I was so proud of them I nearly burst. Hildy gave them each a hug before we started down to the gate to wait on the school van. On the way I checked to make sure they had their meal tickets.

I saw the van approaching as we got to the gate. I quickly gave them all a hug. They got on the van saying hi to Doug their van driver and then turned to wave at me. I stood there and watched until the van was out of sight.

Another school year begins: more adventures; more problems; more independence; more opportunities. I don't know if I'm ready for it.

978-0-595-44639-1
0-595-44639-6

Printed in the United Kingdom
by Lightning Source UK Ltd.
132354UK00001B/297/A